# DEFINING

# PIPER

## O.R

TO THOSE WHO STOOD BY MY SIDE WHEN MY HEAD
SCREAMED LOUDER THAN MY VOICE EVER COULD.

# PROLOGUE (THEN):

There's something about being stuck on a bus for hours on end that makes you notice the little nuances in life. The bus reeked of stale gasoline and body odor from passengers who were escaping their pasts just like I was, and every time there was a subtle aromatic difference, we all inhaled the fumes as if they were a new perfume. I had been trapped on a foxhound bus for sixteen hours, and my body ached from the aged seats, and my bones seemed to be engulfed by the chair's gaudy fabric. I didn't know how much longer it would take or what I would do when I reached my destination. but for some reason, it didn't seem to matter. I was finally free from my past, and no matter how trite that may sound, it was true, and in many ways it still is.

The bus began to slow around lunch time the day I finally found my home. I was just sitting in my seat, breathing in the subtle smell of salt water while trying to write a book that never seemed to be a reality, when I felt the stop. Just another break, just another detour in the trip that felt like it would never end. I had just a few more hours to go until I was in my Father's hometown until I was supposed to be reunited with my estranged Grandparents who reluctantly agreed to "raise me" during my final year of High School.

3

But here I was, in a town in the middle of nowhere, waiting for some supposed fate to unfold before my eyes. Something about the town was enchanting, though, everything from its melodic name, Belfast, to its quaint charm that overflowed like the sea.

I gathered my things off the bus and as the bus driver gave instructions on when to arrive back at the stop, I took off, letting my feet follow an unknown path. I will admit that my actions were strange, that they lacked any actual logic, but I was just a girl back then, searching for answers to questions that couldn't be answered. I thought that the only way I could feel again was to ignore my better judgment and listen to my heart for the first time. An immature decision led me down an endless path of uncertainty and a rough sandy shore. I set up camp along the beach that day, and I watched locals heard their children around in a rushed state while the hypnotic waves became a calming soundtrack for my anxious mind.

When it was time for me to recommit to my journey, I found myself unable to move. I found a nagging sensation of teenage rebellion that I used to embrace for years on end. I wanted to start over, wanted to be a nameless enigma, and I knew I couldn't have that at my grandparent's house. I knew I wouldn't be able to escape the demons that chased me out of my stereotypical Pennsylvanian home. So I sat firmly in the sand, letting the particles slip through the crevices of my toes and my fingers. I let myself relax, if just for a moment, and I hid the guilt in the part of my heart that I left to rot back home. My father didn't have to know that I wasn't where he thought I was exactly, I made it to Maine, and I believed I was old enough to care for my well-being. I made it to Belfast, and I felt as if that was where I was supposed to be.

When I was certain that the bus was far gone, I pushed myself off the ground and stumbled while trying to maintain a decent footing in the unpredictable sand. I was a klutz. I was just another idiotic teenager who believed that I was mature enough to be fully on my own. I wasn't. I was a fool. I was blinded by anger from the world that turned against me. I was a walking cliché. I was turning into the person everyone thought that I would be. I hated it. I hated me.

I threw my mother's guitar case behind my back, and carried a vintage suitcase down the beach, not glancing twice at the locals who looked at me like I was foreign. Well, I tried not to glance twice at the locals because every time I did, I felt anxiety flutter in my heart like a hummingbird's wings. I didn't belong. My cotton-candy pink hair and excessively caked makeup made me look like a Korean Pop Star, and my ivory skin made me look as pale as snow compared to the sun-kissed skin of the locals. I made myself different so that I would be intimidating, so that people would leave me alone, not so people would flock to me like a freak in a freak show.

As I walked down the beach part of me wanted to turn around, head back to the bus stop and tell myself to stop overreacting. Maybe my gut was wrong, I thought. Maybe I should have let my grandparents baby me and express sorrow for my loss. Maybe I should have lived a life of suffering for one more year before taking off to a university abroad, so far away from home that I could pretend to be a new person completely so that I could change everything from my nationality to my name. I didn't have to be Piper if I waited around, but I didn't know who else I could be, and I couldn't take my toxic town anymore. I couldn't breathe. I was dying. I was drowning in gossip that seemed to revolve around my tattered family.

I had no other choice or at least I told myself that I didn't as I paced back and forth, trying to force myself to stick to one decision. Yes, theoretically my options were wide open, but my dilemma wasn't a perplexing as I made it be. I was going to start over no matter what it took, it was just a matter of when. When was now. Well, technically when was then.

Besides debating where I belonged, I started to worry about my future. It was the first time I was truly on my own, even though I basically raised myself for years prior, it still felt different. In my mind I had the choice to do two things, be a kid, or grow up. In the end, I decided to be practical and prepare myself for what life was supposed to be like; I homeschooled myself, found a place to call home, got a job, did things adults were expected to do, and attempted to find myself again, but it was a slow and painful process.

Starting over is never really as easy as we think it should be. In my mind, I believed that a new existence could help me stop living in fear. In my mind, my new beginning was supposed to help me open up to strangers for the first time in my life. In Belfast, I was supposed to become social and become a fearless extrovert instead of being the traumatized introvert who tended to tremble when people made eye contact. With this new start, I believed, falsely, that my problems were over and that things would just instantly get better. I was independent, and yet, in the beginning, I had nothing but big dreams and convoluted plans. I started off homeless, jobless, and friendless in a tiny town that wasn't used to strangers showing up.

I was a stain on society; I was the poster child for things no one wanted to be. I was the kid people pitied while praying to their omniscient Gods, asking for their lives to be spared. And like most of humanity, I did not want to be pitied. I did not want the strange stares from adults as they clutched their children tightly. I did not want people to have hopeful wishes for me. I did not want people to dole

7

out meaningless promises of how my life would get better eventually. I wanted them to leave me alone like they did before. I prayed for the invisible treatment that I once despised.

I walked towards the end of the beach where the sandy terrain flirted with compacted dirt and disappeared into a thicket of trees. I was walking away from the population and into a life full of solace where my only company would be the birds and the bees. I was denying the life I had imagined for myself and instead I decided to stay in my comfort zone, in my metaphorical box. I for some reason was craving isolation as if I were craving a scoop of Rocky Road. I had to get away from everything and everyone, just for the time being so I could think. So I could plan my next move. Deeper I went into the thicket that seemed to be more of a forest than anything and followed the growing darkness. The sun at that point was tangoing with the Earth, the once vivid blues were becoming pinks and oranges, and traces of black lined its edges. I had to find somewhere to rest, and though I had money, I didn't have enough to find a place to spend the night. Farther and farther, deeper and deeper. The more I explored, the more lost I became, the more frigid it seemed to be, the more I regretted my decision, the more I craved for my toxic home. I felt as if I was Snow White wandering through the enchanted forest. The demons of the night were watching my

8

every move through the trees as I became more and more paranoid and my movements became deliberate and quick. I eventually realized that I was just making circles, that soon I wouldn't be able to see my hand, so I moved into a small clearing of trees, pulled out a stolen box of matches and began to collect firewood.

Twigs and branches littered the ground, and there seemed to be no trace of human interaction. I had discovered my own twisted paradise, dark and eerie but also surprisingly serene. I had found my own personal utopia, the one place in the world that seemed to be as paradoxical as I was and still am, and though it sounds foolish of me, and I realized that it was nearly impossible for no one to have ventured into this patch of land, I claimed it mine. I claimed everything as far as I could see my own domain. In this place, I planned on beginning again, and I planned on getting over my irrational fear of creatures lurking in the dusk. I planned on being someone else. I would be the extroverted girl I imagined myself to be by day, and then every night, when the sunset, I would disappear into the woods and become my true self. I would have multiple identities. I would teach myself to wear a mask. I would become so much of a mystery that the world would have questioned my existence. Who is Piper? Who is the loud mouthed girl that disappears into thin air each night? That girl would be the better me, the social experiment. That girl would be the definition of popularity. She would become the girl I once envied and loathed.

But to start over I had to create a foundation. I had to start a home, but that was a task for another day. My focus at that time was solely on surviving the night and organizing a grand scheme on how I was going to get away with my duplicity. My focus was on starting a fire that would warm me on the surprisingly frigid June night. My focus was on everything but home. I was a teen who got away with a metaphorical murder. That night signified the death of the old me. The girl who everyone saw as a freak was now dead to me, and as far as I was concerned, she was also dead to the world.

The darkness overwhelmed me for a moment, then with a flick of a match, my world was ignited. The warm glow was a calling song. A leather trunk was my seat, and for an hour, I watched the flames dance to a fading beat before I pulled out my mother's weathered guitar and gave the flames something to dance to.

The fire's song was thick like syrup and warm like a spring day. It radiated memories of a beloved music teacher. It hummed the secrets of talent spared for a rainy day. As a writer, I always admired my mother's talent to make a story come to life, but as the guitar's vibrato twinkled in the twilight, I knew that I finally was able to tell a story just as melodious, and I knew that my life was finally beginning.

# NOW:

I notice things. I notice the tiny changes in life. I notice people's nervous habits, their subtle expressions that reveal their true emotions; if I played poker, I'd be the best at discovering a person's tell. Although I have no interest in gambling, life is enough of a risk for my taste, but I'll admit, I do find it fascinating to watch a person unfold before my eyes. I guess it's no surprise that I find myself analyzing my interviewer's body language as she analyzes me. Does she like me? Do I even have a chance? Should I have dyed my hair back to my natural color or will she find the fairy floss color that I adore charming?

The skirmish woman taps her foot rapidly against the cracked tile floor, her eyes scan me quickly and sporadically, and she has this annoying habit of chewing on the tip of her pen, leaving a trace of saliva on its metallic end. As she asks me questions, her voice is soft but firm, and after every question I answer, she takes tedious amounts of notes as if she's afraid to miss some important detail or flaw of mine. As the interview progresses, she tries to examine my subconscious by asking me personal questions, questions that technically should never be asked in a formal interview. I don't point that out to her, though; I'm a closed book, and any answer I give her will be vague and professional, just like how answers should be.

What did I like to do on the weekends? She was a churchgoer who was looking to convert others, she said, trying to politely ask if I had a religious affiliation without being caught.  Who did I like to spend my time with? She had a doting husband who worked at home as a journalist for Belfast's online news journal and three darling kids, all kids who would attend the school I was trying to land a job in. She asked everything and anything, but my responses gave little away about my history, and my resumé was somewhat blank, although my few references spoke highly of me. I had only worked in a bookstore and a tiny indie coffee shop right outside of town. I had no experience being a librarian, just a liberal arts degree and the beginnings of a masters in English education.

I honestly didn't even know if the job was right for me, but I had bills to pay. I had to be a mature adult and take whatever job was available to me. Besides, being a librarian sounds quite lovely, besides the fact that I'll have to entertain children constantly. If I manage to get this job my only responsibility will be to care for books and share my love of reading with others, and that was something I always wanted to do.

"Now that I know a bit about you, I have to say, I think you would fit this position quite well, but the final decision isn't up to me. It's up to my boss."

"Wait, so I wouldn't be reporting to you on a daily basis?" I ask.

"No ma'am, I'm just the secretary. If I give you a glowing report you'd have one more interview with the big boss and he'll decide your fate from there."

"Oh."

I take a gulp of air and my toes begin to dance in my closed-toe shoes. I'm barely able to speak to this woman, a woman who has this facade that appears to be so honest and kind though she doesn't even know who I am. How am I supposed to go through the same brutal questioning again? My first true interview and I'm already subjected to go through another one.

"Don't worry sweetie. He's kind of a hard ass, but I swear once you get through to him he has a heart of gold."

"I'm not worried per say, I'm just not sure if I'm prepared for what's next."

"Don't be. You're doing fine right now. Unless you spill your tea all over me or decide to go on a long-winded rant, you are guaranteed my recommendation."

"You'd do that for me?"

She nods and smiles before answering, "I have a feeling about you. Maybe it's just because you're different, but nevertheless, we need someone like you here."

"Thank you, Mrs. Prigette."

"Oh please, call me Cathy."

Cathy flips her strawberry locks and flashes a toothy smile. Her kindness is almost disgusting and seems to be disingenuous. It's as if she has the charm of a southern belle instead of a cold heart that northerners are renowned for. She holds out her hand and grabs ahold of mine, forcing me into a limp handshake.

"I prefer to keep calling you by a title until I get a position here. It's only fair that I give you the respect that you deserve," I mutter politely.

"Well, you are giving me respect by calling me what I want. No one here calls me Mrs. Prigette and I'd like to keep it that way. It's like I'm with my extended family, and if you're going to possibly join the family one day I want you to feel like you're welcome."

I smile and thank whatever omnipresent being is watching over me at the moment. I may not necessarily believe in a God, but I won't deny one's existence when something goes my way. Every time I've asserted myself and tried to find a job, things have gone my way. It's as if people find my quirky attitude charming at first glance. It's as if people here believe in me more than anyone else has, even though no one ever pushes me to my breaking point. I swear, if snow didn't engulf the town every winter, I wouldn't think I was in the North East. People here are so friendly, or at least they're better at playing pretend than people back home. It's like a small town in the middle of the bible belt, and surprisingly I love the vibe it radiates.

"Well then Cathy, I thank you so very much for your time here today, and unless there is more you want to learn about me, I should go. I wouldn't want to prevent you from getting any tasks done today."

I shrink down in my seat as I finish my sentence. I sound like a nervous teenage girl, so I clear my throat and force myself to sit up straight. I force myself to appear stronger and more professional than I truly am. I have to sell my lie. I have to truly embrace my new mask.

*Fake it till you make it; isn't that how the saying goes?*

"Why I guess it is time to wrap it up. If I don't hurry, Mr. Wolf will get very angry with me. It was honestly a pleasure to meet you, Ms. Addison. I will be in touch."

I take hold of her perfectly manicured hand once more and this time I shake it quickly and firmly. I remember reading in a book something that said that handshakes are memorable and important in

15

setting the tone of a work relationship. As soon as the opportunity permits, I disappear out of the conference room and into the halls of the minuscule Catholic School. Part of me wants to explore the building, to find the room I want so desperately to be mine, but I resist. If it's meant to be, I'll be united with the cavern of books eventually.

I walk out of the seemingly rotting doors and sigh before I get into my blue bug. Working with books has always been my safety net, it has always been something I knew I could rely on until I managed to finish my manuscript, but now I don't know what's next. I can't keep being a barista; I'm not some wanna be hipster that tries to fit in at an indie coffee shop just so she can pretend to be over her Starbucks addiction.

For hours I drive around my tiny town, trying to break myself out of my existential crisis, but to no avail. I'm too young to be regretting my life choices, but I can't help it. I've fallen in love with career paths that are being reduced to dust due to the internet and an ever-changing society that has fallen in love with technological advancements. I don't know what I'm supposed to do in this world or how to stop feeling like there is a hole in my heart that's always searching for answers. I'm going insane, and I don't even know if the job is mine or not. I can't even imagine what will happen if I'm utterly rejected. I'm running out of what's left of my brother's college fund, and every spare penny has been poured into my master's degree.

Eventually, I clear my thoughts and head towards my home, my little cottage in the woods, my fairytale hideaway. I pull into the dirt ridden front yard around dinner time, but I pay no mind to my emaciated stomach and instead pull out my only prized possession, my baby blue Imperial typewriter and try to jump into my novel. I've always been a huge proponent of getting the most authentic feel when doing something. I feel as if that's the only way to do anything right. In many ways, I feel as if I have to finish my book this way, or else it won't be any good, and it doesn't matter to me I have the book saved to my brand new laptop, it has to start and end with just me and my baby.

*I spent years in that damned café watching people fall in love, and my copious amounts of notes never led me any closer to the truth. What is attraction? What is love? Scientists claim that it's nothing more than a chemical equation, romantics claim that it's an overwhelming feeling of warmth and joy, but I, I don't know what it truly is. I don't know what anything really is. I'm beginning to regret my life's work. Nothing I've done has* worked out. Nothing I will do will lead to the gratification I've been searching for my whole life. Honestly, I'm just closer to-

My phone rings and I jump out of a trance. Every time I write I become so absorbed that I just forget the world around me. I become enchanted by thoughts that I'm too afraid to say out loud, and so when I get to that point in life, I let my characters speak for me. I let their world become the world of my dreams, and truth be told, it's quite lovely in there. If I could stay in a book for the rest of my life, I'd be perfectly content.

I reach for my phone and answer it without even glancing at the number. No one ever calls me unless it's my Dad. We haven't talked in awhile and the last time that we did it ended in a fight. I honestly can't remember the last time we had a pleasant conversation. I can't remember the last time that we didn't resent each other. I miss my Dad, but I don't miss the man he is now, I miss the man he used to be.

"Hey dad, how are you?"

"Hello?" The voice on the other end isn't my father's; it's deeper and harsher somehow. His voice is rough like sandpaper, but it demands my full attention.

"Oh sorry, sir, I thought that you were someone else. How can I help you?"

When I realize that it's not my dad I start to panic. I'm not good at making first impressions, and I'm even worse at talking on the phone.

"Um yes, I am Richard Wolff, headmaster at St. Agatha's of Sicily. Is this Ms. Addison's number?"

"Yes sir, that is me. How can I help you this evening?"

"First off, I'd like to apologize for calling you at such a late hour especially since you seem to be awaiting an important call," he clears his throat to try to mask his condescending tone, and I roll my eyes. It was just a simple mistake, but I guess that's all it takes. "Secondly, I'd like to offer you the opportunity to come back in and have a final interview with me. Cathy spoke very highly of you, and we are in a tight crunch to find a qualified librarian as soon as humanly possible with the school year upon us, so if you are able to come in tomorrow I'd like to see if we can close this deal."

"That sounds quite lovely Mr. Wolff, what time would you like me to arrive?"

"I think my lunch hour is clear tomorrow, so around noon would be the most convenient for me."

"That sounds perfect. I will be there at noon tomorrow and thank you again."

"Thank you."

I start to speak again, but the line goes dead. *He hung up on me.* I don't know how to feel about this situation, but I do have a feeling Mrs. Prigette was downplaying my potential boss's personality. Just by the tone of his demanding voice, I can tell that he's going to be condescending and I have no time nor patience for that kind of personality.

I pull myself out of my ravaged winged chair and stroll to the kitchen while trying to avoid the unfortunately placed claw-footed tub that lies in the middle of the room. I need a cup of tea. I need tea to think. I need tea to write. I even need tea to sleep. Hell, if I can't figure out the answer to my problems by the time I finish a cup of green tea, it isn't a problem worth fixing. I guess that's why my tub still lies where an island really should, my floors still creak, and the occasional leak in the roof still occurs, but whatever, it works a majority of the time.

I chug the rest of my tea and, in an unladylike manner, strip to my undergarments and run warm water for a bath before dropping in a blue bath bomb that makes the water look like a galaxy. Tomorrow is going to be one hell of a day, so I have to be as relaxed as humanly possible. Green tea, a candle-lit bath, and a bath bomb are ingredients for a perfect night in. To finish the night off, I run to the other end of the room and pull out my favorite record, a worn down album from the forties. I sink into the tub as the jazzy tunes bounce off the wooden walls. My wavy hair rests down the back of the tub, and I close my eyes, allowing my skin to shrivel up like grapes in the warm California sun. This is the way to properly prepare for an interview. This is the way to calm down. This is the way to allow your inner self to shine through. This is the way to be quirky old Piper.

By the time the album ends, I realize that I've spent more than an hour in the tub, relaxing in a pool of glitter, dye, and my own filth. I jump out quickly and fall to the floor, bruising the top portion of my ass. Not surprisingly, I let a few expletives flow before drying myself off and putting clothes back on. I have to finish getting ready, so I drain the water while silently cursing at my past self for being so lazy and so blind to the obvious renovations that still need to be done in my home before running to the wardrobe that seems horribly out of place with its oversized shape shoved awkwardly in the corner.

As I try on an absurd number of outfits, my indecisiveness becomes ridiculous. I have to make a good impression and to do that I have to hide who I truly am. By the time I finally settle on a gray sweater dress and ballerina flats, a mound of clothes sits on top of my bed, and I really don't feel like putting any of it away. I push my clothes off the bed and onto the floor all while telling myself that I'll clean it up in the morning.

It takes me forever to settle into bed, but I eventually fall asleep around midnight, and my dreams are full of fantasies and twisted realities. But of course, reality is not a fairytale, so unlike the princess I dreamed myself to be, I wake up looking like a Disney villain with smeared makeup in the spots I was too lazy to scrub and matted hair that tangled through my tossing and turning in the night.

Making myself look even slightly presentable takes hours, so in a way, waking up at the crack of dawn is a blessing and a curse. After I slump into the small half bath, I splash boiling hot water on my face, and as the rest of my daily mask is destroyed, I apply a new one. A new mask each and every day. Yesterday's was the hopeful teacher who would do and say anything to land a job, and today's? Well, I don't know who she's going to be yet. I'm debating between a persona of an uptight business person who is focused on one thing and one thing only, work, and a girl who wants to do nothing more than spending her days raising someone else's kids. I think I'll go with the first; Mr. Wolff seems to be too serious, too impersonal to appreciate the work of a woman who is truly passionate about teaching.

I start to cake my face with powder and liquid, masking all of my blemishes and imperfections as I begin to bury the girl with the quirks. Then I take out a variety of pencils and tools that look like weapons. Liquid traces my eye leaving a wing at each corner, a brush-like tool makes my eyelashes flutter, and a tiny cotton wand coats my lids in the subtlest silver glitter. By the time twenty minutes pass all I have left to do is to fix my mangled hair and coat my lips with a waxy paint, but those are finishing touches; things I have to wait to do until right before I leave. I'm not stupid; I know if I come out of the bathroom with a completed face and the perfect up-do to match, twenty minutes later it will be falling apart at the seams and I'll look more like a clown than a woman who wants to desperately join the workforce.

I stroll to the kitchen and muscle memory kicks in; avoid the broken kitchen tile, watch out for the squeaky floorboard in the living room, make sure to shimmy around the small desk before eating or else the pile of books you've been too lazy to put away will bury you alive. By the time I'm fully awake and aware that the day has truly arrived, the sun is dancing in the sky, and it's casting shadows through my broken stained glass window, one that I'm too afraid to fix. It's beautiful, and the reflection is something I never get tired of watching. It's as if the hell I go through each morning is rewarded with my own personal rainbow.

Breakfast, of course, consists of tea and a book by the window. Sometimes I even try to get the sun's rays to reflect off the pages, bringing even more beauty to the world that I have called my own, but yeah, that's not really how light works... The light tends to be too bright for my night owl tendencies, and it causes me to retreat back into my bedroom where I again avoid all my responsibilities and finish a chapter or two of my latest obsession before I get dressed and become a full-fledged adult.

Around nine thirty I realize that I'm running out of time, and my reflexes kick into gear. Years of procrastinating the simplest tasks have led to my downfall, but at the same time gives me a strange sense of amusement. I like to challenge myself, I like to prove my fears wrong when I can. I throw on my clothes and run back and forth throughout the house to do simple tasks. Clean the dishes, do hair into a braid, put away clothes, sweep the floor, throw on perfume. By the time I finish everything I barely have time to throw on my shoes and a jacket before running out the door. Catching my breath is not an option, the school is a good twenty minutes away from my house, and it's already eleven.

I force my car to start, and I swear she's slowly dying the whole way there. I've had her for almost ten years, and I'm overdue to get a new one, but then again I'm overdue for a lot of things. If I get this job, things will be easier for me; I'll finally be able to support myself without rationing the last remaining dollars of my college/ "you're an adult now get out my house" fund. I can't afford to be broke, and though I am not in the most ideal living situation, I have avoided slipping into debt my entire adult life, and I plan to stay that way. I can afford to struggle, just like every creative person I know, but I'll be smarter about surviving. I know how to manage my money, I know when my bank is reaching a limit. I know when it's time to change my dreams and adapt them to more realistic ones. I know that playing house and attempting to write a book won't feed me in six months, but a job that promises a constant paycheck will. Most creators will refuse to admit that their work is useless during their lifetime, but I know mine is. I'm just a word wizard; I know how to arrange words and make them sound poetic, but no one in this lifetime will be able to understand my thought process. It will take years of analyzing my every word, every character trait, and every flaw, every minuscule plot detail, for people to appreciate me, but that's okay, that's how all the greats were and how I intend to be too.

Halfway to the school, I feel nerves begin to build up. My foot starts to tremble, and my stomach begins to clench. My lack of sleep begins to seep through my face. I have to pull over to calm down; I have to snap myself back to reality, but I'm running out of time. There isn't enough time to process anything or do anything, so I try to force myself to stay calm as I drive down roads full of potholes that cause me to feel even jumpier.

My slow and deliberate heartbeat begins to accelerate, and I just have this overwhelming fear that I forgot something. I don't know what's wrong with me or why I'm so scared. I don't know why my confidence has suddenly faded into oblivion. I'm being irrational, and I know I'm being irrational. I can't control my own mind, and it's so damn unfair.

*Not now. Please oh please not now. Compose yourself. You can't do this. You can't fall apart now. You have to be the girl they want you to be. Now is not the time to be yourself. Piper, please. Please. Breathe. One. Two. Three…*

The moment my confidence fades I feel like I'm a scared little girl again, afraid of being judged and picked apart. Ignorant and foolish thoughts seem to slip into my mind, and every time I try to reassure myself, things just get worse. It's as if telling myself that I'm overreacting is just causing me to overreact more.

*I really should dye my hair back to it's normal color. He won't like it. He won't like me. Then what's going to happen? I'm going to have to go back to having three to four shifts a day at the coffee shop, maybe even try to get my old job at the bookstore to stay above water and even then I'll be cutting it close. I can't do this. I can't risk the chance. I'll just. I don't know. I'll just pretend I got sick and reschedule. I just need more time to prepare. Time to pretend that I'm still a kid. I can't do this. I can't do this. I can't.*

When I can't take anymore and concede to the fact that my nerves are shot, I force myself to pull over and collapse on the steering wheel. I have an overwhelming desire to burst into sobs while a stupid unnerving feeling sits in the back of my mind. It's that nagging feeling that just pesters you until you realize that you've missed something, but I haven't forgotten a damn thing. I just want to scream at myself. I want to stare my reflection down and ask, *what the hell is wrong with you? Stop shaking! Stop being afraid of the World! We've been through this. As long as we stay to ourselves, nothing bad can happen!*

My shudders quickly transform into shivers which then turn into full out tremors, and all the while I'm still trying to talk some rationale back into my head. Why can't I just have one day? Why can't I have one day where I function like everyone else in this world?

Why can't I shed myself of my true identity? Why can't I live a day where I can truly be the person I pretend to be? I'm so sick of living a life where I'm not even functioning; I'm just coping. For almost my entire life, I've been learning to cope with my defects and I'm tired of relying on pills to fix my problems, hell, they don't even do a decent job. If anything, the medicine is just a foundation, something to put my mind at ease, everything else that occurs during the day is because I've learned how to adapt my persona to every individual situation.

In the back of my mind, I see my bottle of courage, sitting right next to the kitchen sink, untouched. I know I say I don't need my medication, I know I say they're just some temporary fix, but without them, I'm a ticking time bomb waiting to explode. I know that no matter what, words will be censored, but my body language is what's unpredictable, my roaming mind will cause my demise. I can't even remember a day where I was able to function how society expects me to without my pill. Screw what I said before; I'm nothing without it. I seem so over the top; I seem like I'm such an animated person, but in all honesty, I do it to mask the pain I've been through. Broken people do crazy things just so the world believes that they're whole. I mean just look at me. I've had pink hair for over ten years, adopted the typical flower child lifestyle, and devoted myself to constant

28

isolation so that people won't try and get to know me. I want people to think that I'm okay, I want people to judge my appearance rather than the real me. I don't want anyone to discover who Piper truly is. God, I don't know. I'm tired of living behind a wall of PTSD. I'm tired of the panic attacks, I'm tired of the sleepless nights, I'm tired of the stomachaches and lack of appetite. I want to live. All I want to do is to live.

As my body begins to return to slight equilibrium, I force the windows down, ignore the slow demise of my hair, and force myself back on the road. I'm going to force myself to go through the interview even if that means losing the job because of a disorder. I have to prove to myself that I'm stronger than I think. I blast my favorite playlist in the car and force myself to step on the gas, ignoring every legal rule of the road. I'm going to make it in time if it kills me, or any other innocent creature.

I pull into the parking lot and I have just enough time to throw a coat of a shimmery pink lip-gloss and fix my braid. I'm going to walk into the building any moment now and within a matter of an hour my future will become predetermined. My fate is in the stars hands now and if I can pull myself together, I will be leaving this decrepit campus with a job. I just have to believe in myself now. I have to believe that I'm stronger than anything

# THEN:

    I have come to the conclusion that death is misery, but there is nothing more miserable than commemorating a life that was not worth living. There I was, a seventh grader with doe-like eyes and a sunken frame, all alone in a cemetery in the middle of the day. My corrupt brother and angelic mother were both buried that day, and I was the only one to bid them a final farewell. I was the one who had to spread the dirt over their graves, I was the one that was left to put personal items in the casket before they were closed and lowered, I was the one that had to be brave, but I was just a kid.

    That morning I forced myself out of a zombie-like state and trampled through the hollow halls that reeked of beer. My uncle was supposed to be moving in any day, and he was supposed to mend the hole in my broken family. He was supposed to fix my father and bring him back to me, but sometimes plans end up being unreachable dreams instead of reality. My father was too far-gone, destined to live a life of absent-minded behavior, floating in and out of my life when I was incapable of financially supporting myself. I didn't even bother to wake my father out of his comatose state the day of the funeral. I preferred his state of denial, that resulted in blissful

30

sleep, over his drunken state where he'd slur his words until the world couldn't damn him anymore.

That morning I found myself staring at Charlie's door, looking for answers that weren't there. I ended up breaking the door of my brother's locked bedroom before stealing his behavioral pills, the pills that controlled his demons. The pills that, for a time, went untouched for months. The pills created a better him, the pills created a better Charlie, they created a brother I wasn't afraid to love, a brother I was proud of and couldn't fear. My hands trembled as I pulled them to my heart and my eyes wandered around the room that I was banished from; a new foreign land was in front of my eyes but it was too tainted to appreciate. I stumbled farther in, looking for anything that was worth dying with him, and suddenly I had a pang of guilt in my heart, as if I shouldn't be going through Charlie's stuff. My mind was so preconditioned to allow him to have personal space that I couldn't possibly comprehend the fact that he was dead.

*Charlie was gone.*

I shook the morbid thought out of my mind and continued to explore the cavern. Childhood pictures and trophies lined the bookshelves and his books laid strewn about the floor. Charlie didn't understand the value of a book like I did, and no matter how much I pestered him about caring for them, he always preferred people over books. His bookshelves seemed to be a timeline of his life. Memories of t-ball with the boys and learning how to ride a bike lined the bottom shelf, as if he was ashamed of that portion of his life. Transitioning up the shelves, I noticed a gap in time, a time that Charlie tried to desperately hide.

I tried to erase any negative thoughts that floated in my mind, but it was so damn hard. I just had an overwhelming desire to break everything he ever owned. I wanted to know what caused him to break, what caused him to give up everything he had, everything we had as a family. I forced my lungs full of air and by the time I sighed, my anger had vanished, just like that. One moment here, the next gone. I won't even bother making a connection to life, everyone knows that dying just simply is and comparing it to irrational feelings won't make the phenomena less painful. Nothing and no one can fill the void that occurs with a loss, I know that, and I believe in it too.

I forced myself away from his bookshelf and sat upon his unmade bed that reeked of cheap cologne. It smelled like him; the new him, the party boy, the all American-jock, the boy I detested and loathed. The boy I refused to call my brother. I forced the sheets around my shoulders and reveled in their warmth until the sun was floating high in the sky. By midday, it was time to say goodbye to my loved ones forever, but I wasn't sure if I was ready, so I went through

Charlie's closet and pulled out his letterman jacket and threw it over a lace black dress that my father would have scolded me for.

I don't remember how I made it to the cemetery that day. I must have taken my bike or walked the entire way, either way it doesn't matter, my mind has labeled that moment as irrelevant. All I remember is arriving late to two freshly dug plots and a plethora of empty chairs. No one came. No one was there, except me and my reluctant pastor who would soon abandon me to silent grieving.

Charlie's selfish deeds caused a satanic label to be plastered over my family's name, causing all of us to be seen in the same light. My innocent mother, a victim of my brother's rage, was doomed to hell just for raising a boy who was horribly misunderstood. Everyone was against us, and if I was blind to that fact prior, the funeral just solidified the idea.

Isolation was awful for a small girl. No one was there to tell me that everything was going to be alright, no one was there to promise that heaven would welcome my family with loving arms, no one was there to promise to support me through a moment of pain, there was just me and the literal remains of my family.

I pulled one of the eroding foldable chairs and placed it between the caskets while I tried to decide how to say goodbye, I tried to decide if death was truly the end of life or if it was a beginning

33

like I had believed before. Once I composed my thoughts, I got out of the chair and I moved to my mother's side first; her eyelids were shut and her hands rested over her chest, concealing the gruesome bullet wound that led to her demise. I reached for her hands and ignored the feeling of bitter cold. I knew there was no soul left, but I was a kid; I liked to play make believe.

"Mom guess what! I've been practicing the guitar like you told me to. I think I'm even starting to get the chords right. I'll never be as good as you though."

I paused and my eyes perked up, as if I was listening for her response.

"Mom? Did I ever tell you that you that I love you? Cause I do. I love you so very much. For ever and ever. It's true. It's true. You gotta believe me. I know I like to give you a hard time sometimes, but you mean so much to me. You have to know that."

I tucked a loose strand of hair back behind her frigid ear and kissed her forehead, right between the eyebrows, right where she used to kiss me goodnight.

"Goodnight Mom. I love you."

I looked around the desolate cemetery for a while, part of me just wanted to dive right in with her as if I was crawling into her bed after a nightmare, but I couldn't. I couldn't do anything but watch her fade out of my life. I put my hands into my brother's jacket and my finger's flirted with a small figure; one of my mother's spare guitar picks was waiting for me. Fate left an ironic gift, something to bury with my mother, a piece of us that can stay with her forever.

I remember the day she bought me a tiny pink guitar that was no bigger than a ukulele, it was then when I was no bigger than a life sized doll. I was in love, desperately in love with that instrument. I was so determined to learn how to play only to be mediocre at best. I was always afraid that I was going to disappoint her when she learned that I wasn't a virtuosic person like her, but she didn't mind, she just loved the chaos that erupted in the house when music was being made.

I shifted my gaze back towards her and pried open her hand. I couldn't look as her decomposing body began to make odd noises, so I simply dropped the pick in her hand, closed it, and tried to stop my eyes from tearing up as I shut the casket. I had one final goodbye to say but I wasn't sure if I was going to be able to say the right words.

"Charlie, don't get mad at me but I went through your room. Don't worry; I didn't go through your secret stash or anything. I just, I wanted to bring you something."

In my subconscious I looped a memory of him huffing, only to quickly shed his ego and smile wildly at me. Bad boy Charlie had a heart of gold, but he'd never admit it.

"It's your medicine. I know you haven't been taking it lately, but, but I don't know. I just thought that it might help you, wherever you go. You know, It's not okay to be a monster Charlie, and I know deep down you're not so maybe you can take them and they'll let you in those pearly white gates. Maybe the world will see you for who you truly are, and until that day comes, I guess this is goodbye. I have to go live. I have to live without you and prove to the world that I'm better than they think. I have to pretend like you mean nothing to me, but you know the truth. You know I'll never stop fighting for us. Even though part of me hates you, I'll never stop fighting."

By the time I finished my thoughts, my brain was fried and my heart ached. I had to get away; I was falling apart.

"Bye Charlie."

I dropped the container of pills into his casket and tried to walk away, but my knees just collapsed underneath me. A weight was on my chest, and I was not able to move. It's as if my game of pretend was over, and reality hit me like a wrecking ball. It's as if life was tired of my optimism and utter denial. I guess I always believed that death was only for aged souls, but it's for everyone. You don't get to pick when you die, you don't get to map out your life.

It would have been easier for me if I understood that earlier, if I understood that planning and organizing for a future would not prevent the inevitable from occurring, maybe I wouldn't have become a lost cause. Maybe I wouldn't have become a compulsive person whose only crutch was the bottle of pills I clutched to my chest each night. There are a lot of things children are ignorant to, things that should be kept hidden to preserve an innocence that is equivalent to utter bliss. If I didn't watch my mother waltz with death or watch my brother become the grim reaper, maybe I wouldn't have aged faster than I ever did physically, maybe I would have lived a productive life that wasn't defined by tragedy.

I'm not sure why I always come back to questioning what would have happened if Charlie wasn't a murderer when I recollect my past. I can't change anything now. I can't become unparalyzed; I can't become unbroken. I can't change who I was. I can't change what shaped me. History can't be changed, and no matter how many time-travel novels I indulge myself in, no matter how many sci-fi shows I watch, nothing can ever be altered.

For hours I watched the colors of the sky in the ground, my dress caked in dirt and my hair tangled by stray leaves. I watched and pretended to die. I watched and held my breath until my skin became tinted a grayish-blue from lack of oxygen. I played the stereotypical kid in mourning. I played as an adolescent girl that was so attached to her past that she didn't know how life could possibly go on. When the sky turned to velvet, when the trees began to look more like looming monsters than nature's gift, I pulled myself up and realized that the God I once believed in wouldn't let me die.

"It's not fair. It's not fair. It's not fair."

The most common phrase of a spoiled and entitled child quickly became my motto, my catchphrase. I hadn't done anything wrong. I was just a religious girl who believed that loving my family and praising a figment of my imagination would offer protection from the evils in the world. I clearly wasn't familiar with the belief that you had to prove your allegiance by going through a series of struggles, and even now that I'm familiar with the religious theory, I don't know if I accept it.

I cried myself to sleep that night, letting the misery that I had bottled up flow like a river. I just remember praying with swollen red eyes and a snotty nose. I remember praying for death. I remember praying for someone to just put me out of my misery. I prayed for oblivion for months and months until one day I just stopped praying completely. I was tired of being optimistic. I was tired of hope. All I wanted was for it all to be over, I wanted to stop existing, and years later I too would follow down a slippery slope of contemptible acts, though none as bad as murder, none that couldn't be forgiven and excused.

# NOW:

I rest on a wooden seat outside of Mr. Wolff's office. My only companions are school children who keep their gaze towards the floor. The feeling of dread rises back within me, but I try to maintain a steady breath, and I try to keep subtle urges from disrupting my equilibrium. I feel like a small child waiting for a punishment to be doled out. It's so odd, it's as if the manipulative teachings that were hammered into my subconscious are beginning to dictate how I act in social situations; maybe they have always dictated my thought-process and it's taken me until now to realize it. My eyes light up at this idea as I try to make connections to everyday life just to pass the time.

"Ms. Addison, Mr. Wolff will see you now."

I snap out of my daze and my body twitches unexpectedly. I jump to my feet to hide my nerves, and the two children who were once avoiding my gaze, are focused on my every move. By the fear on their faces, it's as if they're silently wishing me luck on my journey into the pits of hell. They're acting as if I'm walking in blind to war. I know I should give them a reassuring smile, to calm their nerves, but instead I duck my head down and follow Cathy into his office.

When I walk in, I'm greeted by the stereotypical alpha male; a man who won't truly acknowledge my presence because I'm wasting his precious time though in reality, he's gnawing on a grotesque looking hamburger. His silver hair is perfectly gelled back and he's wearing a navy blue suit tied together with a maroon tie.

"Piper Addison I presume?" he asks, not bothering to look up.

"Yes sir, that's me."

"Well come in and shut the door!"

I obey his command and tread cautiously into the pristine office. Every corner is decked in masculinity; leather chairs and cool colors signify his dominance over the school. The contrasting red walls signify his willingness to command and lead. Even the motivational posters reek of man, spilling tales of leadership and male-dominated work environments. I know I shouldn't jump to conclusions but this whole situation leaves a bitter taste in my mouth and it's causing my inner feminist to scream.

I sit down on a leather stool that's positioned in a way that he is looking down upon me and it takes all the will I possess to not scoff at him. I can just tell that the longer I stay in the room, the less likely it is for me to get the job, but nevertheless I keep quiet about my enraged disposition, and it's not just because I'm afraid of the repercussions, but because I don't know how to speak up. My thoughts have always been well-crafted, and I often mentally praise myself for a level of raised intelligence, but for some odd reason my thoughts get lost in translation when I try to speak.

"I'm not one for pleasantries and formal introductions, so I'm going to jump straight to the point. Why should I hire you?"

My eyebrows rise at his blunt behavior and I trace a small smirk forming on his stoic face. I see the enjoyment that has resulted from my surprise and I just don't get it. How can a man who runs a school be so stereotypically cruel?

"Excuse me Mr. Wolff, I don't mean to tell you how to conduct an interview but wouldn't you like to hear about my accomplishments and my qualifications? My strengths and weaknesses? The things that would help you assess if I'm right for your establishment?"

"No, and frankly I couldn't care less about those trivial things. There is a method to my madness sweetheart, and there is a reason your first interview was with my doting secretary. You see, she tends to care more about the meticulous things and I don't. I want answers, I want productivity, and I want warriors. I don't need a woman in here telling me about the things that she should keep in her diary. Does that make sense?"

I bite my lip and nod.

"Good," he replies coolly, "Now I'll ask you one more time; why should I hire you?"

"I want to make a difference in this world sir. Just like every other faculty member in this building, I want to do something that can benefit others and teaching is the only way I know how."

"Now I wasn't born yesterday. I've heard that lie a million times and I don't appreciate it. That answer isn't good enough to get you a job."

"Well, excuse me for being a bit confused. You want me to go into detail explaining why I want the job, but you don't want me to go into details about my life and qualifications?"

"Exactly."

"But that, sir, is impossible."

"Make it possible."

"Well quite frankly, I just need a job," I finish my thought and bite down on the corner of my lips as his eyebrows arch.

"That is the answer I was looking for."

"That's what you wanted?"

"I want bitter honesty, and by having you tell me your true motives I know your passion won't die out. You'll always need money so you'll do whatever I say to get it. It's simple math. Good thing you don't want to be a math teacher, am I right?"

"I guess so..."

"Am I offending you? I'm only joking, you do know that right?"

"No sir, you are not."

"Then what's with that grim look on your face?"

"Oh! Um, sorry it isn't intentional. My brother used to tell me that I had a very unpleasant resting face. Well, he didn't use those words exactly but you know what I mean."

Mr. Wolff slides towards the front of his desk and his once "pleasant" demeanor vanishes. I slide back in my chair a bit and I feel the color draining from my face. I've said too much and screwed everything up.

"No I don't know what you mean. Why don't you indulge me and explain."

"Well, I don't want to be impolite, and I like to keep a professional tone especially when giving first impressions."

"Don't make me repeat myself, Ms. Addison."

"He told me I had a resting bitch face."

I barely utter my last word, but it's audible enough to send the big bad wolf into an obnoxious state of entitlement.

"Now, Piper is it, we don't use expletives here at Saint Agatha's."

"But you said-"

44

"Piper, if you're going to work for me you're going to have to learn my basic rules."

"Such as?" I question.

"Never question me."

"Oh."

"Exactly. Now, since my lunch is coming to a close I think it's time that we wrap up this frivolous interview."

"But what about the job?"

"Hm, I'll have to think about it."

"Okay, when should I be expecting to hear from you?"

"I'm done thinking already."

"Oh?"

I don't understand him. How am I supposed to keep up with these constant mood changes? How am I supposed to know when he's thinking or not? I don't know him and he doesn't know me. It's unfair of him to just assume that everyone knows everything about him.

We stay quiet for a while and once I can't take anymore I but in, "So you have reached a decision?"

"That is correct."

"And what would that be?"

My anger begins to boil. I'm tired of his senseless games. I feel as if I have wasted my time, time I could have been spending at home, writing, or finding other job opportunities.

"You can show up tomorrow, I guess. The building opens at six forty-five and classes start at seven thirty, but you won't have anyone to work with until nine."

"Okay and will I have to prepare any catch up assignments since the children are already into the first week of school?"

"Oh don't be naive, no one needs the library. We just need you to check out books and read to the kids so the teachers get a break. You don't have a curriculum. As far as I'm concerned you are at the bottom of the food chain here, right below the music and art departments."

"I'm sorry, I, I wasn't sure of what you expected of me."

"Well now you are. Now get out of here, I have an important meeting to attend."

"Yes of course, thank you Mr. Wolff."

I jump out of the miniature chair and nearly trip trying to escape my horrendous boss. Mr. Wolff just shakes his head as I flee, and as soon as I finally manage to break free of his grasp, I am relieved. I got the job. I get to be surrounded by a plethora of books every day and night. It's the perfect job for me. I head towards the

46

exit but I'm not ready to leave. I have to see it now. I have to see my new home.

"Cathy, I hate to disturb you, but is there anyway I can go look at the library?"

"Of course darling. Did you get the job?"

"Yeah, I did."

"That's fantastic. Do you want me to take you down there?"

"No thank you. If you could just point me in the right direction..."

"It's down the stairs to the right and the first door on the left is the library. It should be open, but if not, just go into the room next door, the music room, and the teacher should have a key to let you in."

"Okay thank you again."

"No problem! Welcome to the family Piper."

I don't bother to reply back, I just give a weak wave before disappearing into the endless halls of the school. If this is supposed to be my new family, I don't know if I necessarily want to be a part of it. I'm perfectly content with my strained relationship with my father. I don't want anyone to pretend to care about me. I don't want to let anyone else in.

I roam around the school for what seems to be forever and when I approached a dusty door in the heart of the school, my heart leaps. It's everything I imagined it to be and more, and even though it's nothing more than a desolate graveyard for books, it has personality, quirks, and more importantly, it has potential.

In the middle of the building, the heart of the operation, lies the underwhelming room. Its condensed walls are filled to the brim with ragged and decayed books that reek from use and lack of care. Every single book is as delicate as a cloud, and I can't help but feel like every book I trace with my fingers is going to disintegrate in thin air. The flickering fluorescent lights don't help the aura of the room, in fact, it gives the room the appearance of a doctor's office, sterile yet dingy. Although, the lighting does help give the room the appearance of having more space than it really does, and yet, the numerous amounts of furniture take up every space that isn't occupied with books. Beanbags and tiny desks are strewn about the space and a unloved rocking chair sits in the corner by a broken and unusable floor lamp. After inspecting each book, my attention shifts towards the oversized check out desk made of solid oak. It looks solid enough, but as I place my weight upon it, it begins to quiver, wobbling underneath me.

I push myself off the counter and run my fingers along its edges, wiping off the dirt, and leaving a residue on my fingers. Even the technology in the room bears an exaggerated age. The computer that graces my desk seems to be a living dinosaur, it's only capability seems to be to check out and catalog books. I sigh and sink down into a broken office chair that's lost one of its wheels.

Every part of the room needs to be fixed, and though I know it'll probably go unfinished, I want to spruce up my work home. I want to make the library a school gem; I want this room alone to be held in such high esteem that the big bad Wolff has no choice but to accept its relevance in education. I can just see it now. New books line every shelf, everything from the typical classics to sinful romances that people can't help but indulge in. Christmas lights will line the edge of a new checkout counter, and the old, floppy disk operated, computer will be replaced by a high-powered and modern laptop. Plush rugs will cover the cracked and appalling looking floors and cozy lounge chairs will replace the crappy bean bags that look more like potato sacks than actual chairs. By the time I'm done with this place it's going to be perfect. I'm going to rekindle or even spark a passion for reading in all my students, or at least I'll try to. It's going to be lovely. It's going to splendid. I can just see it now.

# THEN:

"Dad, dad no. Just listen to me! I know it was meant for Charlie! Dad! Just hear me out. Please. Come on."

After hours of pleading over a sketchy looking public phone, I was tired of arguing with my dad over my financial situation. He didn't understand why I needed money. He didn't understand why I didn't want to enroll in a new school for my senior year. He didn't understand anything. It was as if he believed that all his rules would stop me from aging, maturing, and leaving him. He clearly didn't understand that I was already gone, and not just physically, but mentally too.

"You aren't ready to be financially emancipated Piper. I don't want to give you access to your college fund yet, and I certainly don't want to give you access to Charlie's."

"Why not? Dad I need to buy a car so I can get a job. I have to work, I have to be able to support myself."

"You have your grandparents for that."

"They told me they want me to think of myself as a tenant in their house. I have to pay rent and I can't afford it without getting a job," I lied.

"Do I need to call them and discuss this bullshit? You don't have to pay or work. You just have to go to school and finish up your year right."

I could sense the anger in his voice as he spoke but there was a subtle trace of fear. He hated his parents and as soon as he was old enough, he left their grasps. He never talked about what happened there, but I knew whatever it was made him so determined to be a better parent. Hell, he only agreed to let me go up to Maine because there was no other option. I also think it was easier for him to send me away so I didn't have to continuously watch my father lose every trace of his humanity.

"No, don't piss them off more! I just need the stupid money Dad."

"I won't do it."

"Can you at least think about it?"

"No. I've made up my mind."

"What if we make a deal?"

"What kind of deal?"

"You give me access to Charlie's account and keep control over mine until I actually go off until college."

"No Piper, I'm not letting you use Charlie's money. How many times do I have to say that?"

"I just don't understand why you won't let me though. It's not like he can use it! He's dead Dad. Charlie is dead. He's never going to come back from the dead and decide to go to college. By not letting me use the money you are, in essence, wasting money!"

"How could you?"

"How could I? How could I what? State the obvious? Charlie has been dead for years, him and Mom both. We have to move on. I have to move on. I'm tired of him ruining my life even from the grave. Like dammit dad, I just want this one thing."

"You know what, I don't care anymore. Take his money and while you're at it, take mine too you ungrateful little brat."

I threw my hands up in the air and dropped the phone, not bothering to reply. Dad and I became casual enemies after Charlie and Mom died. He became an angry and vacant man whose soul was nothing more than a glorified shell. He fought his whole life to find love, to be loved. I think my dad would have been okay, been able to survive if it was just Charlie who died, but losing my Mom destroyed him. My Dad was the religious one in the family, but after everything, he stopped praying and believing in a God before I did. It was as if grief turned him into his polar opposite and no matter how hard anyone tried to help, he was never able to liberate himself from the weights that pulled him into an aggressive depression.

I returned back to my dwelling in the middle of the woods. I call it a dwelling but it was nothing more than a sleeping bag made of trash bags. I was running out of what little personal savings I had and I'd only been in Belfast for less than a week. Food consisted of cheesy trail mix and a king sized box of cereal I splurged on, on the trip up to Maine. Since it was summer, the weather was bearable at night, but chills still graced my exposed arms and legs. In my mind, I convinced myself that I was a vagabond, a gypsy, and that my home was the earth. I was desperate to rid myself of the feeling that came with living without a settlement, so I decided to act like I was entitled, like I was above those who lived comfortably in a home. That persona was just another mask that I bore, and not surprisingly, I wore it very easily as if I was adorning my winter coat for the first time in a year; it seemed to be familiar and comforting.

Though I lived without complaints for many days and nights, I couldn't ignore the reality of my situation. I was homeless, and even though it was a conscientious decision, it didn't make my life any easier. I had to find somewhere to live, somewhere to stay.

I ventured throughout the tiny town, looking for a temporary abode, but every abandoned building reeked with water damage and the air seemed to be toxic from mold spores. The only place I had left to look was the woods and the beach. Both places didn't seem to have a secret hideaway for me, and the only money I had left was spent towards food. I was getting desperate. I was waiting for a home, I was waiting for the money to come through, I was waiting for my life to begin as if I thought everything should have been handed to me.

I mapped every corner of the woods that summer, and of course, the last place I checked had everything I was ever looking for. A tiny cottage looking shack, no bigger than a New York loft, was wonderfully misplaced. It's exterior was ridden with weeds but it had lovely bones; it was something I was willing to pour my heart and soul into fixing. I guess if you wait long enough things really do go your way.

I entered carefully through a heavy wooden door, and I tried to keep myself calm. Someone out there had claimed this land as their own too; my domain was now shared by someone who I hoped was long gone. The entire room was decked in wooden features; wooden walls, wooden floors, and even wooden countertops in a half kitchen. The only thing that wasn't made of wood was an oddly place claw foot tub that sat in the middle of the already tiny kitchen and sporadic kitchen floor tiles.

I examined the entire room in thirty seconds, it wasn't much to behold, but it was great. It was livable. The only thing the house lacked was a proper bathroom, but after examining the backyard, I found a detached outhouse. I knew it would take time, years perhaps of saving up, but I planned on connecting the outhouse to the main living space and to have a miniature master bath. Yes, I found my house and ditched my vagabond persona, but I wasn't willing to call the space my home. I wanted to make improvements; I wanted to turn the lofty style space into my version of paradise. I wanted my home to be a lovechild between the houses that were on the home-improvement channel and a homey cabin. I craved a shabby-chic home, but like I've said a million times, I was broke and an aesthetic home wasn't exactly in my budget.

Let me just say that I'm not an unintelligent girl, and though I may not be absolutely brilliant, I was and still am capable of reading my dad's every movement. I recognized his monotone voice as an indicator for when he was angry and trying to keep his cool. I recognized his jaunty walk and incessant whistling as an indicator for when he was happy or when he and my mom had a romantic night. More importantly, I recognized his sudden outbursts and uncontrollable rage as an indicator that he was depressed; that his heart was mangled and tattered. After everything, I was more familiar with his negative attitudes and erratic behaviors, and our last conversation sent him into one of his unpredictable states. I knew he was playing this game, seeing how long it would take me to call him again and apologize.

I knew I would have to wait for him to cool down. I had to wait for just a few days until the angry and bitter man returned to the innocent drunk. He was playing a game, but I was better at it. Enough time had to pass where he missed my voice and would forgive me more easily instead of laughing at the sound of my pleading. It was hell waiting. Honestly, pure hell. Every night I retreated into my new abode and laid on the worn wooden floor, passing the time by imagining how I would manipulate my future. I dreamed about how great my life would be when I truly had it in my hands. For the lack of any better descriptor, it was truly silly and a waste of time. Though I believe all kids play the same game, trying to predict the outcomes to their life choices.

"I can paint the kitchen wall baby blue, fix the cracked tiles while I'm at it. Then I can repurpose the stain glass window, make it look more like a piece of art. What else? What else?" I mumbled to myself, and my thoughts formed endless trains, "I could make a headboard for my bed out of bookshelves. Tons and tons of bookshelves. I'll have to have my dad send me my books though, I didn't pack that many. Ugh no, I can't do that because he'll send them to Gram's. You know what, I'll just buy new books and newer copies of the books I used to have to double my collection. Ahh, I'm so excited just thinking about it."

My days and nights were spent like that. Daydreams and one-sided conversations became an unusual norm, I even got used to referring to myself in third person. I needed a distraction, something to occupy my mind, but every time I tried to maintain some kind of light-hearted and innocent mindset I woke up the demons that rattled my bones and caused even more restless nights. It didn't help that my perpetual loneliness caused paranoia too. Every sound was a threat to my well-being.

*What was that? Who's there? Oh god. Oh god. He's found me. He's going to take me back and force me to go home. I can't go back. I oh my. I just. I what if? Is he going to force me to live with them? Is he just going to leave to rot without the money? I need that money. I need it. I can't survive without it and I don't I. I can't even finish a thought without my heart racing...Oh shit, he doesn't know I'm, no one knows I'm here. Then why is someone outside? I'm just hearing things right? I'm just hearing things. I can just close my eyes and if I don't wake up, at least it will all be over. I just want it all to be over.*

My private thoughts were as unpredictable as my panic attacks. I don't know what triggered me, maybe it was the unknown, the constant isolation I subjected myself to, or maybe it was all just a state of mind. I swear it felt like I was wearing multiple personalities, one that was heavily medicated and fake, always adoring warm smiles and playing immature games, and the other was pessimistic and suicidal, dreaming of the day life would stop teasing her with the end. It's as if I had a broken switch that turned on by itself, leaving me to have an erratic breath, clammy palms, and rampant tremors during one moment, and happy positive thoughts that reignited the diminishing hope in my already charcoaled soul in another. I didn't understand myself, and trying to evaluate who I was caused this divide in my brain. Logic versus instinct. I knew I was crazy. I've always known I was crazy. But I wasn't capable of understanding the severity of it all.

Restless nights definitely took a toll on my mental and physical state. Dark circles and bags began to form under my eyes and I spent more and more time popping pills to keep me afloat. At one point, I would pop five or six pills at a time to just get through the day, though my mind would be clouded and muddled in result. Not surprisingly, it was during one of these mental-comatose states that I dialed my dad and begged him to forgive me, all the while telling myself that I had waited long enough.

"Dad? Dad it's me."

"Is everything alright? It's two in the morning."

"Oh, yeah, sorry. I couldn't sleep. I just had a lot on my mind."

"Are you sure you're okay honey? Is Gram and Gramps treating you right?"

"Yeah, I'm just really sorry. I shouldn't have yelled at you the other day. I'm just scared of starting over Dad. It's all I've wanted to do since we lost Mom and Charlie, but I just don't want to mess up what might be my only second chance."

"I know and I'm sorry that I got so mad. It's been hard on me Piper. It's been really hard. I just don't know how to control my emotions sometimes."

"I know."

"I took some time to think after we talked and I want to trust you. I want you to feel like you do have some freedom. I want you to move on without me, so I called the bank and it's all yours. You can use both accounts, but if you misuse any of it I can regain control of both. This is the beginning you asked for, Piper. Now don't make me regret that I ever gave you the chance."

"Dad, thank you."

"Just don't forget me okay? I can't bear to lose you too kiddo."

"You won't lose me dad. I love you too much to ever let go."

"You always were my girl."

"You should go back to sleep, it's late. I'll talk to you next weekend, and at a decent hour too. How's that sound?" I said.

"That sounds great. I will be eagerly waiting for your call. I love you, kid."

"I love you too."

I hung up the phone and a wave of relief hit me. I was going to be okay. I was going to get money in the morning, then go shopping for my home. After that call I slept like a baby, my temporary worries were over, but my struggle was just beginning.

# NOW:

Everyone in the world gets nervous before their first day. Kids before the first day of school have exaggerated butterflies, singers fear their voices will cut out before their first performance, and jocks fear that the game-winning play will be left in their hands during the season's opener. In every situation, fight-or-flight instincts go crazy, causing odd rituals to make an appearance. In my case, I never sleep on those nights; I write. I write as fast as humanly possible. Things stop making sense, and my brain turns to mush in the process, but I stop stressing; I stop thinking. It's as if writing is a way for me to keep calm, to be under control without the aid of medication.

I don't love. I don't. I can't. It's not that I'm waiting for someone to come save me, or to show me the world; I'm just too much of a realist. My entire life has been devoted to answering the unanswerable. I've answered everything from why we are the way we are, to what makes us hope, to what makes our demons. I've figured it all out except love. I can't love and I can't explain it to others. If I was just able to experience it. If only I was able to have a deep emotional connection with another person in this world. I've spent so many years focusing on my career and because of it I've been unable to grow close to anyone. I don't even have a friend to confide in. I have no one, and to compensate for my loneliness, I bury myself even deeper into my work. It's a continuous cycle that leads to misery, but at least when I die I'll be remembered for doing something great, for helping the world in some sort of way. Goddamn, I just want to be remembered. I just want to be loved. But I can't. I never will. I'm just a waste of space. I'm destined for pure dust. I will

just be another grain of sand that gets swallowed by the merciless sea. It's so depressing. Life is so depressing especially when you realize that hope is just a figment of your imagination.
People say the later you stay up, the more likely you are to divulge your darkest secrets. So many stories and songs refer to these late night conversations as if they're precious things to be cherished forever. It's like people view this grand weakness as something to hold pride in. I find it despicable. Why would people just let their secrets slip through the cracks to the first pair of open ears? Why have the secret in the first place when you just plan to spill it later? I never tell my secrets, or write about them, especially not at night, even though I'm just as vulnerable as the next sleep-deprived human. I just handle myself in a different way. I start talking to the dead, and never mention it to the living. People already believe I'm mentally insane, and if they knew that I believed in chattering with ghosts, that would be the final nail in my coffin. I'd be destined to live the rest of my life in a mental hospital. My brain would turn to slush there, and the only thing I ever pride myself in would become useless with all the heavy medications and sedatives they would force in my veins with tubes.

I'm sleep deprived and when I can't rest I get depressed and I talk to people who aren't really there and my brain just goes all morbid and I ugh. Just ugh. I can't control it. I can never control anything. Why the hell do I think I'm capable of taking care of kids? I can barely take care of myself. What the hell am I doing? This was never a part of the plan. This is not right.

I pull myself away from my desk, abandoning my unfinished book in the middle of a sentence once again. I have to sleep. I have to kill my feelings before I drive myself mad. I work my way into the tiny half bath, pull out a bottle of melatonin, and without thinking, I dump four pills into my hand and swallow them all. If these don't help me sleep, I don't what will. Maybe I'm just doomed to life of insomniatic behaviors and erratic thoughts.

I'm always going to have this deep seeded hatred and brokenness in my heart, and I feel like it's always going to trickle down to the rest of my life in some way or another. I'm always going to have problems functioning even with my coping mechanisms. Coping is just a temporary fix, it's a distraction. I've been coping for over half my life and I'm still nothing more than a miserable and desperate soul at the end of the day. I may only need to cope to survive, but I know in order to truly live, I'm going to have to move on.

I stumble gracefully out of the bathroom and wander around my dwarfish dwelling, waiting for the drowsiness to kick in. Part of me wants to break into the cabinet and caffeinate myself, but that would be ineffective and counterproductive, so instead I grab a pile of pillows and blankets, throw them in the bathtub, and climb in with my latest reading obsessions, The Valley of the Dolls. It's a sinful read, but I can't get enough. I don't know why I become obsessed with characters that have rotten hearts. I don't know why I become interested in characters that are incapable of complex thoughts, but I do.

I fall asleep reading in the tub sometime later, but the entire time I can't get Jacqueline Susann's words out of my head. It's as if they speak to me. It's as if they describe my entire existence.

*"Everyone has an identity. One of their own, and one for show."*

My show is just beginning and, in many ways, it never ends. One identity for strangers on the street, one identity for my coworkers, one for my dear old dad, and even one identity for myself. It's only in these raw moments in the dead of night where I shed my plasticity and the true Piper is revealed. Here I am world. Here I am. Don't you love me? The real me? Aren't you in love with the broken girl? Don't you fantasize about fixing me? Am I defective enough for someone to care yet? Where are my answers? Where is my show? I'm here world, I'm here but my mask is broken and torn. I'm here world, I'm here, but my words are raw and spiteful. I'm here world,

I'm here, but why won't you listen? Why don't you love me? Why

don't I love myself?

# THEN:

My parents used to be that cute couple people would gag over. My dad would spend weeks and weeks pouring all of his free time into planning perfect dates, and my mom had no problem being an independent woman during the day and a doting wife who waited on her husband at night. It was kind of sweet, it was the kind of relationship I saw myself having one day. I remember watching them get ready for their dates, watching my dad softly kiss my mom's neck before helping her put on a pair of pearls. Watching them dance around their expansive bathroom and laughing every time they stepped on each other's toes. Even watching my mom carefully tie my dad's tie was adorable. She used to furrow her eyebrows and lick her lips while her hands moved meticulously, ensuring that my dad would have the perfect tie while he just stood their with a twinkle in his eye from looking at her. If someone were to ask me what love looked like I would just point at those moments.

As I grew up, the more and more my parents felt comfortable leaving Charlie in charge so they could go off on their little dates; instead of admiring their routine that I praised a few years prior, I began to despise them for it. Charlie was changing in front of my eyes and I was forced to watch. I despised who he was becoming. I had to watch him fall out of love with our family, with me, and with himself. No one seemed to notice but me, or if they did, no one seemed to care. I don't blame people for being oblivious; we were at one point the perfect family.

"Charlie? Charlie I'm hungry. Can we order the pizza now?"

During one of my parent's escapades, when I was supposed to be supervised by my "doting" brother; Charlie disappeared into his room for hours, only coming out once to open the door for a girl who I had never seen before. Sure, Charlie brought girls home all the time, but they never met my parents, and they never really met me. I was just there. I was the floor lamp, window blinds even. My job was to stay quiet and invisible until I was needed. Charlie even explained this phenomenon to me and of course I was shocked when he deflated my importance. I was so thrown aback that I expressed my emotions in the only way a child knows how to; I cried for hours. I cried for the return of my kind-hearted brother, but unfortunately he never did. Wallowing in an exaggerated misery, hunger began to envelop my stunted frame, and so I forced myself to regain composer and knocked on his door craving nutrients and answers for who he had become.

"Charlie? I know you're in there open up."

He didn't answer, so I put my ear up to the door and listened. The sounds on the other side sounded mumbled and odd and every now and again I would hear a shrill from both of them. I waited for a good ten to fifteen minutes, just trying to eavesdrop before I knocked again, unable to wait anymore. I needed food, greasy and processed food that would fuel my adolescent belly.

"Charlie open up! If you don't open up in five seconds I'm coming in there," I paused for a moment, "one...two...three...four... four and a quarter... four and a half... five!"

I forced open the door and much to my surprise, I was greeted by two naked teenagers who were dancing on top of each other. This time when the girl screamed, it wasn't out of pleasure but out of pure horror.

"You said she wouldn't come in! You promised me your little sister wouldn't be a problem. Get her out! Get her out, now!"

Charlie's eyes were suddenly lit with rage. I ran out of the room as fast as humanly possible, muttering useless apologies as I went. It obviously didn't help any, in fact it made things worse. Within mere moments the nameless girl ran out of the house, mortified, with her clothes half buttoned and her hair in a disgruntled state. Charlie wasn't too far behind, chasing her in only plaid boxers.

"Come back! Baby, please. I'm sorry about her. Please come on, I'll handle her."

"I can't do this anymore Charlie. I'm tired of your games. Your pervy, freak of a sister was the final straw. It's over. I'm sorry."

She jumped into her car and drove into what seemed to be the dead of night to my younger self. When her car's figure stopped being visible, Charlie stormed back into the house, and instead of retreating back into his room, he picked me up and threw me into mine.

"You little bitch! You ruined everything for me."

As he started his rampage his eyes seemed to gloss over. The brother I knew was gone and in his place was this anger-induced monster that our family tried to hide behind a mask of potions and prescriptions.

"You always ruin everything. Life was fine until you came along. You never listen! Why can't you ever listen?"

"I'm sorry. I'm so sorry."

By that point, tears were streaming down my face and I was shaking uncontrollably. When Charlie was in a bad mood, he was unpredictable. I knew he was capable of destruction. I knew he was capable of more than he could imagine.

"Sorry isn't good enough."

He inched closer to me and his voice echoed off the walls. His eyes were vacant and his breath reeked of booze. With every step his demeanor became more and more calculated. When he got to me I scrambled back into the corner but it didn't stop his wrath.

"You ruined our family. You ruined me, and now you're going to pay for it."

He wrapped his hands around my fragile neck and began to squeeze. Tears started rolling down my face harder and I felt as if I was drowning in them. I couldn't breathe, my sobs and gasps were violent, and stars were twirling around my head as the world gradually began to fade away.

"C-ch-charlie, stop, I-I- can't. I can't breath."

As my lips started to lose blood and turn a sickly blue shade he released his grasp and ran out of the room leaving me to collapse to the ground and force life back into my shriveled lungs. Afterwards, I spent hours in my room, trying to decide if what I went through was reality or just a horrendous nightmare, trying to mask the gruesome bruise that was beginning to form around my neck, and trying to reacquaint myself with life itself.

I almost died that night because of Charlie. I almost died because his anger overwhelmed him and turned him into a demonic being. I was petrified of him after that night. I tried to avoid leaving my room afterwards, but my stomach was emaciated, I was famished. I wasn't about to let myself go through unnecessary trauma for nothing. When I reached my kitchen, the room radiated the gentle aroma of melted cheese and a warm pizza pie was waiting just for me.

As I propped myself on top of a towering barstool to take a slice of pizza, I found a note sitting on the counter waiting for me to read. I knew it was from Charlie, and I was expecting it to go into detail about my impending death, but it didn't.

YOU DON'T HAVE TO WORRY ANYMORE. I TOOK MY MEDICINE.

I read the note but I wasn't sure on how to react. I knew taking a pill wouldn't make what happened go away, but part of me pitied my brother for living with anguishing pain. The other half of my heart loathed my brother for turning into a carbon copy of what society expected of him, yet in spite of everything he did, I couldn't deny that part of me still cared about him desperately. He was my only sibling; he was everything in my life.

"Piper."

I turned around and my hands flailed towards my neck as if it was an instinct.

"Please don't hurt me, Charlie," I whispered and tears began to form.

"I'm not going to hurt you. I'm never going to hurt you again, okay? It was a mistake. I never meant anything I said. I didn't mean to do any of that. I'm so sorry. I'm so damn sorry." His words were slightly slurred and he sounded pathetic. I wasn't sure if he was apologizing because he was actually sorry or because he was afraid to get caught.

He inched closer to me once more and attempted to pull me into a hug, but when he saw me flinch, he kindly retreated.

"Please Piper, don't tell mom and dad. I'm trying to get better. I am going to get better, but you can't tell them. Please."

"I want to believe you Charlie, but I can't."

"Why not?"

"I'm scared." I knew at that point I sounded like a elementary school kid, though I was older by that time, but it's easier to be small than it is to be brave.

"Come here my little Pied Piper, come here and talk to me. It's okay to get close. I'm better now. Can't you tell?"

I nodded hesitantly and my wall fell down. He wrapped his arms around me and sobbed into my wild brown mane. It was stupid of me to just forgive him, to just take his apology and empty promise to get better, but I believed his lie. I believed in the brother who kept me safe from bullies growing up and pushed me on the swings as I tried to fly higher.

"Charlie you have to stop going to those parties and keep taking your medicine. I like you better when you're happy. I like you better when you're my brother."

"I can't Piper."

"Why not?"

"I want people to like me, and for people to like me I have to change who I really am."

"But I like the real you."

"I like the real you too kiddo, but sometimes that's not good enough."

He pulled my entire body closer to him and kissed the top of my head, ending the conversation. He was too far-gone. He had no interest in making people like the real him; he wanted people to approve of his fake identity. Charlie, the popular quarterback, was who people loved, but he was someone who Charlie himself truly despised.

After our conversation, Charlie picked me up gently and carried me into bed, and instead of handing me a book, he crawled under the covers and cuddled me into his arms. Suddenly I wasn't afraid anymore, I felt safe listening to his heart beating so close to mine, it reminded me that he was still human somehow even with sullied soul. Somewhere deep down, the real Charlie was trying to escape his societal chains. I fell asleep that way, listening to his heart's drumbeat, shortly after listening to Charlie's words.

"I'm never going to hurt you again, I swear," he whispered and I thought I heard him cry.

And he never did hurt me again, not intentionally anyways. All the pain and hurt he brought me after that night stemmed from his death when he decided to take the lives of three other females, including my mom's, before taking his own.

# NOW:

I wake to the sound of obnoxious bells echoing throughout my home. They're incessant chimes that are too grating to belong to the church nearby. I force my eyelids open and realize that my alarm clock is croaking for the first time in years. I debate going back to bed but I know I can't be late for the first day of work, so I climb out of the bathtub and run to stop the awful sound. My back aches from sleeping in an awkward position, my eyes have dark rims that frame my face, and quite frankly, my whole demeanor is depressing.

I don't remember much from the night before, just dumping excessive amounts of melatonin down my throat and writing about the lack of love my main character has in her life. It's like a hangover has settled into my bones but not a drop of alcohol is circulating in my veins. I typically live off of sleepless nights; I thrive off of them. Usually I only have problems functioning when I actually sleep, when I actually attempt to be a normal human being.

I slump back towards the bedroom half of the room and begin the same agonizing process that I went through in order to pick an interview outfit. I have to look professional, of course, but I don't want to look like I'm trying too hard. I start pulling out articles of clothing like a mad woman, trying to find everything and anything. I get so frustrated that I just walk away and decide to wash my face and do my hair instead.

That in itself is a struggle. Soap wedges in the corners of my eyes, causing them to burn even more than they already were from the flood of artificial light, and I can't get a braid to lay flat against my neck. I have to settle on a braid-bunish thing that sits on top of my head and is complemented by an adorable black lace bow. By the time my hair's done, I plaster layers of makeup on until color floods my face and my zombie state is fully hidden.

Ruby red lips and snow white skin causes youth to flood my face and as a result, I look eager to start the day; sometimes it scares me how easily I can just change how I really feel. It scares me to think how easily I can fool myself. After losing myself while staring at a stranger who shares the same face, I float back to my wardrobe and continue digging. My indecisiveness is so horrendous but I just want to make sure I get things right. I've already decided on my persona and now I just need something to match. Most people want accessories to match their outfits, but I want outfits to match my personality.

I settle, eventually, after twenty minutes of pacing around my house with nothing more on than a pink striped bra and black stockings, on a black and white polka dotted dress and light pink ballerina flats. It isn't exactly what I imagined myself wearing, but it's cute enough. I've been worried for days about this job, and I know I need to work and grow up a bit but there's a part of me that's just can't. I'm worried that I will be dragged into the spotlight just because I look and act differently. I'm worried that people will see past my plain persona and soft spokenness and expose me as a freak. I want to be forgettable here.

I run out the house with a baby blue briefcase stuffed with my favorite books and my laptop that, unlike the school's, works. I don't even stop to have my cup of tea, or take my medicine, but I do stash the pills in my briefcase and stuff a tiny tea bag in there as well. The car ride is uneventful but I can't get over the butterflies. I'm nervous yet excited; ready to begin a new chapter in life while horrified by the idea of having no control over what's yet to come.

I pull into the school right as the sun begins to rise and the doors open for the day. The start of my workday is going to be filled with staff introductions and cleaning. I won't even get to meet any of the 400 students until midday when a class will stop by for story time.

"Ms. Addison, welcome to your first day."

As I walk into the building Mr. Wolff is standing guard, watching all of his little soldiers rush into battle. I feel my face grow stiff at the sight of him. He seems to be the kind of person who bases everything on a first impression; there is no sense of redemption for anyone in his eyes. It makes me uncomfortable, and the fact is I know he doesn't like me.

"Hello Mr. Wolff. I'm thoroughly ecstatic to get to work today."

"Don't lie to me girl, I see right through you."

"But sir, I'm not lying to you."

"Say what you must, but lies are sinful."

"Mr. Wolff, I didn't mean anything by what I said..."

"Enough, you're fine. You have the job, you don't have to keep trying to impress me. Anyways, when Cathy gets here with her kids, she'll take you around the school and then leave you to your duties. Are you aware of your schedule for the day?"

"I am aware. I have a reading circle with Mrs. Borgin's kindergarteners around ten, lunch at twelve thirty, and then Mr. Shuman's sixth grade class is going to come in around two."

"Sounds like you're ready for the day."

"Yes sir, I came prepared."

"Good, looks like I wasn't wrong about you after all."

"Excuse me?"

Mr. Wolff gives me a small smirk and walks away, not answering my question. I don't understand him and I don't like him. I've fought my entire life to break preconceived notions of who I am, and here he is giving me more. I feel as if I have to prove myself to him, and I know there is some part of myself that should feel that way considering he's my boss, but it's just different. He reminds me of the people that I left behind.

"Piper Addison to the office, please. Piper Addison to the office, please."

I hear my voice called over the grainy PA system and it sounds like an aged record player with its grainy sound and low roar. I walk to the office and pat down my sweaty palms against my dress. I have to be composed.

"I was called?"

"Hi my dear. Richard wanted me to give you a tour of the facility and give you your keys and such. I didn't know where to find you so I just called you over this baby," Cathy says, stroking a decrepit machine that looks closer to a telegraph than a P.A. system.

"Oh okay. I was just heading down to the library. I think that's really the only place I need to know in this building right?"

"Oh don't be silly. You have to know all the good stuff, like which faculty bathroom is clean and smells like roses instead of a moldy stale smell like the rest of the school, and I have to teach you how to get the coffee maker to work in the break room. Stuff like that is how you're going to survive here. Speaking of the coffee maker, follow me, we'll start in the break room."

I follow Cathy and her obnoxiously loud outfit that seems to match her personality perfectly. She's in this bright red top and a blue pencil skirt that somehow makes an exaggerated swishing noise as we walk down a labyrinth of hallways. By the end, we finally reach a desolate section of the school that looks older than dirt itself and she pries open a rusty door.

"It's nicer than it looks I swear, we just, we spend most of the tuition on buying new textbooks and funding our extracurricular programs. All of the money we makes goes straight back to the kids or into our pockets, whatever little is left goes to fixing the school up. Like just last year we had a surplus in our budget so we got to add a water purifier for all of the water fountains. The kids were so excited!"

"They got excited over a water filter?"

"Most of the students are spoiled rich kids who wouldn't even glance at the water

fountain unless they got a stain on their uniform. You wouldn't think it, but as soon as we put in the water filter people starting using them. It's like they stopped being afraid of the 'horrifying' tap water. I don't know. I don't understand most kids. I don't even understand my own."

Cathy ends the conversation by dramatically walking into a less than desirable break room. Middle aged women and men crowd the room and chatter is only facilitated by the share of coffee. I look around rapidly and begin to fidget with my briefcase in an attempt to secretly retrieve my pills without a scene. I'm horrible in new situations, either I'm unable to talk or I talk too much and I don't know which is lesser of two evils.

"Piper dear, come on in and meet everyone."

I shake my head and my body starts gravitating towards the wall closest to the door.

"Darling that wasn't a request, it was an order," she smiles but her condescending tone lingers.

She grabs my wrist and forces me into the center of the break room. She begins to clear her throat and as all the conversation in the room comes to a halt, I feel my heart begin to flutter at a hummingbird's pace. I can't breath; I can't talk. I'm frozen in place, left with nothing more than a vacant look on my face and sudden tremors that cause my fingers to twitch ever so slightly. I feel everyone's eyes burn into my skull, sizing me up ever so slightly, all of them giving me judgmental looks when I'm unable to introduce myself. I avoid giving anyone direct eye contact and I fall into an old routine. I start noticing the little things, describing every minute detail to myself until I'm capable of breathing again.

*Look at that, light orange counters and tiled counter tops. I bet they haven't renovated this room since at least the seventies. Oh and over there, the windows are caked in dirt; do they not have a decent janitorial staff? I mean come on; I could have asthma, get one whiff of the lingering dust and burst into a fit. Hmm maybe I can use that as an excuse for my sudden inability to talk, right? I couldn't breath? Allergic reaction? They're not going to believe me no matter what I say, are they? They're all going to hate me. I can tell. I'm not like any of them. I'm too young, too bold and colorful. What have I done? I just need to get out of here. I need to go take my pill, disappear to the library and have some time for myself.*

"Piper, aren't you going to say hi to everyone?"

"I-I. I have to go to the bathroom," I blurt out to everyone before running towards the door in the far left corner of the room.

As soon as I make it in, I flick on the lights and notice I'm in an unused broom closet. I sigh and an eruption of laughter fills the other room. I haven't even been at work for an hour and I already am the biggest joke around. Tears start sliding down my face and I slump to the floor. I'm falling apart in a broom closet. I finally get my briefcase open so I pull out my pill and swallow it without any water.

82

I'm a fricking mess. My makeup is smearing and running down my face from my lack of composure. My dress now has an odd rim of dirt along its edges, and I'm honestly too ashamed to leave the room.

"Does she realize that she's in a closet?" A man's voice penetrates through the door and the laughter begins to grow.

"She's just nervous. She's a young thing, just teaching for the first time. Give her a break guys," Cathy pleads, defending my tarnished honor.

"She's not even a real teacher, she's a librarian. Her job is a joke and she is a joke," someone else says and this time Cathy doesn't come to my defense.

I stay in the closet for a while, trying to let my frazzled nerves settle. When I hear the first bell ring, the sound of laughter dies and everyone disappears deep into the heart of the school. All of them headed to work with my failure looping in their minds. I sneak out of the closet as soon as I hear the door close shut, but as soon as I step back into the break room, Cathy stares me down with her arms crossed in front of her chest.

"All you had to do was say hi, sweetie."

"I couldn't do it. I tried but I just couldn't."

"I don't understand."

"I don't expect you to."

"I just- how do you expect to work with kids and people all day when you can't even introduce yourself? Are you sure this is the job for you?"

"No I'm not, but I can't see myself being anything else."

"Well then, you should need to go home before your first class. Clean yourself off, change your outfit and come back to school before anyone notices. No one will even remember what happened this morning by the time you come back I swear."

"But what about Mr. Wolff?"

"Don't you worry about Richard, I'll tell him you ran out to grab some school supplies and things to spruce up the library, he may be annoyed with you but you won't get in trouble."

"Thank you, Cathy, for everything."

"Don't mention it, now get out of here before I have to report a raccoon sighting."

She smiles gently at me and I nod in reply before ducking my head and running out of the building. As far as I'm concerned this morning never happened, and by the time I come back to school, no one will remember the girl who couldn't even manage a measly hello.

# THEN:

For a long time I was a stereotypical church going girl. I was destined to stay pure mentally and physically for as long as humanly possible. I was determined to live a life of minimal sin and I never once questioned the lifestyle that I was raised in. Hell, my mother even drove Charlie and I to bible study at school twice a week where more mindless beliefs were hammered into our skulls.

I believed in religion for so long that at one point it defined me, and I even believed that those who didn't believe in anything were just the devil's helpers attempting to tarnish the world with his demonic teachings. I was wrong, so desperately wrong. Believing in something doesn't make you a better person; it doesn't make you superior. Some of the cruelest people I've ever met were Christians with darkened hearts. Good people have compassionate hearts and have sympathy for others, they want to help, they want to make a difference in this world, they don't see people for their faults and they don't condemn the people who don't believe.

After Charlie did what he did, my whole church turned against my father and I. We were the devils, the people who relished in sin. They didn't seem to care that we showed up more in church after the funeral, they didn't seem to care that after every wrong turn we went into confession and prayed for forgiveness, no, they just saw us for our mistakes, for the mistakes of someone else. The people who surrounded me were the people who preached of pearly white gates while having blackened hearts, telling themselves that they were better than I was just because of a broken family.

"Father, forgive me for I have sinned."

"What have you done, my child?"

"I have come to ask for forgiveness for my family, Father."

"You haven't sinned yourself?"

"No, but I feel like I have. Everyone thinks that I have."

"God does not care what others think of you. His relationship with you and your family will be stronger than whatever you are going through."

"But Father, my brother killed innocent people, including my own mom. Now I have to force my dad out of bed every morning. I have to force him to live. I don't even know if he still believes in our Lord, Father. Our family is falling apart and I don't know what to do. I thought that if I asked for forgiveness for Charlie, for my family, that God would let him in heaven. I thought that people would stop hating us."

My high-pitched voice cracked as I finished my thought. Tears were streaming down my face and I was gasping desperately for air as snot shot out my nose. I reached for the tissues that were hiding in a secret compartment in the confessional and blew my nose until it was raw.

"I'm sorry, but it's too late for your brother, and as far as I am concerned, it's too late for your family as well."

"But Father?"

"I can not take away the sins of your family. Only God can offer mercy now, but until he does, you all are doomed for hell. I'm sorry my child, I will pray for you and for your soul to be saved. May the Lord be with you."

"And also with you," I mumbled the last words and forced myself out of the confessional before running a mile and a half home.

That was the moment I lost all faith in religion. I always wanted to believe in an afterlife and a higher being but I couldn't believe in the people who were supposed to teach me it. In some ways I'm not a complete atheist, I believe something is out there, but I refuse to believe that any God would stop loving me or anyone just because of a mistake; just because they were unable to handle their imperfections. If anything I believe in God but I don't believe in religion. I've stopped praying, I've stopped caring. I refuse to let this divine being dictate how I act, I'm going to be a better person because I want to have a good heart and because I believe in the humanity's potential, not because I want to escape purgatory or an even worse fate.

Although, when I was a kid I didn't understand the things that I do now. The idea that the church could turn me away repulsed me and caused anger to linger in my bones. The bitter isolation I faced caused ice to pulse through my veins. I wanted someone to care about what was going on. I wanted someone, anyone to realize that my family wasn't broken because the devil tainted us. We were broken because no one gave a damn about us afterwards. Everyone in that tiny prissy town condemned my father and I to a life full of suffering. They're the reason I stopped looking for the good in people. They're the reason I can't get close to another human being. I blame them for so much of the pain that I hold in my heart, but they aren't the sole cause.

My anger and hatred towards the word was mainly due to Charlie's sin. He was the trigger; he's the one who ended me. Straight after my confession, I ran to the graveyard where Charlie laid dead, and spat on his grave.

"It's all your fault, Charlie. You ruined everything for me! Now I haven't just lost you and mom, I've lost Dad too. He won't get out of bed, he's does nothing but cry about how bad things are for him. God Charlie, you've always been selfish. You've always destroyed everything that got in your way, you even tried to destroy me. I never did anything but love you and be the best sister I could be. Now what? What's next for me? Dad can't love, God's turned his back on me, and Mom's gone. It's not fair. I have no one. There will never be anyone, and it's all your fault! I hate you. I hate you!"

Spite flew out of my mouth and by the time I was finished I had my first panic attack. My airways felt as if they were caving in, my brain couldn't complete a full thought, and my body wouldn't stop shaking. Even now I can't tell you if the tremors were truly from the attack or if they came from me being angry, so angry that I couldn't stop crying. All I wanted to do in that moment was cry.

# NOW:

How long does it take for humiliation to fade? How long will it take for my rosy-pink skin to turn back to its pale shade because it's been nearly an hour and I still can't shake the damn shame? I've already made a bad impression, I've already left a negative mark on the school, I should just call it a day, call in sick with a sudden case of food poisoning and try again tomorrow. Hell I could repeat that cycle for the next month until Dick Wolff catches onto me and cuts me loose with my first two paychecks to ease the blow. Yes, I can do that. I can take the easy route and slip into a life of careless routine. At the same time though, I like to lay down roots so that I don't bring attention to myself. When people get used to your existence you become obsolete.

I should probably just keep working then if I truly do want to become just an invisible bookworm who never leaves her precious library. If the gossip changes faster than it takes for rain to fall then it can't possibly take much longer for people to forget about my blunder. I just have to go back to the school and pretend like nothing happened. I have to radiate the confidence I was unable to radiate before.

I run back into my house just as the sun begins to fully make an appearance and strip my clothes off, discarding them in the middle of the floor. I need a new outfit, so I'm going to have to repeat the same excruciating process that I went through this morning. Create a mountain of clothes that are unfit for the occasion, complain at the lack of available clothes though there clearly is a surplus, throw on an outfit that doesn't meet the expectations that linger in my subconscious, and ignore the mess I've made. My daily routine certainly does cause a mess in my house, but I'm too preoccupied to care. I'll get back to it later.

I run out of my house in a similar panicked state. I have to sell my lie, and market it as if it was the truest thing in the world. I have to convince the big bad Wolff that I was only trying to be the best employee he's ever had. I have to be his warrior though I feel as if I'm truly an enemy in disguise.

I pull into an almost desolate pharmacy around 8:45 and ignore the odd stares from all the middle-aged women in workout gear as I walk through the aisles.

*What do teachers have in their classrooms? Pencils, pens, cute erasers, oh I know I can get some cute bookmarks and have giveaways every month. That'll be fun. Maybe I can even make sticker charts for the younger kids and whichever class reads the*

*most books in a month will win a pizza party. Yeah, that'll work.*
*They'll all love me eventually, or at least tolerate me.*

I rush through the store with random office supplies in a broken cart, whose wheels give off an awful grating sound. At one point I feel an old lady's glare burn into my soul, her body language calling me a hooligan.

"Young lady, your cart is squeaking, you should go switch it out," she presses.

"I'm sorry but I'm in a bit of a rush, I'll make sure to alert the staff about their broken cart though. Thank you for bringing it to my attention."

She stares at me wide-eyed and I swear as I walk away her jaw drops to the floor. It was as if she was expecting me to cuss her out and flip her off, and yeah maybe I was in my mind, but I am not going to give her the satisfaction of being right. I'm so sick of people assuming things about me. This is why I don't leave my house. This is why I don't socialize with other people.

I sigh and continue to rush through the store with a fury. Five minutes later I'm driving back to the school with an energy bar hanging out my mouth and a crappy mix tape blaring from my car's stereo. By the time I get back to school one of my hands is full of useless school supplies while the other is desperately trying to maintain my grasp on my briefcase.

I nod at Cathy as I get back into the building and disappear into the library without a trace. I don't even bother catching my breath and instead use all my energy to blast music from a two-dollar speaker and begin to spruce up my quarters in the neglected building. Clearance sale Christmas lights go up first, I line them along an empty bookshelf that I plan to store all of my recommendations at. Secondly, I set up a lavender candle by my desk and light it to get rid of the musty smell.

Everything after that is just prepping and cleaning. I pour heavy duty cleaner into a cheap mop bucket and start to dance around the room with a slender mop that has the grace of a deer. We waltz around the dingy library and it transforms into a ballroom. My white baby doll dress turns into a golden ball gown and the broom turns into any woman's dream man. I move back and my face turns up in disgust when I see him, and as the man tries to court me I feel impure. I don't want him. I don't want anyone. I simply want to be alone in my fantasy but worldly expectations have managed to seep into my dreams. I back away from him and the warm glow that radiates in my daydream starts disintegrating.

"Ahem, excuse me?"

I turn around and a man with golden brown skin stands at the doorway, eyeing both the mop and I. Part of me wonders how long he's been standing there but I'm too embarrassed to ask.

"Oh, I. Um. How can I help you?" I ask as I bite down on the corner of my lip.

"I didn't mean to interrupt your dancing session, I just wanted to come down here and introduce myself. I'm Mr. White, the Algebra teacher."

"Your name is Mr. White?"

"Yes, why is that so strange?"

"It's not, I quite frankly don't know what I was expecting," I say honestly.

"Well I'm guessing you weren't expecting the only black guy in this place to be named White. Or am I wrong?"

My face turns a brighter shade of pink and his eyes light up and a chuckle escapes his mouth. It's like his soul mirrors one of an old man with a shining soul, not a lengthy nerd who boasts about being a successful teacher in his mid to late twenties.

"I- I really didn't mean anything by it."

"It's okay, relax, I'm just trying to break the ice."

"Oh good, I'm really tired of making bad first impressions today," I sigh and a weight lifts off my chest.

94

"Well you haven't left one with me, if anything you left a grand one with your dancing skills," he smirks.

"You just caught me off guard. If I had known I was having company I would have prepared a better routine."

"You know what, I'm glad I stopped down here. I've heard about you, Ms. Addison, and I knew that what they were saying couldn't possibly be true. I knew you weren't a mute, just a frightened girl."

"I wouldn't use those words necessarily," I muttered.

"Oh excuse me, I meant that you were just nervous for your first day."

"Are you sure about that? How do you know that the rumors aren't true?"

"I stopped listening to what other people say along time ago. I like to come to my own conclusions."

"And what would those conclusions be?"

"That they were right about your hair, it is a lovely shade of cotton candy pink."

"Is that all?" My eyebrows arch and he walks closer to me.

"For now yes, but trust me Ms. Addison, I will figure out who you are soon enough. I will crack your code."

"Good luck with that, Mr. White. It won't be an easy task but I look forward to watching you try, and please call me Piper."

"Well, I have to get back to my class but mark my words. I will discover the true you. I will define you Ms. Piper. Just you wait and see."

"I'll be anxiously awaiting that day, now if you excuse me, I have to get back to dancing."

I pick my dirt encrusted mop and begin to waltz with it once more, and by the time I look back the ironic man was gone.

# THEN:

I was promised a hero when I was little. I was told that someone was going to swoop in and fix my family but instead I was given the biggest bigot in the entire family, my dear old Uncle Mike. The asshole flew into town like a witch on her broom two months after my Mom died, and he did so only because my dad drunk dialed him in the middle of the night sobbing his eyes out.

"Hey kiddo. Look at you; you're so big now. Maybe in a little while we can go out and get ya some ice cream or do whatever kids do now a days."

"You don't have to pretend to like me. I know you hate kids."

"Oh thank God. I'm tired as hell anyways, but I bet you know what that feels like kiddo. I heard you're quite an insomniac huh?"

"I guess so."

"Look I'm tired of small chat and I could really use a beer, can you go get me one?"

"Dad finished the last one this morning."

"Damn, I guess I really do have to fix everything don't I?"

"No, not really. I was handling things the best I could before you got here."

"Of course you were," he nods condescendingly, "but sometimes you need grown ups to get the job down. You need a man's touch."

"Whatever, I'll be in my room reading."

I slumped down the hall and avoided making eye contact with Uncle Mike's new room. I knew that within a matter of days the house would lack any mementos that connected Charlie and Mom to the house. Uncle Mike was a big fan of getting rid of anything that didn't work and starting over. Your girlfriend is too clingy? No problem, dump her for the promiscuous waitress at the Bar. Your car is starting to break down? No problem; reset the mileage and turn it in for a profit before picking out the newest model. Uncle Mike had an answer for everything temporary, but he didn't know how to handle any permanent additions to life. I think that's why he never cared for Charlie and I. We were unpredictable and unlike everything else in his life, we weren't expendable.

As my uncle started to get comfortable in our home, I found myself leaving my room less and less. He and my dad couldn't even do enough to get me dressed for school. My education had to be taught through pleasure books, and even when they did convince me to study, I would lock myself from all human contact unless bodily functions demanded attention.

"Piper, honey come here for me," my dad would try to sound as positive and happy as possible but I could sense his misery.

"Yes dad?"

'We need to talk."

"About what?"

"School."

He took my hand and led me out to the living room where Uncle Mike sat patiently as if he was planning for an intervention.

"Pied Piper, take a seat for me."

"Don't call me that." I cringed at the nickname, only Charlie called me that, and I only wanted to hear it from his lips.

"Whatever."

"Anyways, Piper sweetie, Uncle Mike and I wanted to talk to you about some changes. Is that okay?" My Dad said.

"Of course."

"You're growing up in front of my eyes Piper and you're turning into a wonderful young lady but I'm starting to worry about you."

"What do you mean, Dad?"

"Well your father and I noticed that since the incident you've matured about five years or more. Your attitude is as appalling as a typical teenager and I will not stand for it," My Uncle interrupted. I hated the fact that my Uncle tried to parent me. I hated the fact that he only pretended to care about me when my Dad was around. In all honesty, the two of them together was a toxic combination fueled by beer and poor life decisions about girls. My uncle was probably one of the last factors that signified the end of the relationship between my Dad and I.

"We all grieve in different ways. What if this is my way? Do you just want me to forget they ever existed? I can't forget them. I will never forget them no matter how many memories you try to destroy."

"Piper! You be nice to your Uncle."

"No Dad, he's not my Mom. He doesn't get to tell me what to do. I've been fine by myself before and I will be again."

"Piper, please, just calm down," my father pleads.

"Okay, for you. Okay."

"Your school has been calling a lot. They think it's time for you to go back or switch to a new school."

"I'm not ready to go back Dad. They won't accept me there."

"How do you know that? They said they want to help you, to help us."

"Those people turned me away at church. They said we were doomed to hell. You don't even believe in God anymore so why should I? Why should I have to sit and listen to propaganda all day?"

"That's it, go to your room. You're going to school tomorrow."

"With pleasure."

After I left the presence of my angry father and ignorant uncle, I craved rebellion. I was tired of trying to be perfect. I was tired of trying to change people's minds. I was being a complete cliché but that didn't matter to me at the time. I wanted to give people a reason to hate me, I wanted to desperately get kicked out of school. I wanted to make my dad so mad at me that he would want to send me away. I wanted to be kicked out of town. I needed a reason to leave, to start over. I realize looking back how outrageous and full of angst I really was but I was trapped in a fog; I was blinded by my own anger.

I climbed out my window in the middle of the night with money I stole from Charlie's old room and made my way to the neighborhood pharmacy. I walked down aisles of toxins, junk food, and colorful hair dyes. My school and the church both had a strict no color policy when it came to hair. I knew right then and there that it was the perfect subtle rebellion. It was something to get everyone irritated, but it was something that would come off to my dad as a silent plea for help instead of me blatantly defying authority. I settled on a box with an airy pink color that I knew would compliment my pale skin and walked home with a smug smirk on my face.

As soon as I returned I ran to the bathroom and began the drastic transformation. With the help of strong bleach and an excessive amount of chemicals, my chocolate brown locks turned to the light pink that it's been ever since.

It was at that moment where I felt a moment of happiness. I felt like I was finally shedding myself of the girl who lived in her pain. It was the start of my reinvention. It was the start of my rebirth.

I have never been a good dancer but when I'm alone there's something about the draw of a good song that gets me hypnotized. I just seem to fall into a mindless rhythm. It's so bad that often times I don't even realize where I am until the song is over, or until someone snaps me out of my daze and pulls me back to reality. Just like I met Mr. White, I'm quickly introduced to Mrs. Borgin and her kindergarten class in a similar fashion, caught dancing.

"Um, excuse me?" A stout and curvaceous woman stands at my door with fifteen wanders close behind.

"Oh! Hi there. How can I help you today?" I say, trying to hide the red that seems to be a permanent factor for me today.

"I'm Mrs. Borgin, I'm here to drop off my students..."

Her eyebrows arch and layers of bags are revealed from under her eyes. I can see her sizing me up, trying to decide whether or not she can trust me with children. I smile and usher her and the children in but she just shakes her head.

"You don't want to come in?"

"I'd love to, but it's the only break I get all day and I'm really tuckered out. I'm just going to get myself a cup of coffee if that's okay with you."

"Oh of course, come on in kids. I'm gonna read you a story."

The children all cheer and make their way in the room before settling around the rocking chair.

"Okay everyone. My name is Miss Piper and I'm your new librarian."

The smallest kindergartener raises his hand and as I call on him he moves a pile of hair out of his face.

"You over there, what's your name?"

"Hi, I'm Christian, Miss Piper, what's uh what's a brayan?"

"A librarian is someone who reads little boys and girls stories for fun."

"Oh okay!" He flashes me a smile and my heart turns to goo.

"So now that we know a little about me, why don't I read you guys a story before I learn more about all of you. How would you all like that?"

"Yeah!" they cheer.

"Okay, now what book do you want me to read you guys? How about a fairytale?"

"No," they boo and annoyed looks spread across their adolescent faces.

"You guys don't like fairytales? Hmm okay, what if I told you a brand new fairy tale about a princess who saved a prince?"

The children give each other confused glares and chatter erupts in the library. As if on instinct I shush them all and my voice naturally rises in pitch as if I'm auditioning to be a princess myself.

"Have you heard of it? It's the best story on earth," I whisper and their eyes grow wide.

"I haven't, and I know every fairytale in the whole wide world!" a girl with golden blonde locks and dull green eyes answers as her arms cross in front of her chest.

"This is a story about a new princess who was as little as you guys just a few years ago! I bet that's why you haven't heard of her."

"But Princesses don't save Princes. Princes save Princesses," another voice shouts but I don't see the face it belongs to.

"This princess does. Just trust me guys, if you don't like it, I'll tell you a different story. Does that sound like a deal?"

The cheering returns and so I pull out the largest storybook, flip to a random page, and pretend to read.

"Once upon a time there was a peasant girl with long black locks and silver eyes..."

The children are hanging to my every word as I tell a tale of a girl who wanted to desperately save her family and her people from an evil dictator who kidnapped the royal family and tortured them as a warning to any who tried to rebel. The peasant girl used her beauty and musical talents to win the heart and attention of the evil dictator and he fell so desperately he made her his princess. Once in power, she secretly undermined him and worked behind the scenes to save the last remaining royal, the prince who was not much older than she. As she worked to set him free, she began to court him and he too fell desperately in love and was more determined than ever to defeat the evil dictator.

"...Together the Prince and Princess worked to trap the dictator in prison and when they defeated him together, the Princess and Prince got married and lived happily ever after. The end."

As I finish the story, the children start to get rowdy again, demanding that I read it again or tell another elaborate tale of the Princess being a hero. I insist that there isn't enough time and promise that the next time I see their angelic faces that I will have another story, one that's even better than the one I told before.

"But Miss Piper!" they whine.

"Next time okay? I pinky promise," I hold out my pinky and they all look at one another before agreeing that my promise is valid, "how about I put on some music until we go? Huh? How does that sound?"

I push myself of the broken rocking chair and make my wave through a sea of slobbery yet adorable kids. When I reach the shore the kids start to grow even more rowdy, so I turn on classical music to calm them down, and one by one, they fall asleep on each other's laps.

"Miss Addison?" a knock comes from the doorframe as I tidy up the random crumbs that followed the children in.

"Oh hello Mrs. Borgin! Come on in, the kids loved their story, but I finished a little early so I turned on music and they fell right asleep. I hope you don't mind that they had their nap a little early."

"You got them to nap? I can never get them to nap. Oh my god, you're a natural. Are you sure you're not meant to be a kindergarten teacher?"

"I'm positive. Books are my calling. I mean, I just like sharing them with other people."

"Well you do a fantastic job at it. I swear you're a gift from God. Ugh, I don't want to have to wake them up but it's their snack time. Do you mind?"

"Oh not at all."

I walk through the pile of kids once more and help her wake up each individual child. Most of them try to cling to me as if I'm their mother, other's complain, and some walk like zombies out the door, their eyes still half closed. It's kind of adorable to see them stumble out of the room in one moment and have a burst of energy in another. It's as if they come out of a sugar coma only to get a second buzz mere moments later.

"Well I guess that's everyone. Thank you again for everything. I appreciate it more than you know," she says.

"The pleasure was all mine. I enjoyed reading to them, it was so much fun. I'll see you guys again next week around the same time, but if you need me before then I'll always be right down here."

"Thank you," she starts walking towards the door and suddenly stops in her tracks, "and Ms. Addison?"

"Yes Ma'am?"

"I was wrong about you. I thought you'd be another juvenile delinquent trying to make a quick buck off of shelving books, but I truly was wrong about you. I apologize for my assumptions, sincerely."

"Don't worry about it."

"I hope one day the rest of the school realizes what a gift you are. They're all wrong about you, they just don't know it yet."

And with her final words, she disappears into the hallway and leads her parade of kids back into the endless halls of Saint Agatha's.

# THEN:

Music blared in the nearly empty cabin, library books from the home improvement section were scattered across the floor, and an unused tool box sat on the counter. I had already spent a huge chunk of Charlie's old college fund on the necessities. A bed frame and mattress were going to be shipped to my new home, a mailbox was ordered and registered, kitchen appliances were sent and on their way, and miscellaneous furniture from the local flea market were scheduled to arrive by sundown. It was the first real day of my adult life, which began promptly at five am as I ran around the little town doing errands until lunchtime.

Within a matter of hours I was back at home, with fresh schoolbooks for homeschooling, and a variety of supplies from the neighborhood home improvement store. It was then when I got down and dirty, quite literally. I started with painting the walls a variety of colors as the music bounced off the walls; the kitchen boasted a lovely lime green color that brought out the opaque looking subway backsplash, the living room was coated in a sky blue, and my own little oasis was, of course, painted in the loveliest pastel pink around.

It was the perfect bachelorette pad, my own little woman cave that had everything I ever wanted.

By the time I finished painting, the toxins were giving me such a high that I felt like I was seeing things. I should have stopped then, but instead I kept going. I climbed into my unlit fireplace and began to scrub the excessive soot until the ashes covered me from head to toe, then I began demolishing the outhouse outside, only leaving a brand new pot outside to satisfy my toilet needs. The plumber was due to come in any day, so roughing it didn't seem like too much of an issue. I thought that I could just start work on my own, only leaving the tiniest details for the plumber to fix, but since I was an amateur at home renovations, things ended horribly.

Water spewed from the kitchen sink as I tried to start a new line, and eventually I ended up tapping into the city's sewage line. So not only was all of my water contaminated, but the sewage decided to burst and hit me in the face. It was awful and I was heartbroken. I was already admitting defeat, slumping to the floor and burying my soot-ridden head in my fecal ridden chest. I was over my head, and as if it was an omen, a small rodent danced on my feet before disappearing into a tiny hole in the kitchen's corner.

That day was just not my day, and after screaming and crying bloody murder, I packed my suitcase up, left the house, and finally checked myself into a cheap motel near the highway. I stayed there for a week, until the pest control came, the plumbing was fixed, and the beginnings of a half bath were put in place. Those days went by at snail's pace, the more time I spent in the motel, the more anxious I became. I had to get up and do something, so I started visiting a locally run bookstore in the center of town. At first I didn't buy anything, I just spent my days sitting along a bay window reading the first book I could find, but the more I explored the more my passion for books was reignited.

"Hey, you."

"Me?" I asked as I walked into the store for the third consecutive day in a row.

"Yes you. You've been coming here every day this week and I've been running the shop for thirty five years, and I've never seen your face before."

"Oh well, I'm just new to town."

"You moved here? Most people want to get out of Belfast, not come to it."

"I don't know; I like it. It's very quaint."

"Is that the only reason you came?"

"Yeah, I just needed a change in scenery."

"Well, my name is Mr. Clint and if you ever need anything, just give me a holler."

"Okay thank you. Mr. Clint, can I ask you something?"

"Anything sweetheart."

"Are you hiring?"

He chuckles and pats his bony hand against my back. "We'll see."

# NOW:

I haven't even been at work for one full day, and I've already determined ten upsides to working as a librarian and a smaller list of cons. The list sits on my desk at all times, waiting to be adjusted. Pros: I get to read books all day, kids will never get disappointed in me, I don't have to give out grades, and I can avoid adult contact if needed. I can order books using the school budget and hoard them for myself before allowing the kids to read them. I still have a lot of free time to write and listen to music, and no one will bother me. I'll never have overdue books or late fees, and stress is almost nonexistent. It sounds perfect, doesn't it?

Of course as soon as I convince myself that I've made the right choice the list of negatives stare me down and force me to rethink everything. First there's the obvious, I am not religious and I work in a school that clearly has a religious agenda. Yes it's not impossible to avoid the church's propaganda, and I probably should have considered this issue prior to applying for the job, but I mean come on; technology is making libraries obsolete and so I knew this would be my only option. I would have become a broke and mentally insane woman without it. Secondly my coworkers are already an issue. I've screwed up the most important first impression of my adult life and now I honestly want to curl into a corner and stay there forever. Which I mean, won't be too much of an issue. I can just avoid eye contact, keep conversations to pleasantries, and use the library as a haven. I mean, it's not like I wasn't going to do those things in the first place right? I just feel as if their preconceived notions of me are just like the ones that caused me to act out and run away from my issues in the first place. And if they aren't judging me they think I'm a godsend or they want to "define me." Like excuse me Mr. Ironic name, don't tell me who I am. If you want to define me, fine, but I'm going to define you. It'll be our secret game; no one else will know what our lingering glares towards each other truly mean. Maybe they'll think we're in lust with each other because the idea of love in a place like this is absolutely absurd. I mean I can just see it now; we'd be labeled as the odd couple. The frail nerd with light chocolate skin, untamable curls, and rich chestnut orbs, and the mousy girl with artificially colored locks, ivory colored skin, and dull eyes. It's absolutely laughable, and not because of who he is or the color of his skin, but the idea of me falling in love is not possible. I don't like other people. How am I supposed to love other people when I don't even love myself?

As I was saying, my list of pros and cons isn't exactly the most even, but it's still weighing on my mind as I go through the day, doodling on sketch pads, reorganizing books, and creating lists of new books to buy. I'm indecisive and I know that, and I know that I look for any way to run away from potential problems, but I like to think that the best way to fix yourself is to recognize your problems and make plans to fix them. Well that's what my therapist said during our first session anyways. I thought she was bullshiting me, so yeah haven't gone back there.

By the time my second set of students arrive, the entire library is decked in arts and crafts, an empty tea mug screams to be refilled, and a playlist of eighties pop starts to blare.

"Welcome, welcome. Come on in everyone," I smile and wave goodbye to the teacher, who pays me no mind before disappearing.

A crowd of hormonal sixth graders trample in, almost knocking me over. It's seems as if they have more energy than the little kiddos I had to deal with before. Only one girl even bothers to look me in the eye, but she quickly looks away, her piercing blue eyes leaving a haunting chill against my skin.

"Hi everyone, can I have your attention?"

"Why should we give you attention? You look like you belong at a freak show, what kind of teacher are you?" A bulky boy who looks like he's been benching weights since he could walk spits as he talks.

"Mkay, listen here. I don't have to deal with little ignorant little turds like you. If you don't want to get out of class once a week, suit yourself. You won't hurt my feelings, but I'm pretty sure your teacher won't like having you follow him around like a lost puppy when you should be in here with me."

His jaw drops and it gets so quiet in the room that you can hear a pin drop. Almost all of the kids in the room look to be in absolute shock except the one mystery girl. She just keeps her gaze on the boy with a smug look. It's as if she enjoys watching much overdue karma hitting him in the face. I laugh light heartedly and replace an irritated face with a more pleasant one.

"Now, as I was saying. My name is Miss Piper, and I will be your librarian. I can help make this school year a lot of fun for you guys or absolutely dreadful, and I think you guys would like to be on my good side. My bad side is kind of terrifying."

The petite girl laughs but quickly disguises it as a cough.

"Okay so, I'm going to let you guys pick out books soon, but I'm just going to let you know that the library is going to be changing really soon. I'm going to switch the books to meet the Dewey decimal system to make it easier for me and I'm even going to have a shelf or two for each grade level and some recommended books which will be cool."

116

"Um, excuse me, Miss Piper?"

"Yeah?"

"Um what's the Dewey decimal system?"

"Ah, okay great question. Do any of you know what the Dewey decimal system is?"

The mysterious girl raises her hand and the student scoff.

"Of course Emma Mackenzie knows what it is. Emma Mackenzie knows everything."

Her face turns bright red and she quickly lowers her hand.

"Sweetie. Emma is it?"

She nods.

"Don't be afraid to get something right. Come on, tell me what you think it is?"

"It's an organizational structure for books that all libraries adapted a long time ago. It's a numeral system of some sorts."

"Exactly. Now next time you guys stop by I'll teach you guys how to use it. Until then, go look around for some books, and if you want a book and can't find it just write it down on a piece of paper and put it in the colorful box on the checkout counter."

The kids wander around aimlessly for a long time, talking to each other and whispering endless cruelties to an Emma Mackenzie who slumps down into her bones to appear weaker than she really is, to try to be as invisible as possible. I want to pull her to the side and pick her intelligent brain, learn more about the way this place works with a true insider, someone with smarts and a maturity that surpasses her age. I can't do it right now though. Being a teacher's pet is never a good thing, and seeing how her peers already have an extreme disdain towards her, I rather not make it worse.

"Hey Emma, you know what?" a girl with golden locks and bright blue braces asks.

"What?" she mumbles.

"I bet you're gonna end up just like Miss Piper. You're gonna be an unmarried freak who has to shelve books and promote reading for a living."

"There's nothing wrong with being unmarried or liking reading…"

"Oh honey, you're already too far gone. You might as well just give up schooling and become her little apprentice."

"Nice use of a vocab word Victoria, I didn't think people as dumb as you could comprehend ten cent words."

"What's that supposed to mean?"

"Whatever you want it to mean."

Emma grabs The Great Gatsby off the shelf and shuffles towards the corner without glancing at anyone else. She slumps in one of the decaying beanbags and a puff of dust bellows around the room, causing the class to burst into a coughing hysteria. It doesn't even seem to bother her, it's like she inhales the smell of the dust like I inhale the smell of a used bookstore.

Before long, the taciturn teacher returns and all the children rush towards my desk to check out their trashy popular novels. I swear with each book I check out, the less hope for humanity I have. I guess I expected too much of middle schoolers who are just experimenting with a small trace of freedom. I don't know, I just wanted someone to check out something rather than a typical sports novel or teen romance novel, all of which claim that the girl's first love is the "one." I wish I could yell at all the girls and tell them that their first love won't be real and it'll never last, but I can't, so I just let the hopeless romantics borrow their books, and let the guys explore books where the underdogs always wins. Reality check boys, that almost never happens. I mean do any of them watch TV? Living with two men for over half of my adolescent life, I learned a lot about sports, and I learned one thing from all of them; Cinderella stories are just temporary, they always fall to experienced warriors in the end.

I'm about to give up hope when Emma Mackenzie lays her Gatsby book on my counter. I flash a smile and when I realize that she's the final one, I take the opportunity to start a conversation.

"You know, you don't have to listen to them talk to you like that."

"You wouldn't understand," she bites down on her thumb.

"I bet I do. I was like you before."

"I don't know, it's just like this in every class. I guess I just got used to it."

"You shouldn't be used to it."

I hand her back the book and she glances up quickly before averting her eyes again.

"I need to go before I get in trouble."

"Okay, well, if you ever need somewhere to get away, you're always welcome here."

"Really?"

"Mi casa es tu casa."

"Thank you."

The little girl runs away as soon as she finishes her sentence, leaving me to relish in my thoughts for my final hour of work. I survived the first day. I did it, and I only had one panic attack. Today has been a successful day, but I don't know if I would classify it as a good one. I have so many things to prove to these people here and to myself, I don't know if I'm ready to take on that challenge. I don't know I'm finally ready to face my demons. I don't know if I'm mature enough to move on from my past and create a new identity. I don't even know who I am. I'm constantly changing for other people; I'm constantly changing myself to blend in. Hell, if I can't understand myself, how in the world is anyone else going to be able to?

# THEN:

When I was younger I thought that I could rely on my older brother for anything and everything. When I fell down at the playground it was him who held my hand and cried for our mom to kiss it. When I couldn't understand something in school it was Charlie who walked me through everything. It was as if we were codependent; our lives revolved around each other.

I remember when I was in the first few years of elementary school; I would often call for Charlie to handle my playground tussles. Back then he was only there for me partially, half of him was someone I did not like knowing, but I loved him anyways. It was as if one moment he was the protective brother and the next he was a blood-thirsty demon trying to find his next prey.

Part of me believes that he defended me because he was bored, and because his bottled up emotions were overdue to explode. If I remember correctly, it was during that time where the doctors were experimenting with behavioral medicines. Every other week he would come home from the doctors with the "next best" drug, all of which failed horribly. Some of them would make him depressed, causing him to cling to his bottle as if it was his only escape, others made him hyper and unpredictable, one minute

Charlie would be bouncing off the walls, the next he'd be making a mess in the kitchen, all the while proclaiming that he was the next master chef. I never minded those two types of medicines, sure it hid the real Charlie from me, but those kinds of medicines never left me feeling afraid of my brother. The worse of the medicines made his deep seeded anger worse. It was then when his aggression was at a peak, and no amount of physical sports could reduce the frustration he felt.

"Charlie, are you okay?"

I would come home and ask the same question every day. On occasion, he would shrug me off or answer nonchalantly, but most days he would bury himself into my mousy frame and try to pull himself together. Charlie needed me and I needed him. We were joined at the hip so often that our names were constantly linked, and though he was much older than me, it worked. We worked.

"I'm so tired Piper," he mumbled one day.

"What's wrong? It's it the meds?"

"Kind of. I'm just so angry and sad all the time. Do you understand that?"

"Yeah, mom told me that the medicine can make you a new person."

"But it's not making me a new person," he said, insistently.

"What?"

"It's changing me Piper. I'm not the same big brother anymore."

"Yes you are."

"No I'm not."

"Yes you are!"

"Piper just listen to me already!" He snapped and took ahold of me, shaking my body until I stopped fussing.

"Stop Charlie! You're hurting me."

He stopped and his eyes grew five times his normal size.

"What is it? Say what you wanna; you can talk to me, ya know?" I asked.

"When I'm mad, I hurt people and I can't stop myself till it's over. The medicine just makes me angrier and makes me feel useless. I'm too tired to even play football after school, or help you with your homework. I don't know what to do, I can't take it anymore, but if I don't, I can't get better."

Charlie's words came out with perfect clarity, but his body language showed defeat. He hated himself. He hated who he was becoming. It was as if he knew his fate long before his life ended abruptly.

"Why don't you tell mom and dad then? They'll take you back to the doctor to get better!" I smiled as I said this, as if it was the most ingenious idea anyone in the world had ever come up with.

"Because mom and dad have spent a lot of money on me already, and I hear them talking Piper, we're going to be broke."

"Broke?"

"We won't have any more money."

"What's so wrong with that?"

"That means mom can't buy groceries, we won't have food or new clothes, and during Christmas there won't be any presents."

"No presents! Oh no, you can't tell them."

"Exactly, it has to stay our little secret, okay?"

"Okay."

"Pinky promise?"

"Pinky promise!"

"Good."

"But what are you gonna do if you get angry?"

"I dunno Piper."

"I think I have an idea."

I took one look at him before forcing him to put on a smile. Then I took ahold of his hand and gave him the sincerest look I could give him.

"When you're mad just squeeze my hands and look at me. I'll even sing our song until you feel better, and when I'm not with you just pretend that I am. I can be like your imaginary friend!" I said.

"But you're a real person silly."

"Shh, I'm not here, I'm just make believe."

He broke out into a genuine smile and we both start to laugh. The misery just washed off his face like dirt washes off a car during a rainy day. He seemed truly happy, and by the time I finished my laughing fit his face returned to a stiff line. He became emotionless just as fast as he was able to overcome the restraints his medicine put on him. I knew he was there deep down. He had to be there somewhere, I mean in that moment there was a glimmer of the person that meant the world to me. That moment caused me to believe that he didn't really change, it caused me to believe that he was just tired of fighting. If I was him, I would be too, but I knew I couldn't let him give up. I wanted to be there as much as I physically could, and so I became his warrior, his rock; I became the only person who was capable of reminding him that life didn't have to be a destructive dark hole. I gave Charlie hope.

"Thank you my pied Piper. I love you, you know that right?"

"Yep! and I love you too."

# NOW:

Besides leaving an awful first impression during my first day of school, I manage to avoid drawing more attention to me. In all honesty, the rest of my week is kind of uneventful. I just read to kids daily, let them pick out cookie cutter books, and relax in my own domain. Every now and then Emma Mackenzie shows up, but she doesn't say a word, she simply sits in her dusty dwelling and does her work. I don't blame her for not wanting to hold conversations with me. At least I know she's grateful by her showing up every damned day.

Early Friday morning, I find Emma and I in our normal routine. She's buried in a pile of math homework while I struggle to find an organizational method for the books that is both practical and aesthetically pleasing. Both of us are so focused that we don't notice Mr. White standing by the door until he talks.

"Hello, hello!"

"Hello Mr. White, to what do I owe this pleasure? Have you come by to do more investigating on my life? Have you figured out who I am yet? Can I suggest a google search? I heard the internet is very helpful," I tease.

"Ha, ha. Very funny. I need you to know that your sarcasm is very much appreciated, but I didn't come for that reason. I'm just here to retrieve my favorite student. Come on Emma my dear, I need you for the group work."

"Do I have to?"

Her voice comes out fragile and I swear I see her nervously fidgeting.

"You know Mr. White, I don't mind having Emma around. It's actually quite comforting to be in the presence of another bookworm."

"I understand that, but I just I want to put her out there some more. I can't keep sending her out of class and expect for other students to just be okay with it."

"Why wouldn't they be okay with it?"

"They would ask for the same privileges Emma receives. It's unfair."

"Emma, how do you feel about that?" I ask.

"I-I- I don't want to go back there. I like being in here. Miss Piper leaves me to my work and no one is in here to ask me for answers or to make fun of me. I don't know…" she answers and I place my hand on her shoulder.

"Well, I'll let it slide, but if you want to keep this arrangement up we're going to have to talk to Principal Wolff," Mr. White answers.

"I think I can safely speak for the both of us by saying that we're more than willing to help you get your wish, but we can not fight your fight. You understand that right?" I say.

"Yeah. I think I do. I just don't know if this a battle I want to fight."

"Well we can't decide that for you, so I'll give you the weekend to think about it, and on Monday I'm expecting an answer. Now if you girls will excuse me, I have a class to get back to," Mr. White says.

"Goodbye Mr. White, thank you," Emma says.

I follow Mr. White out the door and as he starts to walk away I just have the overwhelming desire to get him to stay. He's strange and not like anyone else here. I feel as if he's part of the island of misfit toys and that maybe it's a good thing he stumbled into my life. I don't know why I'm feeling this way, but I do. I just feel as if I need to make this abnormality my friend. Maybe I'm just tired of being stuck in my head and want someone around for a change.

"Wait! Mr. White?"

"Yes, my dear?"

"I don't recall ever getting your first name."

"Well only my closest friends call me Clarkson, and the rest of my world knows me by my ironic surname."

"Okay then Mr. Clarkson, hopefully this can be the start of a new friendship. Does that sound okay with you?"

"Of course Miss Piper, I would be delighted to be your acquaintance."

"I'll see you around."

"I'll see you around, mystery girl."

I nod to him and I watch him waltz off towards the labyrinth, leaving Emma Mackenzie to work quietly on a group project by herself. I don't offer to help. I don't even speak to her after that. We have a mutual agreement that we only speak when necessary. It's a term in our nonverbal contact. We wouldn't want anyone to think that I'm favoring her over any other of my students, and even though I most clearly am, I would die if I found out I was causing her peers to harass her more. I just want to help her. I just want to make her life easier, I want to grant her a temporary reprieve from hell. I'm trying to do the things I wish other people did for me long ago.

# THEN:

There is nothing worse than the awkward years, and no I don't mean high school, I mean the middle grades, junior high, middle school, whatever people nowadays call it. Honestly, if I could compare middle school to any part of the body I would compare it to the armpit; unloved, sweaty, and in desperate need of constant attention. Even though my school went from preschool through eighth grade, I did not get to skip out on those brutal years, and the death of my better halves made the whole thing worse. Just imagine my horror when mother nature presented her first gift to me. I thought I was dying, like no one told me I'd be bleeding out for the next few decades. It was even worse when I had to explain to my dad why he had to take me to the hospital.

"Dad! I'm dying!"

"What?"

"I said I'm dying! Everything hurts and I can't stop bleeding. Jesus Christ, it's like a demon is stabbing my gut over and over."

"I'm sure you're not dying."

"I'm bleeding Dad. I'm bleeding!"

"Where are you bleeding…"

I ran into his room and out of mine, covering my lower half with soiled white sheets.

"Do you really want to know?"

He arched his eyebrows and my Uncle wandered in the room. I looked at both of them and as they gave me a quick glance head to toe, I swear even to this day, all of our faces turned as white as a sheet at the same time.

"Oh god. Oh god Mike. I can't handle this."

My uncle snickered and walked out the room, shrugging his shoulders as he left as if he was wishing my dad good luck sarcastically.

"Dad! Snap out of it. I'm dying. You can't lose me too. Let's go."

"You're fine Piper…"

"Do you not see the giant stain right in front of you? It can't be healthy Dad."

My dad shook his hand and reached for my mother's old nightstand. He reached in and handed my a perfectly wrapped gift that had black and red paper.

"What are you doing?"

"Just…I don't know, give me your soiled sheets or whatever and I'll clean them. That gift should answer all your questions…"

I threw my soiled sheet at him and ran off with the gift close to me. I guess I did learn that night, but it wasn't what I expected. Puberty hit me like a truck and it caused this awkward divide between the remains of my family. I mean, it wasn't like I could go talk to my dad about what was going on in my mind or what was happening to my body.

Puberty was bad enough, but I couldn't get a break; school was making my life even worse than it already was. My grand scheme on getting kicked out of school wasn't grand enough, so instead of getting expelled, I was treated like a constant broken soul. My teachers all pitied me and expected nothing but incomplete homework and poor grades on tests. On the other hand, all the administrators kept me close by their sides as they waited for me to exploded like Charlie did. They walked on eggshells around me, and though it sort of made me feel powerful, it was annoying. I just wanted to be normal, that's all any human wants to be after they've been unwillingly dragged into a life of infamy.

The students weren't too accepting of my wishes either. They used my mistakes and flaws as direct hits to my weak self-esteem. I had no friends, and no one bothered talking to me unless it was to mock me or point out my unbiblical ways.

"Piper, you know, I was at bible study last night and I realized that you stopped showing up? What happened? Did you realize that your heart belonged to satan?"

"Screw you Melissa. I'd rather burn in your imaginary hell than go to bible study. I don't believe in what you believe in. I don't believe in your God because I refuse to believe that he would accept bitchy assholes like you and not accept someone who wants to be a good person like me."

"Excuse me? Did you just swear?" she asked.

"Oh yeah I did. What cha gonna do about it? Tell me I'm doomed for hell? Tattle on me? Go ahead, see if I care. Everyone here will just try to rehabilitate me and bring me back to God's side, but it won't work. Do you know why it won't work sweetheart?"

She gritted her teeth, "Enlighten me."

"Because the same people who want to fix me are the people who broke me in the first place. So you know what, I don't need you to question my motives. I know what I'm doing, and I know that I'm better off without all of you."

"Whatever, you freak. I just wanted to know why you weren't at bible study."

"Sure, it's all my fault."

I pushed past her and hid in the bathroom while the rest of my class headed to the church for weekly mass. I was so tired of it. I was so tired of everyone pushing their agenda on me. It was like I was everyone's project. People either wanted to push me until I broke or reinvent me, transforming me into someone I wouldn't recognize.

It was exhausting being in that tug of war. I couldn't please anyone and I didn't want to please anyone, but my defiance also made it impossible to please myself and that in itself caused horrible trauma that lasted throughout my unbalanced adult years.

# NOW:

Humans are people of routine. Routine keeps us from experiencing abrupt changes in life. It is supposed to shelter us from getting hurt, but at the same time, routine keeps people from becoming immersed in true life. I realize that my speech may seem hypocritical, especially due to my tendencies to just run away any time I can't handle a problem, but I don't know. I just get so damn bored of routine. I am so bored of my routine. I'm dying of boredom I tell you, work is driving me to death.

Every day it's the same thing. Emma comes in and does her work before disappearing to who know's where. On special occasions, Clarkson appears and bores me to tears with words of the day, as if I care about a random ten cent word. He tries to change it up on occasion, and at least once a week he tries to update me about Emma's battle with the big bad Wolff. I think she's finally coming around. Pretty soon, she'll be at the point where she may be able to make a convincing argument without stuttering excessively. She's making progress, I can see it, but it's going to take more time if she wants to gain asylum from her devilish peers . She's too fragile and Dick Wolff will eat her alive.

"Good morning Miss Piper."

"Mornin' Clarkson."

"I brought you a spot of tea," he smiles at me and holds up a coffee cup that is decorated with the numbers that compose pi. I tilt my head and he shows me the green tea sitting inside the cup. It's like he's bribing me. If I let him in the cavernous book dwelling, he'll giving me my crack.

"Playing with British slang I see."

"Isn't it just the coolest!" He beams and does this odd little happy dance with his cup. His body sways left and right and his shoulders flirt up and down but somehow he doesn't even spill one drop.

"No, not really. You don't have the look to pull it off, or the accent," I tease.

He tries to fake being offended but ends up laughing instead. I wave him into the room and he hands my my cup. The liquid trickles down my throat and I just feel myself unwind slowly. I never realize how tense I am until I indulge a little.

"So I was doing research right…" Clarkson starts, pulling me out of my daze.

"Mhm…."

"And I found out that there's a synonym for a library!"

"That excites you?" I try my hardest not to roll my eyes, but it's so hard not to. Clarkson is a young adult like me, no more than two years older than I am, but I swear he acts like an old man doing a crossword puzzle sometimes. It's like the tiniest things can amuse him and cause him to go into tangents.

"Yeah, I mean, I'm easily excitable. Anyways, don't you want to know what the word is?" He taps his foot impatiently. It's like he expects for me to give him an excited response.

"Even if I say no, you're going to tell me anyways," I answer, deadpanned.

I lean my elbows on the checkout desk and place my tea next to me. I bat my eyelashes on instinct and try to look interested in what he's saying.

"True. Okay, so it's called an athenaeum named after the goddess of wisdom. Isn't that cool?" He starts gesturing with his hands and I just give him a sympathetic smile as he continues to banter on. He looks like he just hit the jackpot. I mean I don't even really know what he's saying right now but he keeps waving his hands and motioning to random books around the room. I should probably listen to him but It's not interesting.

I try to choke back a yawn and instead I let out an exasperated sigh.

"Clarkson, can I ask you something?" I ask, cutting him off and interrupting his train of thought, sparing me from more tedious drudgery.

"Of course. What's on your mind?"

"Do you ever just get tired of it all?" I ask.

"What do you mean?"

"Do you ever get tired of doing the same thing every day?"

"No, not really, why?"

"Well I do, and I want to do something exciting. I feel like I'm stuck in rut and can't do anything. I'm losing my mind. I'm not even exaggerating."

"So, you're looking for an adventure?"

This time it's Clarkson who leans against the desk. He scans me head to toe, and for the first time I get a close view of his tiny frame. His awkward stature seems to fit his personality. He is the definition of a stereotypical nerd, but I can't necessarily tell him that I see him in that light, and I can't really tell him how I see him as a black Bill Nye.. but for math instead of science.

"Exactly!"

"Well then, I have a surprise for you."

My eyebrows arch and he gives me a devious smile. I don't know if it's possible to have the Hegemon of useless information entertain me, but I do enjoy his company most of the time, and I don't really have anything to lose.

"Meet me tonight at that little coffee shop downtown around eight."

"Carla's?"

"That's the one."

"Alright, you better wow me Mr. White because if not I may just die of boredom."

"I don't think that's possible."

"Prove me wrong and leave me here to die then," I say as I exaggeratingly put a hand on my head and pretend to drop dead.

"Oh no, how ever will the school go on without our precious librarian?" he says in a robotic, monotone voice.

"Ha. Ha. Very funny. But really, I'm dying for some fun. You have to entertain me."

"I know, I know. I will later, but right now we have work to finish. Until then, read a book to some kids, and relax a little."

"But how will I ever pick a book? The inventory is so grand here that I may just get lost in the abyss!" Sarcasm glides out of me like a fish in water. It's my second nature to be sarcastic; it's one of the only ways I know how to communicate with others without tensing up and losing my ability speak.

"Oh stop being so dramatic."

"I can't help it; I was born this way."

"Yeah, yeah, sure. My break is about to be over so I have to run but I'll see you later. Just make sure you don't drop dead before I'm able to come to your rescue," he laughs.

"Of course. I will be anxiously awaiting this grand adventure tonight."

"I'll see you later, Miss Piper."

"I'll see you, Mr. Clarkson."

He waves goodbye, and I pull out my book and attempt to write, all the while ignoring a killer case of writer's block. I know that eventually I'll finish my book but I just don't have the right words. I just don't feel connected to my main character anymore. She and I used to be in sync, and now I find her to be an annoying brat who complains about not understanding life. No one understands life, it's just a game we're all forced to play, so why the hell are you complaining, and who gave you the right to do so? Who gave you the right to be miserable? I may have written her character and given her depth, but I certainly didn't give her the permission to become me. I didn't give her the permission to voice my darkest thoughts and embrace them. That's probably why I've hit a wall, I don't want to dig too deep into who I am.

I stare at an unfinished sentence, a half blank page, and after awhile i get frustrated and put the damned thing away. Every part of me finds my writing completely disgusting, and so I pull out a book titled the *Valley of the Dolls.* The characters in the book are also horrendous, but something about it keeps me compelled. In the story, you have these intelligent women who feel like they need a man to launch their careers and to be successful when they're talented on their own. I wish I could grip on to them and tell them to do something with their life, to stop throwing their talent away. You are not your faults. You are not your ups and downs. Who you are depends on how you handle yourself in terrible situations. Why can't anyone in a book understand that?

I finish the book before the end of the day and end up wandering through the limited selection in my cave. Nothing in here is worth reading, and my budget for the library is so tiny I'd be lucky to get a deal on one class set of books. It makes me sad that books have been reduced to this. There's so little creativity in this room, and all the brilliant classics I love just rot in dust until a teacher forces a disgruntled kid to lug it around.

I feel like my little pupils or adolescents, in general, shouldn't be forced to read literary classics. No one appreciates what they have when it's just given to them, or when it's forced upon them. You have to just go into a classic blind, and once you find that book, you just have to fall into its dimension. Maybe one day, I'll come in here, mix all the books up, and hide all the covers with newspaper. If I did that, then the kids wouldn't be able to pick a book on what they think they should be reading, but on what actually interests them. Hell, maybe I wouldn't have such a big issue with those trashy novels about cliques if people read them because they actually liked them instead of reading them because society tells them too. Like hello? This isn't some big game of simon says; read something because you want to, because it speaks to you, not because you feel obligated. I wish people understood that about the world. We're all going to die someday, and it's better to go out knowing that you lived the life you wanted to rather than living a life everyone else told you to.

As the bell rings, my fingers are still frantically searching for something to read. Nothing is worse than being a book lover who can't have the comforting feeling of aged paper resting tenderly in their hands. Nothing is worse than being a writer who is unable to express their words eloquently, leaving a gaping hole in their soul, and causing the feeling of utter despair. There is nothing worse than feeling useless. I am nothing without words; my identity is completely dependent on someone finding the words I could never find to describe how I feel, or discovering those words for someone else.

I wander out the decaying school as a crowd of vicious children shove me out the way. The entire building is in better shape than the library but barely. The halls are littered with stray pencils and dust bunnies, the trash cans are overflowed with food creations and used tissues, and the vents seem to disperse the smell of sweaty gym socks throughout. The stampede of children cause a larger mess leaving their cares and manners throughout the unloved halls. By the time I get to my car, I'm battered and bruised. I've escaped a war with all my limbs. Those children are vicious I tell you. They'll even turn on each other if push comes to shove. It's as if they have only one mindset; survive. You survive school then you survive a test. Soon after you survive escaping school, and just when you think you're finally granted a reprieve, you have to survive mountains of homework. I feel for those poor kids. Being a student is one of the most soul sucking careers that a human can enter. And why yes, I did call being a student a career. What else would you call devoting over a quarter of your life to a single task?

At home, I load my tub with a mountain of pillows and blankets before curling in and playing Beatles music. As a pure sound manages to slip through the record player's static, I sip on a cup of tea and scan my bookshelf over and over while trying to decompress. I feel tense, anxious almost, though I don't know if I truly need to feel the way I do. I realize that I'm craving adventure in my life so that I can fuel my inspiration. I need to write again. I want to fix my creation, I need to fix my monster before I lose my only way to understand what's going on my brain. Eventually I let my mind wander and time leaves me, causing hours to pass before the nerves resurface.

When I'm aware of the time again, I jump and begin to feel my mind begin to play games. *Why are you going out Piper? Don't you know by now that you can't rely on anyone but yourself? I'm your only friend and I am you. I won't hurt you like he will. I can't. We can just stay here. There's nothing wrong with a little writer's block, right? We can always wait it out and pick up a new hobby until it's over. Oh, or we can try to relearn how to play the guitar. I think that will be fun, don't you? Well of course you do, you're me. Anyways, Piper, darling, don't you see how grand life can be when it's blander than a box of oats? We can be safe. Trust me. Stay home tonight.*

"No!" I scream out loud and my subconscious seems to faded into the background. I was fine before. I was trying to come to terms with leaving my comfort zone, with becoming the confident person Clarkson saw me as, with the person he wanted to befriend. Of

145

course, I had to come in my own way, leaving me with a dilemma that may not make sense on the surface to anyone but myself. If I just shut her up maybe I can enjoy my night with my friend. I don't think I need her; I don't need my doubts.

When it's time to go, I don't bother changing out of my work clothes to meet him and I don't drive my car. The temperature is bitter, and though my faux fur boots keep my feet warm, and a braided beanie covers my head and ears, I'm freezing and alert but I don't mind. I like having the opportunity to make my senses heightened. I like having the opportunity to reduce foggy effects my medicine occasionally gives me. As I make my way towards downtown, my nose starts to turn as bright as a reindeer's and my cheeks become a rosy pink. I probably look like those girls during a cheesy Christmas movie except for the fact that it's not officially fall yet and and there isn't a flake of snow on the ground.

"Piper, is that you?"

I turn around and spot Clarkson driving up besides me. He gives me this goofy grin and I notice that he's changed clothes. Instead of his typical dress shirt and bow tie, he's settled on a nice sports jacket and dark-washed jeans. It's weird to see anyone out of a work setting, but Clarkson is different. No matter how annoyed I get around him, I feel as if trust him, and even if I can't, he's a

146

nonjudgmental person who will talk to me even when I make a fool of myself.

"Hi! I'm so excited for tonight," I say, smiling.

"Me too, hey do you want to hop in? You shouldn't be walking in this weather."

"No I like it, and besides we're only a block or two away."

"You're right, stay right there."

He pulls his car off to the side of the road before parking it and joining me on a brisk walk. I smile at him, and as he gets closer I notice he's hiding something behind his back.

"I know flowers are cliche, and I know you're someone who likes creativity and people who think out the box so I got you something."

"Clarkson, you didn't have to do that." My voice raises a tad as I speak. I didn't think he would get me anything. He shouldn't have got me anything.

"Yes I did, and tonight call me Clark."

"Clark? Hm, okay. I think I like the sound of that. Clark, Clark, Clark."

"Hey come on now, don't wear it out!" His eyes dance as he speaks.

"You're really cheesy, you know that right," I say as I stifle a laugh.

He smiles in reply but I see him shift back and forth on his toes. He's excited and he's making me excited.

"I like being cheesy, it brightens people's day. Now are you ready for your surprise?"

His eyes seem to say *"Come on! Come on! Come on!"* while he speaks. I think I can have some fun with this, tease him just a little bit. I want to drive him insane.

"No I don't think I am. Maybe a little later."

"Are you sure? I mean. I guess I can give it to you later," his voice deflates and I smirk.

"I'm just kidding, of course I'm ready!"

"Oh!" he pauses and color rushes to his face, "Um okay then, now close your eyes and hold out your hands."

"You aren't going to put a snake or spider or something like that in my hands right?"

"No, just trust me on this okay."

"Okay."

I clamp my eyes shut and hold out my hands. I don't know what he could have gotten me. Maybe it's a tea mug or school supplies. It has to be something useful; everything he owns is practical in one way or another, I suspect his gifts will be the same.

Within seconds, my palms are tagged down by something heavy. My eyes flutter open and there in my hands lies an antique version of Alice in Wonderland, lit only by the moon's gentle light. It's even embroidered with red and gold. The book is absolutely beautiful; it's in mint condition, and the hard spine doesn't look damaged at all. This book has been loved and cared for. It must have meant a lot to someone else, and now it's my turn to love it even more than it was before.

"You've probably already read it, but it's my absolute favorite book in the world. Every time I read it I see life in a new way. It makes me feel like a kid again. I just thought that since you needed something to read, you might like this," he smiles but bites down on his lip. He must be nervous, unsure of how I'm going to react to the gift.

"It's beautiful Clark! I love it, thank you so much. You didn't have to do this."

"I know I didn't, but I wanted to. Now let's go inside and get something warm to drink before we turn into popsicles out here."

He holds out his bent arm and our arms soon intertwine as we skip awkwardly into the locally owned coffee shop like two little kids in a toy store. Our whole conversation is just as spectacular as the night sky; he lets me rant about books and work the entire time. He never even loses interest, he just stares at me and soaks in every word. It's really nice to have someone to talk to.

"So, what do you normally get here?" he asks as a wave of warmth hits our faces.

"Well, I don't come here a lot. You know I'm a tea person..."

"That's true... I guess we won't have coffee then. What about hot chocolate? Everyone loves hot chocolate! Right?"

"I guess so, I never really saw myself as being infatuated with a cup of hot cocoa," I tilt my head and think about it. I'm not into soda, coffee, alcohol, cider, or even juice. I just like tea, it's weird. I'm weird.

"Then you've never had the right kind! Okay that settles it, we're both getting white hot chocolate tonight. It'll be the perfect sugar high for our grand adventure."

"Alright, if you insist."

"You won't regret this."

"I hope you're right."

He pats my hand before walking away from our booth by the fireplace as to say he'll be back after he's ordered us our drinks.

When he comes back, I thank him again and the heat from the cup warm my frigid fingers.

"Are you going to drink it?" he asks as he slurps his down.

"Hm? Oh yeah, yeah. Drinking. Right!" This time, color floods my face and I quickly take a sip.

The moment the liquid hits my tastebuds I hear them sing. The decadent liquid is the perfect winter drink, light enough to not feel heavy and slow afterwards, and flavorful enough to savor every sip. I feel like I'm cheating on my beloved green tea but it is just perfect.

"Holy shit, this is great!"

"I told you!"

"You're right! I have to give this one to ya. Oh and excuse my french. If you haven't figured out by now I kind of have a tiny potty mouth, whoops."

"I actually haven't noticed until now. You're much more reserved at work. God, I'm slacking right now. There's so much I don't know yet," he pauses and shakes his head. Of course I'm reserved at work. I'm not going to show my sailor's mouth to a bunch of impressionable kids, especially kids who think that saying the word hell will send them there.

"This just won't be tolerated. I still have so much work left to do till I figure out who you are. I need to start paying more attention to you and less attention to the words of the day if I'm ever going to make any progress!"he sighs.

"Oh give up the game, Clark. You don't have to know who I am right away or even at all. Let's just enjoy our night and have some fun."

"I will never stop Piper. It's not in my DNA."

"Come on, for me? Your little experiment can resume as soon as you get back in your car and drive home."

"I can't do that. The most interesting part of a social experiment is watching people put their guards down. It's the little moments that matter, people's second thoughts. It's how people act and respond after they give off their crappy responses that appease society. I don't know...I'm probably not even making much sense. I'm not good with words. You're the writer, not me."

"You make perfect sense to me, and I know exactly what you mean. I thought I was the only person who notices those kinds of things. I may not see the world as a giant experiment like you do, but I do like seeing how people react when they have no real control over their thoughts."

"No way, I know plenty of people who see the world the way we do."

"I guess I'm learning more about you now. My oh my, look how the tables have turned," I say as I set my cup of cocoa down on the table and cross my arms.

"I guess they have, but there's still so much we don't know about each other. We aren't experts, we're amateurs right now, so don't get too cocky."

"Fine, but what else do we really need to know about each other, Clark?"

"I don't know, the little things."

"The little things?"

"Yeah, like what's your favorite color?"

"Have you seen my hair?"

His face turns as bright as my lengthy locks and my eyebrows arch while my lips form a smirk.

"Okay, that was a dumb question. Let me think of something better. Like, I don't know, what's your favorite book?" he asks.

"I don't know, it depends. I have a different favorite book in every genre."

"Really?"

"Mhm," I say as a slurp down the remaining cocoa and whipped cream sludge.

"Okay then, hmm..."

"When do I get to ask you some questions, huh?"

"I don't know."

He pauses and I look around around the room. Every table is occupied with college kids, buried in their mountains of homework. Part of me wishes that I was in their place instead of mine, but if I was them I wouldn't be here at all. If I was them, I'd be at home, lonely yet too afraid to go out and make a friend.

"Okay, why don't we take turns and by the time we're done with our second cup of cocoa, we'll go on our little adventure, wherever that may be," I say as I shift my attention back to him.

"Sounds like a plan. Why don't you go first?"

"Okay, what made you pick this place as our first stop?"

"I used to come here as a little kid," he pauses for a second and his eyes glaze over just a tad. He's giving himself nostalgia, "I remember running down the icy streets every day as soon as school would get out and doing my homework in here. I remember coming here to ask out this waitress I had a crush on for about a year and a half. She turned me down, of course, I mean look at me. But after she said no, she bought me a cup of hot cocoa and left me to my crying in that booth over there. I've had some really crappy times in here, but I've had good ones too. I don't know, there's just something about this place. It feels like home to me."

"That's really sweet," I smile at him and grab onto his hand, "I love places like this too. Something about the aura in the air. Maybe it's the fact that the owners are real people who care. Maybe it's the fact that the people who come in here are more than just arrogant snobs who brag about their coffee blend. Maybe it's the fact that people have history here, just like you."

"Yeah, it really is something special. Okay, it's my turn to ask you a question. I have to know, out of all places, why Belfast?"

"I think that conversation is just a little too heavy to have over cocoa."

"Oh come on, Piper. I answered your question."

"I really don't want to talk about it."

"Why not?"

"Clarkson, please. You didn't just bring me here to ask questions, did you?"

Why can't he just drop it? I don't want to just open up and tell him why I moved away. I don't even think I can explain to him the entire story, even if I wanted to. I'm a complicated person and I don't want him to scare him off.

"No, I guess not."

"Then drop it."

"Okay, okay, I'm sorry."

"It's alright, let's just skip the questions and get out of here."

"Yeah, let's get out of here."

He leaves a tip on the counter and tells me to follow close behind, so of course I do. Down winding streets framed by colorful buildings and the ocean we walk in silence. Our last encounter was extremely awkward, and I think he blames himself for it. I think I even see him kicking himself but he shouldn't. I don't blame him for being curious, but he needs to understand that I don't want to be pressured into opening up when I'm not ready. I have boundaries and unfortunately I had to set them down pretty early.

"God, it's cold out tonight, huh?" I break the silence.

"Yeah, it really is. It's almost outrageous how fast the seasons seem to be change this year. Do you need my jacket? I don't mind toughing it out, we're almost here anyways."

"Almost where?"

"It wouldn't be an adventure if I told you, now would it?"

I furrow my eyebrows and he throws his jacket over my shoulders without me uttering another word about it. I smile at him and he tugs on my hand, pulling me farther and farther away from

156

town square. When we finally come to a stop, my feet sink into the ground, and right as I try to ask him where we are, he wraps his hands over my eyes.

"Clark, are we almost here?"

"Just a few more steps."

As he speaks I feel his icy cold breath down my spine. I shiver and he notices. He takes his hands off my eyes and adjusts my jacket. I keep my eyes closed and breathe in the ocean breeze that seems to radiate throughout the city.

"Okay, so you told me you want an adventure, so I'm going to give you an adventure. You can open your eyes now."

I open my eyes and right in front of me is a tiny sailboat that looks like it could easily be knocked over by the irritable seas. I laugh and place my book on the sand while he shifts his feet uncomfortably.

"Captain, does this mean I'm a part of your crew now?" I laugh.

"Why yes it does. All aboard?"

"Nice try, but no, don't say that."

"Damnit. I tried really hard to make that work. I guess I'll never be a real sailor," he says as he pretends to pout.

"It's the thought that counts, now come on!"

I take off running to the dock, and without thinking, I jump into the boat and bang my knee. A dark red gel seeps out of my leg and not knowing what to do I sit and let the expletives flow. As Clark lowers himself carefully onto the boat, his eyes widen and he tries to come to my rescue.

"Piper are you okay? Are you sure you don't want me to take you back."

"Hush, we're on an adventure, nothing can stop me, especially not a little blood. It's just you and me Captain, you me and the sea."

"Alright, but at least use my jacket to stop the bleeding."

"Don't be so absurd, I'm fine."

He shrugs and for awhile we just row out to sea. I let the cold air nip my fingers and tangle my hair. As soon as the waves start to slow down I just listen to the oars' ripple in the water.

"So Piper, you seem to be comfortable."

"Are you kidding? It's great out here. I love it."

"Are you sure?"

"Yeah stop worrying."

"Okay good, I just didn't know if you were a beach girl or not."

"I'm not, but I don't know, I'm a girl who enjoys the metaphors in life, and the ocean is one big one."

"What do you mean?"

"Think about it. People romanticize the beach all the time, everything from the tiny grains of sand to the mysteries that lie deep in the ocean blue," I say as I trace my fingers along the top of the water, over and over, barely wetting my pointer finger in the process.

"I mean I guess I see where you're coming from but..."

"Don't over think it. No one truly sees the world in that way. We look back on things in a favorable light even if they don't deserve it."

"Not all people."

"Don't tell me, you're one of those people."

"What, an optimist?"

"No, a dreamer. I mean I enjoy dreams just like the next person but if I'm gonna appreciate life I'm gonna appreciate it while I'm living it, not while I'm withering away in a nursing home somewhere."

"There's nothing wrong with being a dreamer. When you're a dreamer you can see the world in a new light, a better one at that."

"I'm not saying that there's anything wrong with it, hell I like to pretend that this world doesn't exist at all, but I just want to enjoy life while I can."

I spring up in my seat and almost knock us over in the process. Clark pulls me back down and I stumble again, landing in his lap.

"Sorry, sorry I'm a clutz."

"It's okay, what's with the sudden movement?"

"I can't sit still anymore. I want to do something, like rob a bank or egg a house or something. Isn't that what most people do?"

"Maybe if you're a teenager in a book."

"There's nothing wrong with that. Come on Clark, let's live out a book. We can even start with Alice in Wonderland. I'll be Alice and you can be the Mad Hatter. Let's go have an unbirthday party in the woods."

"I don't know if I trust you in the woods, you may try to kill me."

"You're the mad one here, not me. I would never."

"Okay then Alice, is it your unbirthday?"

"Yes it is, is it your unbirthday Mr Hatter?"

"Why yes it is. Shall we go have a party then?"

"Yes, yes we should."

"To the shore!"

160

We both pick up our oars and frivolously paddle towards the beach. It's almost comical to watch Clark paddle. He keeps splashing the water so hard that our boat is starting to slowly sink.

"Captain, our ship is sinking! Screw Alice and Wonderland, we're living out the titanic now. We've found our iceberg and it's your oar!"

"I won't let us die like them. We will not sink with this ship my dear. Man over board!"

He jumps out of the boat and my eyes widen in shock.

"Holy shit it's cold!" he yells.

"What are you doing, you idiot?"

"Being adventurous, like you said."

"I didn't mean for you to give yourself hypothermia."

"It all means the same to me."

I laugh and he starts rocking the boat back and forth. I wobble and eventually, my klutzy tendencies kick in; I fall into the water next to him. At first the water is unbearable, it's frigid and it's enough to rack my bones, but there's something alluring about watching my outfit balloon under me. I feel like a jellyfish or an underwater ballerina.

"This is actually really nice."

"See, I told you that you wouldn't be bored for long."

"Mhm, you were right, but don't get used to that."

"Used to what?"

"Being right."

"Oh god, you sound like my mom now."

"Then your mother must be a fabulous person just like me. Tell me about her?"

"Well she's this frail old woman who has the audacity to believe that her old soul makes her some sort of diva. I swear when that woman isn't lecturing me on the meaning of life, she's running around trying to be a background singer from the sixties."

"She sounds fantastic, but I can't see this wonderfully sassy woman birthing a nerd like you."

"Hey, I am not a nerd."

"You are too. You wear bowties to work and make a point to tell me what the daily word of the day is. If that's not nerdy, I don't know what is."

"I only tell you those because I thought you would like them."

"I do, it's funny to see you geek out over stuff like that. It's like me when I get my hands on a good book."

"Yeah, I've seen you when you're really into a good book. Just the other day, you wouldn't even talk to me, just stuck up your finger and kept reading until you were satisfied with a stopping place."

"Well, that's different!"

"How? How is that different from getting excited over something like a sudoku puzzle?"

"It's very different because when you're interrupting a book nerd whose reading, you're asking them to pause their whole life for you."

"Piper, you're being dramatic again."

"I am doing no such thing."

"Yes you are."

"Clarkson White, I am not lying to you when I say that. I literally just fall into a book and become the main character, and when you ask me to stop reading you're asking me to leave that world and readjust myself to this horrid one."

"You find our world to be horrid?"

"Of course, it's full of lions and tigers and bears."

"I'm not gonna say it."

"You have to say it."

"Oh my," he says deadpanned.

"Ugh, you're no fun. But seriously, the world is full of murderous cheats, and people who are chaotically good and evil, and I don't know. The world is full of bad people."

"Books have those people in them too."

"Yeah but in books everyone gets their due justice in one way or another. All evil people have an inner struggle, something that causes them to be bad something that keeps them down the path they're going on. Good people screw up, they get their karma too. It all balances out in some way or another, in the real world, nothing is guaranteed. Horrible people parade around like they're lawfully good, like they don't have a corrupt bone in their body, but I see through them all and it disgusts me. Like our boss, he can kiss my ass."

"Why don't you talk this much at school?"

"Because I don't talk to people unless I trust them, and I've never trusted someone like this before. God, I'm getting cold, and I'm tired of just wading in the water I'll be on the sand if you need me."

I swim up on the beach and try to gather some warmth out of my soaked jacket but to no avail. I just shiver mercilessly as Clark follows close behind me. He sits down next to me and doesn't say a word as I unbraid my hair and let it fall down my back in untamable waves. I keep trying to change the subject and keep things light but something tells me that this isn't the kind of night.

"You trust me?"

"Yeah, I think I do."

"But you won't tell me anything about your past or even the little things about you?"

"Mhm, that's right."

"Why not?"

"I'm not ready to."

"Will you ever be?"

"Who knows."

"Well, I'll be here for you."

"I know you will be, and Clark..?"

"Yeah?"

"Thank you."

"For what?"

"Tonight, for taking me out and showing me an adventure, for making working at the school tolerable, for giving me a chance when no one else would, and mainly for being my friend. Believe it or not, you're my first friend."

"Your first friend here?"

"No, I mean my first friend anywhere."

"I'm sorry about that."

"Don't be, I don't mind. I'm honestly glad I waited this long, I've found someone who can handle my crazy and doesn't seem to mind it. It's all a girl can ask for."

"Well, I'll try to be the best first friend ever."

"You don't have to try Clark, just do."

I grab my book coated in sand and blow the particles away watching them dance in the dark sky. Once they're all gone I feel my body tremble and shake, the cold is getting to me and in the process a million thoughts flood my mind, causing me to doubt every word I ever said. I don't really know why I'm shutting down but suddenly everything is too much.

"Clark, *Clark*," my throat tightens, "I think it's getting a little late. Can you give me a ride home? Please."

"Of course, is everything alright?"

"Please Clark, just take me home."

He wraps his arms around my shoulders and rushes me off the beach and back into the tiny town. It doesn't even take us fifteen minutes to get to his car but by the time we're driving towards my little shack in the woods, I feel tears slowly rolling down my cheeks uncontrollably.

*He's going to be just like everyone else. He's baiting you in, leading you on to think he's some sort of good guy, and as soon as he think's your wall is down, he's gonna hurt you. He doesn't really care about you. He sees you for who you really are; a weak little girl with mommy issues and a strange ass attachment to your devious brother. But you think I'm wrong, don't you? You think he's going to stay by your side when he learns the truth? I'm you Piper. I'm never wrong. We're never wrong about people. This guy is not your friend, he will never be your friend. We will never have friends. We have each other, we have books, and we have our writing and that's all we need right? You have to get rid of him Piper, for your sake and mine. Have him drop you off and never look back, and think about it this way, you'll always have this beautiful memory of your short lived friendship. Ha, think about it. You'll even look back on it fondly like it was the best thing in the world. Besides, you don't need him to think that you're leading him on. You don't want to be a slut and a satan spawn.*

The negative thoughts are back and I feel so helpless. I was having such a good time and it was just ripped from me. I don't know why it happens, but part of me thinks that it never fully goes away, just waits for the right time to roar.

"Piper?"

"What? Were you saying something?"

"You're doing the thing again."

"Doing what thing?"

"You're spacing out, your eyes are all big and it's like you're just holding your breath. Are you alright?"

"Mhm, I-I'll just be fine. I just have a lot on my mind."

"Oh if you need to talk I'm here."

"I can't. I just can't."

I freeze after that and everything just becomes white noise. Clark tries to start conversations but I don't reply. My vocal chords are ripped out of my throat and my vacant stare puts up a wall. I've shut him out. I was right, there's no hope for our friendship. I just hope he understands that I'm not trying to be intentionally rude; I'm just paralyzed by my thoughts, encaged my by them even though they have a limited amount of logic behind them.

Fifteen minutes pass, or it may be longer, I'm not quite sure, and I realize the car is at a complete stop. Our bodies are both shivering against the cold leather seats though the car's roaring motor gives off the sense of fake warmth. Like yes, I am pumping all the heat I possibly can to the two adults who probably have hypothermia, and no I don't care if it's not warm enough, I'm trying my best.

"Why are we stopped?" I ask.

"I didn't know where to go and every time I tried asking you, you would just turn towards me and give me a vacant look. You looked like you were lost. I don't even know. I swore you were looking through me instead of at me."

"I'm sorry."

"Hey, it's okay. I understand, sometimes we all just retreat off by ourselves where no other person can reach us," he says as he takes my hand and looks at me sympathetically.

"Yeah I guess so."

I pull my hand away and pull my arms towards my chest. I see his face starting to blush and he awkwardly shifts towards his window, trying to give me as much space as physically possible. I have to pull away, I'm not trying to be rude.

"So, where do I go now?"

"Drive into the woods, you're gonna drive straight for a while and once you come to a set of broken umbrellas between two trees you're going to take a right."

"Wait what now?"

"You know how in cartoons they have those umbrellas that get struck by lightning?"

"Yeah...?"

"Well one summer I got bored and went thrifting for some cool decorations and found these two antique umbrellas. I took em home, beat em up a little, took of the cloth off the top, threw on random coats of paint, and bam! I made myself a little land marker."

"Oh... okay. But you live in the woods, should I be afraid for my safety?"

"I like to be by myself if you haven't noticed. I may give the aura of a serial killer, but I swear I'm just a serial loner."

"Do you really like to be by yourself or do you just not have someone you like to spend time with?"

"It's all the same to me."

"Interesting..."

"Hey now, stop analyzing me. You promised, not tonight. When we go back to work you can, but when we're just hanging out you have to relax. You have to let your guard down."

"Why am I the only one who has to let their guard down?"

"Because," I say closing the gap of space between us and getting close to his face, "I only let my guard down when I feel safe, and until you prove to me that you're trustworthy, I won't feel safe."

"But you already said you felt as if you could trust me.. Do I have to prove myself or something?" His voice holds a trace of hurt before he adds, "Why are you so close to me?""

170

"To prove a point. Why, do you find me intimidating? Do I distract you?" I whisper laugh.

"Maybe just a little bit."

I scoot back into my seat and throw my feet up on the dashboard. He pulls off into the woods and I try so desperately hard to ignore my subconscious. I'm fighting myself. I don't want to slip back into my blank state; I want to be the confident girl that although has been quite clumsy, has managed to keep a cool and mysterious air to her.

"You know what Piper, I don't understand you."

"Good. I don't want you to."

"Why not?"

"Because then you'll hate me too."

"Too?"

I sigh, "Another story for another day."

"When will this other day be?"

"When my guard is let down. I told you."

"Okay, okay. Well I'll be waiting for that day to come."

"I know you will. Oh, hey, turn left up here and my house will be in the middle of the clearing."

"Right here?"

"Yep this is me."

Without a second thought, he kills the car's engine and opens the door for me as I clutch his gift tightly. He walks me to the door and throws his jacket over me to stop the excessive shivering even though I'm only a few feet away from the warmth.

"Hey Clark, thank you for everything. I really had fun tonight."

"I did too."

"I'll see you at work?" I say as I open my door.

"I'll see you at work."

I step inside the house and as soon as I walk inside I have an urge to go talk to him again. I rush back out into the bitterness and he looks startled to see me back.

"You're back."

"I'm back."

"Can I help you?" he laughs, as he moves closer to me.

"I feel like I'm forgetting to say something."

"Like what?"

"I don't know. Whatever I'll end up saying will just end up being nerdy at this point."

"I don't mind nerdy. I like a girl who can embrace her inner geek."

He leans in and wraps his arms around me.

"I don't know what happened at the end of the night but I want you to know that whatever it is, you don't have to keep it all in."

"I think I remember now," I mumble, almost breathlessly.

"What is it?"

I'm completely engulfed by his skinny frame and he's surprisingly really strong. I feel protected and warm in his arms, it's really odd. I never imagined friendship being like this. I never imagined getting close to someone so fast and being okay with it, but here I am with Clark and our lives just seem to fit seamlessly into one another's. Maybe I was wrong to think that pushing him away would make things better, maybe I just have to be vulnerable.

"I'm glad that I have you as a friend, and I don't think I'll ever find the words to thank you enough. I just wanted you to know that."

"I do know, don't worry Piper. I'm going to stick around for a long time even after I figure out who you are."

I break away from him and this time I manage to shut the door until I hear the hum of the car disappear. I slump against the door and my lungs become breathless. It's weird, how easy it feels with Clark. I may have chosen an awkward math nerd to be my first friend, but at least I know I can trust him. At least I know that with him my guard can come down. Hell, maybe one day I let him know who the real Piper is, panic attacks, pills, and all.

# THEN:

When you're a child, you have this big picture of what life is supposed to be like. It doesn't matter if you see yourself as a housewife or a corporate lawyer taking over the world; it's the ideal life for you. Then you grow up and see that life never turns out the way you plan it to be, that it's just a domino effect of major disappointment after another.

I feel like love is like this too. Everyone thinks it's such a game, when everyone knows it's more complicated than that. Humans in general try to oversimplify things, life's a game, love's a game, everything's a game, but is it really? I don't have answers to anything, no one does, and in the end we all lose, or we all win, depending on your view of death in itself.

In high school I was obsessed with finding out all the answers to life. I wanted to oversimplify the world for other people because I was tired of the answers people would give me. I wanted to figure out who I was in the world, but it was kind of hard considering my town's population was smaller than a bag of one-hundred calorie popcorn. Everyone knew who I was and it was hard to escape. It took for someone else coming into town for me to to even try to open up for

174

the first time. I wanted a friend, a lover, or even a companion. I wanted someone who wasn't tainted by the truth.

One summer, a middle aged woman and her teenager son, who was just a few months older than I was, moved right down the road from me. He knew nothing about my family, and from what I could tell from my window, he looked normal enough. So one day, I gathered up all my courage and a welcome basket full of cookies, and met my new neighbor.

"Hi! I'm Piper, I live just down the road and wanted to bring you this to welcome you to the neighborhood."

"Oh, Hi. I'm Cam."

"It's nice to meet you. Do you like it here so far?"

"Honestly, it kinda sucks."

"Yeah, I know right. I'm just telling you now, it's all gonna go downhill from here. There's absolutely nothing to do in town except school work."

"That's absolutely disgusting. Hey, I'm gonna go give your cookies to my mom. Wait here for a sec, will ya?"

"Yeah sure."

I waited there, and ended up swinging on a cracked porch swing that demanded to be loved. I kicked my feet higher and higher, ignoring the sounds of the support slowly cracking under me, all the while reaching for the clouds like a child. I was pretending to be a dreamer that day, an optimist. My heart was full of nerves and excitement, if my dad wasn't going to let me start over somewhere else maybe this kid could give me the chance to. We could be troublemakers, the different kids who everyone loathes but slightly admires.

"Having fun there?" he walked out and I jerk the swing to a stop.

"I got bored, what can I say?"

"I don't blame you. Hey, can I ask you something?"

"Yeah, shoot."

"I need something to do here. Anything. I'm bored to tears and my mom is driving me insane. If I have to do one more mother-son bonding thing, I may hang myself."

"I didn't hear a question in that," I smirk.

"Do you know where to have some fun?"

"I mean I did say this town is pretty boring... I guess I could show you around and be your tour guide for a while show you the different variations of cookie cutter houses and prisons that they call schools, but it's going to cost you."

"Cost me? Cost me what?"

"I'll decide that later. Come on, follow me. We'll start our little tour throughout your new pathetic town."

The next few days were spent exploring, and we burned the last few days of summer with each other. It was only three days after I met him when I decided I wanted him to be mine but I wasn't physically or sexually attracted to him. I wanted to know what it felt like to be wanted and to be loved, it was a selfish craving but Cam didn't seem to notice.

It was weird and rushed, our relationship, it was like as soon as we met each other we became an item. There was no official discussion or anything, but it was like we signed our rights away with our tongues during our first kiss. Every free moment was spent with each other doing absolutely nothing. Eventually his flaws slipped through the cracks, and so did mine. It was actually quite a relief to have someone to turn to when I was breaking down. I remember the first time he witnessed one of my panic attacks. I couldn't keep it from him like I used to, my eyes were glazed with tears and my breath was shallow and fast.

He didn't say anything, he just pulled me close to him and waited for me to come to my senses. I just remember looking at him that whole time, while my makeup smeared and my eyes transformed into a raccoon's. He didn't even seem to mind. He was kind and understanding. It was like he understood what was happening to me, but he never asked what triggered me or what caused my unpredictable states. He was my person to cling to.

"Hey, it's okay to break down every now and again. You know that right?" he whispered.

"Is it though?"

"I don't mind being there for you when you're feeling this way. I like it when people are raw to their core. It's like they're not afraid to be vulnerable. I don't know, it's just easier to live when everything is just out in the open."

"It may seem easier, at first, but it just makes stuff so much harder to overcome."

"Why do you say that?"

"If people expect you to be cool about your problems, they'll eventually assume that you have none at all. Then what do you do when you're crippled by the emotional pain?" I asked.

"I'll show you what you do; I'll show you how to forget your problems and be happy. I think it may even help you get over your panic attacks."

He took my hand and led me back to his house, abandoning the desolate park we claimed as our own. When we got to his house, it was eerie and quiet. If I didn't know that his mom was at work, I would have assumed that he lived here on his own. It reeked of him; of leather and wood. He climbed up the stairs and like a tiny puppy, I followed. I didn't know what he expected of me. I had so many questions that were running through my mind.

Living in a house of testosterone, I knew what guys thought about. I knew what they craved, but I didn't want to throw my virginity away to a guy that I didn't even love, no matter how much I tried to convince myself otherwise. I wasn't ready, and as soon as he opened the door to his room I about passed out.

He walked in like it was nothing, and motioned for me to come in too. He grabbed my waist and smiled wide as we ventured in further, but the moment I raised my eyebrows he shrugged it off as if it was nothing to worry about. He let go of me moments later, but his touch seemed to leave a gross impression against my skin.

I watched him carefully reach towards his drawers. His back blocked me from getting a close look, but I saw him clutching a tiny bag. He handed it to me and I dropped it in shock.

"I'm guessing you aren't a smoker."

"My brother was, I never got into it."

"You have a brother?"

"Had."

"Well this stuff doesn't kill you, I promise. You'll be relaxed. You'll feel better."

"I don't know, Cam."

"Come on, you just have to do it once. I'll be right here the entire time and afterwards we can go out or something, get dinner, and wait till the smell goes away. That way your folks will never know."

"Okay, but you're going to have to teach me what to do."

"Of course. Here lemme get something to roll this up in. Sit down, relax. I'm about to blow your mind."

"Alright."

I sat down on the edge of his bed and crossed my legs, trying to keep them from bouncing nervously. I knew what that stuff did to you, the highs and lows, the awful stench afterwards and the vacant eyes. I saw how Charlie acted when he was high like a kite, and I was afraid to do the same, but at the same time I wanted a release. If Cam said it could help me, I wanted to believe him.

"Here, I'm gonna light it for you. Take a deep breath in, inhale the smoke, but don't swallow. When you can't suck in anymore, blow."

I tried to follow his instructions but my lungs rejected the vapor completely. I started coughing like a retired smoker with lungs as dark as charcoal. My face turned up in disgust and Cam broke out in laughter.

"Don't laugh at me!" I wheezed.

"I'm sorry, it's just funny. Here, repeat after me."

"No thanks, I just don't know if smoking is my thing."

"We can work around it. Don't worry, I will get you through this."

He took the joint out my hand and played with his own smoke rings. After a while I felt light headed just by being around him so I excused myself and hid into the bathroom until I regained a clear mind. I couldn't stand feeling that way; light headed and bubbly was not a way I wanted to ever live. Even though my thoughts often caused my emotional and physical paralysis, my brain was and still is one of my best qualities; I'd be nothing without my mind, and I'm not willing to play around with it's chemical makeup for a temporary feeling of euphoria.

"Cam." I knocked on the door but he didn't answer, so I opened the door and covered my face, preparing myself for a blast of smoke, but surprisingly, I was greeted with clean crisp air instead. Cam was no dummy, he was a genius, and a sneaky one at that. His smile led most people to believe that he was innocent; he could have gotten away with murder if he really tried to. In a lot of ways I saw

Charlie in Cam, the bad parts, the parts that I loathed, and even though their motives for acting the way they did were different, they even had the same mentally; fix your problems by creating more. Maybe that's why I was never attracted to Cam, who knows.

"Hey, pretty thing."

"Don't ever say that again."

"Why not? I think it has a nice ring to it."

"Remind me to slap you later."

I plop down on the bed again and he sat down next to me. His dull eyes seemed to have a luster to them, hidden behind a hazy reflection. He reached for my hand and I let him hold it. He felt cold, soulless even.

"I used to have attacks like you."

"You did?"

"Yeah, my mom and dad used to fight pretty bad. Sometimes even I caught the brunt of it. It was too much for me to handle. Then the attacks started, and I swore that made my parents fight even more…"

"How'd you get through it?"

"I told you, I just lay it all out there. I pretend like I have no problems and smoke the real ones away. It keeps me calm. It keeps me from feeling real pain."

I had heard once before that when you're feeling high you're more likely to be open. You aren't afraid to question the world and everything around you because it doesn't feel real. Cam didn't want the world to ever feel real, it was like he built his life on fake dreams and by pretending that his problems floated away with the smoke.

"I'm sorry, Cam."

"Don't be. I don't tell you this stuff for you to pity me, I just want you to know that you're not alone. You'll never be alone as long as you have me, Piper."

"I know, you tell me that all the time."

"I say it because I don't know if you believe me."

"I will eventually, I'm not as trusting as you."

We sat in silence for awhile, holding hands and staring out his window, waiting for his frenzy to alleviate. When he came down from his high, I saw Cam in a new light. He wasn't the kid who didn't care about anything, he was a shattered soul, put together only with duct tape and false appearances. Everyone in this world is broken in one way or another, we all just have different ways of hiding it. For Cam, it was by getting high and for me it was writing and reading.

"Cam, can I ask you something?"

"What?"

"Why did you move here?"

"My mom finally stood up for herself. It was a real ugly conversation, if you even want to call it that. My dad basically told us that we were his property and that we couldn't leave him. He kept going on and on about how we were going to be broke without him, but he didn't even realize that my mom was working behind his back, saving up money for us to escape. He thought it was a game, that we were kidding with him. It was so bad when he realized that we were on our way out the door. He- he hurt her," his voice cracked and a tiny tear slipped down his face. I resisted the urge to wipe it away and he continued, "I don't really remember what happened after that. I just got so angry Piper, so angry that I became his doppelganger. All I remember was the world turning into an inferno before everything went dark. I don't even know how long I was soulless, but by the time I came back to my senses, I was driving on the road with all of my stuff and my mom was knocked out in the passenger seat next to me. If I didn't know better, I would have thought that I just left him standing there while he tried to egg me on. If I didn't know any better, I would have thought that I left the situation being the man my father never could, but at the end of the day, I turned into him. I fight when I'm angry. I stand up for what I love, so I beat the living shit out of him and drove here, I don't need to remember what happened to know that. I still have a bruised knuckle from hitting him so hard, but you

184

know what, he deserved it. That son of a bitch deserved every last punch."

"I don't know what to say," I bit my lip, and my body tensed as his shifted closer to me.

"Don't. I don't expect you to say anything anyways. You're probably halfway out the door in your mind, and I truly don't want to hear another goodbye."

"I'm not going anywhere. I'm staying right here. You need me and I need you. We've both been through shit Cam, and I'm not willing to let go the only person who even comes close to understanding me. And I know what you're thinking, and I know you're kicking yourself right now, but just because you have shitty family members, doesn't mean you're a shitty person too."

"Maybe, but it does increase my chances of inheriting the asshole gene."

"I don't think you have to worry. I'm pretty sure that genes skips a generation," I said as I cracked a small smile, trying to cut the tension that permeated more than the joint's fumes.

"...Hey, Piper?"

"Yeah?"

"Are you ever going to tell me your story?"

"I will one day, but I don't want you to worry about fixing me. It's my job to help you get better instead. One day at a time."

After that day, we made that trite little saying our mantra. One day at a time. Every time Cam's tough facade cracked and weakness seeped through, I would clutch his hand as the words would fly out of my mouth like a melodic tune stuck on repeat.  One day at a time. Whenever anxiety flared in my heart, he would utter those damn words as he stroked my hair, clutching onto my body like the stories said he should. One day at a time. It was our solution for everything. We shoved our issues under a figurative rug in the hopes that our futures would be better than our shitty past. The more time we spent together, the worse our fate seemed to be. We were toxic. Our relationship, or lack of one, was based solely off the promise that we would help each other get better, but you can not "fix" a person, and you certainly aren't supposed to make promises you can't accomplish.

As the first day of school approached faster and faster, our worries mounted like Everest. Cam started relying more and more on getting high, and even though our change of scenery constantly changed, our situation remained the same. Every time he would light up, I would have to excuse myself for a while so that I could get over the lightheaded feeling that I hated so much. I don't know what he did when I was gone, but every time I would come back he would be worse off. Sometimes I would smell a trace of booze afterwards, and sometimes he would be so vacant that I began to second guess myself. Was he really just doing pot? I don't know.

Fall came in with a whirlwind and soon enough our "romance" was disguised. He learned of my unpopularity by the kids who couldn't care less about my existence, by the kids who still believed that deep down I was a murderer too and so our distance grew. He on the other hand, was swept into the ranks of the social gods. Like I said before, almost no one moved there, so any new kids were introduced to popularity before the geeks and pee-ons had a chance to taint the god's meat. After that, he kept this appearance in school, but was still faithful at home leaving me confused when he would make sure that he was there whenever I needed it. I think I liked him best when he was far away, he was happier when he wasn't around me. I know that's because it was a charade, but after you pretend to be something for a while, you actually become it. He became happy, not because he truly was, but because he had to be. With me, he didn't have to worry about hiding his problems, he could be his destructive and depressed self.

But with Cam's popularity came the same perils that plagued Charlie years before. The question of what was more important;

mental and physical stability or a life of fun and games. Of course he chose the later, and with that he flirted with more and more with drugs. It seems to be such a cliche game, the idea that drugs and popularity went hand in hand. If I hadn't seen it multiple times with my own eyes I would have passed it off as a just another myth, hell, part of me still wants to deny the truth but you can't be blinded by ignorance when you've seen the downfall of society so many time.

"Piper, you have to come out with me tonight. This is going to be the biggest party of the year. I wouldn't be surprised if the cops shut it down within an hour."

"You know I don't party, Cam."

"I know, but you should. Partying makes everything better."

"Maybe for you, but I don't know if I believe that."

"I'll prove it to you, just come."

"Okay, okay. I'll go if it makes you happy."

"Perfect, I'll be by your side the entire time. Screw what everyone else thinks. It'll just be you and me."

That night came and went like a summer storm. I remember walking into a house of some kid that I barely knew, wearing a skimpy dress, clinging desperately to Cam's side. All eyes were on us, and I could feel the tension building. Cam didn't seem to notice though, or pretended not to, his main goal was to mingle and let loose.

"Hey, lighten up. People will stop caring once they see that you are one of them."

"But I'm not one of them, I'll never be one of them, Cam."

"Maybe not, but once you have a little alcohol in your system, you'll become a booze brother."

"Booze brother?"

"Ya know, like blood brothers... Whatever, come on. Let's get you a drink to loosen your corset. You look like a walking corpse right now."

"Thanks?"

I took a wine cooler from an unstable and giddy girl and tried to hold down my meal. It was disgusting. I didn't feel better, I wasn't enjoying my time. I didn't and still don't understand the hype. As the music created a deafening heartbeat, Cam chugged on a plethora of cheap beers and got increasingly handsy. I tried to swat him away but he seemed to be hypnotized by the pulse of the room. Everyone swayed drunkenly to the beat while obnoxious chatter and out of tune singing permeated with a layer smoke. It was a pit of all the deadly sins, especially lust and pride. If you weren't hooking up with the closest person to your right, you were a prude. If you weren't drinking your soul away and boasting about every college raves you wormed your way into, you weren't living.

I was horribly out of place, and so I took my place as a wallflower. I observed everyone as I sipped slowly on watered down wine. Goths mingled with preps, laughing over what little they had in common. Jock-type guys flirted with danger and tried to pull outrageous stunts to keep up the party groove. Even hardcore introverts made an appearance, the middle men of the social hierarchy, the people who only got invited to parties because they had access to the greatest party commodity; narcotics, pills, poison, depressants, weed, hash, dope, molly, Lsd, whatever you want to call it, or whatever type you craved, they had it. They had drugs decorated and served in so many ways. You had your choice of baked goods, hard candy, and straight up baggies. It was a buffet and a game of Russian Roulette.

Eventually I lost sight of Cam, who was drawn into the temptations of the night, and so I found myself wandering around the room. Some people said hi to me as I made my way through the thicket of people, but most cleared a path because I was a plague to them. Get too close to me and you'll catch a flaming desire to worship satan, isn't that what they told me at bible study? No? Close enough. It's kinda of ironic that they're all so afraid when they are the ones rolling in sin.

I spent hours looking for Cam. It was as if every time I thought I found his chiseled physique, I was greeted by an ignorant douche who wanted to cop a feel. I was so annoyed and enraged by my fate that I planned on slapping Cam as soon as I saw him. I don't know why I was truly mad but I wanted to take it all out on him. I wanted to hate him because I was so far outside of my comfort zone. When I found him he was slumped against the wall; his eyes were half open, his words were slurred, and his limbs seemed to be sprawled between several other people who were damn near dead. I helped him up the best as I could, and after several attempts of us falling and him breaking out into uncontrollable laughter, I tried to make our way back home. I knew his mom couldn't see him like this and I knew there was a large chance that my Dad would be so out of it himself that he wouldn't even notice, so my house seemed to be our only option.

It was in the middle of the night by the time we made it back, and within an hour or two, I knew the sun was planning on making a lovely appearance. I cracked open my window in the one story ranch house, and forced Cam to climb in. He landed in a thud, and before he could make another sound, I crawled in and covered his mouth, shushing him until I was sure that we didn't wake any of the others. After that, I let both of us curl up in my tiny bed with a pile of pillows separating the two of us. I didn't want him to think that I let him go all the way, especially after the state he was in. I knew he wouldn't even be capable of remembering anything that I did for him or anything that happened at the party, so I wasn't going to let him create his own fantasy. I didn't want my name to further be tarnished.

In the morning, I woke up to my father banging on the door. My head was killing me, my trashy makeup was smeared, and my hair made it look like I survived the electric chair. I pulled myself out of bed and tried to hide the horrible reminders of the night before so that my dad would have no idea what I had done.

"Piper, open up! We need to talk now!"

My father's demanding tone caused chills down my spine. I was screwed. Just by listening to his voice, I knew he was pissed. Maybe he had another failed date, maybe he was suffering a killer hangover that would laugh at mine. Whatever did it, I knew it wouldn't end well for me.

"I-I uh I'm not ready."

"I don't care, open up!"

"I can't!" I screamed.

"Stop yelling!"

"You stop yelling!"

"Not until you open the door!"

"I told you I can't!"

"Why the hell can you, Piper?"

"Because I'm naked?"

"You're naked?"

"Yes, I'm naked. Come back later…"

"You're not naked."

"I am too. What do you want, proof of my nakedness?"

"Nope."

"Exactly, so leave me alone."

"I'm not going to leave you alone and you aren't leaving that room until we have a conversation. I'll be back in five minutes."

He did come back in five minutes, hell he probably even came in faster than that, and the second time he didn't bother to knock. He flung open the door and stopped in his tracks when he saw me, and his nostrils seemed to flare when he saw Cam.

"Piper Addison! What the hell?"

"Dad, it's not what you think."

"What do I think? How are you going to explain this to me?"

"I went to a party and my friend Cam was too unstable to go home."

"Friend? You don't have friends."

"I have Cam."

"The boy in your bed."

"That is correct."

"Piper, I don't understand you. I'm trying my hardest to make things work here, and you keep pushing my buttons slowly but surely...I just don't know what to do with you."

"Dad stop, I'm not a bad kid."

"Then stop acting like one. How the hell is this kid sleeping through this? Get him up and get him out of the house, now."

"He can't go home Dad. Not like this."

"Why not? What else were you two doing last night? Have you lost all your innocence?"

"Dad stop!"

"You're turning into Charlie, Piper. You're following down this dangerous path and you're going to ruin your life just like he ruined his."

"I'm not Charlie."

"Yes, but you always were his shadow, I mean, just look at who you brought home. A party animal who's too knocked out of it to even care that we're fighting over him. You know what, I'll be right back. I know just the way to wake your sweet friend up."

He marched out the room and returned seconds later with a bucket of cold water. He poured it over Cam's head and he jumped up before clinging to my side.

"Morning Cam, meet my dad..." I said sympathetically.

"You can call me Mr. Addison," he said gruffly.

"He-hello Mr. Addison," he managed to talk between shutters.

"So you spent the night here I presume?"

"Yes sir, your daughter took me home so that I could be in a better mindstate before I went home. I didn't want my mom to see me like this, she's worried enough already."

"So you just agreed because you wanted to make your mom proud of you? Would she be proud of you after you ruined my daughter?"

"Dad, nothing happened!" I interjected.

"Shut up Piper, I am not talking to you."

"I'm not going to shut up. I'm not some slut and it's disgusting that you think I am just because I tried to do something good. I wasn't going to let him try to drive home and I sure as hell wasn't going to bring him to his mom in the condition he was in. I was being a good friend, that's all. Stop trying to make things worse than they are!"

"I wouldn't have to assume things if you would tell me what was going on! Maybe if you let me into your life instead of hiding things from me we wouldn't be in this place."

"I don't want you in my life! I don't want a drunken bitter asshole continuously holding me back. I can't wait till I'm finally old enough to get away from you!" I never thought that I would utter such scathing words. I loved my Dad, but I didn't love who he had become. I couldn't take it anymore and because of it I let too much slip.

"Who are you kidding? You'll never be able to get away from me. I'm family, and the only family you have. You're stuck with me, and if I have anything to say about it, you'll be here forever. Living in this hell hole where you deserve to rot!"

I took in a deep breath while i tried to stop myself from fighting my dad. Both of us were mentally exhausted and wore it on our faces. Neither of us were happy people and that was the moment we both let our facades fall in front of each other. Poor Cam shifted awkwardly back and forth on his toes, trying to find a valid excuse so that he could be excused and escape from the miserable conversation. There was no good way out. All of us were casualties.

"Excuse me, Mr. Addison, I think I should go. My mom will be worried about me..." Cam tried to use his mother as a valid excuse to escape, but it just gave my Dad ammunition to kill our tie forever.

196

"Oh I completely understand. Let's go, I'll give you a ride home."

"It's okay, I just live down the road. It's not like it's out of my way to walk home."

"Don't be absurd. I insist on taking you home. Come on Piper, you too. You probably want to have the chance to say goodbye to your little boyfriend."

"Wait what?" I said.

"Did I stutter? This will be the last time you ever see Cam again. You clearly aren't capable of having normal relationships. Hell, you make your first friend and I have to meet him like this? Hungover and in your bed. You sure do pick em, Piper."

"Stop. Dad. Please."

"You're a mess. At least I'm trying to help myself. You've been wallowing in hatred for years now, but you have to grow up, Piper."

"I'm not wallowing in hatred, I'm done with grieving but it's not like I can just wake up and forget all the pain I went through."

"Yes you can. It's not that hard."

"Says the serial drunk."

"My actions and life choices aren't the ones on trial here."

"Fine, it was just an observation," I said.

"Piper, does he even know about you? Does Cam even know who he was spending time with? Does he understand what this is all about?" he said as if Cam was incapable of speaking for himself.

"He knows enough."

"What's enough, Piper. Tell me."

"He knows about the attacks, and he knows that they died."

"Does he know why?" he questioned further.

"He doesn't need to."

"So you're also living a lie too. Great. I raise such great kids. I'm the world's best father. First I raise a fricking demon who murdered half the damn town and took the woman of my dreams away, and now I'm raising you. You know what? Just get in the car and don't even say one word. I'll be there when I can look at you guys without feeling completely and utterly disappointed. Go. Get out my face."

I grasped Cam's hand and took him out to my dad's beat up Camry. We sat in silence for awhile, my head rested on his shoulder, and Cam tried to shut his eyes and pretend that what was going on was all a dream. Our hands stayed intertwined the entire time; we knew that when we let go it would all be over. Cam didn't want us to be over.

"What was your dad talking about in there?" he whispered.

"It's nothing to worry about, just a lot of unresolved issues."

"Piper, you can talk to me, you know."

"I know that, but there's nothing to talk about."

"Stop doing that."

"Doing what?" I asked.

"Pretending that your problems are worthless. It's okay to not be okay. You're struggles are just as important as anyone else's. You don't have to compare your problems to mine."

"I don't compare our problems, Cam."

"Then why won't you talk to me about them?"

"Because I promised you, I'd help you. My focus is on you. It helps me just move on and bury myself into something that's, I don't know, more productive. I can't fix myself but I can help you. That's what's important."

"It doesn't have to be just about me though, Piper. We both know that this is the end. If you really want to help me, you have to let me help you. You have to trust me."

"I can't."

"Piper I don't understand, I told you everything. Why can't you just open up to me just once. I'm not going to judge you."

"I'm trying to open up it's just not easy."

"Nothing in this damn world is easy."

He propped himself up causing my head to roll off his shoulder. I sat up straight and stared dead into his desperate orbs. He didn't want to help me. He just wanted to know that he wasn't the only screwed up person in the world. He wanted to know that he wasn't alone, but he was. He was going through a completely different journey than I was, and I didn't want him to know how broken I truly was. I just couldn't leave him on a sad note. He loved me, and though I didn't love him, I couldn't get myself to ruin his memories of me. I was his manic pixie dream girl. I was his mystery. I was his rock.

"I know," I whispered.

As the words faded off my tongue, my father came in and whisked us both down the street. Cam couldn't even look at me when my father told his mother about his destructive ways. He was broken. I shattered him, just like I was supposed to. I watched his mother turn whiter than a ghost and whisk Cam away. After she slammed the door I never saw Cam again. He fell of the face of the earth. It was as if I was a tornado. I destroyed everything in my path then left the responsibility for cleaning up to everyone else.

After Cam left, I stopped trying to be a better person. I fell back into routine. I fell back into my old ways of hating everything and everyone. I was a hopeless person, and I was someone that I still

200

hate when I look back on life. No one could have loved the girl I became after he left. Hell, my Father even detested me more after the situation occurred. I was my Father's prisoner, and at the same time, I was air to him, vital but invisible.

Months passed and the seasons changed and with the change went my summer lust affair. Snow settled in the landscape and cuddled the foliage into a warm hug. It was then when I heard from him. His mother had sent him away to a rehab facility and though I only received a cryptic letter from him, I could imagine his smile. I saw my mental image of him transform. I dreamed of him no longer being an angry soul. I dreamed of him trying to figure his life out instead of masking his problems behind a puff of smoke. I dreamed of his eyes holding no more pain and his laugh being pure.

I cried when I read his letter, and at first I found myself looking back on our relationship fondly. I started thinking that maybe I did love him but was too afraid to admit it. I thought that I actually was attached, but then I realized my tears weren't because of him. I was crying because Cam got a chance to be a new person, one who wasn't crippled by his psychological damage, and Charlie never would.

# NOW:

Sometimes I dread waking up in the morning. I sike myself out about the horrors of the day before they even begin. I'm dreading going to work and dealing with the angelic brats that will grace my presence, I'm dreading facing the coworkers that have preconceived notions of me being nothing more than a freak, and yet, there is nothing that I'm dreading more than explaining myself to Clark. I screwed up last night. I shut down and ruined a perfectly good night. I saw the look on his face, the hurt behind his eyes. No matter how much he assured me he'd stick around, and that he was perfectly okay with leaving me to be, I saw his discomfort. He felt on edge. He didn't know how to handle my vacantness and that terrified him.

I drag myself to work eventually, taking my new book with me. I don't even bother avoiding Mr. Wolff or sliding in a greeting to Cathy. nothing they say can make the day worse than I've predicted it to be; my pessimism is showing and I have no intention of trying to play it off.

"Ms. Addison, I'd like to have a word with you, if you please."

"Yes, Mr. Wolff, right away."

I follow the villain into his lair of testosterone and sit where I did once before, but this time anxiety isn't fluttering in my gut. I have nothing to worry about. I've been doing my job damn well considering the lack of resources I've been given.

"Okay, so as you know I like to get to the point and I have every intention of getting you back to your duties as quickly as possible, but some things have been brought to my attention and I feel as if they needed immediate attention brought to them."

"I understand completely. What can I clarify or help you with? I'm willing to help in any way I can sir. You said you wanted a warrior, and so here I am."

I clutch my book as I talk. I see him glancing at me up and down, rolling his eyes every time he comes to looking at my pink hair. If I get fired or even chastised for who I am, I don't know what I'll do. I'm doing the best that I can to be professional. I'm doing the best I can to win a losing battle and I feel as if that will never be good enough for anyone.

"Well, first of all, I have been contact by several teachers about your little prodigy, and frankly I'm concerned. This little girl even has the audacity to request that she finish her studies under your supervision. I don't know what this is about, but I had to know what you were thinking? She's an impressionable young lady and she doesn't need to be isolating herself, she needs to interact with children her own age. I can't possibly grant her request."

"Mr. Wolff, do I have permission to be blunt with you?"

"I wouldn't expect anything less Ms. Addison."

"Emma Mackenzie has chosen to be in my care not because she doesn't want to have interactions with her peers, but because the same people you want her to surround herself with have isolated her. They have tortured that poor girl, and I've seen their bullying with my own eyes. I couldn't let her go on like that. I see myself in her sir, so I did what I thought was best. I offered her a haven, and since then she's flourished. Her grades have gone up, her attitude has changed, and she doesn't seem to be dead in the eyes. I told her that I'd help her do whatever she needs to do to be happy. I promised her that sir, but I also made sure she knew that without your permission and clearance from her teachers she'd still being balancing between worlds. Do you know how terrible that is? It's absolutely heartbreaking to watch someone lose their passion for learning and I couldn't just stand by and do nothing."

I begin to ramble on and his face hardens. He clearly doesn't understand where I'm coming from. I've watched Emma secretly, not letting her know that I was on to her little game. She's been pretending that she's invisible to me, burying her head in a book so that I couldn't possibly see her relief. She doesn't want her privilege taken away, and she doesn't want to seem overly grateful.

"Are you trying to make excuses for her? I don't care if she's making leaps and bounds, she's gone behind my back and so have you. You think that just because you're new you can revamp this place and make your program relevant, but you can't. I have established a successful program here that can survive without you. Reading isn't pertinent in today's society and quite frankly one girl's social life isn't pertinent either."

"Her name is Emma sir, and I hope you realize that reading never loses its importance. It's essential and it helps so many people. Books let people know that they're not alone, that they are understood, and books spark conversation and explorations of unknown concepts and worlds. Without books, human society is useless, we'd all be nothing more than glorified neanderthals. Books make people better if you believe it or not."

"Books can't make people better, it just gives them a false hope, and that is pathetic. Reading won't make a person successful, but communication skills will, persuasion techniques will, and power will."

"There's more to life than success, sir. Power isn't everything. If you just take some time out of your day and see how she acts with them and then with me you'd see the difference. You'd make a positive impact on her life, and who knows what that'll lead to one day?"

He laughs at me before sliding to the edge of his desk. He's so close to me that I feel his dragon breath against my face. He's trying to intimidate me, and though I know I shouldn't fear the man, I do. It's something bothersome about him. He craves power and will destroy anyone in his path. He must be emotionally corrupt or ignorant to the world around him because he sees no compassion. He doesn't know what it's like to feel anything, I pity him and envy him for this same reason. I feel too much, he feels nothing at all.

"Power is everything in this world, and if you don't have power, you're a slave to the system. I have power and I have every intention of enforcing it, so I'm not going to let you or whatsherface trample over my establishment. She will go through the curriculum like it was intended and that's final."

"Allowing this exception will not diminish what you've created here!"

"Maybe not, but if I allow one rebellious child to break the system, who's to say that others won't follow suit? I have to stick to what I know is best and let God guide me to running this school. At this point in time, I am confident in my decision, and that's the end of this discussion. Do I make myself clear?"

"Crystal," I mutter and try to leave the room as fast as humanly possible so my face doesn't fall.

"I'm not done just yet Ms Addison, we have other matters to discuss, so sit back down. We have a lot of ground to cover and not much time."

"Fine, but first I need you to answer something for me. That is, of course, if you don't mind. I wouldn't want to be a bother."

"Make it fast."

"Who is going to tell Emma that she can't study in the library anymore?"

"Why you of course."

I shake my head, but he pays me no mind. He's the alpha dog, and I despise him for it. I can't take this away from Emma. I don't want to watch her reaction as I send her back to her bullies. I see so much of myself in her and I don't know why. I just can't cause that little girl pain.

The entire conversation from there on is one sided. My replies are short, his are lengthy and condescending. Apparently, my impressive disappearances during weekly mass are starting to leave a sour taste in the priest's mind, and my unwillingness to participate in faculty events goes against everything the school stands for. I don't think Mr. Wolff understands that I isolate myself to preserve my integrity. I'm aware that I am not the perfect faculty member,but I rather not participate in events that would leave people more inclined to hate me. If only I knew how to present myself better maybe then I wouldn't be sitting around like an idiot agreeing to everything he wants.

"Okay sir, I will try to better represent the school. I'm sorry for not living up to your standards."

"It's okay for now. Since you're new I will cut you some slack soldier, but remember you work for me and you will always answer to me. If I say something's wrong, you fix it. If I want you to do something you do it. I'm tired of our debates. I don't want you to question my motives, just accept that they're true. I'm trying to train you."

"You're trying to train me?"

"See there we go again with the questions! By the time this school year is over, you'll see that everything I've done is in the school's best interest."

"I hope so because at the moment I believe that you're trying accommodate things that are in your best interest."

"Sweetie," he chimes and his voice rising several octaves, "What's in the school's best interest is what's in my best interest."

"I hope you're right about all of this. I better get down to the library, I have an early morning class today. I have the second graders today."

"Then go, you don't have to read off your schedule to me."

"Yes sir."

I run off without looking back once at the wicked man. I know he has a wide grin spread across his face. He thrives on chauvinism. He thrives on degrading others to secure his sense of superiority. He makes me so angry. How is it still okay for a woman to be viewed as less than a man? We're both doing good work, we're both trying to shape future generations. How is it still okay for people like him to even exist? He seems to have nothing redeemable about him and I hate it.

I huff when I get into the library. I feel like I've been broken down and destroyed. Everything about the situation makes me feel wrong. I'm so angry. I need to write or read or do something, anything to get over myself, but I know anything I'll do will be destructive, so I pace around. I pace around the room and every now and then I stop and reorganize a book that seems out of place. Everything seems out of place. I pick up another out of place book and it falls apart with my touch. I pick up the remains and chuck them, letting out a silent scream in the process.

"Ms Piper? Am I-um-am I interrupting something? I can come back later?"

I turn around and I feel my heart beat out of my chest. Standing at the doorway lies miss double name, and she looks absolutely terrified. I open my mouth but no words come out, so she comes in the room and makes the smallest gesture, she takes my hand.

"What happened to you?" she murmurs.

I slump down on the floor and she pulls up a chair besides me, being careful of the tattered pages scattered around the room. She doesn't say anything at first but as my breath slows, she decides to open up to me.

"You know, I wanted to thank you for everything you've done. I know we really don't talk much when I'm in here, but you've helped me. I actually don't mind going to school anymore. It's like a weight has been lifted off my chest."

Her eyes twinkle as she talks, though her voice is soft and passive. She acts as if she's afraid of everyone and everything, but I know that's not who she really is. I can see the fire in her, and one day when she learns to open up to the world, everyone will appreciate her for who she truly is. I hope so anyways.

"Don't thank me."

"I have to. No one else in this place even cares about me except you and Mr. White."

"I'm sure that's not true."

"It is. No one in this world even cares if I'm alive or not."

"Oh sweetie," I feel my throat clench as I hold back tears.

"I'm sorry, I've said too much."

This time, I grab her hand but she quickly pulls away. Bracelets line her arms, and her excessive layers of clothes fall off her tiny frame. I've never noticed how much she needs someone. I never noticed that she felt so alone. I understand now why she's always reading, or trying to avoid comments from her devilish peers.

"No, it's okay. You can talk to me. Whenever you need me. I'm here for you. I know I'm not supposed to say stuff like this at school, but I want you to see me as your friend."

"Really?"

"Yes. I know how you feel, but you're never alone as long as you have a good book. Ya know? I swear if I didn't have books to read when I was your age, I would have gone insane. I probably wouldn't be alive either. I owe everything to reading and writing, that probably doesn't even make sense but..."

"So you're like me too?"

I shake my head and pat her arm. I have to break her heart soon, but I don't know if I should wait and make her feel better, or pile it on all at once.

"How do you get better? How do you convince yourself that you're worth the universe's time? I just feel like a waste of space."

"When I figure out the answer, I'll make sure you're the first person I tell."

"You're still fighting it?"

"Fighting what?"

"Don't make me say it. If I say it, I have to admit to the world that there's something wrong with me. I don't want them to be right. I can't have everyone be right about me."

"Okay then don't say it. You don't have to. But now I'm fighting a different battle, one that's different than the one I was fighting when I was your age. That's the thing about growing up, it never gets easier, but you do become more prepared to fight the next battle. Now's not the time to give up, you're a warrior, Emma. You just have to believe in yourself."

"I guess so."

She shifts uncomfortably in her seat, pulling her legs towards her chest and burying her head into her knees.

"So I talked to Mr. Wolff today about our proposal…" I say.

"What did he say? Can I stay with you?"

"Unfortunately, he shot us down. I tried everything and I fought so hard. I've noticed how happier you are when you're in here, so I thought if I reasoned with him he would understand, but he just didn't."

"What do you mean?"

She bites on her lip then starts biting her thumb. In the moment, she ages backwards. I'm not looking at a six-grader, I'm looking at a innocent girl flirting with adolescents.

"Some people in this world will do whatever it takes to get power and keep it. Mr. Wolff is one of those people, so he asserted his dominance. He made sure that I knew that he was in charge. He wants to destroy us and our free thinking, but he can't. I think that's why he said no. No matter what he does to us, he can't take away our passion for reading, or our desire to stay by ourselves. That's what makes him mad."

"I hate him What did I do to deserve this? I've done nothing but be a good student. I've even been a good catholic. I've done everything he's ever wanted me to do."

"Sometimes you don't have to do anything. Life sucks and it's unfair. I just don't want you to think that I'm throwing you out. I'd love to have you here during the day. You keep me sane."

"I would never think that. Are you sure there's nothing we can do?"

"We can keep fighting, but I don't know what good it would do," I say bitterly.

"I can't just go back. They hate me, Ms. Piper."

"We'll come up with something. Until then, you can spend your lunch in here, or study hall. Every free time you get, you just walk down here and he won't be able to stop you. That way you have some sort of escape. That way you won't go mad."

She looks down at my new book, sitting not to far away from us, and gives me a frail smile before saying, "We're all mad here."

"Indeed we are. Indeed we are."

"I better go back to class then. Thank you for everything Ms. Piper. I'll see you around, I guess."

"Things will work out exactly how they are supposed to. You and I just need to have a bit more faith."

She wraps her arms around me in pulls me into a hug. I melt down and fall to my knees so that we're equal in height and hug her with all my might. She's a warrior, and I want to aid her in her fight. I

214

want to save that poor girl, but I don't think that I can. Some things are just impossible to save, like the tattered book on the ground, her broken heart, and mine.

# THEN:

Being broken doesn't excuse someone for being horrid. Most terrible things are committed by the people with the saddest hearts, but their anguish, their cries for help go unnoticed because they never learned how to handle themselves. They never learned how to express their pain and move on. I too, played a stereotypical role when it came to the archetype of being broken. I flirted with danger and I did everything I could to prove to myself that I was better than the labels bestowed upon me. I hated that word and the idea of being broken, but I couldn't convince myself that I wasn't, so I drove myself insane.

It was right after the church condemned me when I gave into the world. I let myself rot, and toyed with death. I could have ended my life, and so many times I tried to. It was as if waking up each morning was it's own personal hell. It even became a routine, every awful thing would occur in a cycle, each time ending and beginning with my acidic tears. Every morning, I would wake up from nightmares covered in sweat, go to school, find a demonic symbol or another unclever relic by my locker. Then I would eat alone at lunch while trying to ignore the stares and whispers. After school I would block out my father's cries and my uncle's ignorant demands while trying to do schoolwork, but within time I would give in to my own sadness, flop down on the bed and cry until I felt numb.

I was so unhappy. I was so weak. I couldn't see a way out. I wanted to wake up one morning to find out that the months prior were all just a lengthy nightmare so that things would be okay again. It was half way through the semester when my school picked up on my habits and tried to do something. They noticed that I stopped eating, they noticed that I started to wither away and the bags under my eyes were piling up along side schoolwork that went untouched and incomplete. My school demanded that my health was evaluated. They demanded that my mental state was assessed. They didn't care about my well being though, they just wanted to make sure that I never had an episode like my brother.

The tests came back on my state and they all stated the blatantly obvious; I was depressed and was experiencing anxiety from post traumatic stress. The team of psychiatrists suggested rounds of extensive therapy and they even threw the idea of me going to a rehab into a mix. Both ideas were rejected furiously, and though my father and I debated profusely over the proper way to handle the situation, I decided to go on a medicated route. Pills in the morning to calm my nerves, pills in the evening to curb my suicidal tendencies, and a mixture of experimental drugs that did who knows what. For a while I took them and faked being better, but every night I would clutch the pills in my hands, trying to decide whether or not that was the day to end my life.

It was when I would debate ending it all that I found myself unable to say goodbye. Even when pills flowed in my bloodstream, I couldn't get myself to write a letter. I didn't know how to explain how I felt, and I knew that whatever words I could manage to scrawl would just hurt my Dad more. My inability to do anything left me feeling increasingly numb. Though I felt like dying, I had to feign okay. I had to cover up the look of death and put on a mask. People knew that I wasn't okay but they didn't know the severity of it all. They thought that my simple rebellions were all I needed to grow up whole. They didn't know how bad off I really was. I wouldn't let anyone know.

I kept up my charade for months and months, never once being suspected for having suicidal thoughts. I found it amusing that I was able to fool the world. I became so good at fooling everyone that I began to convince myself. I convinced myself into believing that the social isolation was the best option for me. I fooled myself into believing that living a decent life was possibly by relying on conversations between fictional characters as a form of social interaction. I bought into a fake world to hide how reality made me

218

feel. It was pathetic and sickening, the person I became, though parts of her still remain. I'm just as introverted and cynical as I was back then, and I still rely on charades to mask my true emotions.

Only once was I caught. Only once did anyone manage to discover the raw girl that drained her wrists and medicated herself until she was numb, and it was by accident. One night, my father was whisked away to a local bar where he was a frequent visitor. It was there where he preyed off desperate widows and bored housewives with my uncle, and since I knew I was going to be alone for the night, I took another chance to claim my own fate. Since I have always been terrible at saying goodbye, I decided to lay out one of my short stories about a tortured girl who was confined in a prison that she referred to as her mind. I hoped people would understand my choice for selecting that piece, then again, I wasn't sure if anyone would care about my cautious choice at all or even notice the connections to my real life. I then made my way to the bathroom and played bartender. I created concoctions of pills to numb any and all pain before surgically opening myself up. After that I just remember the eerie calm that overcame me. It was like I enjoyed dying. I was a serial killer fascinated with the way death washed over people, but the only victim I murdered was myself. I just remember watching the stream of red rush out of me as my pulse slowed, the color drained out of my body, and as my vision began to blur. I even remember cherishing every last breath as my world became a spectrum of gray.

I would have died that night, and discovered what's truly beyond life, but my drunken father returned home too early. He stumbled into me, quite literally, and it was after he purged himself of the toxins that withered his liver when he realized that his little girl had decided to play grim reaper. I don't remember much after except piercing wails that filled my ears. It was like I was fighting death after I had accepted its conditions. Doctors brought me back to a shaky reality and patched me up like a quilt. This time the professionals shoved rehab down my throat saying it was the only way to get better. They didn't understand that I thought it was impossible to get better in my condition. No matter what I did, or what medical miracle that they performed, part of me would always be erratic. My father understood what the doctors couldn't comprehend, but only because he was experiencing the same thing that I was. He never sent me away, no matter how many times he threatened to, yet afterwards, he tried as hard as humanly possible to form a new bond with me. It worked, because of him I stopped trying to play God, but I never escaped the thoughts that hid in the crevices of my skull.

# NOW:

I am not quite sure if I should be classified as an adult. My childish behaviors and outbursts are not only frightening but annoying. If anyone were to find out about them, I'd be fired and I wouldn't get a chance to plead my case. Part of me secretly wants to believe that other adults act in the same way they just know how to clean up their messes better than I do. I can fake a smile, I can distort reality, but I can't keep up a persona without letting the girl I try to hide break through.

When my first class comes through after my meltdown, I try my damned hardest to be okay. I plaster a smile across my face, grab my book, and let dozens of tiny eyes watch my every movement.

"Ms. Piper, what are we reading today?" a boy with layered hair and chocolate orbs asks.

"I thought that we'd read a classic if that's okay with you all!"

Another child, a girl with curly black locks and caramel skin raises her hand.

"What's a classic?"

She stutters as she speaks, trying to process the foreign word. My eyes light up as she tries. These kids haven't been introduced to classic literature, they've only been introduced to carbon copy books made for kids. They don't know creative worlds out there exist; they're used to their world being manipulated and dumbed down simply because they're kids. The people who are the most creative are children, they're differences should be celebrated. They should be able to tap into their creativity, to create new worlds that are as strange and beautiful as the minds that make them. I want to inspire my students, no matter how cheesy that sounds. I want to help create the next inventors and entrepreneurs and by showing them a world that's bigger than their own, by showing them different types of literature, they'll learn it's okay to be different, it's okay to be exceptional.

"A classic is a book that people love for a really long time. A book becomes a classic the moment that people realize the talent and the meaning of the book. Does that make sense?"

Some of them shake their heads, while others stare at me intensely. It's fascinating to see their little minds work. They're forcing their brains to work so hard, to make connections that don't exist yet; they're trying to become enlightened.

"Okay, let me try this. So when a lot of people like a book and feel like it's worth talking about it becomes popular. Over time, if people still feel the same way, it becomes a classic."

A round of oh's fill my ears and I reach for the book. I fade into my character slowly, making sure I explain difficult words before rounds of questions are asked, but eventually I become so immersed that time seems to stop completely. I'm Alice now, a dreamer and book critique, desperate for adventure. My senses are heightened and everything is so vivid. It's beautiful, it's frightening, but it's all mine.

When the teacher comes to gather the kids, even she becomes enchanted by the tale. We all just fall so seamlessly into childhood dreams that it's hard to return back to reality. We could have stayed absorbed for hours and hours until I finished the book or until the school bell rang, but my dear friend walks in and joins the conversation, pulling me out of the world of pretend and back to a world that I quite frankly despise.

"How is a raven like a writing desk?" he asks, walking into the room, pulling all eyes towards him.

"I haven't the slightest idea, Mr. White. Do you?"

"Not a clue," he says, flashing a bright smile.

"Well class, I think that's all we have time for today, but we'll pick up from here next week, okay?"

They let out a disappointing groan and I swear, the teacher even joins in. After her lapse of adult behavior she reassumes her role as a shepherd, herding her stubborn kids out of the athenaeum. Clark smiles and I awkwardly place the book back on my desk, marking the spot I have to pick up from.

"So you do like the book."

"Of course I do; why wouldn't I?" I ask.

"Well I don't know."

"You don't have to pretend like everything went perfectly last night. It's okay to say it."

"I know it wasn't perfect, but I'm not afraid of admitting that."

"What are you afraid of then?"

"I rather not come off as rude."

"Mr. White, I thought we decided to be frank with one another."

"Yes, we did, but I don't know."

"Clark, it's okay," my voice softens.

"It just seems like you left me in the middle of everything. It was like one moment you were there and in the next moment you were nothing but a shell."

"I'm sorry about that."

"What happened? Was it something I said?"

"Oh no, not at all. You were fine. I just, now it's me who doesn't know what to say."

"It sounds like we have a lot to talk about. I mean if we ever find words other than I don't know," he teases.

"Yes we do, perhaps over a cup of tea."

"Over a cup of tea sounds perfect."

"I shouldn't have led you to believe that everything was your fault. I hope you know that I never had any bad intentions yesterday. I really did enjoy myself, I just screwed up a bit. Anyways, I'm sorry for everything."

"It's okay, I just want to understand."

"I know."

"Piper."

"I'm sorry, Clark."

He walks over to me and takes the book out of my hands before interlacing his fingers in mine. I raise my eyebrows but he ignores me.

"I'm your friend Piper, you can confide in me."

"I understand that, but there's nothing wrong. I just zone out sometimes. I promise, everything is okay."

He looks at me and cocks his head to the side. "Are you in denial over something? You weren't okay yesterday and you're doing a terrible job convincing me otherwise."

"Mr. White, I need you to stop. I'm a human made of many faults but I certainly don't need anyone to try and fix me. Our friendship is still so new and I'd like you to see the best of me. We'll get to the point where we'll divulge all of our secrets like middle school girls, but just not yet" I say as I pull my hands away.

"But Piper…"

"If you want to stay friends, I suggest you respect my space. Now if you'll excuse me, I need to get back to work. I have to order some new books for the library."

"Ms. Addison, are you trying to get rid of me?"

"No, I'm trying to keep you from knowing me."

Clark and I lock eyes for just a moment before I look away, drawing my eyes down towards my book, his book.

"Well, I guess I should get going then," he says.

"I guess you should, and here... take your book back. I don't feel right about taking it from you. It is your favorite after all."

"Keep it, it's a gift. Besides maybe it'll help you, maybe you'll see that we're all mad in some way or another."

I sigh, "You and your damn book quotes."

"You're just as bad, my dear. You're just as bad."

# THEN:

I am a woman of many cultures and worlds. I am a traveler, yet I never leave my house. I am knowledgeable and accepting, yet there are many things I never have and never will experience. I've been transformed by literature so much so that all my best traits come from reading in one way or another. The summer moved to Belfast I read so many books that at one point my house had more books in it than furniture and it changed my life. Actually, now that I think about it, my house still does have more books than furniture. I guess some things never change.

Most of the books came from the excessive amount of time I spent in the bookstore. I wanted to get Mr. Clint to like me so that I could have a home away from home. I wanted to live in that bookstore. If it wasn't for that place I probably wouldn't have majored in library studies in college.

"Good morning, Mr. Clint!"

"Well hello there, Piper. Did you come to buy more books?"

"Probably. I just needed somewhere to go."

"I don't understand you."

"What do you mean?"

"Out of all places, you come here. This place is falling apart at the seams. Almost every book goes unloved, and everyone I know wants to give their money to an established company instead of here. And yet, you come by everyday still wowed by this place's decrepit charm, but why?"

"I don't know, I just feel like I belong here. I find myself drawn to this place."

"You don't have to romanticize it. This place is as weathered as I am."

"I'm not, I'm being honest with you. There's nothing better than the smell of aged books that flirt with new titles on the shelves, nothing better than the subtle creaking of the floorboards, and there's nothing better than finding a new crevice to read in, one that's been overlooked for so long that it's only company seems to be the sunshine itself. It's quite beautiful."

"You're a dreamer, aren't you? It seems like you're incapable of seeing the bad in things."

"Oh I'm not a dreamer, I'm actually quite the pessimist."

"Then how do you see the beauty in things that have none?"

"It's all about perspective. You know how pickers say that one person's junk is another person's treasure? They're right, it all depends on who's looking and how they see it."

Clint smiled at me and I pulled out whatever book I was reading at the time before disappearing into my little corner. A blanket was waiting for me there, and the sun was shining bright, creating the perfect book light. I fell into the pages for hours and when Mr. Clint came to check on me, he stopped in his tracks and didn't say a word. I don't know what was so interesting to him, but he observed silently in an attempt to not bother me. I kept reading until I found natural stopping place, the end of the book, and then he finally approached me.

"I've been thinking about what you asked me a little while ago," he said.

"What did I ask you?"

"About the job. Anyways, I realized that you were right about what you said earlier. You do belong here and I'd love to have you work for me, but I don't know if you really can. People just don't read as much anymore, so I wouldn't be able to pay you often and when I would be able to pay you, your paycheck would be worth almost nothing."

"I don't care about the money you can pay me."

"Well I can't just make you work for me for free, so how's about I make a deal with you? If you like it, you can start working tomorrow."

"Okay, let's make a deal."

"Okay, so if you work for me, I will pay you in books and tea until I can pay you with legitimate currency. In return, you will basically be my apprentice, learning the trade of books and helping me run this place. I just want to know that my old girl will be taken care of even after I'm long gone."

"That sounds...perfect."

"So do we have a deal?"

"Yes we do."

I shook his frail and bony hand before he ushered me out of the store and into the warm darkness. Walking home that night felt like I was walking on air. This was where I was supposed to be, no matter how many ups and downs I had to go through, I knew I had found my calling, I just knew.

# NOW:

What is more intimate than a church? Everyone's grievances are voiced softly here, everyone's hopes and dreams are expressed while weights are lifted off weak hearts. I never imagined myself back in a church. I never thought I would find myself sitting in another wooden pew that bruises the top part of my bum. I shift uncomfortably in the back row and I cross my legs, rooting myself down in the wood in an attempt to not draw any attention to myself.

I find it amusing watching the kids rise up and down. Pray, sit, stand, pray, sit, sing, listen. They're oiled machines who seem bored with their routine. Life lessons go in their ears and out another as they try to keep their eyes open. No one questions the message, and no one speaks out of turn. The room has a melancholy feel to it and the priest's words echo off the cavernous walls.

It doesn't seem to be a place of worship, I guess I distorted my memories and thought of church more fondly as a child. The more I think about it, the more this situation makes sense; everything seems to be a mirror image. Everyone is so caught up in their worldly problems that they can't even appreciate all of the good things in their life. They can't even thank their own God, all any of them know how to do is apologize for their shortcomings. By the time service is over the kids are pinching each other to stay awake. It breaks my heart and I don't even believe in what they do.

If you can't even accept your own beliefs and pride yourself in them, how do you expect a skeptic to view it in a different light? How is someone supposed to concede and accept the possibility that your God is omniscient when you have doubts yourself, when half the people have darker hearts then the people they persecute. I shouldn't be so cynical. I respect them, I really do, but part of me will always feel hurt for the Church turning its back on me. To be honest with you, I still think someone's out there, I just don't know what they're doing or what that God really believes in.

I try to walk out of the church shortly after the children, but the priest stops me, and calls me towards him.

"Hello father, can I help you?"

"No, not really. I just wanted to introduce myself. I'm Father Michael."

"It's a pleasure to meet you, Father. I'm Piper Addison, the new librarian."

"I've heard of you," he nods as he recognizes my name, "I just wanted to make sure I had a face to place with the name."

"Oh my, I bet the things you've heard about me aren't the

greatest. I've been kind of a clutz and a little antisocial since I started work here."

"That's okay, not everyone is a people person. It's not right for people to pass such harsh criticism on you, you're just trying to adjust."

"I guess so, I don't blame them though. I haven't done anything to prove to them that I'm anything besides the girl they don't particularly care for."

"Ms. Addison, why are you trying to prove your worth to other people? You don't have to explain your actions to anyone on this earth. Don't even bother, they aren't worth your time."

"You're right Father, but sometimes it's hard to be an outsider. Everyone in this world just wants to be liked in one way or another. Anyways, I should be going."

"Okay, I'll let you get back to work. I'll see you at the next mass."

"You probably won't I'm not the religious type, but I'll see you around," I smile.

"Well then feel free to just stop by when you need someone to talk to. I'm not going to condemn you for not believing in anything, or try to force my beliefs down your throat. So if you ever need to get something off your chest, you know where to find me."

"Thank you Father," I say, trying to mask my shock.

I walk out the church in a rushed pace, and never once look back. Father Michael seems to contradict this idea I have built up in my head. After everything that happened before I told myself that the church was a corrupt institution with horrible people. I found myself buying into stereotypes just like the people who condemned me. Maybe the world isn't as black and white as I thought it to be. People keep proving me wrong, that they're more than who they come off as. I really need to work on accepting that, but it's so hard to change your beliefs when they were put in place to protect you.

# NOW:

I am a hard person to figure out. I can't figure out myself sometimes. I find myself in moods where I crave changes in my life. Nothing can be predictable. Sometimes I crave the companionship of other people, and other times I want my only friends to be the records I play and the books I read. I'm a walking paradox, and when my beliefs are questioned I don't handle myself well.

I feel myself being slightly over dramatic. I feel my mind panicking more than it really should. I know I shouldn't be questioning my beliefs completely, especially not over one incident, but I can't help it. I was wrong and I don't know what to do with myself because of it. Even though I tend to stay by myself, I feel terrible when i pass judgments without any merit. People did it to me and so I've always wanted to avoid doing it to anyone else. I can't believe I let my heart turn so cold to other people. I told myself that I was going to be better and I ended up being like everyone else.

*You don't have to be right all the time Piper. You don't have to be perfect. You aren't perfect, you know that. Come on it's okay. Stop being so dramatic. Get out your head and move on. This isn't a life or death situation. Everything is going to be okay.*

I try to get myself out my head by pacing around the library a bit, and since no one is around, I start to think aloud.

"They never were the bad ones, were they? They never really hated me or wished me to hell, did they? They just wanted someone to put their blame on so they could grieve. People aren't inherently bad... people are mainly good. We're all good deep down, we just get a little lost in life and our morals change to match that. I know I don't have to hate them. I don't have to be angry at everyone. I know it's going to be hard for me to forgive them. They caused me to hate myself. They caused me to be a shell and they caused Charlie's condition to be dehumanized. And right now I do blindly hate them all, I hate every last one of them but I can't keep holding on to this feeling forever, can I?"

I mumble to myself over and over, trying to get my mind to shut up and stop overreacting. I'm so consumed by myself that I don't even notice a ghostly Emma wander in my room. She doesn't question my sanity when she sees me, and instead she slumps down into her chair and begins to shake as her face slumps into her palms. I'm not able to regain composure until I see Emma break.

"Emma, are you okay?"

She nods but doesn't lift her head.

"Why are you here? Shouldn't you be in class?"

"It bell rang fifteen minutes ago. School's over."

"Then why are you still here?"

"I don't have a ride home and I couldn't get myself to take the bus. I just can't handle their voices; they're looping in my head over and over. I can't handle them pointing out every little thing that's wrong with me anymore. I needed to get away. I have to get away," she cries.

"Okay, okay let's get out of here."

I try to take her hand but she won't do anything except stare at me vacantly until I start walking out the door. She follows close behind me as tears trickle down her face and I guide her to the parking lot. In the car, I try to get her to open up but she's rooted down in the seat, and her hands are clasped around her knees. I don't know whether to drive off or wait until she opens up to me. I honestly don't know what to do when I'm on the receiving end of vacant stares. It's haunting, the way her face looks frozen. She looks like a porcelain doll. I need to help her, I need to do something, but I know she's buried in her thoughts. She's too far gone. I pull out onto the uneven road and drive around slowly. When we pass the desolate beach I start to slow down even more. The waves calm me, their sound and their predictability makes me feel safe.

"Hey Emma, can you talk to me?" I ask softly.

Her head turns in my direction but her gaze goes right through me.

"Okay, well at least listen to me. Since I don't know where you live, I'm going to take you back to my place where I can give you a warm cup of tea and a nice book to read. Then when you're ready I'll take you home or I can have your parents come and get you. Everything is going to be okay, just keep breathing for me, sweetie."

I start driving off towards my makeshift road and slowly but surely her glossy look starts to fade away. She still won't talk and tears still run down her face, but she's responsive now. Her numbness has faded and now she feels. I know feeling numb is easier but it isn't a good way to live. When you're numb, no one can reach out to you. Now that she's in a different mindset I can get her to open up, and I can help her.

I pull into my house and she follows, once again, like a lost puppy. I guide her to an aged winged chair that looks like it should fall apart, though it's comfortable and strong, and hand her the first book I see. I sit across from her and put my typewriter on top of my foldable table. I see it catches her eye, but when I try to create a conversation she just goes back to her book in an attempt to keep composer.

"You know, you're my first guest ever. I probably should have cleaned up a bit, but I wasn't expecting company. I guess I should be prepared but I mean no one visits the woods..." I start mumbling but she doesn't seem to care. "are you a tea person or a coffee girl? I have a tea set but I'd have to run out to the store if you want anything else. That's not a problem with me, but yeah, I don't want to leave you alone right now."

"I-I um. I think I'll be okay." Her voice is so high pitched and small that if I didn't know better I would think she was a mouse. I shrug and try to tidy up in response.

I start picking up clothes that are scattered through the house and shove them in the corner. I throw books back in their places and cringe when I realize that my shelf has to be reorganized.I try to make a good impression, I try to prove to my lifeless guest that though my house is not the most beautiful or perfect in the least, at least it's loved.

"Miss Piper, um, I uh..." She calls for me and I drop a stack of books on the ground, shifting my attention to her.

"Yes?"

"I think..I think I should get going.... I kinda imposed on you and that, that wasn't right of me."

"I don't mind. You don't bother me," I smile.

"I don't know how I don't..." her voice trails off as she closes her book, "everyone else says that I do."

"I know how you feel Emma. I've been in your shoes before. I told you that I'll be there for you, but I can't help you unless you talk to me. I hope you know that things won't get better if you hold it all in."

For some reason I'm extremely flustered and I feel a rush of rage pulsing through my veins. Was I like Emma when I was younger? Was I completely hopeless and vacant? Is that how people see me now? I don't want to be that way. I don't know what I want or who I want to be, but I don't want to be that. I don't want to see any more of myself in her. It sickens me. She sickens me.

"Maybe I don't want you to fix me! Maybe I just want someone to understand."

"No one is ever going to understand unless you speak up. You have to stop blaming everything else in the world for your problems. You create your own problems! You are the problem! People suck! But what are you going to do? Cry about it? Lock yourself in your room? Look at you, you're nothing more than a shell. You're pale and frail. When's the last time you've tried putting yourself out there? When's the last time you tried sleeping? I see the bags under your eyes. I see what they've done..." My voice trails and my vision blurs. I'm no longer yelling at Emma. I honestly don't believe I was ever really yelling at Emma, instead I'm here yelling at a younger version of myself. A girl who has ballerina pink hair and horrid roots, a girl who has a blackened heart, a girl who has a vendetta against her loved ones who have already passed. I see a girl with tattered skin, I see a girl I tried so hard to separate myself from. "They've ruined us. They ruined you and now I can't fix myself no matter how hard I try. I-I...Damn it I'm so sick of you. I hate you. I hate you so much," I finish my thoughts and the girl I loathe disappears and Emma is put in her place.

Her body is trembling now and I see that she's numb all over again. I pull my hands to my mouth to stop myself for spilling more spiteful tales and I too find myself breaking down. My anger was misdirected to a girl who just needed a friend. She came to me for help and what did I do? I picked her apart, I blamed her for having a terrible fate. I blamed her for being like me.

"Emma, I didn't mean any of that... I wasn't... I didn't mean to offend you. It's been a bad day for me too and I took it out on you. I shouldn't have done that. I- I'm so sorry."

I shuffle my feet and bite down on the corner of my lips. I look like a frightened child, but then again I guess Emma and I are just twins by fate. This time our roles are reversed. She's the one in utter disgust while I'm drowning in embarrassment and misery. She won't even reply to me, she simply hops out the chair, throws the book on the ground, and walks out of the house with nothing but her backpack and a cellphone. I run after her. I yell her name, but she doesn't look back. I run around the forest for a while, looking for her, but give up when the sun starts to set. I don't know what I'm supposed to do.

I make my way back to her chair and find a note written by her, thanking me for everything. I feel more guilty now than ever, and I hate myself for taking my problems out on her. I start to dial a number scrawled on the bottom of the note, but she doesn't answer. I call again and again until she sends me a text. Don't worry, she says. She's home and safe, she says. I don't know if I really trust her, but there isn't much I can do now.

Before I question myself and my sanity any further, I plop down in front of my desk, and do the only thing I know how to do correctly; I write.

I feel as if I'm aging faster each day. Utter loneliness has become so damning that my thoughts age me thirty years. I've wasted my time. I've wasted my life. I've never lived. I don't know how to live because I've trapped myself.

I've become so horrible and unstable with my thoughts, and now I can't remember a time where my heart was still pure.

I just keep thinking that if I channel all my energy into my work that my problems will just go away. I've somehow managed to convince myself that the formula to living is to work until I'm able to reap the rewards of my labor. I want to have a moment of utter bliss where unresolved issues aren't dictating my every emotional reaction. I need help, but I can't open my mouth. I can't let more hatred spew from my tongue.

As I look around my disorganized home, I find myself throwing my work into the air, letting papers fall like flakes of snow. I feel defeated. I am defeated.

# THEN:

There are so many ways to describe the things that destroy us, so many ways to describe our flaws, our sins, our burdens. We wear them all like a scarlet letter, a symbol of shame that is persistent in our daily lives. You can't hide from your flaws no matter how hard you try. Everyone is weak on the inside.

I've watched people throughout my life pretend to be someone else, including myself, in order to seem impenetrable, in order to seem unbreakable. I used to see so many strong-willed people that would have a symbolic heart so battered and bruised that their bitter remains were a constant reminder of the pure hearts they used to posses. The weakest kind of people I knew were scattered and few, but they were only labeled as such because their gentle hearts were so desperate to see the good in people that they would forgive and love when no one else with common sense would. I personally used to be the latter, but as time passed and my soul grew bitter, I became the former.

Watching your soul harden is a slow and gruesome process. You don't just wake up and have a vendetta against the world. Sometimes you see the hatred form in a person, sometimes you feel it growing inside you instead, but then there are those who know how to hide it so well. They know how to bury their insanity until the moment they snap. They know how to be normal until their time runs out.

"I don't want your help. I just want you to leave me alone!"

When the leaves began to ripen and the sky began to pump warmth back into nature's bloodstream stream, I realized that my brother's composure was beginning to fade away. I saw his scarlet letter.

"Piper? Piper, where are you going?"

I ran into the house after an awful day at school. The kids had decided that my passion for books was something to target me for. It was my first true taste of peer-inflicted torture. Two kids, who had the combined strength of an adult, pinned down my limbs while the ever-so round Chase Tirans ripped up my books. I tried to put up a fight, but wiggling my limbs and screeching did nothing. No teachers were around, and the more I resisted the asshole's "power" the more he relished ripping up pages of my precious books.

When I came home from school, my mother insisted on badgering me with questions. Questions that I, quite frankly, did not want to answer.

"Piper, sweetie, just tell me what's wrong. I can help you."

"I don't want your help! Just leave me alone."

I stormed to my bedroom, and as soon as I collapsed on my bed, Charlie came in and decided to wreck any chance of obtaining peace.

"Piper, what happened today? It's not like you to yell at mom."

"I told mom already. I don't want to talk about it, Charlie. Can't you just leave me alone? Can't anyone in this house leave me alone!"

"I just want to help you. Jesus Christ, Piper."

"I don't need your help. I need you to leave me alone."

I took my backpack and threw it at him, causing folders, art supplies, and paper to spill everywhere. Charlie looked at me completely dumbfounded before storming off. I swear I heard him throwing a fit to my mother from the other room because of how I reacted, but she shushed him and sent him back into battle.

"Charlie, why are you back? I told you to go away!" I yelled.

"I understand english Piper, I heard what you said."

"Then why are you here?"

"Because mom asked me to talk to you. Do you think I want to be with you when you're being a complete brat."

"I am not," I huffed.

"Are too."

"Am not."

"We're too old for this game Piper."

"No we aren't."

"Stop trying to pick a fight with me. It's an awful way to shift focus from the main issue. I'm not leaving here until I find out what's wrong."

"I don't want to tell you, so you should at least sit down and relax. It may be awhile."

He glared at me and popped down on the wooden floor. The floorboards creaked as his weight shifted and he threw his hands behind his head and sighed.

"I could stay here all day. I might even read a book or two while I'm at it. I don't have anywhere to go."

"Have fun trying to find anything decent to read," I mumble under my breath.

"What was that?"

"Nothing. I didn't say a thing."

"Whatever."

He started to shuffle through my bookshelf but nothing interested him. Then he picked up my discarded backpack and did the same.

"Where's that one book you were reading? The ones with the wizards."

248

"Harry Potter?"

"Yeah, that's the one. I want to read something decent rather than all these girly books you have. Anyways, where is it?"

"I dunno. Look on the shelf."

"I already did. Are you hiding your books from me?"

He paused for a moment and waited for a response, a response I wasn't about to give.

"Piper, I'm not going to hurt your stupid little book," he said, completely deadpanned.

"My books aren't stupid!"

I tried to give him the most menacing stare as humanly possible but I wasn't able to. Within moments, my weight seemed to collapse and my body began to shake. Tears flooded my eyes and I felt my heart rattle. The broken pieces were everywhere, and I felt overwhelmed. I wish I could begin to explain why I was so emotionally attached to my books, why they meant so much to me, and why books still do, but it's almost impossible. If someone asked another to describe what they love, would they be at a loss for words, or would they spew cheesy details? I'd do the former. Books understand me. They get me and accept me more than people do.

Charlie locked eyes with me before the tears began to flow, so in a poor attempt to save my angry composure, I buried myself in a mound of pillows.

"Piper, I'm sorry. I didn't mean it like that. I just don't understand why you love those things so much.. Um. I uh.. wait are you crying? I didn't mean to make you cry."

I stayed silent and tried to pull myself together. I didn't do a good job at composing myself though and that's because I believed I was perfectly justified in my reaction. I believed that I was allowed to mourn the death of my books. Little did I understand then, I was being immature by letting the actions of other children dictate my emotions. They were trying to change me, program me to believe that there was something wrong with me by destroying my pride and joy, by trying to dictate my behavior. Sure, I could have always bought myself another book, but instead I preferred letting their vicious behavior penetrate my heart like a knife.

I don't understand why I was obsessed with the beliefs of others. I fell into society's trap at an early age. I tried to conform, minimize, and even apologize for my differences. I wish I could say with confidence that I broke away from its deadly grasp, but I'm still enslaved. People are still able to make me feel inferior when they mock my social anxiety, when their loud chatter suddenly dies as I enter a room.  People are still able to shatter me by mocking what makes me different. No matter how much I try to preach self worth, part of me has always and will always bow down to society's whim.

"Piper," his voice was gentle as he said my name, pulling me out of my thoughts. "look at me. Please."

I felt my brother's warmth as his arms engulfed me. I tried to fight him, I tried to regain what little composure I had, but somehow I just crumbled. I let my walls come down. I stopped being an utter brat and let Charlie in.

"I have a feeling that I'm not the reason you're crying."

I let out a soft laugh before I choked on my own tears.

"No, you aren't," I forced a smile to spread across my face and Charlie attempted to clean up the flood by wiping the steady flow of rain off my face.

"Then why are you so blue, my little Pied Piper?"

"It doesn't matter. I'm fine. I'll be fine."

"You aren't fine if you can't stop crying."

My smile immediately faded and I slumped my face into my hands before sighing heavily.

"I just can't do it anymore. I can't go back there Charlie. Not now, not ever."

"Go back where?"

"School," I said aggressively.

"You can't just not go back to school."

"Why not? I hate it there. I hate the people and the teachers. I just hate everything that dumb building and the people in it stand for. I don't want to go back. Please don't make me go back."

"Piper, what happened in school today?"

"I don't want to talk about it. I told you that already."

"Then you have to go back to school."

I rolled my eyes, I knew I wasn't going to win the battle.

"They tore apart my books. All of the new ones you and mom got me are gone. I just want to sit here and cry and not go to school, so if you'll excuse me."

He released his grip and my body turned away from his.

"Who tore apart your books, Piper?" his voice was stern and I could only imagine the look of his face as anger grew in him.

"It doesn't matter."

"Yes it does. I want to help you."

"You can't help me. You'll just make it worse!"

"Don't be crazy. I can help you."

His hand rested on my shoulder and I sighed. As a child I was never able to conceal my emotions. I wore my heart on my sleeve and that made me easy prey. I didn't understand that when you hide

252

your feelings, people get disheartened and eventually leave you alone. I wish I could have prepared my little self to bottle her emotions. If I could have, maybe things would have ended up differently for me.

"You promise?"

"I swear."

"Pinky swear?"

"Pinky swear.

# NOW:

I am a warrior, or so I like to think. I am a pioneer. I am a force to be reckoned with. In many ways I am against the world. I fight against the corrupt, the vocal evils, and the ones who stay silent, the passive minds.

Okay, none of that is true, like whatsoever. I'm just trying to make myself seem less of a horrific person especially after what I did to Emma. I didn't mean to stomp on her soul, I didn't mean to scream at her. I didn't mean to do a lot of things but they just happened. I don't know what's wrong with me.

What's going to happen when I see her at school? Why am I so worried about it? She's just a stupid little girl. I don't have to worry about her. I'm an adult. I can live my life without any emotional attachment to a student. I can do whatever the hell I want to. Yeah. I'm not a bad person. I just have to snap out of it. Can you tell that I'm failing at convincing myself?

I push myself away from my desk and my body is physically trembling. My toes are humming, my heart is radiating out of my chest, and my fingers are twitching. What's wrong with me? What's wrong with *me*? What is **wrong** with me?

I force myself to walk to the bathroom, and as soon as I catch my reflection, I'm haunted. Her wild eyes peer into my soul and war paint is smeared across her face. I'm looking into the soul of a demon, an animal looking for its prey. Who is this girl? She can't possibly be me because I don't know who that person is. I don't know what it's like to stare down a person whose eyes are filled with hunger and despair.

I don't think I'm her, I don't feel like I am her, then again my emotions seem to be uncontrollable these days. Maybe the only time I'm truly myself is when I'm in the company of others, when I can slip into the role society created for me. That life is easy, in that life I don't have to think so hard because everyone else dictates how I live. I don't have to discover who I am because someone has already done it for me. Maybe this whole time I've been lying to myself. I've always tried to rebel against society, but it's the same institution that keeps me sane.

I wipe the muddle masterpiece off my face before trudging back into the main room. Gliding along the uneven floors, I wander aimlessly. I feel like a puppet dancing with strings. Come one, come all, see the freak show, see the unbecoming of Piper Addison. Come one, come all, see her twirl, see her leap, and watch her go insane.

Come one, come all, it'll be a treat I assure you. Isn't it glorious to watch someone else fall?

I feel as if wanderlust in bubbling in my core, giving me an excuse to run away. I feel as if it's trying to cut me free. It's trying to unravel the chains around my heart and liberate me. Oh, how easy it would be to just walk out and leave. It would be so damned easy to start over and create a new identity. There's only two steps to it: pack up and never look back. How easy it would be to live the life I always planned for myself. All I have to do is walk out that door and drive until everything I know is no longer in my rear-view mirror. I can do this.

I start walking, but with each step, with each agonizing creak of the floorboards, I move slower. I find myself changing my mind. I'm starting to do a complete 180. I'm indecisive. I'm afraid.

There's no guarantee that life will ever go my way. I failed to escape my past once before, who's to say that it won't haunt me until I'm in my grave? Things haven't always been perfect for me here, but I've made the best with the cards I've been dealt. I've made a home in the middle of nowhere and I've fallen in love with the idea of reinvention. They say Rome wasn't built in a day, well neither was a human. It's going to take me time to be comfortable with myself. I have to be patient. Maybe I just have to stick it out.

But what if things never get better? What if I live out the storyline of a manic pixie dream girl? I can drive until I reach the other side of the country, find a cute guy along the way, string him along until he falls for me, and then leave tragically, causing his heart to break into a million pieces. Wouldn't that be nice and predictable? I just don't know what I want so it's easier to live a fantasy. I don't know why my heart wants to lay roots one moment, and then pack up the next.

I sigh and stumble away from the door. Somehow in the process, I end up in the kitchen, clutching a bottle of unopened vodka, covered in dust. The only way to mask a craving is to cave into another one, and so in an attempt to stop my head from spinning, I pop open the bottle and drink.

Eventually drinking become a game, and I somehow convince myself that I'm winning. If I trip over my own feet, I take a sip. If I fall while dancing, I take another. Every and any arbitrary task is topped off with a taste of poison. It actually feels nice after it trickles slowly down my throat, leaving a burning sensation. The alcohol makes me feel warm and alert, but lose and lighthearted. It makes me feel freer than I've felt in a long time.

I'm invincible. I'm free. I can do anything. I can do everything. I can leave. I believe I can. I know I can. Don't look back. Take one step at a time. Don't trip. Don't fall. Keep your head up tall. Smile and keep poise. Let's make little noise. Let's tiptoe through the woods. Let's move on.

I reach for the handle once more, and as my finger grasp the handle, my vision blurs. I feel a drunken haze wash over me. I pry open the door, and begin to stumble out into the night, but I don't make it far before my world turns into a black abyss.

# THEN:

I walked towards the trenches of hell, prepared for battle. The school yard was a living example how society expected the odd to conform. Those who didn't fit in were prey, and unless you managed to gain favor with a predator, you didn't stand a chance. Bullying and teasing were constants. No matter how many patronizing talks adults gave, no matter how many children gave up their lives, no matter how many times parents begged for future generations to be better, it was never ending.

Bruises and mental scars don't stop the pain, It encourages the privileged to take advantage of the weak while they're down. I used to wear my heart like a girl scout badge, on display for the world to see. It was so easy to take advantage of me. It was so easy to make me fall. No wonder I did. No wonder I still do.

"Piper, what do you normally do at recess?"

Charlie's voice sent a wave of calm down my childish frame. He had managed to convince his teachers that he needed to spend the afternoon with me. He had somehow managed to convince my teachers that I needed him by my side, and he had somehow managed to convince me that it was okay to need him.

"I normally sit on the swings and read until someone kicks me off," I muttered.

"Well then, why don't we go on the swings?"

"I don't know if that's a good idea."

"Why not? If that's what you like to do then it's a great idea."

"I don't think there will be enough swings for Chase and his friends."

"If there aren't enough swings, they'll just have to wait their turn."

"Charlie, don't make me do this."

"I'm not making you do anything. I just want you to be able to have fun without getting picked on. You deserve to be happy."

Charlie squeezed my hands and then took a deep breath in. In that moment, I believed that he could feel my heart race. I was partially scared for what would happen. There was just this feeling in my gut I couldn't shake. I wasn't necessarily afraid of Charlie's actions when he came faced to face with my tormentors, or how the boys would react to him, but I was afraid of how the boys would treat me when Charlie was gone.

"Let's go Piper, I see two swings by the slide with our names on it."

"Charlie..."

"Come on, don't you trust me?"

"Of course I do."

I flashed by brother a nervous smile and he just smirked in response. He was up to something, his gears were set in motion, the cranks in his brain were whirling.

"Do you want me to push you?" he asked.

"I can do it myself! I'm a fourth grader not a stupid second grader" I huffed, slightly insulted.

"I know you can. I know you can do anything you try to do because that's just how big you are, but sometimes it's funner to have someone help you out."

"I don't know if I believe you."

"Of course you don't," he laughed and started to tickle me.

"Stop Charlie! Stop!"

I threw back my head and tried to control my laughter as tears streamed down my face. In that moment, I was happy. I wasn't afraid of the inevitable. A smile spread over Charlie's face, and when he let me go, I wrapped my arms around him and hugged him tight.

"Okay, I'm done for now. Now, are you gonna let me push you, or do I have to tickle you some more?"

Gasping for air, I answered him sarcastically, "Hm, I don't know. I really don't trust you after that! I think you're secretly the tickle monster who is just wearing a Charlie costume. Who are you, and where's my brother?"

"I'm right here, Pied Piper; I'm always right here."

I let go of him and glided over towards the empty swings and sat down with confidence. I wasn't going to let anyone or anything move me, no matter how hot the plastic under my butt was, no matter how many people tried to push me off. I was a rock. I was going to stand up for myself and assert my own will because my brother was right by my side.

Inhaling the smell of a warm mid day, I took off. My legs were pumping furiously and as soon as I gained momentum, I was flying. My arms were wings and as the air rushed into my face I felt utter bliss. Nothing could take me out of that moment, not even the mess of wind blown hair that rushed into my face.

"Piper, you trust me. Don't you?" he asked.

"Of course I do," I whispered quietly and tried to hear my voice fade into the wind.

"Then close your eyes, I'm going to push you higher."

My eyes clamped shut, but light still seeped through my lids. Within mere seconds I was flying higher. The only thing connecting me to the earth was Charlie's steady hand, leading me to the sky, keeping me from falling.

262

"Is this how the birds feel?" I whispered.

"No, I don't think so. They're used to walking so they can't love it the way we can. Does that make any sense?"

"Yeah, I think so."

I cranked my head back and let my feet stick in front of me. My body was a board in the wind, floating gently as the sun tickled my skin.

"Hey Charlie, can you do somethin for me, please?"

"Of course, what is it?"

"Will you sing our song for me?"

"Now? In the middle of the playground? Aren't you afraid of what the other kids will think when they hear your big brother singing badly?"

"No, I don't care what they think when you're around."

"Why's that?" he prodded me as I swayed with the wind.

"You know why."

"No, no I don't."

"Yes you do; you just want me to compliment you."

"So what if I do? Just tell me! Or else."

"Or else what?"

"Or else I stop pushing you."

I snorted and opened my eyes to look Charlie dead on. He wasn't kidding, he had an underlying fire that was hiding in his eyes, and he was just waiting for a moment to ignite it.

"I can always pump my legs Charlie. I don't always need you."

"Whatever Piper."

"Oh come on, don't get mad at me."

"I won't get mad if you say it."

"Why are you so stubborn?" I huffed as I pumped my legs.

"Why are you?" he fired back.

"You keep me safe, Charlie, okay? I need you. I need you to protect me. I'm just a stupid little girl who needs her brother to keep her safe. I'm a girl who can't do anything on her own."

After the words flew out my mouth, I felt gravity weigh down my chest and shackle my feet to the ground. I couldn't swing. I felt nervous again.

"Piper," Charlie's voice was soft and sympathetic, "you don't need me. You're the strongest and bravest little kid I've ever known. I wish I was more like you when I was your age."

"Don't lie to me."

"I'm not. I'm serious, you don't need me, but I need you. I told you that."

"You're a bad liar," I said.

"I'm going to change the topic now. I don't want to talk about this anymore."

"Ugh, Charlie."

"Come on, cheer up."

I didn't answer him.

"Piper, come on. Smile for me."

More silence.

"I'll sing. I promise I'll sing."

"Prove it."

I pushed my feet off the ground, kicking dirt toward my brother. He was annoyed by my attitude but didn't try to argue any further. Within moments, I was flying again. The fear of falling made my heart skip a beat, but the adrenaline rush that came with soaring uncontrollably made up for the rest in my heart's rhythm. As my body danced in the air and flirted with the ground, I heard my brother and I's song. Here Comes the Sun by the Beatles was flowing out of my brother's mouth.

I couldn't help but smile at his failure. His song was out of tune and flat. It was horrific but yet perfect. No matter how hard he tried to sing, he just couldn't do it right. He inherited my father's athletic traits, not my mother's musical ones, and that was okay with me. Charlie being different always made me happy because it was in those rare moments, when he wasn't trying to be someone else, when he was truly happy.

"You're terrible!"

"I may be terrible but...*it's all right ba dun na na nuh nah na nuh nah dum..*"

As he tried to sing acapella, the song looped through my head. Once again, I clamped my eyes shut and let myself go back into time. In that moment, I wasn't listening to my tone-deaf brother. I was living in a world of technicolor, where everyone around me was screaming and fighting over their favorite beatle, where my hair was cut into a bob and my flared bell bottoms were bluer than the morning sky. In that moment, I was reliving beatlemania, I was watching them sing for me.

Screams pierced my ears and I let out a fangirl's shrill back. I thought to myself, if I stayed up in the clouds, if I stayed captivated by my imagination, I'd never have to worry about reality ever again. Twirling around the the weed-filled ground, I danced with people who only existed in my dream. It was perfect until I heard another scream. This scream was different, it sent a shiver down my spine.

The anguished cry tugged on my heart and my universe began to disintegrate. As my dream disappeared, the cries got louder, and other voices began to scramble. I fluttered my eyes open, and as reality came into focus, fear made my blood run cold.

"You're going to leave her alone from now on. Do you hear me? My little sister is not your toy. You and your little friends are done."

"Stop, please! I'm sorry! I'm so sorry!"

Chase was shaking, his body curled in a ball in an attempt to lessen Charlie's deadly blows. I could see where bruises were starting to form, and I could see a pool of blood spreading throughout the playground.

"Charlie stop!" I screamed, but he didn't hear me.

"It's too late for sorry! You're going to remember to not hurt her ever again!"

Charlie kicked Chase and with each blow, Chase's fight got weaker. He was giving in to the pain. I was horrified at what I was watching, but I was up too high up to break up the fight myself. I tried screaming at Charlie again, and again, but nothing. He was gone. Charlie was gone and his inner demon had surfaced to unleash hell.

I felt the sun's warmth piercing on my skin, the ground wasn't getting any closer to me but my only option was to land and pray that I wasn't too late to save someone. My eyes fluttered shut again, and with one final kick, my body flailed in the air while gravity grounded me. Gravity wasn't too kind to me; my limbs couldn't help but flail in the wind. It was as if spending all that time in the clouds caused me to believe that I truly was a bird.

"Charlie!" I screamed as my body tumbled in the air.

I felt as if I was falling for hours, though everything around me was moving at a warped speed. Every blow to Chase's body, every explicit scream that escaped Charlie's mouth caused me to feel as if I was falling slower.

As the ground met my body, my arm twisted and my weight collapsed. A bone was projecting out of my arm and not even Chase's screams of horror could drown out my sobs of pain.

"Charlie! Please. Help me," I cried.

It was my final plea that broke him.

"Oh my god Piper. Are you okay? Oh my god, your arm," he paused and turned around to face the battered child curled in a fetal position. "this is all your fault. You caused this you little piece of shit. I should kill you!"

Charlie began to pull back his leg, preparing for the final blow, but I grabbed his ankle and pulled with my usable arm.

"Look what you've done Charlie," I whispered.

He looked at me and said nothing else, just lifted my fragile body and carried me off towards the school for help. His wild eyes

268

faded as we moved away from the crime scene but the blood stains on his clothing told a gruesome story; Charlie was not my savior but a predator looking for helpless prey.

# NOW:

Before I explain the horrendous shape that I am in, I'd like the record to reflect to the fact that I am not a drinker; I am not a binge drinker, a casual drinker, or even an emotional one, but every now and again the human conscious cries out for change. You can't always help yourself. You can't always save yourself.

Now that I have set the record straight, I can truthfully proclaim that I remember absolutely nothing about the night before without shame. Okay, not without shame but, whatever. I feel like shit! My head hurts, my eyes have fifty pound weights on them, and never in my life have I ever hated the birds chirping out my window more than I do in this moment.

I rub my eyes open and try to prepare myself for the blinding glow that seeps through. By the time I adjust myself to the light I unsuccessfully attempt to pull myself out of the bathtub, which might I add, I have no recollection of getting in. Eventually I stumble towards the bathroom and try to wash the regrets out of my mouth and off my face.

"I hate everything," I whisper.

"Are you sure you hate everything? I mean that's not what you said on the phone."

I stop dead in my tracks and turn around to face the voice. Sitting at my kitchen table, peering at a newspaper is Clark, hunched over in the chair with a bagel hanging out of his mouth.

"What are you doing here? Did...did we?"

"Oh Piper, I thought you knew me better."

His eyebrows furrow and he sets down his newspaper, revealing a t-shirt that has a cat holding a science beaker on it.

"I'd never take advantage of a lady especially when she's going through a personal struggle. That would be utterly despicable of me."

"I'm not going through a personal struggle, Clarkson. I'm perfectly fine, but I do appreciate you not being a pig. Gentlemen are truly hard to find these days," I snarl.

"If you weren't struggling, you wouldn't have called me last night, drunk off your ass. You begged me to come here Piper. I know someone who needs help when I see it, and you do. Don't deny it, it's very unbecoming."

"I'm not in denial Clarkson White. I had a bad night and made a few bad decisions along the way. I'm human, and I'm young, so my behavior, although you may view it as deplorable, was completely normal. Now if you'll excuse me, I have to get ready for work."

"You're not going into work today."

"What do you mean, I'm not going into work? You don't control me or my work schedule. I have a job, and I have no intention of losing that job so I need to go to work no matter if I'm hungover or not."

"I'm not trying to control you, I'm trying to help."

"I don't need your help," I cross my hands in front of my chest and Clarkson shakes his head.

"Okay, you don't need me, but can I stick around anyways? I can take you into work. Please, Piper, for me?"

"Whatever, let me go get ready for the day. I'm not in the best driving shape anyways."

"Alright," he grabs my hand and smiles, "but don't disappear on me."

My body tenses at his words. The only thing I remember clearly is wanting to leave everything behind. I remember envying ghosts and their anonymity.

"Clarkson, if you don't mind, can you start up the tea kettle? If I'm going to make it today I'm going to need some caffeine in me."

I worm my hand out of his and try to change the conversation. His eyebrows arch at my actions but he says nothing and moves towards the stove while I retreat towards the bathroom with the first outfit I can find, a black lace dress with matching stockings.

"Piper, what kind of tea do you want?"

"Surprise me."

I slam the door and throw my clothes in the sink before slumping down on the closed toilet seat. I wonder how long I can stay in here without him bothering me? I don't want him here. I don't need him getting close to me. I don't need a friend. I don't want to hurt anyone else.

"Piper?"

I look up at the sealed door and every bone in my body stiffens. I've lost track of time.

"Piper, are you alright? You've been in there for like a half hour."

"I- I'm fine. I just need to be alone. Maybe you should go to work without me."

"How many times do I have to tell you that I'm not going to leave you here alone before you accept it?"

How do I respond to that? How do I convey to him that if he doesn't leave he'll get hurt? I hate the fact that I'm like this; a whining self-serving little girl who runs away from all her problems.

"Piper, stop ignoring me. Please, just talk to me."

His hand rests on the doorknob but he doesn't turn it. We both listen to the sound of each other's breaths. After a while they start to sync, rapid breaths with no relief.

"Are you decent?" he asks.

"One moment."

I throw my dress over my head and hop around as I attempt to pull my stockings over my legs. As I try to pull them up the last little bit I end up falling on the ground, proving once again that I am the definition of beauty and grace.

"Shit! I can't do one goddamned thing right!"

"Miss Addison! That is not language a lady should be using."

"Oh shut up, Clarkson, I'm sick of this gentleman act."

"I'm not acting."

I grunt, force myself off the floor, and open the door. I take two steps toward him and he takes four steps back. He can see the rage in my eyes and he's afraid. It's funny how people want to change you until they see the dark side, until they see that you're completely and utterly hopeless.

"I'm tired of this game Clarkson White. I'm sick of you trying to figure me out like I'm some of mystery. I'm not your pixie manic dream girl. You can't make me your project. You can't fix me. I'm not a damsel in distress looking for a prince. I'm fine, and you need to accept that and stop treating me as if I'm constantly on the verge of destruction."

Fire spews out of my mouth, words that I didn't know I had in me are thrown at an innocent victim. I know he means well. I know he only wants to be a good friend to me, but I don't need a babysitter. I need to be by myself.

"Piper, I'm not playing any games here."

My eyebrows arch, and he takes a step towards me, closing the gap that he created just moments before.

"I just want to be your friend. I'm not trying to make you mad, here. Please, stop fighting me," he says.

"Why? Why me?"

"Because when I first heard about you, I knew you were different. I thought you were someone who embraced her quirks. I thought you would be able to change how this school looks at people like you and me."

"Clark..."

His voice lowers to a soft mumble, "I was wrong."

"I'm sorry. I wish I knew, I would have stopped you-"

"Stopped me? Stopped me how?" he cuts me off, "Piper, you hide your true self behind crazy pink hair, an amazing collection of literature, and this odd personality that I don't understand. You would have thought that the fact that you were nothing like I'd imagine would stop me from trying to figure you out, but by the time you revealed your warped soul I realized I couldn't imagine life without you. The ghastly truth of the matter is that as soon as you started pushing me away, I came to the conclusion that you were the only true friend I had."

"That's not true. That can't possibly be true."

"It is, and it pains me to admit it."

The destruction I left can't be ignored any longer. I can just see it in Clark's face, pushing him away dismantled him. I can't even begin to imagine how my actions affected Emma if Clark's as shaken up as he is.

"I'm sorry, Clark."

"Stop apologizing for things beyond your control. You can't fix how I feel."

"Yes I can."

"And how do you intend on fixing this situation?" he taps his foot impatiently.

"By helping you forget me. I've led you to believe that I'm invincible, but now that you've seen the real me, maybe it will help."

"I don't want to forget."

A cackle escapes my lip and I grab Clark's hands, steadying them with my grasp.

"I'm sorry," I say between laughs, "but are you really trying to sell that bullshit line to me? You aren't Peeta, Clarkson, and this isn't the Hunger Games."

"Stop, Piper. Listen to me."

I meet his gaze and the laughter dies.

"I am not an act. I have never been anything but myself around you, and do you know why that is? It's because we're friends. It's because you're weird just like I am, and I don't have to worry about what you'd think about me when I wear my favorite cat shirt, or when I tell you about a new way to learn times tables. It aggravates me to the core that you think I'm being anything but honest with you," he says.

"Clark."

"No," his voice bellows and I drop his hand. "No, it's my turn right now Miss Addison, so you will have to wait your damn turn."

As he finishes his sentence, I'm the one I who takes a step back. I have never seen him lose his cool, in fact I've never seen him be anything but happy or disappointed. I didn't think that it was possible for him to experience pain, to experience utter disgust.

"If anyone is a liar in this botched friendship it's you. I know nothing about you, Piper. I'm trying my best to be a good friend, to be someone you can talk to, but I'm starting to believe it's hopeless."

"I'm not a liar. I'm just a private person who prefers to stay to herself. Not everyone is comfortable with embracing their individuality. I'm not comfortable being an open book. I can't tell you everything about myself, Clarkson."

"Why, not?" he asks.

"I've gone through a lot of shit. My emotional baggage is too large of a burden to expect anyone to deal with me."

"It distresses me that you view yourself so poorly, Piper."

"Again I say, how I view myself is none of your concern, Mr. White."

"Again I've noticed, we've slipped back to using formalities."

"Touché, Mr. White."

"Well, Miss Addison, I'm tired of bickering. I say we put this conversation on hold and make our way to school."

"I think that's the best idea I've heard all day."

Clarkson saunters over to the decaying coat rack that is hopelessly displayed next to the door and puts a tweed blazer over his t-shirt. My eyebrows arch and I hold back a snicker. Clarkson's convinced that he's this perfect gentlemen, born in the wrong time

278

period with one mission, to spread manners and algebra. I can just see it now, Clarkson bustling up and down the streets of New York City after the first World War, dancing with every lady until her feet could take no more twirling, giving the first cold woman he saw the coat off his back. I can see him hailing cabs for pregnant women and paying for their outrageous fares. I can see him settling down with a lovely darling who'd call him honey and offer to be his southern belle though he'd insist she assert rights as an individual. I can see him having a little girl and calling her princess. I can see him moving to the suburbs and growing his family, watching as the world unfolded in front of his chocolate pools. I can see Clarkson being happier in a different time, regardless of the pigment of his skin, and that makes me somber. He would be happier if our lives didn't become entangled, but here he is, trying to save another damsel in distress. If only he understood that the only dragon that needs to be slain is myself.

"Are you coming, or are you just going to stare at the cat on my shirt all day?"

Clarkson's snarky comment releases me from my trance and forces my blurred reality to come back into focus. I shrug at him, and before following him out the door, I rush to the kitchen and take my pills while trying to avoid eye contact with the mathematical gentleman.

"Uh, Piper…"

"I'm a closed book, Clarkson."

"Alright, alright. Should I be concerned at least?"

"Were you concerned about my well-being when you met me?"

"Um, no..?"

"Then you just answered your own question."

Before he can ask any more questions, I make my way out the house and usher him to his beat up, gas guzzling, death trap that he calls a car. In a bold attempt to piss him off and stand my ground, I walk over to his side of the car and open the door for him.

"Ladies first," I smirk.

I see his body tense as my comment penetrates his fragile ego. No matter how progressive he claims to be, he'll always try to be a provider.

"You make my blood boil, Ms. Addison."

"I have to my dear, Mr. White. If I didn't, who else would keep you on your toes?"

I flash him a toothy grin and shut the door before trotting over to my side. As I glide into my seat I pretend like there is nothing

280

unusual at all. He huffs and turns on the radio, causing a jazzy melody to come out.

"You are a walking cliche, Clarkson White."

"What did I do now?" he frowns and turns off the radio.

"Nothing, you're just so sure of your antique disposition."

"I am very comfortable with who I am as a person. Does that irk you?"

"No, not at all. It actually is very refreshing to see someone be so comfortable breaking all of society's norms."

"They may not be the norms of this generation, but if I was born in another time I would be nothing short of a carbon copy. Isn't that weird to think about? Living in a different time, a different place, or even having a different name could have changed your entire identity. It could have defined you in such a different light that the person you are today would be completely unrecognizable."

I shift awkwardly, but Clarkson doesn't notice, his eyes are glued to the road.

"I think life would be better if we were given an opportunity to start over."

"I don't know, Piper. Part of me wants to believe in fate, like no matter what we do, we'll always end up with the same consequences. I guess we'll never know."

I shrug when his eyes meet mine, and to break contact I reach for the radio and turn it up as high as it can go. I just need to get to work and I'm free from entanglement. In my library I'm home, I'm safe. Books can never hurt me the way people can, they can never let me down, even when they have a bittersweet ending.

"The object of my affection can change my complexion from white to a rosey red," Clarkson starts singing along with a girl group, singing as loud as the creaky stereo emits white noise that sounds just like a record player would.

As he sings my head pounds harder, my breath dissolves, and my hands clench the car door. I wince in pain, but of course Clarkson doesn't notice. The man is delirious, entrapped by his own personal reality where everything is sunshine and pi.

"God, I just love this time of year. Don't you?"

He glances over at me and turns down the radio immediately.

"You alright?"

"I was woken up by the welcome committee, why wouldn't I be alright?"

His voice lowers just a tad, but his eyes shift back to the narrow winding roads.

"I'm serious, are you okay? You look like you're being tortured."

"I'm fine, even though I am being tortured in a way."

"You're so difficult, and for no reason at all."

"It's because you're too pleasant for me, now if you don't mind, can we keep the music down? My head is killing me at the moment, and if I'm going to be working with a bunch of screaming kids all day, I'm going to need all the peace and quiet that I can get."

"You were the one who turned the music up in the first place? Whatever, I'll be quiet, but only after I say one more thing."

"What is it, Mr. White?"

"I'm sorry."

"It's okay," I whisper.

He smiles at me and rolls down the windows to let the crisp autumn air whisk away the tension. It seems as if it was yesterday when I watched summer fold into autumn, but now it's here to stay, to chill my bones and remind me that in just a few weeks I will be alone during the holidays with nothing more than haunting recollections of my mental scars. Air swells in my lungs and my eyes flutter close. I become perturbed at the thought of another holiday, and the more I think about it, the more upset I become.

I was always told that as time goes on it gets easier. I was told that grief was nothing more than a wave that resurfaces and fades with the changing of the tide. I was told that there were only two ways to dull the ache: live in your dreams, or move on completely, never looking back. I tried the latter before, but I haven't managed to escape anything but a father who let his soul die alongside the rest of my family. I have to get this to stop. I have to stop letting what happened to me as a child transform me into a terror. I have to stop cowering behind a diagnosis that seems to have defined me more than it ever should've. I have to escape my own mind. I need to find my happy place, and so I try, and try, and of course the moment I think I've cleared my head, I hear his voice.

*"Hey Pied Piper, how've you been? You look absolutely radiant, my dear sister."*

I hear his voice, I see his face. His being must have been preserved by some God, because as I see him, no part of him has aged a day. His mop-like locks swoop in front of his face, hiding eyes that hold more depth than the night sky, and a devilish smirk creeps up his lips causing my heart to skip a beat. He's here, but he's gone. He can't be anything but a hallucination. His ghost is taunting me, forcing me to bring up emotions that seep through the cracks of my faltering mask.

*"Charlie, I hate to be the bearer of bad news, but you're supposed to be ten feet under right now, having a tea party with my good friend oblivion,"* I say, concealing my sorrow with a level of

284

*cheekiness that would only amuse him.*

He laughs and takes a step forward in my subconscious.

*"You never fail to make me happy."*

*"Well, I'm glad that you're easily amused," this time I smirk before him, and for a brief second, I start to believe that he's going to reach out to me and break the inevitable fourth wall that keeps us apart.*

*"Piper, can I ask you something?"*

*"Anything."*

*"Do you hate me?"*

His voice jumps octaves, and all of a sudden, he looks so small, so weak and innocent. He reminds of me of the person he used to be, the person afraid of the monster he was becoming, the little boy who just wanted to get better.

*"Go on, Piper. Tell me the truth."*

The gap between no longer exists and his hands dissolve with my touch. My knight in shining armor is also the devil who made me fall. How can I love a devil, and how can that devil share my blood?

*"I'm so sorry," I mumble.*

He kisses my forehead, and I feel nothing. I watch him walk away, and I feel nothing. I watch my parallel universe transform back into reality, and again I feel nothing. I'm empty and nothing can fix how I feel.

One, two, three, breathe. Four, five, six, breathe. Seven, eight, nine, breathe. Pull yourself together, you're fine, we're fine. Monsters are wandering enigmas who destroy everything in their wake in a quest for legitimacy. I can't let him continuously destroy what's left of me. Ten. Ten. Ten. It's over, it's not real.

"Piper? Piper are you okay?"

Clarkson's voice pulls me from my daze as my eyes dart back and forth. I've been thrown into the deep end with weights shackled to my wrists, pulling me down. I didn't realize that I was crying throughout all of this. I didn't realize that my safe place was also my eternal hell.

"What?" I ask.

"You're crying."

"Oh am I? It's just my head is killing me so much. I don't ever drink, and obviously I can't hold my liquor well if I feel this horribly. I'll be fine, I just need to get my mind to relax."

"I don't believe you."

"That's fine, I expect as much considering my recent behavior."

"I guess that plays a factor, I'm not as concerned with your recent behavior as I am about the trigger of said behavior. Does that make sense?"

"I think so."

"Something had to have happened for you to lose grip on reality, Piper. People don't just fall apart."

"They do when they can't keep a charade going any longer."

"What charade, Piper? Who are you really?"

The car comes roaring to a stop, and the school's grounds comes into perfect view. A prison disguised as a place of privileged learning, a gothic dream, a student's nightmare. The only thing that seems to keep anyone going is the belief that a break is around the corner, and the only thing keeping me afloat is the belief that my stories are making people happy.

"What happened to your little game, Mr. White? Have I not proven myself to be a worthy competitor for you? If you want to know who I am, figure it out yourself."

Though I wait for a witty reply, he doesn't retaliate, his eyebrows simply furrow as he unlocks the car door. I thought that that would be the end of it, that once Clarkson got me to work he would leave me to my words, but as he helps me out of the car he tries to lead me towards the towering chapel attached to the school.

"The school's the other way," I chime.

"I'm very well aware. I called in sick for both of us, we're not going in today."

"Where do you get the perception that you have the authority to make decisions for me? I'm quite sick of you forcing your agenda on me, and quite frankly I don't think you realized what gossip will follow both of us due to your little call."

"I don't care what other people think Piper."

"Well I do."

"I don't understand why."

"I just do."

I fumble with my words, relying on simple answers to hide the looming depression that lingers in the crevices of my heart. How am I supposed to convey how I feel without sounding like hysteria inhabited my consciousness? How am I supposed to convey the pain without sounding like my livelihood revolves around flirting with the grim reaper? How am I supposed to convey how I feel without seeming dramatic, annoying, or hopeless? I can't. I can't say anything, so I hide behind by fumbled words, desperately trying to mastermind an escape from Clarkson's grasp.

"While I applaud your simplicity and attempt to avoid the real question, I think we need to go inside. Someone is waiting on us. Answers will just have to wait until later."

"I don't particularly want to go into the church Clarkson. I don't hold faith in my soul, I lost it a long time ago and can't seem to find it."

"That doesn't matter one bit. I'm not even Catholic, I'm a proud Baptist who hums hymns during mass while the choir seems to sing some cultic chant with no emotion. What you define yourself as has nothing to do with the location. A church is just a building where people go to get advice, to find themselves, and I believe that is exactly what you need."

"How do you know?" I say, and for the first time my voice holds no hatred, no sass, but curiosity masked in desperation.

"I see it in your eyes. My first expectations of you may have been wrong, but ever since I haven't been."

"I don't know if I should be offended or grateful at the the moment."

"Why don't you keep pondering that question and tell me what decision you've come to after we talk to Father Michael."

"Do we have to?"

Clarkson laughs and grasps onto my hand. It's funny how my hand folds perfectly into his and how I instantly feel slightly better with his presence. I guess I just can't stay mad at my dear Clarkson White. I guess I've made myself a best friend who won't let me go.

"Come on, let's get this over with."

# THEN:

There are some things that are never spoken about. My mother has seemed to fall into this damning category for me, but I'm not quite sure why. I grieved over her death differently, experienced more in-depth sorrow than I ever did before. My mother was my everything, but her memory was sullied by Charlie's misfortunes. I wasn't even given time to process what happened to her before I was forced to grow up. Due to this, I feel as if I need to conceal her memory, keep it hidden from everyone. I need her image to stop flickering in my subconscious, but I don't want anyone altering how I view her. I need to feel her music in my bones, but I don't want anyone to teach me how to. I want my mom back, I want to move on with my life with her as something other than a bitter feeling, but I'm not willing to let anyone help me grieve.

A woman who possessed a soul more gentle than a baby's didn't deserve such a horrific ending to her life's composition. She didn't even have a chance to resolve the last dissident note, causing a sour, unsettling feeling to forever permeate around her name. My mother was a woman who revolved her entire life around music and children. She was a woman who only knew how to love unconditionally.

Sometimes when my mind permits me to drift off, I see her before the nightmares come. She's the siren's wail, the calm before the storm. Every time I think of her, her shadow tries to protect me from myself. That's all a mother ever truly does, protect their child from themselves, but unfortunately my mother has done nothing but catalyze my self-destruction. She's my bad omen, she's the phantom that only lurks when hell is nearby. I love my mother, I do, but the more I think about her the more engulfed I become. It's as if she has to lurk in the crevices of my subconscious, in this sense she has to be nothing more than a lingering memory because anything more is simply too much. It's all too much.

"Baby girl, baby girl! Come here! Momma's got a surprise for you."

I liked to tell myself that I was her favorite, her sun, her moon, her world. There was nothing that she wouldn't do to make me happy, but she was like that to everyone she nurtured.

"But mom, I'm studying for my test tomorrow!" my voice ruptured and her hearty laugh carried into my bedroom from the den.

"Nonsense, you've worked for long enough. Come here, come here!"

Dragging my feet across uneven wooden floors, I trudged into the great room, also known as the gaping hole connecting the den and the kitchen. My mom was coated head to toe in paint the color of yellow daisies while her brown locks were thrown into a heap on top of her head by an oversized red bandana that too looked to be coated with the wall's dressing.

"What do you think about painting your room this color?" she smiled as she talked and at the same time she managed to adjust her glasses, a pair that aged her ten years in all the right ways. She looked a mess in paint splattered overalls and "artsy" clothing, yet she was picture perfect, worthy of a polaroid.

"Is that why you called me in here, mom?"

"No, of course not. I just wanted your opinion, my darling."

"I don't know, I think I'm more of a light pink sort of person. Something girly but mature. Something I can grow up with!"

"Oh, oh oh!" she threw up her paintbrushes and mocked me, "Something mature? Who are you little lady and what have you done with my offspring?"

"I'm serious!"

"I'll see what I can do. Now go look on the kitchen counter, I picked up something for you on the way home from the music store."

As I took the twenty steps that it took to walk into the kitchen my mother's smile pierced the back of my skull. She was so proud of this discovery, this great treasure for only me to possess.

"Come on Piper! Don't take all day!" she yelled and I jumped, causing her to laugh so hard that her body shook like an earthquake ran through her.

"Just because you said that I'm going to walk in slow motion!"

"Oh you just want your poor mother to die, don't you?"

I sighed and grabbed a brown package tied up with string before rushing back to my mother's side.

"Well go on, open it already!"

I carefully untied the package and unfolded the paper revealing a beautiful lavender leather bound book that made my heart swoon.

"Well! What do you think?"

"Oh momma, it's beautiful!"

I brought the book close to my chest and inhaled the scent of worn pages. It was absolutely lovely, but so is every book that's properly loved. Knowing that someone gave this book away so someone else could love it is one of the best things in the world. My mother loved books, but she never understood my deep fascination with them, and yet she never stopped me from pursuing the addictive hobby. I believe she understood what books meant to me is what music meant to her. Something that defines you, something that brings joy, something that brings clarity in a muddled world. Nothing is better than finding what makes you whole, what makes you unique. Most people search their entire life for their niche while my mother made sure I never gave up on mine.

"Oh good, I'm so glad you like it! Do you know what makes this book so special?

"No, what?"

My mother's lips curled into a smile and seconds later my dad waltzed into the room, making his grand return from work. As soon as he saw the book in my hand he rolled his eyes, and then kissed his beautiful bride.

"Why are you feeding her habit?" he asked, trying to suppress laughter.

"Because she's a young lady who needs literature that will empower her, my dear."

"How did I end up with marrying such a passionate feminist?"

"I'll tell you how. You chose me because I'm intelligent and a proponent of making this world better for everyone, and I plan on instilling the same principles in our daughter."

My mother shrugged as my father stared dumbfoundedly before going back to her painting and ceaseless humming. It took him a second to process but then a stupid grin spread across his face. In his eyes there was a dull twinkle, a pride that ran so deep that it could never be explained. My father loved how she stood up for what she believed in and never apologized, he loved her fire.

"I don't think she needs a book to learn those lessons my dear, not when she has you as a teacher."

"Don't flatter me!"

"But it's all I know how to do."

I miss my mother, she brought out the best in all of us. She taught me how to love, how to live, and how to make the best out of everything. Without her I've lost a sense of myself that I didn't even know existed, but I tend to suppress the feeling of loss. I tend to repress her memory. Her warmth brings me joy, but I don't like to think about her. I don't like to bring up the dead, it's too morbid, and it makes me too sad. The thought of her leaves a bitter taste in my mouth.

# NOW:

An intelligent man once wrote that people are made of string, and his characters dared to question what causes a person to unravel, for their strings to break. I as well have decided to figure this out, to figure out why I can't put myself back together like any normal person after something so basic as a wretched day. My hypothesis is that when forced to face the darkest parts of one's soul, a person goes into panic mode and completely shuts down, leaving a physical body without a subconscious or an able soul. I never thought that I would ever have to try out my hypothesis, but here I am, about to run an experiment on myself due to the one dimensional and stereotypical Clarkson White, and the unstereotypical young priest who I know absolutely nothing about, Father Michael.

"Miss Addison, Mr. White, it's a pleasure to see you both."

"I wish I could say the same Father," I flash a smile and Clarkson elbows me in the stomach causing me to double over. "God, Clarkson what was that for?"

"Mind the language Piper."

"I could knock your teeth out right now."

"Both of you stop quarreling, right now. Ms. Addison, you are not only an adult but a role model in this school, you need to stop acting like a child. Mr. White, stop egging her on. Now both of you, in my office."

"Just when I thought you were starting to become likable," I sneer, so silently that Father Michael doesn't hear my snide remark.

"I'm sorry to disappoint you, my dear colleague, but I remain the same. You, on the other hand, seem to change your opinion of me far too often for my enjoyment. Now, go on in before I have to drag you by your chemically processed hair," Clarkson says.

My mouth drops and Clarkson smiles before escorting me into the church. I don't get why he's pushing me toward religion, or why it even matters at all. I'm okay. I had a rough night. I had a bad day. It happens to the best of us, so why can't he just let my mistake go? I can't stand this. I told him before that I don't need him to save me. I am not his girl to fix. I need a friend, not a lover, not a professor, not a mentor, a friend. If Clarkson White can't figure out what a friend truly is then I just don't know. I like him by my side but I just can't deal with the back and forth. I thought friendship was supposed to be easy.

"I'm sorry, that last comment was a little too much, but come on Piper.  Just do this for me. I promise I'm not your enemy here."

"I don't want to, but I guess there's no turning back now."

I walk deeper and deeper into the quaint church and with every step my stomach churns. I know I've messed up but I don't want to let that define me. I can't let my mistakes make me who I am. I've done that my whole life, but enough is enough. The whole reason I moved to Belfast was to start over, I can't say that enough. I can't convince myself enough that this is all better than what I left behind. Bad times define me, but I can't let them do that anymore.

The aged floorboards crack underneath my feet, tiny rays of sunshine seep through stained glass windows bringing life to the room, and all the while a steel cross pulls focus. It seems out of place, an industrial piece of work juxtaposed in the gothic church. Maybe it's an extended metaphor for people like me; you can stand out and still belong. Churches are supposed to stand by that motto.

"My office is just this way," Father Michael says.

"I didn't realize we were going on such a long journey," I remark, "I would have packed a snack."

Father Michael laughs and opens the door to his office, which coincidentally is right next to the confessional. I shuffle in as Clarkson brings up the rear. His hand touches my shoulder, and when I flinch he just gives me a sympathetic smile.

"Everything is going to be okay," he whispers.

"Of course it is, why wouldn't it be?"

Clarkson doesn't reply, but his carmelized eyes darken and a tiny grimace creeps up on him. As I sit down on the wooden chair across from Father Michael, no more comfortable than a pew, I feel the grimace creep up on me too.

# THEN:

How does a person get lost in their mind? How does one clean out the cluttered thoughts, the things that keep them awake even in the darkest of hours? What makes the mind feel free even for a moment? These questions aren't hypothetical because I truly want to know the answer. Even as a kid my mind was scattered, and it's just gotten worse as I've aged. Maybe it's because I clung to whatever tiny remnants of my childhood I could find.

After reading twenty books in a row, questioning my sanity and the world itself, I wasn't in the best state of mind. It was as if a tornado ripped apart my subconscious, scattering memories and thoughts alike. Still I was determined to work in the bookshop, to prove myself worthy to a man who was as fragile as glass and small as a child. With dark circles around my eyes, a swirling mind, and a tattered heart, I made my way back to the place I was desperate to belong.

"Piper my dear, you look absolutely dreadful. Come in, come in, I was just about to open the store for the day. Would you like something to drink? Perhaps some coffee?"

Mr. Clint ushered me into the shop and sat me in my corner before probing me more.

"Do you have some tea? I think that's all I really need at the moment," I yawned and mumbled words manage to slip through.

"Of course, but I think you need a bit more than just tea. Have you been sleeping at all?" he asked.

"No, my mind is cluttered, my house is unsettled, and I have to sign up for online school sooner rather than later but I don't have a connection set up yet. My whole life is a mess, so instead of sleeping I just read. I read all of the books you gave me, and now I'm back, ready to talk, and ready to work."

"You're in no position to work my dear. Relax, I'll go get you a cup of some tea."

After he left me I felt my eyelids droop. My body began to slump, and within moments I was in a temporary state. Somewhere in between a sleep paralysis and reality my life blurred. My hands trembled, and the world turned dark but specs of light floated around like an 1980s rave. Soon enough my body mellowed, but I felt as if I was fluttering in thin air. I still don't know what happened after that. Thirty minutes of my life were erased from my memory completely, and when it returned I was sitting upright, sipping on a cup of watery tea.

"Piper? Are you going to answer me? Piper?"

"What? You said something to me?"

"Oh no, you're in worse shape than I thought. This is what happens when kids grow up too fast. All of your energy is gone, and now look at you. You're a moving corpse."

He shook his head, and left me once more. I tried to follow him, but my feet gave out leaving me to fall on my face. I was a hot mess. I wasn't prepared for the realities of the real world. No one gave me a crash course, I learned everything on my own by trial and error. When he came back he was holding a tray of cookies and forced me to eat one.

"You need to take better care of yourself. Just because you're on your own doesn't mean you get to stop living. Eat, sleep, dream, love. These are all of the things that are expected of you, nothing more. Don't worry about all of the little things, I'll help you, and you'll work here with me."

"Thank you, I don't deserve your kindness," I said.

"Nonsense, finish eating your food. I need help stocking my books."

I spent hours upon hours there, working through every break Mr. Clint tried to force me to take, working until I was pushed out the door every night. That store was my haven, and while I worked through the nights making my house a home I dreamed of coming back. I dreamed of having running water and lights, of a non sketchy toilet. I wanted to get my life together.

After a few months time, I saved up enough money to afford finishing my house without dipping into my college fund. Working helped me become an adult, it came me a sense of responsibility, one that wasn't forced upon me but chosen. I wish I could say that afterwards I got better, as if a distraction was all I needed, but life doesn't work out that way. Sleep was still a mystery to me, and just when I started to believed I had my life managed, nightmares would plague me leaving me to be nothing more than toxic combination of medicine and caffeine.

"Piper, are you still not sleeping?" Mr. Clint asked a month after helping me on my feet.

"I'm trying, but some things I just can't manage to fix, my mind just happens to be one of those things. It's quite unfortunate really, but what can I say? I'm a trooper."

"Oh my dear girl, I do worry about you."

"You have no need, Mr. Clint. I promise you I'm as right as rain."

"I don't think that's the truth. People with clear minds, people who aren't as mysterious as you, people who don't have monsters locked in their closets are able to sleep soundly."

"Well what do you want me to say, Mr. Clint? I moved here for a reason, and that same reason is why I'm alone pretending that I'm a real adult."

"Piper do you need to talk?"

"No, thank you, I've never been one to just open up, I'm more of an observer."

"Then how do you expect for anything to get better?"

"I don't, I just hope that they will eventually. Don't they say that time heals all wounds? Who am I to argue with that? It must be trite for a reason," I said.

"Perhaps, but the people who say that first have to come to terms with their past, but I don't think you have, now have you Piper?"

To this day, every time I replay our conversation in my head I think the same thing. *No, of course I haven't come to terms with my past.* I was barely able to comprehend the idea of death when my loved ones were stripped from me, how was I supposed to understand what it meant to grieve?

"Maybe one day I will, until then I think I can survive the lack of sleep. It builds character, and it's a small price to pay for a new life."

"I won't win this battle will I?" he asked, and a chuckle escaped his somber face.

"I don't think so," I smiled in reply.

"Well, do you at least do something with all those endless hours?"

"No, I mainly just listen to the record player I found at the flea market and wait to come back to work. I keep thinking that maybe the music will help, but it's gotten so bad that I know the number of skips and scratches on each track. I'll figure something out eventually, I always do and I always will."

"I think I may have an idea for you."

"And what would that be?" I asked.

"You should try writing. You never have to show the world your words, but writing will allow you to stop holding yourself back. It will help you feel alive. Books are good when you want to disappear, but if you want to live you have to let the words come out of you like a roaring volcano. Does that make any sense?"

I laugh, "I think it does, but I've never been much of a writer, I can never find the right words to say. I wouldn't even know where to begin."

"Then let the words come to you. When it's time they will, and when they do you'll thank me. Trust me, Piper, you were meant to live in this world, and you're going to do it whether you think you're ready or not."

His frail hand grasped my shoulder and he smiled at me. I touched his hand back and it felt as if I was holding onto air. That was the last time we ever talked about my past, after that moment he always tried his hardest to keep the conversation lively, though I could tell his life was slowly fading out. Years later, he died, from what, I couldn't say. His family refused to tell me anything; they treated me as if I was the one that caused his death. They never understood his love for his shop, so much so that they sold it to the highest bidder who turned the damned place into a bank. I wish I could go back and thank him. For helping me open my eyes, for helping me learn to read, to write, to live, and to grieve. For the first time in my life, I was allowed to fall apart without having to grow up and piece myself together. I wish I could tell him that all my war scars have faded, but I like to think that he knows I'm getting better every night as I use his typewriter. Mr. Clint, I'm trying. I'm going to live. I'm going to do it for us, old man. I'm going to do it. I have to.

# NOW:

My heart is crawling up my chest. My throat is beginning to dry up, and all the while I have four eyes peering at me, waiting for me to crack. Forcing myself to sit as straight as possible, I do what I do best, stay silent and let my mind wander in endless loops. What have I done? What has happened to me? One misstep and my whole identity seems to have fallen at the seams.

"Miss Addison, your friend came to me in confidence and we're both a bit concerned about you. Do you know why that could be?"

"No Father, I don't," I reply, and avoid looking both men in the eye.

Lord only knows what they think of me. They probably see me as a drunk, a loner, unstable, straddling between life and death. They probably believe that I have no right working with books and even more so children.

"Should I explain, or would you like your friend to?"

"I'm not sure I want to hear much from either of you. I don't think you understand my situation, and so you believe that the problem at hand is bigger than it truly is," I mumble.

"Piper, please. Let him talk," Clarkson begs and my nose scrunches in disgust.

"Both of you know my stance on religion, well at least Father Michael does, and so I'd like to politely ask you to hold your opinions lest they leave out religion all together. I'd like to get back to work as quickly as humanly possible, I'm still new here and haven't earned my keep, I wouldn't like to get fired."

"Of course not Miss Addison," Father Michael says.

"Please, call me Piper, if this is to be a normal discussion we should drop our titles and talk one on one."

"Fine then Piper, if that's how you would like to be addressed I wouldn't want to offend you. Is it safe to assume that you'll call me Michael then?" he says.

"Jesus Christ, can we just move on already! We know each other's names, and we are familiar with each other. She knows this isn't a casual visit so can't we just tell her the truth?" Clarkson blurts out and Father Michael cringes ever so slightly.

I can sense the tension between the two men, both may be on the same side, but they each have a different approach to handling their dilemma. For some reason, Clarkson is on edge, even more so than I usually am. He won't sit still, fidgeting with everything from his tweed jacket to his glasses. I just want to grab his hands and tell him to stop, to stop worrying about me. I know, I'm unpredictable. I know my mood changes quicker than leaves can change colors in the fall, but he keeps trying. I'm this way to protect myself, to keep prying eyes from tearing me down, but he doesn't get it. He refuses to believe what's in front of him, he refuses to believe that the mess he sees isn't a gem in disguise.

"Clarkson White, I thought we came to a mutual understanding about how we were going to handle this." Father Michael almost radiates anger. You wouldn't be able to tell it by his mellow demeanor but I can tell by the subtle movements. His hand is clenched around a pencil, his foot keeps tapping ever so lightly so he doesn't draw any attention to it, and his whole body jerks just enough for me to notice anytime he says anything with passion. It seems as if the perfectly well-rounded preacher has a character flaw; he's human after all.

"Now, now, boys. Settle down, I'm nothing to fight about," I say sarcastically.

"Piper, I'm trying to be serious here, and I need for you to do the same. Alright?" Father Michael asks.

"Of course, Michael. I never meant to be impolite."

"I know you didn't. Now, Clarkson tells me that you've been hard on yourself lately. Why is that? What's going on?"

"I've always been hard on myself. Ever since I was little I have striven towards self-love, but in that process I have somehow turned myself into a perfectionist who loathes her own flaws. It seems absurd, but it has turn me into a goal-oriented person, and now I can use that self loathing to motivate me."

"Piper, this isn't an interview. You can relax, this is a safe place here."

"You can say that all you want to, Michael, but I am not comfortable in any religious institution."

"And why is that? All religions were based upon bringing peace to this world, and all churches strive towards that same goal. This building was meant to better you, to better us all."

"Religion may have been founded on good principles, but the moment people like you started to use 'God's words' to justify your hatred of others was the moment I decided that places like this will never be safe for me. Now if you'll excuse me, I need to go to work."

I start to walk out the church, and I won't look back at the two men exchanging troubled gazes. I know what I'm doing. My memories aren't faulty. I can trust in myself. I am all I have, and so I have to start accepting that and take care of the only thing that matters in my life, me.

"Piper! Piper, please wait."

Out of the corner of my eye, Clarkson comes running out of the church and stops me at the school's rotting wooden door. He keels over, but the entire time he keeps one hand on the door knob and his eyes on me all the while trying to force air back into shriveled lungs.

"What is it Mr. White?"

"You don't have to go through this alone," he says.

"I'm sorry, I don't know what you're talking about."

I flash him a smile and move his unfit body out of my way, but as the distance between us grows, the churning in my stomach does as well. I know Clarkson, I don't have to be alone, but even when you're there loneliness is all I feel. I know Clark, you won't let go, but you'll never understand me. *I know Clark. I know.* I just wish you would leave me alone.

# THEN:

I am not a good person. I am not religious, I am not friendly, nor artistic, nor talented. I am as useful as a particle of dust. I try to justify my actions with faulty logic. I try to convince myself that I am not as bad as my brother, but at the end of the day I am flawed. I guess that's why it took me over a year and a half to tell my father the truth about where I was living.

I can remember the day clearly, it's ingrained into the back of my mind, stuck there like a stain that just refuses to fade. It was a sunny day without a cloud in the sky, but I felt as if a raincloud was hanging above my head. I couldn't shake the deceit. I felt it growing with every call back home. I would disguise my phone number, refuse to skype or facetime, and even pretend to always be out with friends just to avoid him, just to craft my perfect life. Lying was absolutely exhausting and with time I grew tired of it. Once upon a time, my father knew the real me, and our bond was different than the one I had with my mom and Charlie. My dad understood me, he kept me safe while my mom was the one who shaped me through passion. He was my guardian angel, and Charlie was supposed to be his apprentice. With time and grief we grew apart. I thought that nothing could break a familial bond as a child. I thought that even the

313

most inexcusable action could be forgiven if it was done by someone you love, but children don't know anything. I didn't know anything at all.

My residual raincloud drowned me, it pulled at my strings. I knew I owed my dad at least a call, and I knew he would accept my lies because he wanted to believe that I was getting better. He wanted to believe that at least one of us was going to be able to move on. My dad wanted to be optimistic. He wanted to be a good man, and a good father towards me. I don't blame him for what happened, but I just wanted him to be there for me after everything happened. I needed him. I needed him to raise me, to love me when no one else would, but instead I got an absentee father whose soul died right along side his wife's and his only son's.

"Hi Dad, it's me. Piper…"

My voice raised an octave while my knee bounced up and down. I wanted to convince myself that he would understand, that he would be happy that I've made a life for myself, but how much hurt can a person take?

"Piper! It's so great to hear from you my sweet sweet girl."

His words slurred as he spoke, and I could only imagine the smell of booze that traced his breath. It's almost comical to think that prior he never took a sip of the damned thing. Since the accident my father craves it like a newborn baby craves their mother's milk. It's disgusting, but I don't have any resources to help myself, let alone him.

"How are you, Dad?"

"I'm holding on. Your uncle is still trying to find me another girl, but I keep trying to tell him that you're the only girl I need," He laughed and my heart wrenched.

"Dad, you need to move on. I don't want you to be sad your whole life. You deserve all the happiness in the world. You deserve so much better."

The words escaped my mouth quietly, so quietly that I barely heard them myself. My dad paid my words no mind though. He never did when I talked about his life. He thought that he was coping. My father truly believed that he was a survivor and that's all he had to do to make his life worth anything.

"Did I ever tell you the story about Charlie breaking your favorite tutu when you were little? I don't think I did, but then again I don't remember much these days…"

"Dad, stop. Please. Please, you don't have to do this for me."

"Do what, Piper?"

"Pretend to be brave," I said.

All of a sudden his act slipped away, and his anger surfaced. I knew he blamed himself. I knew he put on a brave face for me, I just never expected it to be so bad. I never wanted to look beyond the surface of his depression, I never wanted to see the man I always loved. I wanted to run away and take charge of myself. I wanted to save myself before I became just like him.

"I am not pretending to be anything! I am trying to make the best out of my life, but you wouldn't know that. You're gone. You've left me. You were all I had and now look at me."

His voice faded out and all I could hear was him breathing deeply. He did that everytime he got emotional. He would try to breathe his problems away, or at least until he control himself. My father was not a man who believed that emotions were feminine, but he hated showing any emotions that didn't show off his charming personality.

"I'm sorry. I didn't mean to upset you Dad, I was just calling to talk," I said.

"You don't do that enough," he mumbled.

"I know. I know. It's because I'm afraid of how you'll react."

"React to what? I know you've been spending Charlie's funds and I know you're about to burn a hole through yours with tuition."

"Money has nothing to do with the truth, unfortunately."

316

"Then what is it, Piper? What do I owe the pleasure of your voice to?"

"Promise me you won't get mad first. I need to know you'll be okay even after I hang up."

"Piper, what the hell? I am a grown ass man. I know how to wake up, and live. I am fine, I will be fine. I am not as broken as you think I am."

"Dad, I didn't mean it like that."

"I know. I know you just want the best for me, and that's all I want for you too. You're my princess, Piper. You can tell me anything."

"I'm not with Grandma and grandpa, and I never was."

"What do you mean?"

Neither of us spoke for awhile. I was surprised in myself. I didn't think I would have been so easy to just tell him the truth. Lying became almost natural to me, but at the end of the day my dad deserved to know. No matter how angry he became, he deserved to know that I was okay, that I would be okay in the end.

"On the bus ride up to their house, there was a stop in this tiny town called Belfast. It was the kind of town that no one would ever find me in. It's the type of place where people just disappear.

After I stepped off the bus, I never looked back, and now, somehow, this place has become my home."

"What else about your life is a lie, Piper?"

His voice turned even and cold. He sounded more sober in that moment than he did years before, when alcohol was nothing more to him than a bitter man's drug.

"I don't know where to begin," I replied and tried to mock his cool tone, though nerves couldn't help but slip through the cracks.

"I don't even know what to say to you right now. I'm really disappointed in you."

"I'm sorry dad, but I knew there was no way for me to get better unless I started over completely. I needed everyone to be ignorant to who I am. I was tired of being an outcast and being pitied."

"I tried to give you that opportunity and you took advantage of the situation."

"I didn't mean to. I just did what I thought would be best. I listened to my heart for once, and look where it's gotten me."

"Piper, do you even have friends? Do you even go out and live? Are you homeless? Is that why you asked for more money? Oh my god, I am a horrible father. First I drove my son to his death, sent my wife out to hers, and now you? I tried to make things better. I

318

wanted us to be happy, Piper. All I wanted was a goddamned happy ending."

By this point in our conversation both of us were crying. My tears were silent, and his were ugly and loud. This juxtaposition alone describes how we both preferred to grieve. My father wanted the world to know his pain, while I just wanted the world to simply go away.

"Don't say that. You didn't cause this. You didn't cause the end of our family. We're still alive and we're still a team. I don't care if I'm a thousand miles away, you are still my dad, and I love you. I don't care how drunk you get, or how sad you are. I will always love you and try to protect you. That's why I lied to you. I just hope you understand why I did what I did."

"I wish I did. I really do."

He hung up on me, yet his conversation clung to my heart for months. I believe it was almost a year before I heard from him again, and even now our relationship is fragmented. He was so hurt. It was as if I shattered the remaining pieces of his heart. I broke my father. I broke the only person who understood the pain I was going through. I drew him in close with distance and fairy tales, but in the end I pushed him out of my life with the truth, just like he shut me out after the accident.

"Hi Dad, it's me. I'm just calling to catch up. I hope you're not still mad at me. I really am sorry. I wanted you to think things would be alright in the end. Everyone deserves a happy ending, and I wanted you to believe in mine. Please forgive me. Please call me back."

" Dad, I love you, I hope you're doing okay, and in case you're wondering I'm doing okay too. I may have lied to you about a lot but I never did about that. I'm better. I'm not fixed, but I'm better, and isn't that all you ever wanted for me? I'm sorry. Call me back when you're ready. I'll be waiting."

# NOW:

Inside the school, a wave of terror washes over me. I can't move. I can't speak. For some reason the walls seem to be moving in closer. I feel as if I'm hallucinating. Maybe that's why the air seems thinner. When Clarkson stumbles in the building after me, tremors shoot up and down my spine. I try to control myself but I can't. I can't do anything at all but stand into space and watch myself unravel.

"Piper, are you okay? Earth to Piper?"

Clarkson clutches onto my shoulders and shakes me as gently as humanly possible. I wish I could tell him to go away. I wish he would stop coming to my rescue every time I need help. I can get through this. I will get through this. I can do it. I just have to calm down. I have to do it. I can't do it. I can't do it.

"Piper, I'm going to sit you down alright? Come on, shift your weight on me."

I shake my head and focus on my contracting lungs. I need air. I need to breath. I need to. I need to do something, but I can't leave.

"Come on, it's okay. It's going to be alright."

Clarkson gives me his hand, and my clammy palm latches on to his.

"Take me to my library," I stutter, "take me to the kids."

"I will. After."

He sits me down on the worn carpet and my face droops into my palms. I can't stop crying. I can't get rid of the fear. It's everywhere, but nowhere. It has to be irrational, it has to be, but why then does my body accept it as truth? I feel as if I've missed a step on the stairs. As if I'm stuck in a dream where I'm endlessly falling. Clarkson tries to keep talking to me, but I don't want to listen. I need to move around, and get to work. I need something to focus on. I need to pretend it's over until it truly does end.

"I think I'm okay now," I mumble and try to mask a stutter.

"Piper, it's okay you have time. Everyone thinks you're at home," he replies.

"Well, if you really want to help me please tell Mrs Cathy that I'm here and if any teachers want to drop off their kids I will be opening the library in twenty minutes."

I try to stand up, but my legs wobble and I almost fall. Clarkson reaches for me, but I snatch my arm away.

"If you really want to help, you'll do that for me. Okay?" I ask.

322

Clarkson nods, and I stumble down the steps into my haven. I'm safe in any place where there are books. I have to be. Books can't judge you, or hurt you. Books are abstract worlds. They hold places where I am not a person, but a mere spectator that ceases to exist on the last page. I am safe there, and I will be better when I make it.

Once I make it away from Clarkson I feel the air pump back into my shriveled lungs. My body won't stop shaking though. I have too much energy pulsating through my veins to relax, but it's better. I am in a better state. Better is okay, better is something that I can live with. Better is something that I have to live with. In the library, I collapse in my reading chair, and try to clear my mind but I can't. I've worked myself up too much and negated any possible help that medicine could give me. I'm a freak that's buzzed on her own stress because I'm too afraid to talk about my past and let anyone in. I fear the truth and I fear the repercussions of people knowing who I am.

A half hour passes and my jitters fade. I'm back to a state where I can work without drawing too much attention to myself, but not back to the point where I don't jump when I walk on a creaky floorboard under me or when I hear the children running down the hallway singing songs. I'm in my head and it's driving me insane. It's no surprise that I knock several books off the shelf while attempting to dust when I hear Mr. Wolff call my name.

"Miss Addison, my dear girl ,I thought you were sick today?"

"I ate some bad shrimp last night and stayed up very late, but I want to be dependable and I feel bounds better than I did before."

"What did I tell you about lying to me?" his voice raises and I think he expects me to cower.

"I'm not lying sir. If I wanted to play hooky I wouldn't have shown up at all."

"Very well, but I'm watching you."

"I wouldn't expect anything less, sir."

"Good, now enough interrogation. We need to discuss Emma once again."

"What for? I thought we discussed her doing an independent study with me prior," I say.

"Yes, but that is not what I mean. I received a call from her parents this morning saying that she never came home, but that she supposedly got a ride from you. Is that correct?"

"Why yes, but she messaged me saying she was home safe."

"Well she never got home, and her parents are concerned, as you would be if your child went missing."

"I'm sorry, sir, I don't know what you want me to do."

"You're going to have to find that little girl, or your ass is fired. I don't need any parents suing this school so you need to take responsibility."

Mr. Wolff didn't even give me a chance to answer before he stormed out, leaving me to my fear. I didn't know that my words would cause such a mess. I didn't mean to hurt her. Emma Mackenzie is essentially me as a child, and I guess I forgot how easily offended I was. She trusts no one and expects no one to help her out. I don't blame her, I do the same thing, but doesn't she understand the longer you keep to yourself the more you self destruct? It doesn't matter if a person is an introvert or extrovert, we were designed to be social in some form or another. We were designed to confide in each other. If she doesn't learn now she'll be like me, a woman composed of childish tendencies, book attachments, and bottles of anti-anxiety medication.

I can't let her be by herself. I could care less for my job, jobs are replaceable but I need to help that little girl. I don't know why I feel so obliged to, but I have to. I have to. Emma Mackenzie I will help you. I will prevent you from becoming me. I will.

It seems as soon as I get to work I'm leaving again because moments after talking to the Big Bad Wolff, I'm running down the dust covered cinder block hallways in an attempt to get Clarkson's car keys from him. It hasn't been too terribly long since we got to work, so hopefully he hasn't sent his substitute away, or maybe he'll just give me the keys, but I doubt it.

"Mr. White, do you have a moment? I need to speak to you."

"Of course Ms. Addison, give me a moment to pass out the worksheet for today and I will right there. Is everything alright?"

"Everything is going to be okay, but I am going to need you sooner rather than later."

Clarkson arches his eyebrows, but when he sees the color drained from my face and a maddening spark twinkling in my eye he simply nods, and motions for me to wait just outside the door. I feel like a kid again, waiting to be yelled at by the teacher. I can't help but continuously peer into his classroom through the cracked glass in the door. He's running up and down the uneven black and white titles, weaving through wooden desks trying to answer as many questions as possible. His face is getting so red, it's even starting to match the blush paint on the walls. When he looks my way I duck and I swear I hear his laugh on the other side of the door. He wasn't supposed to know I was looking.

"Piper, what on earth are you doing?"

He opens the door and finds me sitting on the floor, trying to look as casual and unembarrassed as humanly possible.

"Just waiting for you."

"On the floor?"

"Still trying to compose myself."

"I can tell."

He helps me up, crosses his arms, and just waits for me to speak.

"Well... um, when I told you that I don't need you help I kind of lied."

"You think? What on earth led you to that conclusion!" he says sarcastically.

"Don't be cross with me. Emma ran away and I have to find her. I need your car keys. I promise I'll get you after work."

"Piper, what happened?"

"I don't know where to begin."

"Well then you can tell me after we go find that little girl."

"But your students?"

"The sub hasn't left, it's okay. Let me just get my coat."

"Clarkson, you don't have to do this."

"Don't, Piper. I'm not doing this for you. I'm doing this for Emma. I'm still mad at you. I'm so tired of pretending like I'm okay with you pushing me away. You're so self absorbed that you don't even realize that you chose to be alone. You picked this life, you have to deal with the consequences, and quite frankly, I'm tired of trying."

He leaves for a moment and lingers inside his classroom. He wants me to feel guilty, but little does he know. I'm not as shallow as he thinks, I do care about him and Emma and this whole situation. I know what I've done but he can't see that. Hell, he sees what he wants to see. Our friendship is dysfunctional at best, but what am I going to do? If I continue to go through life alone I'm going to end up living a life filled with sour memories and bottled up nerves, but at the same time I've managed to convince myself that if I let anyone close they'll just run away. Wouldn't you? Who would ever love a girl that carries a tragic childhood around like a weight on her chest? Who would ever love a girl that is so self aware that she doesn't even know how to help herself? Who would ever love me? No one, but it's not my place to complain.

# THEN:

The memories of my family come in waves. Some memories are whole while others are just fragmented pieces. Sometimes when the dreams seem too perfect I doubt that the memories ever existed. Nostalgia distorts our view of the past and its reality, and that fact makes me uneasy. Have I oversimplified the murder of my mother? Have I excused my brother's crime? Have I repressed memories to keep me safe, to keep me sane? I'm not sure.

When I first moved from home, the hallucinations were the worst. My family seemed to always be there. My dad's lighthearted chuckle, my brother's obnoxious scream, and my mother's melodic hums made up my scenery. It seemed to be that the noises in the woods were them, no matter how crazy that sounds. Some nights I found myself following the noises, leading me deeper and deeper through the trees. I thought that if I wandered enough I would wake up and realize the second half of my life was all a terrible dream. I thought that I would wake up and realize that my family was just around the corner.

"Charlie? Mom? Dad? Is that you all?"

My feet were covered in mud as I trudged through endless trails. The cold wind caused me to wrap a sheet around my arms, pulling it close to keep me safe and warm. Every time I heard a leaf crunch I jumped in the air and turned around, with the hopes that I would see them. I knew it was delusional. I knew it wasn't realistic, but I couldn't stop myself.

"Piper!"

My name echoed off the towering trees, and I came to a stand still. He was there. He was always there watching me. His voice was always the one that left me on edge. His voice was always the one that kept me up at night hoping it would all end. The cause of my misery and pain decided to stick around and watch my life unfold.

"Why are you still here? Why can't you ever leave me alone!" I said.

"Do you remember that story mom used to tell you when you were a little kid?"

"Charlie, please I need you to go away. I can't sleep with you here. I need to start over, please just let me move on. You're killing me."

I watched his face twinge, but he wouldn't reply to my pleas. He enjoyed holding a one-sided conversation. Charlie enjoyed pretending that everything was okay, that our lives were back to normal.

"The day you were born she let me hold you. I was so afraid I was going to drop you I started crying. Mom just wrapped both of us in her arms and started singing to calm me down. When I finally stopped crying, she made me promise that I would always be there for you, that I would always keep you safe. I'm going to keep you safe, Piper. I have to. I need to."

"Charlie, please. Go."

"Piper, what happened to mom's guitar? Did you take it when you left? I miss hearing her play, and I miss you failing at playing."

"I-I can't do this."

I turned on my heels and ran back to my house, never looking back. His voice didn't leave, but he faded into the background. He stopped calling for me eventually, but I knew he was out there. I heard his laugh, his cry. I heard our memories come to life and die. I felt haunted. I felt insane, yet I never spoke a word about my delusions and simply passed them off as insomnia taking a toll on my subconscious.

At one point, I would triple the amount of medicine I took a day just to stop it all. I know that it's bad, but I was more ill than I cared to admit. I just wanted to believe that I could push through. If you talk about seeing and hearing people they lock you up in a mental hospital and throw on a straight jacket, but once you've had a traumatic experience no one seems to object to writing an endless stream of prescriptions for PTSD pills as if they are the cure to any mental issue.

"Just call the office whenever you need a refill and we'll call it in! If the attacks get worse or more frequent please let us know so we can up your dosage. Have a nice day, and stay strong. You will get through this, and we're here to help you do just that."

Every doctor told me the same thing, and so I stopped feeding into their attempts at apathy, and I ignored all the pamphlets that tried to tell me how I was supposed to grieve. Every person reacts differently to traumatic situations, so I didn't think my pain was something that was to be simplified. I decided early on that my path to 'recovery' would not be a cookie-cutter program that sounds as effective as those seen on tv weight loss commercials that promise to help you lose ten pounds in seven days.

I know that moving on is about coming to terms with the past. It's about accepting your losses and pain. It's about accepting the shitty things that made you you, and understanding that you'd be nothing without it. I know what it will take to get better, but I'm still sitting at the bottom of the mountain with the little girl I used to be, listening to the hums of my family's dead souls. My problem is, if I know what it takes to get better, why do I keep failing at actually feeling that way?

# NOW:

I feel as if there is no sense of urgency in Clarkson's driving. The car is dead silent, and Clarkson's eyes scan the roads slowly opposed to me, who is frantically processing everything in my view. Tonight, the town is dead, not even the bay's waters move. It's as if the world is holding its breath, waiting to see if the little girl is still alive.

"I can't believe you got into this mess," Clarkson says.

I divert my eyes away from the window and a look of disgust plasters itself across my face.

"Do you think I meant to do this? I care about Emma, I would never do anything to hurt her. I made a mistake and I'm trying to fix it."

Clarkson slams on the breaks, and my body crashes into the dashboard. Before I even have the chance to give him my mind, he let's me have it.

"You're an ungrateful piece of shit, do you know that? You turn away anyone who wants to help you, and you push away everyone that needs you. I swear to god, once we find Emma I am done with you. I never want to see your face again."

"Wow Clarkson, I'm surprised you have some sass in you after all. I thought you were just a little cry baby that I could clearly walk all over!" I say sarcastically.

"Don't Piper. I'm done with your games."

"I'm not playing any game! Hell, just let me out the damn car and you will never have to see me again. I don't need your bullshit."

"No, I'm not letting you run away from yet another one of your problems you're going to see this one through."

"Um, excuse me?"

How dare he? How dare he think that he has me pegged. He doesn't know shit about me. I'm just his mystery girl that waltzed into his life on accident. He imagined me to be something that I'm not, it's not my fault that I failed to meet his expectations. I'm not a fictional character, I am a human being. I can not be defined into some simplified description. I have strengths and weaknesses that define me. Maybe I'm not ready to share my life story. Maybe I'm not ready to be vulnerable again. Why does that make him better than me? Why does that justify his constant interrogation of my life?

"I've figured you out, Ms. Addison. You think that dying your hair and rejecting mainstream culture makes you blend into the background. You think that rejecting any notion of you having a problem makes you stronger when you probably moved to this town to escape reality. I've figured you out. I see right through you, and the fact that you think you're better than me sickens me. You're no better than any of those people at work that make fun of you daily. How does that make you feel? Are you even capable of feeling anything at all, Piper?"

"Please stop. You don't know anything at all. You don't know me," I whisper. He's getting to me. He's somehow managed to peg me and it scares me. I don't know how he knows so much, or how I let him get so close to me.

"And why don't I?"

"Because I don't want you to. I don't want anyone to know the real me. Alright? Just leave me alone. You have more important things to worry about than me, so please. I don't care what you think, I'm sick of caring what people think, let me live. Let me be."

"Piper..." This time it's him who regrets his words.

"Don't."

He reaches for my shoulder but I turn away from him. I don't want to give him the satisfaction of seeing me cry. I don't want to give him the satisfaction of seeing me break down because it's true, he knows me.. He knows me better than I know myself and it's sickening.

"I never meant..." His voice trailed off and anger bubbled over in me. He didn't mean to say what he did? He never meant to make me upset? How the hell did he think I was going to react to him telling me that I couldn't feel? How the hell was I supposed to react to someone telling me that I'm as worthless as I feel?

"You never meant to do what Clarkson? You're so desperate to learn how I feel that you're willing to tear me down? Is this what you wanted? A broken shell? Well congratulations, you won. You've defined me."

Clarkson pulls the car off to the side of the road and puts it in park. When I try to escape he grabs my hand, and then wipes the tears streaming down my face as I fail to compose myself.

"I never meant to hurt her," I whisper.

"I know, and I never meant to hurt you. I just wanted you to be okay, Piper. I just wanted to be your friend, you know that right? You have to know that."

"I do, I just wish you didn't try so hard."

"Why?" he asks.

"Because you make it so hard to push you away."

"You don't have to push me away. Let me be there for you, let me be your friend."

"We- we should get back on the road. We need to find Emma."

"Piper."

"What?"

"I'm sorry."

"I forgive you."

He grabs onto my hand, and this time my fingers intertwine in his. A sad smile creeps up on both of us; we want to have hope but it's been drained out of both of us. He's lost faith in me and I've lost faith in the world. When he let's go the car pulls into the road and we go back to filling our roles. Clarkson is back to being the world's sweetheart, and I'm back to being the cold-hearted girl with a pathetic backstory.

Hours pass and the scenery stays the same, although, the sun is beginning to flirt with the earth while the moon comes out to play. I can't find her anywhere. I imagine her cold, sad, and alone. I see her like I saw myself. Running doesn't get you anywhere, and apparently hiding won't either. Come back Emma, come back. We can get through this together.

"It's starting to get really dark. I don't know where else to check. We've been to the park, done circles around the bay and downtown, where else could she be?" Clarkson asks.

338

"I don't know, where do people go to disappear in this town?"

"I don't think you can in this town, it's too damn small; you'll always be found."

"Then why can't we find Emma?"

"I don't know. I'm trying to think of something."

"Is it possible she went to the next town over or something?"

"Not unless she took the train. There isn't another town nearby for miles."

"Then it looks like we better go to the train station."

The whole ride to the station I hold my breath. If she's not there I don't know what I'll do. I'm afraid that, if we don't find her, Emma Mackenzie will stop existing as a person and become a cautionary tale, what happens to little girls when they feel as if they have no one, what happens when they are no one.

"What happens if we don't find her?" I ask.

"We'll find her."

"Clark..."

"We will."

When the car pulls into the train station, I jolt out of the car and run down to the platform. Clarkson tries to follow, but I yell at him to stay put. If she's here it has to be between the two of us. I may not

339

be able to continue going on life alone, but I know this situation has to be handled in exactly that way, alone.

"Emma? Emma? Are you there?"

I pull out my phone, using it as a flashlight as I wander down empty train tracks and uneven platforms. The trains barely ever run anymore, and if Emma did manage to catch a train there's no one here to tell me where she went.

"Emma! Please, I'm trying to help you."

By the time I reach the last platform my body is as cold as ice, and any traces of sun are long and gone. The seasons are starting to change once more, with fall merging into winter quicker than it really should. Maybe I missed her, maybe she faded into the background.

"Emma! Emma Mackenzie!"

In the corner of my eye I see a figure curled into a ball. I take off running, but it's not her. I try to climb back on the tracks but I end up faceplanting, causing blood from my noise to trickle onto the ground. After forcing myself back on my feet, and wiping the blood off using my conveniently white shirt, I trudge on. Calling her name, rushing up to things that aren't there. Emma where the hell are you?

"Emma. Please, I need you to be okay," I whisper.

"Piper, come on it's time to take you home," Clarkson says.

"No, no go back in the car. I'm not ready. I have to find her. She has to be here."

"We've done all we can for today. We'll go out looking again after work tomorrow."

"They say if you can't find someone after the first twenty four hours it's very unlikely that they'll be found," I say.

"Statistics have a large margin of error. Don't worry there is always an outlier, and that outlier will be Emma."

Clark puts his hand on my back and guides me towards the car, it isn't until we're under the fading streetlights that he sees what state I'm in. The blood is no longer pouring out of my nose, but it's all over me. It's dried on my face, my once clean shirt, and traces are splattered on my knees, but then again I could have also skinned my knees and not noticed at all. I mean, it's possible, but whatever, it's casual.

"What happened to you?" he asks.

"What? You mean this? Oh nothing I just got into a fight with the ground and lost. It's no big deal, I'll be okay."

Clark starts laughing hysterically and I go to scrunch up my nose in disgust but it hurts too much. Of course that fact just makes him laugh even more.

"It's not funny!" I cry, trying to hold back my own chuckles.

"Yes, yes it is."

"Okay, maybe a little bit. But, just a little!"

"Whatever helps you sleep at night, Piper."

I smile at him, and show off the warrior scars of a five year old. He winks at me and I recline as far back as his car will let me. I like moments like this, when Clark and I aren't fighting, when we truly are friends. It's nice to have someone to laugh with. I can't remember the last person to make me happy before him, is that bad?

"Piper, wake up. We're here."

"Huh?"

I brush the hair off my face and rub my eyes only for them to adjust to utter darkness.

"You're home. Go get some rest, I'll see you tomorrow morning, okay?"

"Alright, but will you give me a ride again tomorrow? I just don't want to look for her alone... I don't want to be alone anymore."

"Of course, I'll text you when I'm on my way."

"Thank you, Clark," I say.

"Don't mention it."

I watch Clark drive off before I go inside, lingering on the front porch for longer than I really should. I don't understand how our relationship can change so fast. We go from hating each other to being best friends within a few hours, but it feels like longer. I feel as if I need him in my life. I need someone to confide to. I need someone to come to me and tell me about the word of the day, or rant to me about how there aren't any motivational posters for a classroom that aren't disgustingly tacky. I need a friend like that, and I need Clark to bear with me until I can get my shit together.

When I walk into the room I plop down on my favorite writing chair, and as soon as I try to start writing, I hear her voice.

"Miss Addison?"

I jump out of my chair and there she is, cowering at my doorway. Dirt covers her face, and her mud colored hair is tangled in the wind. What happened to her? And why the hell did she come to me first?

"Emma, where the hell. Oh, sorry, I mean... no I meant what I said. Where the hell have you been?"

"I had to get away. I had to clear my mind."

"Then why didn't you go home first?"

"I thought I owed you an apology. You probably got in trouble because of me and I never meant to take advantage of your kindness."

"I'm just glad you're okay. Come in, you need to clean up before I take you home."

"I don't know if I should," she says and her voice trails off.

I eye her up and down and fear still hides behind her eyes.

"It's okay, I'm not mad at you. You're safe here."

She reluctantly shuts the door behind her, but stands no more than five feet away from it, just incase she has to make a close escape.

"You and I are a lot alike, you know that right?" I ask.

"How so?"

"We both think that we can get through this world on our own, and instead of trusting someone we both go to literature, as if that can solve all of our problems."

"I don't think that I can get through life alone, but I don't have a choice. No one likes me."

"Isn't it funny that even though people like being alone, no one likes being lonely," I say.

She gives me a small smile, and I wrap a blanket around her shivering body before ushering her towards the bathroom to clean up. It's going to be okay, Emma. You don't know it yet, but it will. It's going to be better for both of us.

"Can you take me home now?"

"Of, course, but I need you to promise me one thing."

"What's that?"

"Whenever you feel sad like this again, you have to go talk to someone. I don't want you to grow up and be like me. Books are good things, but they can't replace a good friend and they can't listen to you when all you want to do is cry."

"But, books are the only things that make me happy, and all I want is to be happy," she cries.

"I do too, that's all anyone wants, but we can't be happy all the time."

"I wish we could."

"I do too, Emma. I do too."

# THEN:

My teenage rebellion came in many shapes and forms. Changing my hair color, sneaking out, and shutting the world out were just some of my shining moments. It got so bad that my Uncle would literally pick my body off my bed, throw me in the car, and drive me to a psychiatrist. They thought it would help me, but it just made me worse off.

"So, Piper. I heard about what happened to your mother and brother. Do you want to talk about that today, or would you like to talk about something else?"

My straight by the book psychiatrist was obnoxious to say the least. Nothing about that woman was genuine, not her fake empathy, and certainly not her bottle blonde hair. Hell I'm pretty sure her glasses were just for show as well, she liked to fix them every time she wanted to make a point as if they gave her authority.

"Not really. I don't like talking much these days," I answered.

"And why is that?"

"People get through things differently. My father grieves, others pretend to go through the motions of life, and I stay to myself. I live in my head."

I feel as if my so called emo phase lasted longer than it should've. Poetry about dropping off the face of the earth was too frequent in my life, so was having characters commit mass murder. I understand now that my writing was a twisted way of understanding what happened to me. Hiding in my own subconscious felt safe, no one could judge me in my own mind, and there I was allowed to be as wicked as I pleased.

She held the gun in her hand, and for the first time that night, she was entirely calm. She wanted revenge, she wanted to cause all hell for what they did to her. Locking the gun into place, she made her move, calling her suitors out to play, luring them into a trap. As soon as they were close enough, she fired her gun, launching each bullet in their hearts.

As a sea of red poured out of their chests, she smiled, thinking about the ruby red kiss she placed on each bullet. It was her token, her signature, letting people know to fear her. Little did she realize, she was not a girl to be feared, she was simply a girl with a jumbled soul and twisted mind. She was a victim of her surroundings.

Soon enough, the body count soared. One, two, three, four, five. The pile of dead boys left the grass stained and the world quiet. By the time she released her last bullet, her facade faded. Her body trembled as she lowered her gun, her brain was beginning to connect the dots, there was no way for her to hide. There was nothing for her to do but to try to get rid of the bodies before they were ever found.

One by one she dragged them, deeper into the open field that she committed her crimes. She planned to return, to finish her deed, and escape her hellish life forever, but she couldn't with blood stained shoes and jeans. Cautiously she stripped, laughing at the fact that she was finally giving her suitors what they wanted, then left her bottoms before running towards the road.

She had her story all planned out. She was going to say that a guy tried to rape her and that she needs a ride home. It was the perfect excuse, not only for her lack of pants or shoes, but the perfect way to buy her time. She needed gasoline, something, anything that could cause a massive fire, destroying her evidence.

"Can you help me?" she cried when a lone truck driver pulled to the side of the road.

"Sure thing darlin, hop on in. Where ya headin?" he said.

"Just into town, about five miles down. I'd walk but it's too dark, and I don't have any shoes."

"What happened?"

"Some boy thought he'd take advantage of me, but I don't go down without a fight," she forced a smile though every part of her was afraid.

For a long time, I was invested in writing that horror story. I wanted to create a person who was unforgivable. I wanted to create a person like the Charlie the world saw. I just didn't know it at the time. I thought I was creating a book that hadn't been done before not trying to process through my life. I was so naive it's funny. The bad part is that I'm probably no better off than I was before, I've just adapted to this life. I know now what my issues are, and I think I know the root of all of my evils. Yet, somehow I find myself consistently incapable of moving on all the while passing the time on my therapist's worn couch.

"Piper, you're going to have to tell me something eventually sweetie. I can't just have your dad waste money for you to sit on my sofa and stare blankly at me for an hour," my psychiatrist said as she intertwined her fingers and sat up as straight as she could. She did this every time she wanted to squeeze a confession out of me. I knew she was evaluating my state of mind, seeing if I needed medication or if I needed to be locked up forever.

"I'm sad. I'm always sad. I just want to be happy."

Those were the last honest words I ever told her. Soon after both my father and her gave up trying. Medicating me was their only answer.

*"Oh she'll be fine with time. Just give her this pill to sleep, this one for her panic attacks, and this one when her depression gets to be too much! It'll all be okay!"*

Fake smiles and swallowing down mountains of pills only got me so far. They were temporary fixes. I felt as if the pills were just bandaids over bullet wounds. A temporary euphoria did not help me feel less empty and alone. Yet, I stayed silent. Yet, I suffered alone but that's only because it was the only way I knew how to.

# NOW:

I feel as if I should label myself as an insomniac. I can never sleep, and when I do it's restless. Dreams are too trippy, my mind is too scattered. My brain is good for nothing except for reading and writing and I don't know if it's even particularly good at that. I wish I had a way to escape myself the way I escape the rest of the world. I know that I like blaming everyone else for why I am the way I way I am, but I stopped trying to improve myself, so in the the end, I caused my own ruin.

I spend my entire night pacing back and forth, staring at the books I should read but have no patience for, staring at my typewriter waiting for words to come to me, staring at a dark world that is fast asleep. I know things are going to turn around for me in work, yet another can of worms is beginning to open. I'm starting to believe that I thrive off drama, that I hold grudges longer just to fuel my mania, that I turn everyone away so that I can justify my insanity. I have to move on, it's time for me to let what happened in the past go. I keep saying it, but I need to believe it. I need to believe in myself.

When the sun comes up, I find myself in the bathtub with no recollection of how I got here and a laptop on top of me. The laptop burns the tops of my thighs, and when I bring it to life I see all the stories I tried to forget. Descriptions of my nightmares pile up in the hundreds. Murder, slaughter, and death are buzzwords that are included way too often. It makes me sick. I try so hard not to look back because the girl I used to be disgusts me. I may not be better completely, I still have baggage, but now I'm self aware, now I don't think that it's selfish to be happy.

My creative writing projects from college are less violent but more questioning. I sound like a philosopher in some, and in others I sound plain cynical. It's no wonder my main character in my novel is a girl who believes she's incapable of love. After awhile, I can't take anymore of my pity party and so I shut my laptop and peel myself out of the tub. My joints crack as I roll my shoulders and spine before telling myself that today must be a new day.

Dancing over to the sagging wardrobe with chipped paint and broken handles, I pick out a sky blue sundress. I want to feel lively, pretty, and comfortable in my own skin. I want to be happy, so today I will be. Today, I will dance to the sounds of acoustic guitars and melodic piano chords. Today, I will eat cookies with my tea even though it's barely breakfast time. Today, I will read and write stories that don't include tragedy. Today, is the day I'm going to redefine myself. I can feel it, I can see it.

A knock at the door a few hours later causes butterflies to rise in my stomach. Today, will be a good day and I will find security in my own personality. I will be okay with being myself completely. Running away left me emotionally fatigued, I put all my eggs in one basket, but nothing ever changed. I may have pretended to be happy, but nothing was ever resolved. So now I have to change my mindset. No more running away, I just have to deal with everything head on with a smile spread across my face.

"Come on in!"

"Good morning, Piper," Clarkson says. He walks into the house and wanders straight over to the books. He smiles when he looks at them, and then back at me. I wonder what he's thinking? Does he feel the way I do? Does he know today's going to be a good day?

"You seem different this morning," I say.

"You do as well, but I can't quite put my finger on why... You just seem more lively. I think I quite like the change in attitude," he chuckles.

"Excuse me for being cheery today. Don't get used to it, I may just snap and attack you. You never know, I am unpredictable."

Clarkson huffs and crosses his hands over his chest defiantly, as if he were a small child in the midst of throwing a fit. He doesn't last like this, before long, a smile creeps up on him and he's laughing once again. When he laughs his whole body shakes as if the positive energy can't be contained. I swear I see his chest explode out of his denim button up when tears start rolling down his face.

"You okay there?" I ask.

"Never better. I'm just in a really great mood."

"Me too, my friend, me too."

I walk over to my phone and change the song blaring over the cheap speaker. Next thing I know, Michael Bublé's Sway comes on and I start to twirl around the room all by myself.

"Come on and dance with me!" I plea.

"I can't dance, Piper, so unfortunately I'll have to pass."

"I don't buy that bullshit for one moment, come here I'll teach you."

I hold out my hand, and he takes it hesitantly, unsure of how to act or move his poorly coordinated body. One foot forward, one foot back, we move around the house, laughing whenever Clarkson steps on my bare toes. His face gets so flustered he starts to look mad. He just wants to keep count, but I don't let him. Feel the music, feel the beat.

"Do you want to try to spin me?" I ask.

"No way! I'll drop you. Besides, we have to get to work."

"Don't be such a downer, Clark. You can do it, just trust me."

He spins and drops me, causing my dress to poof up. I laugh and pat my dress down while Clarkson watches me nervously. He thinks he can break me over something as small as this. He doesn't know that it takes a lot more to hurt me, I'm stronger than anyone thinks. I'm a warrior.

"You look like you've seen a ghost. Have you never seen a girl fall before?"

"Why of course I have, but I've never been the cause of it."

"Don't be so hard on yourself, shit happens. Come on now, help me up."

He extends his hand and after I pull myself up, I wrap my arm around his and give him a cheeky smile.

"Can you escort me over to my shoes? I wouldn't want to fall again!"

"Oh get away from me!" he says, slightly peeved.

"Suit yourself, I can dance all by myself."

I waltz around the room, collecting my things for work, and twirling around Clarkson just because. He doesn't know how to react to me when my good mood is sustained, and quite frankly I don't either. I have too much energy and I'm ready to take on the world, and by take on the world I mean say hello to my coworkers without wanting to run in a broom closet and hide.

"Do you remember the first time I met you, just a few months back? he asks.

"I think so, why?"

"You were dancing with your broom, around and around you twirled, with your books as your only audience. Well, what you thought was your only audience. It was at that moment I knew you were the person the school needed to liven it up. I hadn't seen that girl since that day, but here she is again, and I hope this time she's here to stay."

"I do too, Clark. I do too."

"Come on, let's get goin, we have a long day ahead of us."

In the car we're both completely silent. The windows are down and the bitter air is blowing on my face. I know my body is trembling, but I like the cold, and I like the sun beaming down on my face, attempting to undo the damage that the wind has done. Eventually, Clark turns on the radio and its static overpowers the tune of premature Christmas music, but I don't mind. The sound reminds me of what home should feel like.

"I can't believe they're playing Christmas music. For God's sake, we haven't even had Thanksgiving," he whispers.

356

"I don't mind it, it's nice."

"You're one of those people?"

"Hmm?"

I prop myself up and open my eyes to find Clarkson looking quite bewildered at me. He looks angry almost, but I don't really get why. I swear I didn't do anything, this time.

"You're one of those horrible people who listens to Christmas music before Thanksgiving. I'm sorry but I don't think I can be your friend if you're that type of person."

"Oh please spare me, Clarkson White. I could not give two shits about when I want to listen to Christmas music. It could be summer for all I care, and I'd still break out the here comes Santa Claus."

Clarkson puts one hand over his heart and acts as if he's been shot.

"Why do you keep hurting me in this way?" he cries.

"Shut up and drive, stupid."

I prop my feet up on the dashboard and go back into my little trance. Today is a good day. Emma is back home, Clark isn't mad anymore, and I'll finally be able to move on. I'll finally be free from myself, and damnit it feels great.

At the school, Clark and I say our goodbyes and I head down to my cavern. I have my little ones again today, and so I spend most of the morning tidying the reading rugs and moving books down to their level. I think today I'm going to let them actually touch the books, but probably not for long. The kindergarteners may be cute, but they are still grimey, and I'd like my decaying books to last a little longer than my first year here.

Mrs Borgin troops her kiddies in after their lunch and just prior to their nap. She waves at me before running as far away from the kids as she can get in a school full of them. I can't imagine how she does it all day, I can barely do it for a few hours.

"Good morning my cuties!"

"Good morning Ms Addison!" they say in a failed attempt at unison.

"What should we read today?"

"Princess story!" the girls yell.

"No we want pirates!" the boys croak.

"What about both?" I suggest.

"Yay!"

I wait for them to settle down and curl up next to one another before I start crafting a tale. A story of a made up princess who falls in love with a pirate seamlessly flows off my tongue. Though cliche, children seem to love forbidden romance, even before they know what forbidden love truly is.

"The princess and the pirate met every night at the docks, talking to each other about how lonely they felt. After a month, they realized they were falling in love and wanted to run off together and live happily ever after, but that could never be. The princess was engaged to a handsome prince, whom she didn't love."

A brunette with pigtails and two yellow bows containing her curly waves raised her hand, causing me to stop before I could continue my next thought.

"Yes Mara, sweetie?"

"But princesses are only supposed to marry people they love!"

"Yes, that's right, and that's why the princess was so sad. She wanted to marry her pirate, the man of her dreams. For a year they continued to meet in secret, always after the sun went down, and before the church bells rang for the last time each night. It was then when the two made a plan. The pirate was to kidnap his princess, and make him her bride, that way they could live happily ever after on the sea."

A boy with scruffy blonde hair was the next to interrupt me, but as I try to listen to him, he fidgets with his overalls and stumbles over his own words.

"But what about her mummy and daddy?" he asks.

"They didn't know about her pirate, and neither did the handsome prince. On her wedding day, the pirate stormed down the aisle and grabbed his sweet girl. The king and queen were dumbfounded, but before they could get the guards to save the princess, the pirate was already on his boat, sailing off with the love of his life. The two sailed around the ocean world for years, and the pirate named his bride the princess of the sea. They were happy together, and they knew they belonged with each other. The end!"

"But, Ms Addison!" they all cry out.

"But what, my kiddies? Did I forget something?"

"Did they live happily ever after?" a small voice breaks through the controlled chaos and a smile spreads throughout my face.

"Oh lordy me, I forgot, didn't I? I'm so sorry!" I say, pretending to be shocked. "Of course they lived happily ever after! They're in love," I conclude, leaving all the children satisfied.

They all smile and soon enough Mrs. Borgin waltz in and rounds up her troops, all the while trying to mask the exhaustion that wears her so well. It's honestly so crazy to think that at one point in time, everyone on earth was that small. Those kids all have an uncorrupted heart. They all believe that every story has to end with happily ever after, or it's not a true story at all. Just wait my dears, wait until you grow up and see the world around you. I wish I could tell them that things will be great, perfect even, but the real world is plain old shit. For every good thing that happens, five crappy things follow, and it's up to any individual to decide how that's going to shape them as a person.

I was dumb enough to let the negative destroy me, and so I admire the people who manage to stay positive. They give me hope; children give me hope for the future. Maybe one day everything will be better because of people like them.

The rest of the day is spent cleaning up after my little ones, and checking out books about genocide for the seventh grade history project. As the school day winds down, I find myself becoming increasingly worn down and my happy facade begins to falter. I have to stop questioning my reality and just live instead.

"Piper, you ready?"

Clarkson peaks his head in the door and I drop the pile of books I was holding, causing him to rush to my side. I roll my eyes, but Clarkson doesn't notice.

"I don't need you to save me," I whisper.

"I'm not trying to, I'm just here to be your friend."

"Clark, I'm starting to over think again."

"It's okay, Piper. Just remember that no matter what, today's going to be a good day."

"Today's going to be a good day."

# THEN:

After the incident, I was a child who suffered from terrible disillusionment. Think Santa Claus type disillusionment and magnify it by one hundred, or a thousand, or as big as you can imagine. This was how I went through life. Even as years past and my father's excessive drinking habit mellowed as he returned to work, my heart was stuck searching for something more. I needed to fill the holes, or understand why I felt so empty in time all the time. I couldn't let the past go. I wanted to be the nerdy sister who had prince charming for a brother. I wanted to be the perfect daughter for a musical mother and poised father. I wanted a perfect home.

I became obsessed with what should have been my perfect life, with a life that I believed was unsullied as a child. I even began to alter my memories, to make them better, to make the disillusionment go away. It didn't work, and it couldn't. I knew the truth and that was enough to sober me up.

People crave perfection, people want to have what is unobtainable. For a large portion of my life, I saw my life as something that people wanted to have. My brother was perfectly poised, his temper and emotions hidden behind closed doors. My mother was a fallen angel, her song was used to pull us from our dreams and to calm even the rowdiest of quarrels. My father was a technological wizard, spending his days behind a desk while his mind decoded not only the tech world, but his world at home. Then there was me, plain jane with a silent soul and a book fetish. I was the black sheep, but I made them whole. We loved each other. We were perfect. We were. We were.

My delusions were blown out of proportion. There were days when I would lock myself in my room and pretend that the world that was in front of me was all just a dream, and then I would live the world in my head instead. A world full of music shaped waffles, sun covered streets, endless music, and nothing but happy faces.

"Piper, darling wake up! Wake up!"

My mother's lips grazed my cheek as she tussled my caramel colored locks to life. Immediately I latched onto her warmth, trying to convince myself that morning hadn't come. I didn't stay long in her arms because soon enough she was propping me on my feet and telling me to get ready for school, trying to mask her exhaustion with a fake falsetto.

"Today's going to be a great-great day!"she sang.

Walking out of the room, I tiptoed behind her and made my way into the kitchen. My father paid me no mind as I piled waffle after waffle on my plate, instead, he read his newspaper and pretended like the simple act didn't age him beyond his years. By the time I was five mouthfuls in, my brother slumped to the table and didn't say a word until he took his pills. I always wondered why he never said anything until after the medicine was in his system, but I know now that he was afraid of who he truly was so he refused to speak until he was the person he wanted to be. The silence was how we got through our morning routine, listening to the irritating birds sing outside of our stereotypical Pennsylvanian home, and munching on a labored breakfast. My mother never sat with us, she kept on her feet, sneaking mouthfuls of food between chores that my brother and I offered to help with one time too many.

"Okay you two, your dad and I will clean up, go get ready my darlings. Off you go, we don't have much time! We can't be late."

Every time I was ushered off, I would run and put on my navy blue jumper and white polo shirt as fast as I could so that I could beat Charlie to the bathroom, but I almost never won. Most of the time, though, he let me in with him, allowing us both to get ready at the same time. He only wanted to know he won, gratification was all my brother needed to fuel his prideful spirit.

With my hair brushed into two pigtails my mother would come to rescue, braiding them precisely and tying them with two coordinated bows. I was her little doll, and all she wanted to do with her life was play house and make music. My mother was a simple woman and prided herself on her work and family only. I admired her for that, especially how everything she did was done with not only heart, but relative ease.

"Charlie! Charlie! Where are you! Come on! Charlie!"

My mother's voice shifted from composed to strained. All of a sudden my reality shifted, and my nightmare was revived. I was transported into the back seat of my mom's car and body sitting in the driver's seat was bloodied and cold. My brother was found just a few feet away with a gun in one hand and his backpack in another, his body frozen in a similar state. I started to scream but no one heard me. I started to cry but no one could see me. It wasn't until I took ahold of the gun that I became visible. It was all my fault. I'm to blame. I'm the reason they're dead. Murderer. Murderer. Charlie may have pulled the trigger, but it's you who's to blame. You shouldn't have survived. You were an accident, and you should be dead too.

Violent shakes were how reality came back to me. My hands were cautiously hovering over the computer keys and my body was as stiff as a board. Running my fingers through my hair was how I tried to calm myself, but as tears poured I could feel nothing but entrapment. Somehow, someway, I forced myself to finish out my delusion, and by the time I finished I went numb once more.

We weren't perfect. It's all a dream. The life I have created is the only place where perfection exists. I wish we were perfect. I wish, but we weren't. We weren't.

# NOW:

I think I've made a terrible mistake. I'm setting myself up to face my fears and it's not good. Somehow Clark convinced me, that since I was feeling better, it was the best time to try and speak to Father Michael. Yet, as I walk on uneven pavers my stomach churns. I keep mumbling to myself that today's going to be a good day, but with every step uncertainty brews. I'm not ready. I haven't even talked to my own father about this, why in the hell should I feel comfortable talking to a virtual stranger who believes my existence is a sin?

"Piper, are you going to come in?"

Unknowingly, I find myself staring at the church doors, unable to move.

"I don't know if I can do this. I don't know if I can go in there."

Clark grabs a hold of my hand but says nothing more. He wants me to think that his physical presence is enough. It's not. I feel alone. I feel like I can't handle what's next.

"Clark, I can't go in there."

"Why not?" he asks softly.

"Last time I ever talked about myself I was told that my soul was doomed for hell."

"Oh Piper…"

"I thought I would be able to. I was so excited. I'm sorry. I don't understand what happened to me… I thought I was ready."

"You don't have to go in. You don't have to do anything."

As he speaks, I wrap myself in his arms and start crying. He thinks that I'm an alcoholic or just another stereotypical depressed girl that people write about to progress a shitty plot. He doesn't understand. Clarkson White is incapable of understanding, but only because I can't open my damn mouth. My life has become a secret locked in a vault for no good reason except for my insecurities. I wish I could just get my thoughts out. I wish I could explain to him why I am the way I am, but I don't really get it.

"Why don't you sit down on the stoop and I'll be right back, okay?"

He talks into my hair and I just slump down in defeat. Up and down my emotions go. I can be trusted. I can't be tied down. I'm destined to drown in my own self pity, aren't I? I'm disgusting and despicable. I've let one moment define every part of me. I am no one without my pain, and no good person is defined that way.

When Clark comes back he brings Father Michael. They both kneel to my level and offer to help me up, not telling me anything about where we're going. Past the church my heart rate slows, but I still feel unsteady with the two men. Where do I begin? Where do I end? What changes with the truth? Does the world stop turning? Does the world stay the same? My exaggerated thoughts only swirl in an attempt to lighten the situation, but in all honesty, I make fun of myself to hide my terror.

"Piper, everything is going to be okay," Clarkson says.

"Whatever you say."

"Trust me."

He takes ahold of my hand once more, and leads me to the grassy hill that overlooks the parking lot that the teachers call a "playground." On top of the hill, there's a lone pavilion covered in wilted wildflowers and browning leaves. Both of them make sure I sit first, then Clark sits next to me while Father Michael sits across, eyeing us both carefully, as if he fears that we're going to disappear in front of his eyes.

"Okay, so let's try this again, shall we?" Clark says, smiling.

"Well where do we begin?" I reply.

"Well, Clark came and talked to me after your little outburst and both of us are growing concerned that your strange behavior at work is due to some underlying circumstances," Father Michael speaks as I bite back an angry laugh.

"I know what you two think of me, but let me start off by saying I am not a drunk nor am I addicted to pain medicine."

"Then how would you explain your erratic behavior?" Father Michael presses.

"I suffer from PTSD and got it at quite a young age, young enough where I'm unable to deal with the most basic social cues, young enough where anxiety attacks and depression spells have become so routine that I mock myself in my mind as everything occurs. I don't particularly enjoy the taste of alcohol. When it comes to medicine, I only take what I need. I am not what you think of me, and I-I just ask that you try and reserve your judgment," my voice cracks as I open up.

"Piper Addison, what the hell have you been keeping from me?" Clarkson asks.

"Everything, my friend, everything," I say resting my hand on his forearm.

I can't compose myself to say anything more. I just watch them look at me in disgust. They don't know what to do, what to say. I was right. Once people know the truth about me, they avoid me like the plague and deem me to be too broken. I can't be loved, nor cared for. I am a lost cause.

"Well, it looks like we need to change course a bit, now don't we?" Father Michael forces out a laugh.

"I think so."

I start laughing, and tears rain down even harder. I'm a mess, and an ugly crier. There's no going back now. Piper Addison welcome to the world. Take off that mask. Find out who you are. Trust people, Piper. Love yourself. Find out what it means to love other people. Life can be good for us eventually, but hell, there's a reason for the saying that to get a rainbow you must first have rain. Here is the downpour, but I see it far in the distance, can't you? Here comes the sun, Piper, and it's going to be alright.

"Well Piper, why don't we get started?"

"Well Father, where should I begin?"

# THEN:

After Mr. Clint died, I was jobless and restless. Shelving and organizing books kept me busy all day and my mind clear. While I worked for him I felt not only stable but independent and free. I needed to get back on my feet, but I also needed to hide behind a pile of books and forget the world. This desire is what caused me to horde the want ads of every town's newspaper in a 75 mile radius.

It got to the point where the stack of newspapers overtook my house more than my books did. Everywhere you looked, discarded ads lied scattered across the floor. In the bathtub, on the kitchen counter, in my bed, in my backyard, everywhere. Every paper fell short, and the jobs online were even less helpful. Books were dead to the world. No one needed to flip through the pages of a book to find out what they wanted; it was all at the click of a button. It got to a point where I believed that I, just like my passion, would soon become completely obsolete.

After six months of hopelessness, my funds began to run dry. I used all of Charlie's bank accounts for my tuition as well as my not so spectacular renovations to my shack. It was at that point where I was eating more ramen and white rice than a freshman in college. I needed to survive, but I couldn't settle. I was tired of settling. Belfast was my opportunity to do what I wanted, and I was determined to live that way, so much so that I was willing to starve for a job that never truly came.

It was at my low point when the job at Saint Agatha's was brought to my attention. I was so excited and full of hope when I saw the ad. I wanted the job to be mine. I knew it was meant for me. My only apprehension was the fact that I knew I would be subjecting myself to the same hatred that drove me away from the religious life in the first place. Some religions are very forgiving, and some aren't. My childhood painted the unseemly image that led me to believe that the Catholic church was not a forgiving one, and I was also led to believe that anyone associated with them would see right through me.

Still I believed that things could work out in the end. I told myself that all I would have to do is play normal, read to children, and give out worn out books as if they were iphones on Christmas Day. My beliefs didn't have to be tampered, I thought. I didn't have to give up anything about myself. All I had to do was spend five days a week with books and children, and that alone sounded perfect.

I convinced myself to sign up for that job, and now I don't know if I made the right decision. I'd like to think that by the time I leave Saint Agatha's my life will be completely transformed, but it's going to take a lot of soul searching for me to get anything right.

# NOW:

They're both watching me. They're both analyzing me. When they aren't looking at me, they look at each other with perplexed faces. They don't know how to handle me. It looks as if they're trying to figure out how to defuse the bomb ticking in front of them.

I'm okay though, I think. I'm starting to regain composure, and besides the occasional sniffle, you wouldn't be able to tell that just moments before I was emotionally raw. Maybe that's what scares them most, the fact that I can be so open and emotional in one moment, then cold and heartless in another.

"Well, let me start out by asking you a question. Is that alright?" Father Michael asks.

"Was that your question?" I joke.

"At least those tears haven't washed away your sense of humor," he retorts.

"Sometimes it's the only thing that I have to keep me grounded."

"Well then, may I ask that question now?"

"Of course, Father."

"What brought you to Belfast?" he asks.

For some reason, I don't even hesitate when I answer. "I wanted to escape. I thought that if I could get far from home, I could move on and forget everything. I was horribly mistaken, but at least I'm now in a more positive environment. At least now, I believe that progress is attainable."

"But this is such a tiny town, how did you find it?" Clarkson breaks in, and I turn to find his leg bouncing up and down under the table.

"My grandparents live a few hours north of here. I was supposed to go there, but the bus stops here. I don't know why I picked here, but I told myself to never look back and so that's what I did. For awhile, I lived off the little money I brought. Eventually, after months of fighting with my dad on the phone, he gave me access to my brother's old bank account and I had enough money to settle down and get through college. The rest is history."

"Your brother?" he asks.

I shift away from Clarkson and take a deep breath. I feel trapped. I can't get out of this. The only way is through. I must get through this.

"Piper, you're shaking," Clark says, grabbing my hand and closing the gap I just created.

"Am I now? I didn't notice."

"Did your brother do something to you?"

Clarkson's voice lurches. He's jumping to conclusions again. My brother may have been a murderer, but he was no rapist.

"No, besides the occasional fight, I can't bring myself to complain about him. He was my knight in shining armor as a kid, until he got older anyways."

"Piper, what happened?" Clarkson presses.

"Nothing, nothing I want to talk about."

"Piper, you can't expect to get better if you don't talk about anything. Don't shut us out now. You're getting somewhere, can't you feel it?" Father Michael asks.

"Last time I talked about any of this..." I stop myself.

"Piper, come on. Do one thing for yourself," Clark whispers.

"I've done everything for myself. I'm a horrible human being Clarkson White, a selfish one at that."

"At least finish your sentence," he pleads.

"Last time I talked about any of this I lost all my faith and all my friends. I don't know If I'm ready to do that again just when I'm starting to find my place here."

"Piper, you are not going to lose me. I told you, I'm here for the long run. I need someone to help me takeover the school, and you're my perfect partner in crime."

"Stop being... I don't know.. Stop being you," I say.

Clark arches his brow, but doesn't push me any further. He's figuring out my limits, and I find myself sighing and shifting my weight on him.

"I think I've said a bit too much. Maybe we can try this again another day? If not, it's perfectly okay, I'm fine. I actually feel better now that I've told someone the truth. At least someone will know now that I'm not crazy."

I muster up a fake smile at Father Michael before squeezing Clark's hand. If I can get home, I'm free. I just have to do what I do best, pretend. I can still save the day. I can make it better if I can get home in one piece.

"It pains me to see that you are unwilling to get the help you need, Piper. Although, I have a feeling that even getting this far was an enormous step. Once you are ready, I am here to talk to you. I hold no judgments, that is not my job but the job of our Lord," Father Michael concludes.

"Thank you." I extend my hand across the picnic bench and shake his hand. Not moments after he lets go I find myself bolting.

Down the hill I appear to be a child. My arms are flailing by my sides as I attempt to prevent myself from falling. Right behind, Clark is booking it too. He's trying to keep up, but he trips over a rock and falls flat on his back, knocking the wind out of him.

"Clark! Are you okay?"

His glasses are crooked on his face, and he's covered in icy mud. I bite my lip to hold back a chuckle, and when he notices my look, his face blushes.

"I-I should be fine." He wheezes and forces air back in his lungs with every syllable. He sounds like a smoker after their last puff, or an asthmatic kid.

"Do you need me to help you up?"

"No, no, I can take care of myself, Miss Addison!"

I scowl at him for the subtle jab. I'm trying, you prick. He stumbles to his feet and falls straight back down, sliding the rest of the way down the hill. I watch as he tries to pull himself up, as he tries to maintain his pride, but once he's given up, I help him to his feet.

"I thought you said you could take care of yourself, Mr. White?"

"I thought you did too, Piper."

I drop his hand, and walk off, not wanting to finish an arbitrary conversation. I don't want another fight. I don't want to answer any more questions. I want to sleep and pretend like this day never happened. Is that too much to ask for?

Another silent car ride greets me home. Clarkson White looks perturbed, he doesn't know what to say or how to process my selective information. I sit angered, clutching onto the handrail while letting the crisp autumn hair rustle my hair.

"We're here," he states the obvious.

"Oh are we now? I thought this was a five star hotel! Thank you for alerting me, I never would have guessed it!"

"Don't be this way."

"Don't be what way?"

"Today's supposed to be a good day," he murmurs.

"Well life doesn't always go the way you plan, now does it?"

I hop out of his car and wave him off, but he won't move out of my dirt covered driveway.

"Why would you keep this from me, Piper? Why have you been lying to me this whole damn time? I know nothing about you, do I?"

And so it's revealed. What's been on his mind since I spoke my mind. He feels betrayed because I've stayed silent. He doesn't know that my silence wasn't meant to hurt him. He doesn't know that

I was trying to shield him from the truth in an attempt to preserve our friendship. He doesn't understand that I don't owe him anything. He isn't entitled to know anything about my life, but I let him in. I was stupid enough to let him in thinking he'd be satisfied with living in the in between.

"I don't have to tell you everything. You learned what I wanted you to learn about me. Emphasis on the I."

"But, don't you think the person helping you through everything deserves to know the damned truth? If you want me to stop seeing you as broken you're going to have to give me a reason to see you whole."

"Get this through your head, Clarkson white; you don't own me. And get this through your head, I never came to you for help. I am a big girl, so I can and will take care of myself. You keep saying that you'll be there for me, and yet you stay on my toes waiting for me to stumble. Maybe our issue is that you're incapable of seeing that what breaks a person also makes them whole. Maybe our issue is that you can't realize that I don't want a savior, I just want a friend."

Clarkson looks dumbfounded, and he bites his tongue so he doesn't say anything. He knows he messed up. I hate how he thinks he can constantly fix me. I know I can't get better on my own, but I can't go on the way he wants me to.

I find myself missing my family the most after Clark leaves. I need a hug. I need to be reassured that I am loved no matter my mental state, no matter my outbursts, no matter my mistakes. I just don't know how anyone could love a broken girl who can't even love herself.

I curl up in the tub again with a mound of blankets to warm my worn heart. I finally let my emotions get the best of me. I cry and scream without any logical train of thought. I'm convinced that I can't be happy. I'm convinced that I can't go a day without my emotions spiraling. It's not healthy. It's left me insane, but I can't change.

Reaching for my pills I turn sour. I rely on the medication to mask it all. I rely on a fog to get through the day because without it I am nothing and yet I feel everything. As I swallow them, only one bitter thought crosses my mind.

"Today's going to be a good day."

# NOW:

There are nights when I crave for someone to understand me. I want someone to be able to look at me and know when I'm happy or when I'm sad. I want someone to be able to look at me and know when I need to hear that things will be okay in the end. I don't think that's possible though, I'm in a world full of constant isolation and sometimes I don't mind it, but every now and again, I get lonely. I realize that I need someone to help me escape myself. I need someone to confide in, yet I only have the words on a page to comfort me.

Throughout the night I find myself roaming. I can't sleep, but I long for it. My feet glide on the wooden floors, from the bathtub to the bed I dance. I bounce back and forth, trying to become comfortable. Anytime I fold into a ball, the savages come out to prey. My mind is a battlefield, and the only casualty is my sanity.

I wake up screaming, recalling nothing more than images of dead bodies scattered across my family home. I drift off and it repeats, though it increases in clarity with each repetition. I feel the pulsing beat of the party. I feel the electricity that was once there. The careless attitude radiated out in the open. Everyone was free before. Then a rash decision throws me in chains. I am a domino in a
384

chain reaction, unable to move on, unable to look away, forced to relive a night I didn't even witness first hand.

After torturing myself for far too long I find myself at my desk, laughing at my stupidity, laughing at my own damn pain. I can't take myself seriously. It's a game. It's all in my head. Everyone was right about me. I am a freak, and I know it. Yet, how do I make it all stop? How do I get out of my own damn head?

I down four sleeping pills and force myself back in bed, setting ten alarms on my phone for the next day. After I medicate, I dream of nothing, I think of nothing.

In the morning I move through the motions. My body is sluggish, and there's a hole in my soul. At work I don't smile, I don't talk. The little ones have faces of worry plastered over their face, I give them a sad soft smile to ease their worries. They ask me for stories, but I have none I want to tell. I want to hide, I want to disappear.

I know I can't keep running away from my problems, but wouldn't it be easier? I hate the fact that I constantly say that my main goal is get better, but anytime something goes wrong I fall back down. I have let every event in my life shape me, form me, and morph me into a trainwreck. I want to be emotionally stable, I want to stop fearing life and the unknown. I have to stop being such a human contradiction but how? How do I get better? How do I turn my mental state around?

Around noon, I hear a knock at my door, and I know who it is. I told him to leave me alone, I told him to go away, but of course he doesn't listen. Clarkson is incapable of understanding the meaning of anything worth something. He is two dimensional person, a fly on the wall, a cloud that refuses to go away.

"What do you want?" I croak.

He slinks in and his demeanor is sullen. I know he's remorseful by the fact that he's trying to hide a book behind his back. He's trying to apologize to me, but I don't want to hear him out. I'm done with Clarkson White.

"I come in peace."

"What did I tell you yesterday? Did you not hear me? Go away."

"Just hear me out, please? I won't stay long."

"You have five minutes."

"Okay but first-"

"No, put down the damn book. I don't want it. If you want to talk then do so," I say.

"Fine."

He sets down the book and stares at me, watching my every move. Why does he care so much? Why won't he just give up on me?

"I don't have all day."

"Jesus Piper, stop pretending like everything's about you. I know you're mad at me. I know I went too far. I'm sorry, I am. I can't pretend to understand what you're going through, but you can't pretend like the whole world is out to get you when no one knows a damned thing. You can't pretend like you're the only person in the world who is going through something. Stop being so ignorant and stop pushing me away. I'm done with this. I'm tired of the fighting. I shouldn't have to fight to be your friend, and I shouldn't have to fight to get to know you."

"Then stop fighting! I don't know anything about you either. Why should I have to be the one to throw myself out there when you won't? I'm not comfortable with it, so stop forcing me. No means no Clarkson White, and if you're such a gentleman you will respect my wishes."

"You're right, you don't know anything about me, do you?"

"I know your name and I know you're a nerd, that's about it," I say.

"Fine then, let's make a deal."

"What kind of deal?"

"I'll let you into my life if you stop pushing me out of yours."

"I don't know."

He holds out his hand and takes ahold of mine. We just watch each other, not knowing how to react. I can't trust him. He's a person made a paper. He has no depth to him. Maybe I should just humour him, keep him at an arm's length by making up some fake tale. That way we're both happy, that way he'll leave me alone.

"Please, Piper. Please," he murmurs.

"Okay, Clarkson White. I guess it's time for our roles to reverse. It's now I who get to define you, and not the other way around."

"Alright then, bring it on. What are you doing tonight?"

"Wait what?" I stammer.

"You heard me, what are you doing tonight?"

"Nothing, I guess."

"Alright, then meet me at the pier at six. Come hungry."

"Are you asking me out, Clarkson?"

He gives me a coy smile before answering, "I am a gentleman Miss Addison, and I just want to get to know you. Oh, and enjoy your new book."

He waltz out of the room and I can't help but radiate anger. He thinks he's got me right where he wants me. He thinks he knows everything. I hate his cockiness. Why is he determined to drive me insane? Ugh I hate him, but I find myself unable to shake him. I guess I'll play his little game, but I'll be damned if I let him win.

# THEN:

People never are how we perceive them to be. We see the pretty popular girl as someone insecure, someone who uses bully tactics and cliques to hide her problems. We see the jock as a pinnacle of society, someone to be praise, someone to be protected. We see the nerd for their intelligence, we see them a weakling, someone to be molded, someone forced to obey society. This social construct has been around longer than I can imagine, but how accurate is it really? How can people be defined into simple groups? How do stereotypes restrict us, and how can we set them free?

As a child I thought about that a lot. I wanted to question the world and break free of society's mold, but instead I adapted to it, and I let it blacken my heart. How many masks do I wear? How many people am I? I think of my childhood memories and allow them to dictate my life with a sense of bitterness. I let generalizations bind me though I realize this flaw of mine. People can not be defined so easily, but I still see them as paper-thin. For some reason people seem to be nothing more than black and white to me.

"Charlie, why are we so different?"

I walked outside and sat down next to my brother on the front porch, letting the street lights illuminate our faces while the stars attempted to poke through.

"What do you mean? We just like different things, what's so wrong with that?"

"I don't know."

"Piper, what's on your mind? You can talk to me."

'Why don't people see us like we see ourselves?"

"Everyone has an opinion; but it takes longer to change someone's mind then it does for them to form it. People just can't see you as you unless you make them, so in the end, it's just easier to change so you're like how they want you to be," he stated.

I shivered and Charlie wrapped his arms around me. I couldn't remember the last time he let me close to him. As he got older, we grew apart. Whenever he would open up to me he would quickly backtrack, pretending like his life was picture perfect. He wanted me to see him how everyone did, but I couldn't, I wouldn't.

"Why should you have to change for anyone other than yourself? I don't get it. Why isn't being yourself good enough for everyone else?" I asked.

"Because in this world it doesn't have to be."

"That sucks."

"It's not all bad, if people didn't believe in me I wouldn't have any friends. Things are so much better now than before, Piper. Sure, I lose my temper now and again without my medicine, but I'm happy now. I belong now."

"You don't have to belong to be happy, Charlie."

"I don't know my little pied Piper, maybe I'm wrong, but I'd rather fit in than feel alone."

"You're never alone, you have mom, dad, and me. If no one else in the world sees you as you want to at least we do, at least I do."

Charlie looked at me and gave me a sad smile. I couldn't help but hug him. He had changed over the year, but he was still my brother. I always loved him, and I always wanted him to be okay. I needed him to be okay. Nothing hurts more than to see your hero as an actual human being. Over the years, he deteriorated. No longer was Charlie my superhero, no longer was he my monster, he was simply a boy, he was simply my brother.

"Even you see me as something else, Piper."

"No I don't!"

"Don't get all worked up, it's okay. I like that you see me as a better human being than I really am. Maybe one day I'll actually live up to it. Maybe one day I'll make you proud, lil sis."

"Charlie, don't say that. You're fine just the way you are. Besides, who wouldn't want to have the most popular boy in the city as their brother?"

"You're too much."

"I know," I smiled.

It took years for me to believe that I truly did see Charlie as something else, and to this day I guess I still see him in another light. It's so hard to see another human being as a human. We want to glorify them. We want to highlight their flaws. If I can't be courteous enough to see someone else as who they truly are, why do I think that I'm entitled to having people understand me?

# NOW:

My feet dangle off the warped dock, my shoes are tossed to the side, and I sit watching the sun dance with the water's edge. With every approaching day, the sun lingers for less time, reminding me that the season's end is close approaching. I can't wait for winter to come. I hate the loneliness that occurs with the holidays but I love the excuses the cold brings. I can hide inside all day, bury my head in a good book, and not have to associate with any human being. Winter allows me to justify my antisocial tendencies. Winter allows me to recharge and it lets me forget that humanity exists even when I will it to vanish. Winter allows my dreams of a sugar-coated world to appear right outside my window, and it allows me to thrive.

Sitting on the dock, letting chills run down my spine, I let myself fall into my routine. I let myself dream of a perfect snow, the perfect cup of hot coco, and the perfect winter holiday. It's not until Clarkson parks himself right beside me that I fold back onto reality's grasp.

"It's a lovely night tonight, isn't it?" he asks.

"It really is, too bad you're here to spoil all my fun."

"Oh stop pretending like you loathe me. We both know that it is impossible for you to stay away from me."

"I hate to break it to you, but I'm not a fan. You're the one who's obsessed with me, hence the reason we're even here tonight," I state.

"I'm not here to fight, Piper; are you ready to go?"

"Where are we venturing to, Mr. White? Are you taking me to your lair?"

He doesn't respond to my taunting and instead proceeds to help me up, escorting me off the dock like the gentleman he wants me to believe he is. I loop my around his and let him lead the way. We stroll down the city's square and my stomach begins to growl. I feel my cheeks flush and Clarkson simply laughs at me.

"I see that you get grumpy when you're hungry," he smirks.

"I don't think I do."

"Hm, then what causes it?"

"I would have to contribute my mood to shitty know-it-alls, to be quite frank with you. Are you familiar with any of them?"

"No, I don't think so. You know what boils my blood?"

"What would that be?" I question.

"People who pretend like caring is a villainous trait. As if the moment you show them common decency, they're expecting for you to have a motive. Why can't a person just be kind without having a reason?"

"Because that's not human nature, Clarkson."

"I think that's bullshit. Not all people are inherently bad!"

"Perhaps, but people aren't inherently good either."

"Why do you always feel the need to quarrel with me?" he asks.

I shrug and I can tell he's getting flustered. Clarkson must have had a privileged life. He must have been sheltered from the realities of this world. There is no way he would have survived if not. The only true optimistic people are crushed at a young age. Hope dies as hate flourishes. I don't care what he tells me tonight, this is the reality of humanity.

"I don't get you. One day you're energetic and lively, the next you won't even get close to another human being. What happened to you as a kid? What made you stop believing in everything?" he presses.

"I thought this night was about getting to know you."

"Piper!"

"Your story for mine, we agreed upon it."

"Fine, let's get you some food."

Before long we're walking into the only decent restaurant in town not known for their seafood, a small soul food spot sitting just a mere block from the pier. Clarkson walks straight in, waving hello at the wait staff before ushering me towards a quaint booth with worn leather in the back of the restaurant.

"You're full of surprises, Mr. White," I say.

"How so, Piper?"

"Well you just waltzed on in to one of the best restaurants in all of town without even batting your eyes. How'd you do it? Are you a food critic in disguise? Oh, no that can be. You must do the owner's taxes for them, right? Am I even close to guessing the answer?"

"No, not even close."

"Hm, well then."

"My parents own the place, and since I know the people my parents hired, they probably blabbed to them about your presence already, so prepare yourself," he says, sighing.

"Why would they care that I'm here with you? Is it the hair?" I laugh.

He doesn't answer and within a few moments, a petite woman heads our way with a muscular man following close behind. The two of them look to be in their mid-fifties. The woman has a creamy complexion and lengthy chocolate waves with whispers of gray, while the man has a rich burnt caramel look to him but no hair to show his age. He wears an off-white apron stained with food while hers looks to show no sign of wear.

"Mom, Dad," he says.

"Hello son," his father replies and Clarkson's parents plaster smiles on their faces, anxiously waiting for him to introduce me to them.

"Why have you two ventured from the kitchen on this fine evening?" he asks, baiting them.

"Can't a mother take her own son's order without the fifth degree? I just wanted to make sure your service was up to par tonight. Some of the waitresses have been slacking and I only want the best for my son. Now, stop being rude and tell us who this lovely lady here is!" his mother says.

"Mom, Dad, this is Piper Addison my new coworker down at Saint Agatha's."

"Piper, it is a pleasure to meet you, I'm Sarah and this is my lovely husband Michael. Clarkson didn't tell us about anyone new at work!" she says.

"Oh the pleasure's all mine Mrs. White. Clarkson didn't tell me his family owned the best restaurant in all of Belfast," I say.

"He didn't? Son have you been slacking on your job? You're supposed to help us advertise this place!" his dad teases.

"Please stop, you all are embarrassing me," Clarkson whispers.

"I didn't know it was possible to embarrass a grown man, I apologize sweetie. We'll get out your way as soon as you tell us what you want to eat," his mom says.

"Just chicken and mac please," he says.

"What about you, dear?" she asks, looking at me.

"She'll have the same mom, now go!"

His parents shrug at me and make their way back to the kitchen, flirting with each other the entire way while Clarkson sinks down in his chair like a teenage boy. He's completely mortified and it's kind of amusing to watch. I just don't understand why he would bring me here if he knew this would happen. That boy really wants to know my story and is willing to reveal even the most mortifying parts of himself for it.

"Clarkson White, a mathematician of mystery," I laugh.

"Are you even capable of not heckling me for one moment?"

"I don't think so. I'm not programmed to sympathize with people."

"You are absurd, Piper Addison."

"Whatever you say... but really Clark, why did you bring me here?"

"You said you wanted to know the real me, and this is the real me."

"What? A privileged little boy whose mom and dad waited on him hand and foot? Really Clarkson? This is what you want to show me?"

"Open your eyes Piper, I may have a complete family but my life isn't perfect and never was."

"How so? Did you have to work nights at the restaurant when you were short staffed? Or maybe you had to learn to cook for yourself when your parents had to close up shop late? Am I being more accurate now? Were these your struggles because if so I'm going to walk out of here laughing my ass off at you," I say.

"Stop being such a bitch. Your struggles do not cancel out mine. Pain isn't something that should be compared, everyone is different so everyone is going to have a different experience." His body seems to tremble slightly with anger, but his voice doesn't waver, and there seems to be no more light in his eyes.

"I don't care!"

"Then why are you still here?" he asks.

I drop my face into my hands and rub my temples in an attempt to knead out the tension building in my brain. I don't know why I'm here. I don't know what I'm doing with myself. I want someone to understand me. I want to understand someone else.

"Piper, I don't know what you've been through, but if you keep pushing me away I can't help you. I can't keep saying it. I can't keep doing this," he whispers.

When I look up at him I can see his anger is resided, coming just as quickly as it left. He tries so hard to be kind, and I can tell he beats himself up anytime he makes a mistake.

"I'm not trying to push you away. Sometimes I just get a little frustrated with you. You're impossible to understand, Clarkson White."

"You aren't too easy to understand either, Piper. You can't just put all the blame on me."

"I'm not trying to!" I say.

"Piper, your defensive wall is up. You need to decide if you want to trust me or not because we're just wasting each other's time, talking in circles like this."

"I want to trust you."

I'm sure I want to trust Clarkson. I'm sure I want to move on with my life. I'm sure I want to come to terms with the deaths of my loved ones, but just because I'm sure of it, doesn't mean I have the confidence to fulfill anything.

"Then do you want me to tell my story?"

I grab ahold of his hand and nod, but I quickly pull away when half the wait staff comes out of the kitchen to serve us our food. We're on display for them. I know in everyone's mind we're an item, but they can't see the truth. We're dysfunctional friends bonding over the mass amount of things that make us different.

"Go ahead, I'll try not to be such a jerk," I say, cracking a smile in an attempt to deescalate the mounting tensions in the room.

"Okay well, Belfast has never really been a diverse kind of place. There aren't people like me around here, and there never has been. Even as a kid I couldn't find a place to fit in. I was too white for the black kids and I tried too hard to fit in for the white kids. It drove me crazy. I didn't belong anywhere, and once I figured out that I liked math I became even more isolated. Can you imagine being rejected by everyone simply because you knew who you were when everyone didn't? I couldn't even openly claim to like the things that I was passionate about. It came to a point where my identity was a stain in the eyes of my peers. Everyone had that one thing that defined them, but that defining quality helped them fit into a crowd. My defining quality led me to be ostracized and because of it my life has been a series of people telling me that I don't belong. Even now, I feel as if I can't escape my past. I still have to fight to be me."

"Clark, I'm sorry."

"There's no need to apologize. You didn't do anything. Why do you think I try to joke about who I am so much? Why do you think I refuse to give up on you? You understand that feeling of loneliness. Sure, I don't know where it comes from, and I don't understand you, but we're more alike than you know," he says. I see tears bubbling at the corners of his eyes fighting to escape, but he forces down a glass of water to distract himself. He's trying to show me that he's strong, that he's moved on, but part of him still feels like the little boy that could never belong.

"How could people be so cruel? This isn't the 1950s and we don't live in the south, aren't people here are supposed to be more open?"

"People here are more open to liberal ideas, I guess. No was ever blantly racist towards me, they just didn't understand me as a person. I think the issue people have with me is that I don't identify with one culture. I don't try to define myself; I just try to live for me. That scares people; no matter where on earth you live, people want to be able to classify everything and everyone. Abnormalities are thrusted into a social darkness, they become beggars for justice, and their cries for help are ignored. I don't know, I'm tired of trying to figure out how to be liked and instead I want to focus on how to make myself happy. It's the only thing that I can control, so I might as well do my best, ya know?" he says.

"How do you pretend like it doesn't still bother you? How do you bury your skeletons? It's not like it just gets better when you grow up."

"I mean...it does get better as you get older, but just not in the way everyone expects it to. Old feelings are like the last bits of a fire, waiting to be rekindled."

"What do you mean?" I ask.

"I mean that no matter how old I get, no matter how much I grow as a person, I'll always remember what people said to me. I'll always be emotionally scarred, but because I don't hear it everyday anymore, I feel happier, I feel as if life is better. It's like even though the pain will forever linger in the darkness, one glimmering star is all I need to fight even the bleakest of nights."

"So you're saying it doesn't really get better? You just learn how to cope?"

"Basically," he answers, and I notice him playing with his food. His mind seems preoccupied, and his entire demeanor has changed.

"When I moved here, I thought it would that everything would be different. I thought that the people would be nicer in Belfast. I thought that I could escape what I left behind. I thought that maybe people in my hometown were just inherently evil, and that everywhere else would be heavenly in comparison. I still don't think that people are inherently good, but maybe people aren't inherently bad either; maybe we're all just victims of our surroundings. Maybe we are all slaves to the world around us," I mumble.

"No we're not. How could you say that?"

"Just think about it. We're punished for being different, we're punished for blending in. There are no happy endings, just consequences."

"Not everything in this world is bad, and we do control our own lives. It's up to you to decide how you're going to react to what the world throws at you, Piper. It's up to you to decide how the world is going to perceive you. Who you are is up to you, though what makes you that way is a different story."

"You're too much of an optimist for me, Clark. I just can't see the world the way you do."

"I don't expect you to."

I push my plate away from me and fidget in my seat. Meanwhile, Clark won't take his eyes off me. Maybe he's waiting for me to talk. Maybe he's waiting for me to runaway. I can see that he's never told anyone what he's told me. He's never felt the need to be so honest with anyone, maybe he expects the same in return from me.

"Hey, I think I'm done eating. Do you want to go for a walk?" I ask.

"Sure, let me just go say goodbye to everyone. I'll be right back."

A faint smile flickers on his face but within seconds he and his warmth are gone.

Maybe I'm overthinking everything, maybe I'm wasting his time and mine. I should just blurt it out. What happened didn't directly happen to me. I'm not a murderer. I am a side effect of tragedy. It's nothing to be ashamed of, right? I didn't pick my family. I didn't choose for my life to turn out this way. Everything that has affected me has torn me apart, but it has also made me who I am. I just don't know how to convey that without seeming like a child asking for pity.

When Clarkson comes back so does the warmth that makes me feel safe. No matter how much he angers me. No matter how much our ideologies differ. Clarkson White has made Belfast a home for me.

He grabs my hand and rushes out the restaurant. My feet are dragging behind him and the friction slowing us down is small in comparison to the turmoil of the night. It isn't until we're half way down the block that his posture relaxes and his pace slows.

"Clark, what was that all about?"

"I love my family, don't get me wrong, but I can't take their constant analysis of me."

"Oh, so that's where you get it from?" I smirk.

"Ouch, I walked right into that one."

"Yes you did my friend, no, but really, that's what families are supposed to do right? They're supposed to bother you for the rest of you life. They're supposed to care."

"I guess you're right. I just thought that it would get easier as I grew up, but I'll always be a kid to them," he laughs.

"Well I hate to break it to you, but you still kind of dress like a little boy going to church, so no wonder they baby you."

"Hey now, my style is refined."

"Even your bowtie and graphic tee combo?" I question.

"That too."

"Whatever you say.... so Clark, where are we going?"

"Wherever the wind blows."

I roll my eyes, and he shrugs before we trudge along. The streets are lonely in Belfast, and the town seems to hold its breath waiting for snow to be at its feet. The lights in the town are so scattered and few that my eyes only see shades of black and gray. Still I walk, and still my mind runs faster than prey runs from their predator.

"Piper, you never talk about your family at all," Clark says gently, bringing up the conversation again, "it couldn't have all been bad. Why don't you tell me about the good times?"

"I don't like talking about any of it. Every last memory leaves a sour taste in my throat and the longer I ignore them the more the pain fades."

"Pain seems to make you who you are, doesn't it?" he asks.

"I'm not sure why I tick this way."

My footsteps become heavier the longer we walk. My mind starts to whirl the longer we don't talk. I hate that this internalized conflict prevents me from living, but I'm too afraid to see how the world is without it. I believe that being cynical and cautious has kept me safe, but what if that same belief has also kept me from happiness and life?

"Clark, have you ever seen the movie the Notebook?" I ask as we cut across an empty street.

"I have, but you can not tell anyone that. I'd lose my geek card!" he whispers.

"I'm pretty sure that face just reaffirms your dorky character, my friend, besides, who would I tell? I only have you."

"Fine, fine, but back to what you were saying."

"Okay, have you ever wondered what it would be like to lie in the middle of the road?" I ask.

"No, but I'd imagine it be very dangerous and a dumb idea."

"But that's the point."

He walks over to the sidewalk and I just drop to the cold pavement and close my eyes.

"What the hell are you doing?"

His voice bounces off the cracked ground, and I ignore him. This is what staring death in the face looks like. This is what going insane looks like.

"Come on no one is even awake in this sleepy town anymore."

There's an awkward silence, and the wind rustles my hair and chills my bones. Within moments Clarkson drops down next to me and sighs, though his heart causes tremors underneath me.

"You know, when I was a kid I thought about how easy it would be to just lie down in the middle of a busy street and end it all, but I don't think it has the same effect now," I whisper.

"Why do you say that, Piper?"

"Because it's true. After my brother and mom died, I thought it would just be easier to end my life too. Yet, I could never pull the trigger. I wanted to prove everyone wrong, but the only person I proved wrong was myself."

"Piper, I think you're being hard on yourself."

"Clarkson White, I am a mess. I don't deserve to be here on this Earth."

"Are you okay? Are you..." his voice fades out I know what he's implying.

"Yeah, I'll be okay don't worry about me. Besides, I couldn't kill myself even if I tried."

"Piper, I don't even know what to say right now."

"I'm sorry, I don't mean to make you uncomfortable. I can stop."

"No, it's okay. I'm just worried about you."

"Don't be, my little nerd. I am just a wandering soul pondering her life."

"Then keep talking, and I'll just listen."

He reaches for my hand and, just like every other time our hands lace, I feel less alone.

"I've always wondered what it's like to live. To have a near death experience like this and feel alive instead of dead. I'm talking too much. I've said too much. I'm sorry for babbling."

I prop myself up, dust the cracked pavement off my legs, and saunter over to the sidewalk that we were journeying to, but Clarkson doesn't follow. He watches me in awe. He watches me in confusion. It's all coming clear for him. He's figuring me out. He's defining me before I can even define myself.

# THEN:

People never know when something bad is about to happen. We're blissfully ignorant creatures at birth and it's a apart of who we are as a whole. Anyone who says differently is full of shit. People can be inclined to think something will happen, but human beings aren't capable of knowing the inevitable. The day my brother and mother died there was no gray sky hanging over my Pennsylvania home, there was no boiling tension at home. There was no way for me to know that a storm was silently brewing, waiting for the soul-less night to unleash its wrath.

The more that I think about that day, the more I doubt the normality of the situation. You never hear stories about a day going wrong that started out perfect, but that was my reality. The morning greeted me with with my mother's radiating song, causing me to float to the kitchen for french toast with cinnamon maple syrup and dancing sunbeams. Even Charlie was in a good mood, which was a rarity, but no one questioned it, no one wanted to ruin the start of a good day.

"Good morning my darlings, how'd you sleep?" my mother asked.

"I slept on a huge cloud while angel babies in diapers serenaded me," Charlie teased.

"Oh Charlie let's not start the day off on a rough foot," my dad reprimanded Charlie.

"Relax, I'm just joking around. Mom knows that I love her and just like to give her grief every now and then, right mom?"

"Whatever you say Charlie. Alright you two need to finish eating so we're not late to school. I have to post the cast list for the musical today before a group of stay-at-home moms lynch me," she laughed.

Charlie rolled his eyes before shifting the attention back to him, "Blake and I are throwing a party together at his house tonight, so I will not be making curfew."

Blake was Charlie's partner in crime. They were never apart, but the funny thing is, the person who claimed to know the most about him couldn't know any less. The Charlie Blake knew was artificial, the poor bastard just didn't know it.

"Excuse me, you don't get to decide if you can break curfew or not," My Father fumed.

"But it's Friday, and not only is it right down the road, but I also told you that I was going to be delinquent, therefore you should just accept that it's going to happen."

"I don't appreciate you thinking that you just get to run all the shots. This is my house, and as long as you live under my roof, you listen to me!"

My Dad slammed his mug of coffee down on the table and a miniscule earthquake rocked the kitchen. The air seemed to stiffen at my Dad's outburst, and yet, the earthquake's only damage was the coffee pooling on the table. Soon enough, my mom swooped in and not only saved the table, but also the day itself, or so I thought.

"Both of you hush up. Charlie, you are not going to ruin the start of a good day. Now apologize to your Father, right now," she commanded.

"But, Mom," Charlie protested.

"If you want to go out tonight, you have to apologize. Got that?" she said.

"I'm sorry Dad," he murmured.

"Now, my love, tonight is Friday, and Charlie has been doing well in school lately, so I think we should treat him by allowing him to extend his curfew for the night. Don't you think that's a great idea?" she said, shifting her focus to my Dad.

My Dad scowled at Charlie, but his sour face soon transformed to defeat. He looked worn. He looked tired of fighting. He looked as if he was accepting the fact that he could never protect his broken little boy from the horrors of the world, no matter how hard he tried. My Dad really did try his best.

"I think that I'm okay with whatever you think is best, my love. Happy wife, happy life, right?" my Dad replied.

"Perfect, now both of you stop bickering and get out of here. We're running late."

# NOW:

I feel tired but my mind is wide awake. I don't have a true grasp of time, but I know that if i stay up much longer I won't be able to wake up in time for work.  Still I don't want to go home, I want to stay and talk to Clarkson. I like when he listens to me. I like when I can listen to him. I like when neither of us say anything and let the world talk for us.

"Clarkson White," I say. My feet dangle off the aged boardwalk once again. I'm back where I started, but I'm not angry anymore. This night has given me a sense of clarity that I truly needed.

"Yes, Piper Addison?"

His gaze shifts from staring out into the dark soulless sea, to meeting the restless waves that reside in my eyes.

"Thank you for being my friend."

"It's my pleasure. I don't think I would prefer to talk to anyone else at work. You're crazy and it's wonderful, annoying sometimes, but mainly wonderful."

"Oh look at you, such a sweet talker," I laugh easily and it seems as if there isn't a weight on my chest. My emotions feel more tangible, more real, but I'm not sure why.

"Yeah, yeah. Back to earlier though, I feel like every time we take one step forward you just shut me out completely. Is it something that I've said?"

"No, not at all. I've just never talked about my past in full detail. It hurts to remember."

"But it would hurt less if you let it out in the universe. Wouldn't you like to stop carrying your past around like a battle wound? Piper Addison, you're stronger than you believe. Stop fighting a war against yourself."

I feel as if I'm a soldier in a never ending battle. I know I'm a woman who passes off my fears as pessimism so I don't get hurt, and because of if I can't fully trust anyone. I guess it's why I hate telling a story that doesn't directly affect. It makes me question whether I'm important at all. Am I a secondary character in my own life story? Am I forced to face the repercussions of someone else's evil?

"The problem, my friend, is not that I don't want to say anything, but that I don't know how. I am afraid of being myself and I am afraid of moving on. I don't know what you want me to say."

"Just keep taking it one day at a time. You can even write it down instead of talking about it. Maybe that will help. I don't know, Piper."

"I'll try, but can you promise me something?"

"Sure, anything. What do you need?" he asks.

I reach for his hand and our fingers intertwine. He has this look of worry plastered on his face as if I'm about to ask him to kill me. I just need him to stay by my side. I need someone to help me because I know if I do this to myself, there is no going back. "Promise you'll be there for me, even after you learn the whole truth."

"I promise. When you need me, I'll be there."

# THEN:

The rest of that day seemed so unimportant. It was just normal. Tests and endless lessons greeted me at school, while hundreds of kids swarmed the halls with talk of plans for the weekend. I just blended into the background, walking without anyone by my side, watching people with their friends, trying to hide the jealousy that bubbled in my stomach because I never really had friends.

After school, everything was still in order, and our house was running like clockwork. Everyone was doing their own thing, letting life run them down. My mother was occupied with auditions, my father was working late, and Charlie was getting ready for the party. We were all in our bubbles, separate yet together under one roof.

Before he left, Charlie ordered a pizza for me gave me money and told me to tell our parents to not wait up for him. It was going to be a long night, he said. It was supposed to be the best party of the year.

"Have fun,"I called out to him as he slammed the door and drove just a few neighborhoods over. "Be safe, Charlie."

# NOW:

I wake up in a pool of my own sweat, my skin clings to moist sheets, and aged tears mingle with the perspiration. Even the idea of opening up causes nightmares to return with full force. Nights are so long, and days are even longer. I'm constantly on edge. I don't know if I'm fighting with reality or flirting with insanity.

I pry myself up and the world is still in its twilight. I could make myself a sleeping concoction, but those just heighten my fears when I'm in this state. Everything is so surreal. I feel the need to scream, but when I open my mouth no words come out. I feel the need to cry, but tears refuse to flow unless I'm in a restless trance. I feel the need to figure out what the hell is wrong with me, but my heart won't stop racing, and my head won't stop swimming.

My typewriter ends up calling for me after moments of looking for a purpose. If my mind is restless, I force it to be productive. The sound of the keys clanking and the gentle bell at the end of every line calm me down a bit. They are my lullaby, and at the same time they give me a sense of purpose. Hours later, papers are sprawled over the uneven floors, dark rings form around my eyes, and my brain succumbs to the deprivation.

You would think that the voices would stop when my brain just gives in. You would think that the nightmares would go away. They don't, they just get stronger, and I'm too tired to fight them. Some nights my mind creates a reality based of the stories of that night, the gunshots, the supposed torture, and the end of the town's peace of mind. Other nights I am forced to face myself, I am forced to become what society expects of me, I am forced to look at myself as the damned monster I truly believe I am. I don't know what's worse, in either reality, I lose a part of myself, either to the pain that my brother left or to the pain that I've cultivated throughout the years. I know I did this to myself, and now it's too late. I have to live my nightmares.

When the morning comes, the alarm doesn't startle me. My mind is almost too eager to stop fighting sleep. Bad nights tend to go that way. You fight to sleep and when you can't win you just give in to delusion until you're forced to face reality. Another day of work waits, and with work comes another day of pretending that I'm okay.

A navy blue sweater hugs warms my frigid heart while black pants latch onto each leg. My hair is a mess, and a mountain of makeup can't hide the air of desperation that my under-eye bags reak. I look as if I'm falling apart, but truly I'm just trying to hold myself together.

I grab my pills on the way out and a to-go cup of tea before I'm rushing back to my hole in the wall, the library. At school, I avoid all the teachers, like normal, and I avoid Clarkson's request to talk over lunch, citing that I have to rebind books before the day is over. I don't want to deal with people, I don't even want to deal with the kids who haven't done a damn thing to me.

I don't know why I feel so bad today. I don't know why I can't get out of my head. I can't help but wish I wasn't real. I wish that this was all some dream. I can't pinpoint what's wrong with me. I feel confused, and I don't know how to convey that to people without them thinking that I've lost all sanity. Maybe I'm just burned out. Maybe if I keep myself busy everything will just go back to normal, with me successfully pretending that I'm always okay. God, what the hell is wrong with me?

Of course the day goes by excruciatingly slow. Of course, I hear snickers in the teacher's lounge when I go to heat up my lunch like I'm back in highschool all over again. Of course, I get yelled by the Big Bad Wolff for not trying to insert more religion into my story telling. Of course, today is not my day.

When I see Clarkson during my planning period I can't help but pull him into a hug and cry into his shoulders. His scrawny frame somehow seems to keep me stable, and he doesn't ask why I'm upset, he just lets me cry and runs his fingers up and down my spine.

"I don't know what's wrong, or what's happened, but I'm here, and I'll do whatever you need me to okay? I'm here for you, Piper."

"It's just been a really shitty day."

"I know, I know. How about tonight we go and do something fun, huh? That'll make you feel better?"

"That does sound nice," I say as I try to regain composure, "why don't you come over tonight, and instead of us going out, I'll make us some dinner. I think I need a night in."

"Perfect, now shape up. You have fairytales to make for eager little kids."

"Thank you for being here for me."

Clark holds my shoulders and our eyes meet. He shakes his head at me before saying, "I meant what I said before. I will always be here for you. I don't care that you haven't had someone to care about you before because now you have me. Your problems are valid with me, your tears are valid with me. Piper Addison you are my best friend, and though you irritate me quite frequently, I would jump off a cliff if you asked me."

I give him another hug before both of us retreat to our own corners of the world. I honestly think that Clark may be the best thing to come out of this town, and I'm so glad he's in my life. I don't think I'd ever tell him that though, he'd start gloating and I'd get annoyed.

At the end of the work day, I drive to the store and pick up chicken and some pasta to make the only adult type meal I know I can succeed at. I know it won't live up to any meal a restaurant can produce, the type of quality food Clark is used to, but it's okay, the food doesn't really matter. All that matters is that I'm trying to get out of my head.

For the first time all day my mind is occupied by something else. I'm running around the house like a madwoman trying to cook and clean. I don't know if I should change or not, and I'm trying not to overthink the situation more than I already am. By the time the house is starting to come together I plop myself down in front of my desk, pull out my typewriter and start writing what I know I should say though I know I never will.

# THEN:

When you are a person who is desperate to fit in, your personality molds to those around you. When the popular crowd adopted Charlie, his mood turned sour, his ego inflated, and his habits became reckless. Although his personality shifted, I could see insecurities bubbling under the surface. The look of fear, the look of someone who was perpetually lost, rested in his eyes. I knew in my heart that he wasn't happy with how his life was going, but we weren't close in the last few years of his life, and I had no place to tell him how he was supposed to live.

Of course I wasn't at the party the night of murder, but gossip spreads faster than lightning can strike. It took years of eavesdropping to figure out fact from fiction, but I was so determined to figure out why I lost my soul to my brother's crime.

They said it was a crime of passion, done by a boy who was angry over rejection, but that wasn't true. No one knew that Charlie was mentally ill, they didn't know that changes in his mood caused him to be everything from a protective loving brother to a menace. No one knew the real Charlie except those who shared a roof with him. No one knew how unhappy he was with his life. No one knew that he believed his medicine made him weak. He even stopped taking his pills at a point, believing that it was clouding his thoughts and preventing him from doing well in sports.

Charlie's humanizers grew dusty with time, but no one said anything. Mom pretended like her son was okay, though she saw the emptiness in his eyes and chalked it up to teenage rebellion. Dad pretended like his son was just going through a bit of teenage rebellion causing him to threaten to take away Charlie's freedom only to let go of the reigns and let Charlie roam uncontrolled. I pretended like I didn't see a thing, and eventually I became blind to the chaos around me. I guess when you come to terms with a twisted reality you don't really know what's corrupt and morbid.

Anyways, they said that the party was a true rager, or whatever they call cool parties now, I'm not really up to date with slang. Booze was flowing, music was blaring, and parents sat quietly by their phones, giving the teenagers time to be free but waiting patiently for their time to expire. They said that during the night there was an odd couple hooking up at every corner.

With an aura of unrestricted freedom, Charlie let his demons escape him. He drank, he flirted, he smoked, he did everything and anything there was to do at that party. I wish I could say I know why he did it; I'd like to think he did all those things to forget himself, but it clearly didn't work if that was the case.

Sometime later, a fight between two of Charlie's girls broke out. Neither of them knew that the other one existed, and both were jealous. Neither of them pointed the blame at Charlie, but instead to the scandalously dressed peer in front of her. When Charlie found out, he ran to break up the storm, but instead got thrown into the middle. They wanted him to choose, they wanted him to pick a girl and announce it to the world. He was enraged by the idea and stormed off as they were screaming and crying.

As he walked away, his morality escaped him, anguish filled him to the brim, and suddenly he couldn't take the voices in his head any longer. He went into his friend's room, retrieved a gun and calmly walked out of the party as if he was planning to play a harmless game of Russian Roulette. When he reunited with the girls he did not show them what he was hiding in his pant's pocket, he simply led them to a stretch of field at the end of the neighborhood where no one went unless they had something to hide. At this point, my glitzy narrative fades away as reality begins to break through.

They were in that field when he shot them in cold blood. He killed the girls for resembling his inner demons, for representing his indecisive nature, his inability to open up to the world, his constant paralyzing fear of the future. He killed them to make the voices stop, and as the last shot rang through the air, the voices grew silent and so did the world.

Realization set in slowly like a calm tide, but once he realized what he had done his body dropped to the ground and he curled up into a ball. Once again, the vulnerable Charlie had managed to make an appearance, revealing how unstable he truly was. He was a child pretending to have grown up. He didn't know how to deal with the consequences of his actions because he refused to admit that he wasn't like everyone else. He put himself in the situation and he knew that all hope was lost.

When too much time had passed, he finally got up and began to attempt to fix his mistake. He knew he had to get rid of the bodies, and so one by one he carried the girls in his arms. With their lifeless bodies clinging to his chest he decided that their final resting place would be our backyard. Often times, in my dreams, their bodies aren't completely cold when Charlie starts digging them a grave. It makes me feel like he could have saved them if he tried, but I think he was too caught up in his own ego to hold compassion for anyone else. I mean, he didn't even give them a proper grave. Their burial place was nothing more than a shallow grave next to a vegetable garden. As he tried to bury the girls he laced flowers from the neighbor's yards into their hair and between their hands. It was his way of saying he was sorry. It was his way of asking the angels for forgiveness. His only bit of redemption on that seemingly perfect night.

As he covered the body of the first girl my mom came home and found Charlie. She was confused over why he was covered in dirt and blood, and the animalistic look on his face frightened her. She tried to talk to him, to ask him if he was okay. He wouldn't answer her question, but he spoke to her with a heavy heart. At this point, it's easy to question how reliable of a source I am, but I have nothing to gain or anything to lose by telling the truth. I might not have seen the first two deaths, but I did hear the last two.

"Charlie, my love, what happened to you, you look like you've killed a man?"

"You weren't supposed to see, you weren't supposed to be here! It's too late. It's all too late."

"Charlie, what are you talking about? Please, let me help you."

"It's too late, we're both dead anyways."

When my mother stepped towards him and tried to pull him in for a hug he reached for the gun once more and pointed it directly at her heart.

"Mom, I'm sorry. I wanted to save us. I wanted to save myself, but it's too late. It's too late."

"Charlie, don't do this. Put it down."

"I love you," he whispered as his finger rested on the trigger.

"I love you too, my sweet, sweet boy."

Tears streamed down my mother's face as she resigned to her fate. She couldn't reach him; her baby boy was gone and was replaced by a monster. Suddenly, a woman whose life could only be described as a beautiful composition ended in dissonance without a true resolve. When the shot rang out, it echoed through the house and the neighborhood. The game was over, police were on their way to find their criminal, and to break up the party going on just a few doors down.

Once more, Charlie dropped to the floor, but this time he kept the gun in one hand. He cradled our mother in his lap and kissed her forehead. He never wanted to hurt anyone, especially not her, his mother who he loved with his whole world. With two scorned lovers and a beloved mother, the massacre was almost over. It was then when I turned on my ipod and blasted the only song that brought me joy and comfort. It was then when I was blissfully unaware of the tragedy, but frightened by the terrors of the world that accompany a gunshot.

*Here comes the sun, here comes the sun, and I'll say it's all right…*

At the end of the song, one last gunshot was fired. The massacre was complete. Four lives were ripped from reality by a tortured soul. Even to this day, I wish I knew what he was going to do that night. I wish I could take my brother back and help him through life. I wish I could have made him feel less alone. I wish I could have had him listen to that damn song just one more time.

*Here comes the sun Charlie, here comes the sun. It's alright, Charlie. We're going to get through this, just you and me, just like it's always been, just like it always will be.*

# NOW:

In my house, there is a table set for two for the first time. The plates aren't matching, the silverware looks dingy, and in the middle of the table a small stack of papers stare me down, but there is a table set for two for the first time. When Clarkson rings the doorbell, I straighten out my black skirt and greet him with a warm smile. He walks in holding a bouquet of daisies and behind the flowers there is a scrawny nerd dressed in plaid.

"Well come on in!" I hum.

"I'm mighty glad to be here, these are for you."

He hands me the flowers and I walk into the kitchen and pull out a giant water bottle to house them. My face turns bright pink when he notices that's what I'm doing, but I don't own a vase and all my mason jars are too small to house them.

"Thank you so much, I love them."

"I'm really glad."

"Here, why don't you sit down, I'll get you a drink. Is water okay?" I ask.

"Water is fine by me."

I fidget with the water and spill some all over myself. I don't know why my nerves are out of control and why my body seems to be fluttering. Clarkson comes up to me when he sees me panic and grabs my hands to steady them.

"Are you okay?" He asks.

"I finally wrote everything you wanted to know down. Well, the start of it at least," I whisper.

"Is that what's on the table?"

"You should read it before I do something stupid."

"Even more stupid than spilling water all over yourself?"

"Hey, watch it now. This could easily go all over you."

I give him a small smile, and gesture him to sit down. Moments later we're talking and laughing, but I know he's only try to calm me down. Half way through the dinner, the conversation starts to slow and so he reaches for the papers and starts to read. He scans through it quite quickly, only stopping after every few paragraphs to take a bite of food, and it puts me more on edge. He looks up at me after but I can't make eye contact; I don't want to see him judge me.

"Piper, I'm so sorry. That must have been really hard to deal with," he mutters.

"It's fine, it's just my reality."

"I guess I get why you moved here, to get away from it all, but I don't understand everything about your situation?"

"What do you mean? Just ask me, I'll do my best to be more open."

"How come you blame yourself? Your brother was the murderer, not you. He was the bad guy, not you. You did nothing wrong."

Clark reaches for my hands but I pull away. He doesn't get it. I hate myself because I can't hate Charlie. I don't see him as a bad guy. I hate myself, and blame myself, for letting the world convince me that I was sinful, broken, and unworthy of any love. I hate myself for listening to lies for so long that they've all become true.

"It's not what I did do, it's what I didn't do. My brother was never the demon the world made him out to be, and I was never a devil spawn who needed to be watched."

"Piper, he killed three people before he killed himself."

"Clarkson White, people do the darndest things when they need help. I was supposed to be there for my brother. I was supposed to be his rock like he was mine. It took me years to realize that the only people we had were each other. When I was a kid, he protected me from bullies, he helped me feel less alone in a school full of people who just saw me as different. And at the same time, I

434

helped him through so many medical treatments, I listened to his troubles and made him feel less alone too. We were a screwed up pair, but he was my family. He was one of the only constants in my life until that night, even factoring the years where we started to drift apart."

"I didn't mean to offend you…" he starts to talk, but I don't want to hear it.

"It's okay," I lie on impulse. It's easier to say that you're okay than to explain all the reasons why you aren't.

"Just help me understand how you turned into a shell of a human? Help me to understand how I can help you."

"I don't know how to. I don't know what I'm doing in general and it's just really hard for me to trust. I always feel as if my back is against the wall. I feel as if I'm always fighting a battle I know I can't ever win."

"Listen to me, you are not solely your faults or what you think are your faults. You need to let someone help. You need to let someone in," he says.

"I tried that before."

"What about religion? What about giving it another chance? Maybe if you believe in something you can find the emotional strength you've been looking for this entire time."

"I don't think I'll ever seek solace from religion again, Clarkson. Those were the people who turned their backs on me. Those were the kinds of people who made me feel as if i was doomed for hell before I had a chance to decide who I wanted to be in the world. I can't put myself back in that place."

"But not all Christians are bad, not everyone who believes in a God is out to get you."

"I understand that, but I am unwilling to go back down that route and set myself up to be hurt all over again. I'm trying to prevent a cycle of mental abuse."

"Piper please, maybe if you just talked to Father-" I cut him off.

"Clarkson, it's your turn to listen to me. I respect the fact that you have faith, and I respect the fact that you believe wholeheartedly that it will lead you to any and all closure that you seek, but you and I have different viewpoints. If you can't respect the fact that I am not religious, nor have any intention to turn to religion to figure out who I am, I'm going to have to ask you to leave. I can't keep having the same conversation with you, I'm not changing my mind."

"Piper, don't be this way."

Clarkson reaches out to grab my hand but I move away. I thought he was starting to get it. I thought that he wouldn't try to change me. I thought that I could open up to him and he would just understand.

"I'm sorry, thank you for the flowers. They're lovely."

"It doesn't have to be this way."

His eyes are staring me down, trying to process me as fast as he can. He's shutting down too. Poor fool thought he could help me. He thought he could save me from myself. I don't need to be rescued. I never needed to be rescued. I've only ever needed a friend. When I stand up and move towards the door, Clarkson doesn't budge from the table. He stays, he waits. He wants me to say that I don't want him around, but I can't say that.

"Thank you for coming, Mr. White."

He realizes that I'm too firm in my beliefs when I call him by his last name. He realizes that I'm too far gone, that he pushed me to my brink. I don't hate him for not understanding. I appreciate the fact that he tried, and that's more than any other person in this world has ever done. I just need space. He moves from the table, and extends his hand. Of course I don't take it, my pride is too overwhelming, and my heart is too bruised to forgive. I see the look of defeat in his eyes. He thinks he's failed me, and so I watch him walk away, just like everyone else did before and everyone else will after.

# THEN:

You sit on an aged pew, waiting for your name to be called. You wait to confess your sins, and you wait for an unfair burden to disintegrate into thin air like a gentle breeze on a sunny day.

"Forgive me father, for I have sinned" is a saying that has been ingrained into my subconscious. Forgive me. Forgive me for all the shitty things I've done. Forgive me for forgetting to do the dishes and blaming my brother. Forgive me for yelling at my mother when she took away my favorite book. Forgive me for being human because I am flawed.

At one point in my life, my worries, just like all my other classmates', were simple. There was no question as to if we were to be forgiven, we were just children. Yet, as I aged I found it harder to apologize. It was even worse after Charlie did what he did because I was not only apologizing for my sins, but for his. I wanted to believe that I could take on Charlie's sin. I wanted to believe that if I took on his pain, we could both be forgiven, we could both move on. I wanted to take on his suffering so that I could be happy again, and so that he could end up in heaven instead of the hell everyone else told me he was in.

Even after I was told that I would never be forgiven and my whole family was doomed for hell, I kept going back. I kept believing that I could change the church's mind by becoming extremely subservient and obedient. I fought my own disillusionment and attempted to become some sort of evangelist. I attended church whenever I could, I ignored the jeers from my peers, and I prayed. I prayed for my voice to be heard. I prayed for some understanding. When I didn't get any answers, when life started to get worse, I found it hard to keep trying.

Many people see suffering as some sort of test from God, to prove their faith, and I won't knock on the experiences of others or their beliefs, but I was tired of proving myself faithful. I wanted a moment of clarity. I wanted to believe that after every low there was a high. I wanted God to save me, and I don't think he ever heard my cries.

I don't know when exactly I just stopped believing. I don't think any person just gives up something they believe in all at once, I think it has to be gradual. You start finding flaws in your logic until one day it isn't your logic anymore but the logic of others who were just naive as you once were. It's then when you stop believing. It's then when you stop praying asking for answers that will never come. It's then when you stop looking for redemption. It's then when you are

able to take fate into your own hands and control your own destiny.
It's then when your will is as free as your corrupted thoughts. It's then
when you see the world for how it truly is.

# NOW:

Sometimes you wake up with a pit in your stomach. You dread the idea of the day ahead and you just want to feign ill and go back to sleep. This is how I feel today. I don't want to face Clarkson White. I do not want to see what I've done to him. He feels as if he broke me, so he in turn is broken. The fault is solely mine, and I don't think I am ready to handle the consequences.

The night was going so well, if he just stopped trying to force me to change, things would have gone right. I want to trust him. I want to open up to him because I feel as if he's in my life for some reason. I just have to fight a battle against myself to prove my instincts wrong. It doesn't make much sense and my emotions are muddled because of it.

At work, I try to sneak into the library without anyone noticing me. Most of the time people don't. It is as if my existence begins and ends in the library, and I like it that way. I don't like bringing attention to myself, I like to exist behind the scenes. Figuring out who you are is easier when no one else is watching. Yet, of course, I'm only ever found when I don't want to be.

Clarkson stares at me as I walk in, he is silent but I can tell that his mind is racing. I don't know what he wants or expects out of me, so I pretend like he's not there and start checking in the books from the drop off box. I don't think his eyes leave me once. We wait in silence, neither of us know what to say. It's rather ironic that in a room full of words, both of us find it difficult to compose our own.

"I'm surprised you haven't kicked me out of here too," he starts and I hear the underlying pain masked by a sarcastic tone.

"Clarkson White, please don't be that way."

"I just don't get why you can't see that I'm trying to help you."

"I don't want you to fix me, I want you to be there for me. Those are two different things and I don't think you understand that," I say.

"I don't want to fix you, I want to help you. Those are two different things too and I don't think you understand that," he fires back.

"How? How do you plan on helping me then?"

"By having you come to church, by reintroducing you to the thing that gave you hope and stability as a child. You don't have to be catholic if that's what makes you uncomfortable, it can be anything, I just want you to believe in something."

"Stop! Enough. Stop trying to make me into something that I am not."

"Piper- I..."

"No, stop Clarkson. I am tired of people trying to change me. My entire life no one has thought I was good enough. There was always some improvement I had to make, some person I had to please. It destroyed my self worth. It destroyed me. If you aren't happy with how I am you don't have to deal with me at all."

My words start off strong but turn into a whisper by the end. I'm vulnerable. I want to be accepted. I just want someone to look at me and realize that I deserve to be loved. I want someone to validate me. I want to be able to love and validate myself. I just don't get it. I thought he was my friend.

"I'm not trying to change you. I just want to make you happy. I just want to be there for you, Piper. Stop pushing me away."

"I'm not always a happy person. I'm not super bubbly or bright and upbeat, and besides you, I don't think there is a person in this world who is like that all the time. If you can't handle that, if you can't handle the fact that when my emotions truly come out everything is intense then you need to let me know. You need to tell me that you can't handle me. You need to end the friendship now because I can't get hurt anymore. I'm tired, Clarkson. I'm really tired."

Clarkson walks towards me and grabs me by the shoulders. The library is empty and so it feels as if we are the only two people in this world, and as I look at him all I feel is complete and utter emptiness. I want to walk away from him now, I want to turn into a puddle of tears and disappear, but I can't. I hate him, I hate him so much. I hate that I opened up to him. I hate that when he's around I feel comfortable, I feel happy. I hate this constant battle of emotions that I feel when I am around him. I hate that every part of me loves every part of him and that in itself has left me nothing but completely and utterly vulnerable.

"You're pushing me away. You aren't listening anymore. I don't know what I can do anymore. Just please Piper, let me be by your side. That's all I ask. That's all I want."

He lets go of me after that and once again the staring returns. Who's going to leave first? Him or me? Who's going to give up on this toxic friendship? Who's going to break first?

This time it's me who walks out the door, and with each step out of the school my heart breaks just a little bit more.

# NOW:

When I get home I call into work, feigning an illness before I admit to myself that I truly feel ill. I'm shutting down, and my being feels absolutely empty. There is no part of me that feels okay, I've opened a door in my past that I desperately tried to keep closed. I've allowed my mask to fall and for my true self to slip through. She's a mess. She's a nightmare. I hate her completely.

After I get off the phone, I find myself writing again. Emotions that I didn't know existed pour out onto the page while my brain is still searching for answers. It's then when I realize that though the characters we write are not always a complete representation of us, their words are. Their emotions, their love, their pain, it's all a part of us. Feelings I've repressed for so long come out so freely when it feels like no one will see through my guise. Writing helps me be myself by pretending to be someone else.

With a new identity, I write about how I feel by taking myself out of my own situation. I talk about love though I don't understand what it is. I talk about fighting through life though I'm still in battle. I talk about being so much wiser than I really am. If I could take all the advice my characters give, I'd live a much better life, but I'm too stubborn to listen to my own heart.

There are ways to pretend that you are okay when you're not, and writing is my way. I don't stop for hours, I keep pressing on. I ignore my responsibilities, I ignore my body's cry for food, water, and a bathroom break, and I ignore my phone as it slowly fills up with messages.

I'm not okay, but I will pretend to be so until I feel that I am. If that means writing until my heart stops hurting, so be it. If that means locking myself up in this house until I can think clearly, so be it. If that means packing up and starting over again, so be it. I want to be happy. I want to feel happy. I'm tired of pretending.

As the dark night blurs my already tunneled vision, my eyes grow heavy. Just a few words more, just a few more pages, and it's all over. To my character,  there is no point in her work, nothing can explain the pain that love brings whether it be platonic or romantic, it hurts all the same. To my character, there is no point in her being. She can't understand her life and she spent all of it looking for answers to questions that have none.

After all this time, the only thing that I've learned is that I never lived because I was too busy trying to find out why I do. I've tried to force love, I've tried to force faith. Because in my eyes everything was an experiment I didn't allow myself to believe in fate or hope. I didn't allow myself to believe in fantasies or have happy endings. I ruined myself.

446

Maybe I'm turning into her, maybe I've been her all along. I live miserably under a cloud of synthetic happiness. I am quiet yet odd, and yet I'm exactly who society wants me to be. My character hates that about her, and I think I hate that about me too. I hate her so much I've never even given her a name. Maybe that's because she's who stares me down in the mirror every day. It's all just maybes with me. Unanswerable questions are only met with halfhearted answers that will never help me find my truth. I think I'm going to kill her off and end the story. I'll make her do something I never had the guts for. I'll give her the relief I've never been able to find.

Her story ends and mine still goes, and yet as she ends her life questioning whether her story will ever be worth reading, I ask myself the same.

# NOW:

It has been days since I've moved from my bed. I've done nothing but call in sick to work. My body is weak and I don't really want food. I don't want anything but peace of mind. I wish I could sleep it all away. I read somewhere that two nights sleep is all you needed to fix your problems, but it's been more than two nights and I don't feel better at all.

After three days of not showing up at work, Clarkson reappeared in my life. He shows up before work and after now, trying to talk to me, trying to keep me alive. I don't know what he wants from me, or what he's hoping to gain from all this. He doesn't get that I'm not good enough for him, or worth his time, and that's because my core has slowly rotted with time.

"Good morning Piper, are you going to get up today?"

Every morning he asks the same thing, and every morning I don't answer. Some days he leaves me food and water for the day while other days he sits right next to me and tells me to go back to sleep. I see the worry in his face and it makes me sadder. I warned him, didn't I? I told him to stay away from me, that I was no good. Yet, he's still here. He's still fighting even though I won't. I don't know why he won't just give up. He won't ever figure me out, so he needs to walk away before it gets any worse.

"Why do you always come back?" I whisper.

"I told you I'd be there."

"You're wasting your time on me."

"Shut up and go back to bed."

I laugh, I always seem to laugh when I feel like I should just stop caring. I laugh at myself. I laugh at the situation. I laugh at my life. I just feel so fed up with everything.

"What's so funny?" he asks.

"You're being pathetic. That's what's funny. You don't see when it's time to give up. You don't see when it's time to let go. I never understood why you said people picked on you when you were little, but now I do. You don't get social cues, do you?"

My words are vile, my thoughts are bitter. If my sadness isn't enough to deter him, then I have to push him out. I'm sorry my dear Clarkson, but I have to hurt you to save you. I have to hurt you to save me. I can't have any more attachments.

It takes him a while for my words to register and he immediately backs away. He can't believe me. It worked. He hates me, at least for the moment anyways. I watch him leave the house with a pile of graded papers crumpled in one hand and a half opened briefcase in the other. He doesn't even take his coat with him, and I don't have to go outside to know that a fall morning in Maine is pretty bitter.

I hurt him. I got my wish, but that doesn't stop me from feeling shit about the whole thing.

# NOW:

He comes back the next day, he always comes back. He doesn't say anything when he comes in, just makes breakfast. He sets the food by my bed and watches to see if I'll move, if I'll say anything. I won't apologize to him, but he's expecting one.

"You need to get up," he says.

I don't answer him.

"Piper, get up. You're going to get dressed and go into work. This is all getting ridiculous. Don't you think I know what you're doing? Stop playing games. You're fine. You're just pretending that something is wrong with you."

"You don't know anything about me." I spit.

"Prove me wrong then, get ready."

"I'm not going back, Mr. White."

I feel a wave of red rush into my cheeks. I'm angry. I'm angry that he doesn't see that I'm trying to keep him from getting hurt. I'm angry that he doesn't see that there is something seriously wrong with me. I don't want to be here. I don't want to be anywhere. My brain is this tangled messed and I don't feel as if I can trust anyone, especially not myself.

"Why not?"

"I can't do it. I can't do it anymore."

"Do what? Use your words Piper!"

"I can't keep pretending to be happy being someone else. I can't keep pretending to be okay with everyone trying to change me. I can't keep living this fucking lie that I have been since I was a little girl. I can't handle any more. I'm so tired. What more do you want from me?"

"I didn't know you felt that way."

"I know."

I sigh and melt further into my bed. I feel myself tearing up. I feel the vulnerability seep into my bones. Clarkson White this is exactly why I played shy this entire time. This is why I kept you at an arm's distance. When you defined me you figured out how insane I am.

"I don't know what I'm supposed to do with you," he says.

"Please, don't make me go."

I clutch onto his hand and my childish demeanor slips through. Clarkson doesn't say anything but his fondue colored eyes hold nothing but sympathy. He thinks he destroyed me, made me unravel and unfold with truth. If only he understood this was a long time coming. A person can only hold on to fake sanity for so long before madness slips through.

"We'll try again tomorrow, okay?"

I sigh again and bite my lip. The world seems so heavy and here's a person who keeps trying to share my load to only mess me up even more. As our hands unravel, I watch Clarkson hold onto his breath and watch me cautiously. Yes, I'm a bomb. Yes, I'm fragile, but please, please, look past that. If you're so determined to stay by my side, if you're supposed to be the one to help me put myself back together you have to be patient with me. You have to just let me find myself the only way I know how. Please, you're the only person that can. You're the only person who can see me. Please, don't lose faith in me even though I've lost faith in myself.

"I'm going to go to work now, okay? Just go back to sleep. I'll be back to check on you later."

Before Clarkson leaves my side his fingertips intertwine with my unkempt hair, and he shakes his head.

"I'm so sorry I did this to you," he mutters and as he finishes his words, the last bit of my heart breaks. It's not your fault you wanted to help, Clarkson. It's not your fault that you didn't know you were only trying to save me from myself.

# NOW:

He tries several mornings in a row to get me out of bed, at school they've stopped asking if I'm going to come in; they just assume I'm sick now. Clarkson lies to them and tells them that it's very serious, that I've been in and out of the hospital. None of them question him and none of them check up on me. They don't care, and this lie plays right into their fake narrative of me. After a while, even Clark stops trying to get me to do anything, he stays by my side and I stay in bed. It's a role we've both accepted playing.

"Morning Piper."

"Good morning, Clarkson."

"So I called in sick today, would you mind if I spent the day with you?" He asks.

"No matter what I say, you're going to stay here anyways."

"You're smart."

"Well what are you going to do all day then?"

"I have papers to grade, but I'd really just like to talk."

"I don't really have anything to talk about Clarkson..."

He pauses for a moment to think. He won't give up. He always come back, but I don't get why. You don't just keep trying when there is no reward. I don't understand him. Helping me won't help him, and there is no person in the world that is that selfless. We all have selfish motives but what is his?

"Then maybe we can just read, do you have anything on your shelves that you haven't read? Or maybe a favorite of some sorts?"

"Anything I have is worth reading."

"Okay well what's this Looking for Alaska book about?" he asks.

"It's an angsty teen book, it's absolutely wonderful."

"Then I guess that's what we're going to read today."

And that was all we did. At one point, I found myself shifting my body weight towards his as he acted out the book. He shifted towards me too, and by the middle of the book, we were both sitting up sharing my messy bed. We're both part of the story, we've both fallen into the pages, and it's here where I feel the safest.

"Piper," He stops reading. "You remind me of Alaska, both of you are so free spirited but at the same time there is just an utter darkness that envelops you two. It's crazy."

"Really? I never liked her, I thought Pudge was crazy for loving her."

"I think that we're compelled to hate the characters that remind us most of the unsavory parts of ourselves, but you know what?"

"What?" I ask.

"If I was Pudge, I'd fall in love with her too."

"Don't lie to me, Clark."

"Haven't you realized by now that I don't lie to you? Pudge saw through her faults, and yeah, it was dangerous for him to fall in love with the idea of her, but I don't think he ever saw her as someone to fix; he saw her as someone who deserved love."

I don't respond to Clark, I don't know how to, so he just starts reading again, and within time I take over. He smiles when I read, living on my every word. I even get him to tear up as I make it towards the end. Who knew the power of John Green could get him to blubber?

When the day morphs to night, he falls asleep on my shoulder with one chapter left to read. I don't move him, I just kind curl up next to him and start drifting off myself. We spent the entire day together without fighting and it was really nice. He's like this constant distraction that makes things seem okay for short bits of time. I may not know why he sticks around, but it's days like these that make me glad that he does.

The next morning things start out the same, he doesn't make a scene that we woke up tangled into each other, he just smiles and whispers good morning.

"Good morning to you too."

"Will you get out of bed for me today? Maybe we can get some food in you."

"I do believe that if I try to consume anything my stomach will then try to consume itself. It's gotten quite used to being malnourished, and I wouldn't want to make it uncomfortable."

My voice slips out but it sounds foreign and cracked, like uneven pavement.

"Piper Addison, there are children dying of malnutrition and here you are, mocking their pain and suffering?"

"I'm not mocking them, I'm simply joining them."

"I don't believe that is something worth joining."

"Oh Clarkson, it is. Fasting is quite admirable, and so is self sacrifice," I state bluntly.

"You must be having a good day, you're joking around again."

"Well I do hope so, the sun is shining, the birds are chirping..." I tease.

"Oh please, don't start up with that nonsense. Alright well, I need to run home and get changed before work. I don't want to miss two days in a row, if I do they're start to think I'm playing hooky with you!"

"You're absolutely ridiculous Clarkson White."

"In all seriousness though, I'm gonna run. Please try and do something today for me, even getting out of this bed will make you feel better. I'll be back after school and maybe we can start another book?"

"That sounds really nice," I pause. "You know what, I really don't deserve you, Clark, not one bit."

"Nonsense, you just don't see what I do."

He peels himself off the bed and squeezes my hand before running out the door. It's funny how quickly things can change between us. It's this constant back and forth that's exhausting but I wouldn't trade it for the world. If only things were different our friendship would be unstoppable.

After he leaves, I do get out of bed, I do clean myself and the house up, but somewhere along the way I get the idea of reinventing myself again. I don't have to run away to start over, I just have to change how everyone sees me and how I see myself. Maybe that way I can move on and be happy. Maybe that way I won't find myself glued to my bed for weeks on end. If I change I can stop worrying about everyone else, I can worry about me. My opinion is going to be the only one that matters but first I have to change. I'm going to reinvent myself, and everyone will love who I will become, including me. With those thoughts in my head I leave the house and make my way to the drug store. In order to start over, I need a new few things,

I need a new look.

# NOW:

It takes hours to undue the damage that has spanned years on end. My little piece of rebellion is gone. The light pink shade that defined my individuality is gone. The chocolate locks I grew up with have returned. No longer do I stand out to the world. I'm plain once again, with my simple face and typical eyes. It's the start of a new identity.

When Clarkson stops by after school his jaw drops. He looks dumbfounded and I don't know how he feels about the change. I was hoping he would like it, but if he doesn't, it doesn't really matter, I'm not trying to make him happy.

"Piper Addison, what have you done?"

"I wanted a change, do you like it?"

"Why did you decide to do it?" he asks, ignoring my question.

"I think I'm going to go back to work tomorrow, start over with everyone. Be normal, fit into the fold. I think it'll be nice." I ignore his question back.

"Are you sure you're ready for that? Today is the first day you've even left the bed."

"Don't worry, I'm okay now. Everything is fine, trust me."

"Piper, I don't want you to take this the wrong way but..."

"But what?"

"I'm not sure if you're stable enough to go back. I don't want you to go back to work until you're feeling one hundred percent better."

"Okay Clarkson, what do you want from me?" I roll my eyes. Of course he isn't happy. I'm ready to go back. I'm ready to force myself to suck up the pain and put myself back together again with some duct tape.

"I want you to be better, I want you to take your time."

"I'm ready, stop worrying. Tomorrow will be fine and it'll be the start of a new normal. I don't want you to remember me as the broken girl, but I want you to remember the one who was always able to herself back together again."

"I feel as if that's more of what you want for yourself, Piper."

"So what?"

"Fine, fine. If you're happy, I'm happy for you."

"Thank you, that means a lot to me."

"Now that this surprise is out of the way, what are we going to read tonight?" he asks.

"Let's just finish Looking for Alaska and talk, how about that?"

"Sounds perfect to me"

As we finish the story, he plays with my hair. It's like he doesn't know who I am. I don't know if this is what I was expecting but it's still a start. School tomorrow will be the true test, I'm going to have to force myself out my shell. I'm going to mingle with people who find me undesirable and god damnit I'm going to make them love me.

"You know what, Clark? This was my hair color before I dyed it pink." I whisper after we finish reading. It seems better to stay quiet, to let the world be louder than us for a change. I like when we're quiet. I like when I can hear our breaths fill up the room. I like when they sync together and dance with the air around us.

"I always thought that the pink suited you."

"I did too."

"Then why change it? Why won't you tell me?" he keeps prodding.

"I'm tired of running away from my problems. This is my attempt to start over without leaving. This is my attempt to pull myself together."

"You didn't have to change."

"Didn't I though? No one likes me like this and so I'm just going to move on. Keep moving forward, never look back, you know?"

"I guess so. I like you as you are though," he says.

I laugh, he says what he knows I want to hear. I know he doesn't believe it. If he did, he wouldn't have done what he did. It's okay though, we've moved past it all, well for now anyways.

"Are you staying over again?" I ask.

"I don't know, I wasn't really planning on it. I didn't mean to yesterday too, but your voice was just really calming by the end."

"Oh okay, that's fine."

"Do you need me to stay?"

"No, no, I'm fine. I was just wondering."

"Alright, well it's getting late anyways. I should probably get going…" he says and by the end of it his voice is drifting off, his mind is somewhere else.

"Oh okay then, I'll see you at work tomorrow?"
"Most definitely." He squeezes my hand and makes for the door, and this time he doesn't forget his coat.

# NOW:

In the morning, I find myself in black slacks, ballet flats, and a baby blue blouse. My hair waves gently down my back though part of it is braided into a crown. My face is painted, but barely so, and I look as if I'm radiating calm but in all honesty, I'm nervous.

With a cocktail of tea and medicine, my anxiety begins to quiet. If I'm going to survive today my brain has to get it's shit together, my emotions can't control me, I have to take control of myself. I walk to the car and drive down the winding road with this pit in my stomach, all while trying to control my heart with deep breaths.

Everything will be okay if you just believe it. You can only control things till fate kicks in and if this life isn't my destiny, if I can't really start over, then so be it. I'll figure out something for myself, no matter how long that takes.

Pulling up to the school, I feel as if I'm reliving my first day all over again. I feel as if I'm forcing myself to have a second chance, so as soon as I walk into the building, I make my way to the teacher's lounge. Everyone stares at me, and at first no one says a thing. I think they're afraid that if they open their mouths I might just run into the closet again, honestly, I don't blame them. When someone does have the courage to talk to me it's Cathy, of course. It never occurred to me til now that she's the voice piece of this place. She knows all, she runs all.

"Piper? Goodness, hun, is that you? You look like a new woman!"

"Yeah, I thought it was time for a change."

"Where've you been?"

"Well I was fixing my hair and got a horrible allergic reaction to the dye, they changed up my formula or something and so I had to go back to my normal color. While I was all sick my immune system couldn't catch a break and I ended up catching the flu too. It took me until yesterday to really get moving around. I'm just glad to be back on my feet."

I smile when I answer, I'm clear, loud, and concise. I peak their curiosity but quell it at the same time. I do exactly what I'm supposed to do. I'm becoming the girl I always wanted to be.

"Oh you poor thing! I'm so glad you're feeling better!" Cathy pulls me into a hug and I melt into her arms.

"You know what? I really need to get down to the library and clean up a bit before the kids come through. We really need to catch up though, is lunch okay for you?" I ask.

"That's perfect with me. Just meet me up here later then!"

"Sounds like a plan."

I start to walk out the door with my head held high, but she calls my name and stops me in my tracks.

"Piper dear?"

"Yes?"

"You've really come out of your shell, I don't know what did it, but I like this girl. She's not only beautiful, but a total gem on the inside as well."

"Why thank you, that really means a lot to me."

I leave the lounge and my face is flushed with color. I didn't embarrass myself, I feel confident, I feel like I can do this. Cathy likes the new me, and if she approves of me, so will everyone else. Down the halls I float, and once I get into the library, I find a single daisy on the desk waiting for me with a note.

TO THE PINK HAIRED LIBRARIAN WHO DANCES WITH BROOMS,

WELCOME BACK PIPER, GOOD LUCK TODAY.

YOU'LL DO GREAT.

FROM THE GEEK WHO JUST WANTS YOU TO BE HAPPY.

I smile at his letter and prop it up by my computer so I can look at it whenever I feel the nerves bubbling over. Throughout the rest of the day, the kids come in rounds and books pile up with the compliments. Everyone likes this girl better. She's happier, more outwardly kind, she fits in, and she doesn't question the world because it's never done her wrong.

At lunch, I chit chat with Cathy, at one point, I feel my legs vibrate; I feel my heart beat out my chest; I feel my throat tighten, but I don't let her see my panic. I leave for the restroom and I cry. I let my mask fall in the privacy of chipped paint and dirty tiles. The girl behind the happiness is still horribly insecure; she still feels anxious when it comes to making impressions, she still doesn't feel good enough, and no matter how much I try to repress her, she still seeps through.

Changing yourself is a war, not a battle. I can not give up any time soon. I have to convince myself that the new Piper is here to stay.

The rest of the week, I keep up my act. I play along, I feel relieved that everyone is responding so well to it. Mr. Wolff even complimented my eagerness to "conform to the school's hierarchy." The only thing that's wrong is that my panic attack still sneak up on me, at least twice a day. I'm better at masking them now, no one has seen me crack, but I hate it. I hate that it's the only thing keeping me back from fully belonging. Well, it's not the only wrong thing but it is the most worrying. The other thing, is that I haven't seen Clarkson all week. He never visits me, he's never in his class when I go to see him, and he never comes by the house anymore. I don't know what I did to make him go away, but I guess that's what I wanted, wasn't it? People only leave when you want them to stay.

On friday, I finally see him. He wanders down to the library and it takes all that I have in me to not run towards him and pull him into a hug.

"Hey stranger, it's been awhile," I say trying to hide a full grin.

"I know, I've just been real busy lately..."

"It's okay, I get it..."

"You know, I've heard that you've become quite popular around here lately. Congratulations, Piper, you got your wish."

His voice has this sarcastic undertone, and he seems to have an attitude about the whole thing, I just don't get what I did. I don't know how we can constantly go from being so close to complete strangers over and over again.

"You're not mad at me are you?"

"Not mad, just disappointed."

"And why's that? People finally like me, Clark."

"They don't like the real you though, so what's the point of it all?"

"No one ever liked the real me, and now she's gone."

"I liked the real you, Piper. I did," he says.

"Don't be ridiculous."

"I'm serious, the best parts of your persona are and have always been the best parts of you. Everything else is just a game, and if you took time to think, you'd realize that who you've become won't bring you happiness."

"I just want to be accepted. Honest to God, I think that's all I've ever wanted."

"I get that, but you'll never be accepted until you learn to accept yourself. You know what, I should probably get back to my class. I told them all that I came down here to ask for some workbooks for next week's homework. I'll see you around."

"Clark, don't go."

"I'm sorry, Piper. I just can't pretend to be okay with all of this."

As he leaves I find myself wanting to yell, "You promised you stay by my side. You lied to me." Instead my words come out as whispers, and once again the feeling of abandonment bubbles over. When I'm me, I'm not good enough. When I'm someone else, I'm not good enough. What do I have to do to be good enough for someone, anyone? I just don't get it.

# NOW:

It's a week until Thanksgiving break and throughout the school there are murmurs of excitement. Everyone is in need of a vacation, including myself. I'm tired of the act and I've found myself more prone to panic attacks and crippling insecurity. Now, I don't know if my plan is so grand after all. I honestly need time to decompress and unwind, but I can't afford to take any more days off of work, so I've rekindled my reading passion with the hopes of finding a distraction.

I've tried to write again too, but I don't have any decent stories to tell. I have no incredible insight that needs to be shared, and I've seem to have lost all of my melodic words. I wish I could get myself through it all through writing about characters with lives that are worse than mine, but none of them seem to exist anymore, which is strange because my life isn't that bad. My problems are self manufactured, and I hate being aware of it.

I really just feel as if I need a friend to talk to, to help me figure out my next move. I can't keep changing who I am with the seasons. I need a balance. I need to figure out who I really am, but I need an outside opinion. Ha. How ironic.

The only problem is that the only person I trust enough to talk about this too has avoided me for a week. I miss him, I miss him a lot. I should swallow my pride and talk to him. I should just ask him to meet up. With a single flower in one hand and a note in the other I walk into school the next day, early and leave them on his desk. If things go as planned he'll meet me at the boardwalk and we'll talk like we did our first night along the beach.

When the sun sets, I make my way out to the boardwalk. I'm wearing my favorite lavender colored sweater with leggings and ugg boots that are too comfortable to admit how unfashionable they truly are. For some reason butterflies flip in my stomach. I'm just meeting Clarkson but for some reason it feels different. I feel as if I'm fighting for his friendship.

"Hey stranger, it's been awhile."

At the boardwalk he waits for me, staring between the sunset and the water's gentle waves. When he hears me, he stands up and smiles but it seems more forced. I don't care though. I kind of rush towards him and give him a hug that he eventually reciprocates. He's fighting himself, just like I am. He doesn't know whether he wants to be around for the trainwreck or save himself from any possible domino effect. We sit at the edge and our feet dangle off the weathered wood. He doesn't speak one word, just waits for me to start.

"You know, I've really missed you, and I hope it wasn't wrong of me to be so forward asking you to meet me tonight... You seem kinda distant," I say.

"I just don't know what to expect. You're two different people and I'm not quite sure if I like both of them or not."

"Clarkson White, I'm here as your friend. That's all that matters, or all that should matter anyways..."

"Well then, I'm glad to have the real Piper Addison back."

"Clark, I don't get why you're so upset with me. I don't get why you just left."

"Because I admired the real you. I liked you because you weren't afraid to be yourself. Sure, you didn't just let me into your life, but when I got to know you, I just knew you weren't just another eccentric wannabe. You were an original. You were unique."

"People change though. Isn't that the point of life? We learn, we grow, we change until we die. That's how it's always been and that's how it always will be."

"I guess that's true, but we change in order to grow as people. We change to progress our humanity. You never changed for yourself. You changed to make other people happy, Piper."

"I already told you why I changed, I'm not going to keep repeating the same thing over and over," I mumble and I feel so deflated.

"You never had to change though. Piper, let me ask you a question."

"What is it?"

"Why did you move here?" he asks.

"I moved to get a new start. I moved to find myself and escape what everyone expected of me back at home."

"You moved to escape what everyone expected of you, and yet you conform to the same idea now."

"I didn't mean to…"

"I know, and that's what makes me so upset."

"Why do you care so much about me, Clark?"

"Because you're my friend, and that's just what friends do."

"Okay, then what am I supposed to do? I can't just go back to being myself after all of this. I don't want people to go back to thinking I'm a freak. I don't want to turn everyone against me again. No matter how much I hate who I pretend to be, I like being liked. I thinks it's daft of anyone to say they don't like being liked, it's human nature, ya know?"

"You just have to start figuring out the real you a bit at a time. No one is against you, and people may not understand why you're doing what you are, but they'll respect it. It's time to realize that the world will only be on your side if you let it," he says.

"It's easy to say, 'just figure out your life' but it's a hard thing to do. It's what I've been trying to do."

"You have to grow up, Piper. No one has it all figured out, but you have to find peace with yourself. I can't fix anything for you. I can't tell you what to do. You have to come to terms with that. I care about you, and I'll always be there for you, but I won't baby you."

"I didn't know you were so mad at me."

"I'm not mad, it just hurts to see you this way."

"Sorry. I never meant to put my problems on anyone else, I hope you know that."

"I know, I wanted you to talk to me about everything. I just never would have guessed that it would all lead to this."

"No one could, it's alright."

"I want you to be alright instead of just pretending."

"I am trying to be okay. I will figure it out someway somehow."

"Why don't you start with tackling your problems head on. Figure out what parts of you like and what you want to change, so that you can become the person you want to be, not who everyone else wants you to be."

"Maybe that's what I'll do."

"Don't just say maybe, do it. Let's start with this, how do you feel about pink hair?" he asks and his eyes twinkle with a soft laugh that rings out on the water.

"I think it suits me quite well."

"Looks like we're finally getting somewhere, huh?"

The rest of the night we talk about nothing and everything simultaneously. He asks me questions about myself and sometimes I surprise myself with the answers. It's like this wave of judgment is gone and we're back to normal, once again. The pendulum swings and some days it's for the better. I know it sounds like I'm wrapped up in my own life and just using Clark, but I do care about him, and surprisingly while I'm learning about myself I'm learning about him too. It's just the little things though, like how his favorite candy is smarties, how his favorite color is yellow, and how he always knew he wanted to be a teacher. I feel as if I knew so much about him before, but now the picture is a little clearer. Maybe the little things were the only things I had left to learn and just didn't realize it.

# NOW:

I can't say that things just get better overnight. I can't say that getting to a good place takes anything more than hard work and a ton of self discovery, but I can say that I'm making progress. My hair, though chemically fried, is back to it's rightful color, pink. My coworkers are back to be standoffish with me, but none are outright rude anymore. Clarkson is back to being my friend, and he stops by every day to see me and talk about life. It's as if my life currently is starting to balance out slowly but surely. Things aren't perfect, the nightmares still come, the panic attacks are still frequent, but now I'm in a place where I can celebrate any and every success.

I'd be lying if I said that I didn't dream of waking up fixed. I'd be lying if I said I get up every day with a smile on my face, but I'm trying to accept the idea that the journey really does matter; the journey is what defines the end result. It's all about self discovery, but more importantly it's all about self acceptance.

Two days before Thanksgiving break starts ,I find myself sitting in Clark's apartment in the middle of town, watching a premature Christmas movie while shoving my face full of popcorn. It's one of those movies where you can't help but want to hold on to your family by the end. It's as if we're only able to appreciate what we

476

have when the holidays come around. By the end of the movie, Clark has a single tear running down his face and he's calling his mom to check on her and the family restaurant.

"I love and hate these stupid Christmas movies at the same time," he says as he gets off the phone with his mom.

"And why's that? You afraid to tap into your sensitive side?" I arch my eyebrows and throw back my head to laugh. Clark rolls his eyes at me and throws popcorn at me. I dodge the food and it falls on the floor, mixing with a pile of ungraded math tests that cover the room.

"Those movies always make me feel like I'm a horrible person for not cosntantly keeping tabs on my family. There's only so much family bonding a guy can take before he loses his mind."

"Hey, at least you still talk to yours."

"I guess that's true. Do you ever miss them?"

"Of course I do, this time of year is the worst too. I miss them all the time, but I don't know if I miss them or the memories we had when my family was whole, ya know?"

"Maybe that's what missing for you. That missing piece that still keeps you up at night."

"Who knows. I haven't talked to my Dad in what feels like years."

"Well maybe you should go up and see him for the holidays. It be good for you, Piper."

"I haven't been back home at all. I never looked back, Clark. I don't think I could handle that place, let alone handle it by myself."

"What do you think would happen if you went back?" he asks.

"I don't know, I feel like I'll just slip back into old ways. I'm afraid to face everything and everyone. I don't know, maybe I should, I just..."

"I get it, Piper. You don't have to do anything you don't want to."

"I feel as if I should though. I think you're right, it's the last thing I need to do to move on. I just don't know if I'm really ready to do it," I say.

"Well if you want to go through it, you don't have to go through it alone. I'll come with you if you want me to."

"Do you really mean that?"

"Of course I do. If you want we can head down there the first few days of break, and if all goes well we can stay down there for Thanksgiving, if not, you can come back with me and eat with my family."

"Clark, I can't ask you to skip Thanksgiving. Your family is important to you and you should be with them instead of trying to help me."

"Piper, you're like family to me, if you genuinely want to do this, we're going to do it."

"I guess it's happening then...Oh god Clark, it's really happening."

"It's going to be okay Piper, I promise you."

The last two days of work go by quickly after that conversation. Everything's a blur, from the rush of books out of the library to the mound of clothes that I try to pack quickly. Part of me doesn't want to go home. I don't want to face my past, I've been trying to hide from it this entire time. Maybe that's been my problem all along. I'm just afraid to see what's changed and what's stayed the same. I'm afraid to see if going back will cause me to hurt all over again. They say you shouldn't live in the past, that you should only look forward, but how can you move forward if you never resolved your past?

When it's time for us to go, we make our way to the same bus that took me to Belfast in the first place. Clark wanted us to drive, but something felt right about finishing things the same way we started. With a three day ticket and the promise to return to my real home, we set off. Everything is just as I remembered it. The bus reeks of stale gasoline and lingering perspiration, the chairs are still broken in and the gaudy fabric swallows me whole. It's just another endless trip, but this time I am not alone, I have Clark by my side.

Of course, the entire ride we read together and end up going through several more cheesy Christmas movies. Although, most of time I can't keep my eyes open. I feel energy drain out of me as my anxiety rises through the roof. Clark doesn't mind my drowsiness, or doesn't say anything about it when I fall asleep on his shoulder and end up waking up on his chest.

"I-I'm so sorry. I keep falling asleep on you…" I murmur.

"Hey, don't worry about it. I don't mind. It's better that you sleep and keep yourself calm you know?"

I smile at him and pull him into a hug. "How many times have I told you that I don't deserve you as a friend?"

"Too many times to count, if I'm being honest with you."

"Well, my dear Clarkson White, I mean it more every time."

I fall asleep again soon after, but the closer we get to our destination the more restless I become. In the middle of the night, I wake up screaming. Clark doesn't even bat an eye, he wakes up and pulls me towards him, shushing me while running his hands up and down my back. Every fiber of my being is shaking, but he is determined to be my rock. Clarkson White doesn't want to fix me, he wants to help me be comfortable in my own skin.

Early sunday morning, we pull into the town I once called home. The periwinkle sky greets us with a rising sun while the earth is coated in white. It's bitter cold out too, and I can't stop myself from shaking. I tell Clark that it's because it's so cold, but Maine weather is harsher at this time, so I know he doesn't buy it, but he doesn't question it either.

"So where to first?" he asks as he lugs our suitcases off to the curb.

"I don't know. I guess home first. I honestly didn't think this all through."

"Well then, should we get a cab and head over that way?"

"No, we're only five minutes away from my house. We can walk it."

"Alright then Miss Addison, lead the way."

Down the white-washed streets everything seems to be the same. The houses are quiet but picturesque; pine trees line every street and they're already covered in strands of lights for the holiday season. I remember loving this time of year growing up. The world just seemed to be so still and perfect to me, but now it's unsettling. I feel as if people are watching Clark and I walk home.

"Do you mind if we take a detour first?" I ask.

"Wherever you need to go, Piper. I'm one step behind you."

We pass my house mere moments later and there's just this part of me that feels as if it's the coldest house on the street. All the love in the house died a long time ago and now it's a place haunted by lost souls. I can't look away and yet I can't convince myself to stop and walk back in. I'm on another mission, I have another plan. I finally find myself stopping at the end of the street at the small field where everything began. It's changed since I've left. No longer is it an empty field near a pond that was only ever good for ice skating on snow days, now it's a park with a memorial for the two girls my brother killed.

"Is this where?" Clark's voice fades out when I nod.

"I always asked myself how he could do it. I saw him lose his temper so many times as a kid, but most of the times it was to protect me or someone else he loved. I just never fathomed things would end up this way."

"What do you mean? Did you expect your mom and brother to be here too?"

"My mother maybe, not Charlie though. I don't know what I expected. I know how everyone feels, I just didn't expect this."

"Maybe we should get going then. You don't want to upset yourself too much."

"I guess so. God, they could have at least remembered my mom. She deserved to be remembered..."

Clark doesn't answer me but places his hand on the small of my back and guides me towards the street. I feel myself bubbling over, I feel myself wanting to cry, but I can't. I have to hold myself together. Clark talks to me the entire way to my home, he tries to keep me upbeat and lively, and he tries to fake comfortability.

As we walk up to the house, I see how run down it's really gotten since I left. The front porch used to have an uneven step masked by flower boxes, but now the plants are all dead and the boxes all broken. The front door used to be a brilliant blue, but now it's chipped and faded. With the house looking as bad as it does I don't think Uncle Mike lives with Dad anymore. He was the only person who kept my Dad going on a daily basis. I might not have liked my Uncle, and I might not have agreed with his methods of helping my Dad cope, but he kept my Dad from losing every bit of humanity he had

"Dad might not be happy to see me, so I apologize in advance for any and everything that comes out of this," I say.

"It's okay, don't say sorry. I signed up for this, remember?"

I nod my head and knock on the door. Part of me hopes that my Dad won't be home while the other half of me wants to hug him so badly. When he opens the door, both of our faces drop. Time and unresolved grief has aged him quicker than it should have. My Dad was once handsome but now he's worn. His once fit figure now hides behind a beer belly and unshaved face. He seems to be a new man and I must seem to be a new person to him too.

"Piper? Is that you?" he asks.

"Hi Dad, it's been a while..."

"It's you, oh god, it's been so long."

My Dad pulls me into a hug, and though he smells like stale booze, I don't want to let him go. It's him who let's go first, and it's not until he realizes the present of Clarkson that his mood changes completely.

"And who, may I ask, is this young man?"

"Dad, meet Clarkson White, my coworker and my closest friend."

Clarkson extends his hand to my Dad and he takes it hesitantly.

"A real friend? Or is this young man like that Cameron boy?" he asks.

"Dad. Are you really going to start this up again? I was sixteen, and I know that this is going to fall on deaf ears but nothing happened with Cam."

"No matter, both of you, come in. I don't know if you two want to stay here though, I haven't really cleaned the place up. I wasn't expecting company."

"It's alright, Dad. I'm just going to set our stuff in my room for now, but we'll get out of your hair as soon as possible. Come on Clark, follow me."

I walk into the house as my Dad frantically cleans the house, moving years of spam mail into trash cans, hiding pizza boxes, and crushing empty beer cans that are scattered around the kitchen floor. I guess I wasn't wrong when I said that the soul of the house died.

Besides the mess in the kitchen everything else is sterile and quiet. It looks like no one has lived in the house since the day I left home. I usher Clark into my room with it's light pink walls and light oak furniture, and set our bags by my book collection that looks pathetic compared to the one I have now. Clark's immediately drawn to the books and starts talking about all the ones he read as a kid, but I'm drawn to a small window in my room and I don't hear a word he's saying.

In my room there are two windows, one I used frequently to escape, to leave the place I believed was suffocating me slowly, and the other was gateway to the garden. I find myself freezing at the sight of the withered garden. Nothing's changed since the police finished their investigation. Police tape still wraps around the tomato poles, and two giants patches of dirt still loom in the back. The graves of the girls were never sealed once the police removed their bodies. It's seems to me like my Dad wanted the constant reminder of what had happened; he wanted to feel the pain on a daily basis. Just standing here now I feel my whole body crumble and ache.

"Piper, are you okay?" Clark's voice breaks through my thoughts.

"You know, I was home when everything happened. I heard a large bang but I didn't know what it was. I didn't want to know. I don't know how I didn't see anything. Maybe because it was dark out or maybe because I wanted to deny what my heart knew was true. Just right out there the tragedy ended and my nightmare began."

"Don't blame yourself. There was nothing you could have done."

I turn around and he's closer than he was, but the empty space between us speaks volumes. He doesn't know how I'm going to react, if I'm going to lose my mind or cry or both.

486

"The funny thing is, I just played our song and pretended like things would be okay in the morning. I just had the line *It's all right* repeating in my head over and over, but when I woke up it wasn't." I face the window again and begin to hum the song.

"It might not have been okay then, but you know what, it's okay now."

"Is it? You see how my dad is, he wasn't like that before everything happened. You know how I get when things get bad. You know how easy it is for me to fall apart. Did things ever get better? Or am I just getting so good at playing pretend that I've managed to convince myself."

"Piper…"

"What is it, Clark?"

He places his hand on my shoulder and when I turn to face him he doesn't say a thing. He just stares at me and I realize it's not pity in his eyes but heartbreak from seeing me hurt. He brushes one finger against my cheek and I feel my stomach flip. I close my eyes and sigh. It feels like we wait that way forever and I find myself wishing that he would just make a move. It's when I make the wish that he leans in and kisses me and my heart melts completely.

"I'm sorry that was a bit inappropriate of me, I just had to get you out your head."

"Oh, was that all?" I ask and my voice deflates a bit.

"Honestly? No. I've wanted to do that for awhile."

"Is that why you came all this way with me?"

"No, you know why I'm here. I don't lie to you."

"Promise me?"

"I swear, Piper. I'm not that kind of guy."

"I know."

I don't know how we're going to change now, but at least he's by my side. At least I know at the end of the day someone will be there to talk to.

"We should probably go out there and talk to your dad before he gets the wrong idea, he seemed a little angered by me," he says.

"You're right. Let's go."

"Wait, I have a question for you first, who's this Cam guy?"

I laugh and roll my eyes, "That's a story for another time."

We walk down the hall hand in hand, but when get to the lemony living room we separate to face my Dad. I feel like I'm hiding some secret from him, but honestly this man knows nothing about who I've become and who I am as a woman.

"So, what brought you home?" my Dad asks.

"I thought it was time to try to let everything go."

"I thought you did that when you left here."

"I tried, but the whole situation messed me up. It broke us, and I'm finally in a place in my life where I'm willing and ready to try to piece myself back together."

"Well I'm proud of you for getting this far, I just wish you would have been ready sooner. I've missed you, and this damn house drives me crazier every day."

"Why won't you move then? You don't have to stay wait for the world to just end, Dad."

"Because no one in their right mind would buy a house that had 3 murders and a suicide on the premise. Besides, this was your mother's dream home and it's just something I don't think I'll ever be willing to let go."

"I worry about you," I say.

"Clearly not enough to call me though."

I clear my throat as the tension builds. It's weird to think how much this place has stayed the same but changed at the same time. The furniture is all the same, worn down and blue, while a polkadotted rug sits under the same square coffee table that I used to run into as a kid, yet instead of feeling comfortable, everything feels stiff. Nothing lives here anymore. The light doesn't even seep in through the windows like it used to.

"Every time we talked we fought and you were drunk. I couldn't take it. I'm sorry, but I'm here now, can't that be enough?" I ask.

"You weren't the only one who was hurt, Piper."

"I know. I'm sorry. I'm sorry I left, I'm sorry I didn't call. I wasn't a good person, but I'm trying to be better."

"I want to believe you, but after the incident you became a liar."

"Dad, what on earth are you talking about?"

Clark reaches for my hand and his thumb draws circles on the top of it to calm me down.

"Remind me how long it took you to tell me the truth about where you live?" my Dad asks.

"Dad, I..."

"You lied for so long, played me like a fool, told me you were happy starting over."

"Dad, I was happy starting over. I was happy in Belfast. It wasn't the perfect place, but I felt as if it was where I belonged."

"You know I never really believed that you made to your grandparents'. I felt as if you were too happy, especially someone living with them. Yet, I wanted to buy into your idea of a new life. I figured that if it got too bad you'd ask for help, but when you told me

490

the truth it just hurt. It hurt me that you lied to me; it hurt me to know that my gut was right along; it hurt me that no matter what I did, I still wasn't good enough for you to come to me. Lord knows I'm a shitty parent, but I just wanted what was best for you, so I believed in you. I wanted you to be happy. I wanted to try to be a good parent for once in my life."

"I am happier. Starting over was the best decision I've ever made. Besides, you did do what was best for me. I hope you understand that I can't thank you enough for giving me the chance to escape this hell. I just don't want you to hate me for starting to find peace. I feel like you've hated me since you learned the truth. Dad," I pause to look directly at his weathered face. "please don't hate me, It's not too late for you to get better too. It's not too late for our family to begin again."

"Oh my sweet girl," he gets out of his chair and lifts my chin to get a good look at me. "I died with your mother and brother. There's nothing left in the world for me. That's why your Uncle left me. I'm a ghost stuck in purgatory. I'm glad you're getting better, but I'm a selfish bastard and I hate that I'll never be happy again."

"I'm sorry."

"It's not your fault, it's only mine, but I don't know if it's a good idea for you to stay here. I've built myself a wall to protect me from getting hurt again and I think you being here will ruin me once more."

"I understand, we'll be gone tomorrow morning on the first bus back. Until then, there are a few more things I think that I need to do," my tone shifts to professional and all of a sudden my Dad is gone and a loveless old man is in his place.

"Okay, well I wish you the best of luck."

"I love you, Dad."

"I love you too, good bye my sweet girl."

My Dad excuses himself and disappears into his room without another word. I never thought that I wouldn't be able to restore the relationship with my Dad. I never thought that he'd send me away and drink away his pain for the rest of his life. Seeing him like this makes me realize that though I am broken I can still be redeemed. I am not dead, and the fact that I can still feel the same pain year after year let's me know that I am alive.

"So where are we off too next then?" Clark asks.

"I need to go to the cemetery, but I think I should go alone."

"Piper, I don't feel comfortable leaving you."

"I'm okay, honestly. I need to do this. I need to talk to Charlie and my Mom."

"Are you sure?"

"Positive. If you need anything, there are takeout menus in the drawer next to the sink, and I'm pretty sure we still have a collection of Christmas movies saved on my computer for you to watch if you get bored. My Dad won't bother you."

"It's not him I'm worried about."

I give Clark a sad smile and kiss his cheek before bundling up in my winter coat and braving the cold again. As I walk down the deserted streets, I feel as if I'm heading to the funeral all over again. Back then I had basically aged five years in a matter of days. I had lost my innocence, I had lost my youth. The years that were supposed to be the best part of my life were the worst, but I don't know if I would ever change it. Changing myself has only brought me more grief and confusion. I'm only truly happy when I'm not worried about being anyone else, when I'm not pretending to simply fit in. Being myself may not be the easiest thing in the world, but I'm stronger person because of it.

At the cemetery, I find myself kneeling by my mother's grave first. My jeans are coated in snow and as the water seeps through my layers I clean off her tombstone. It's too cold to leave flowers, and I have nothing to give her but my pure honesty.

"Hey mom, it's been a while. I've missed you. I'm sorry I haven't come to visit you. It was just too hard for a while. I lost myself without you. You were the glue in our family. You were the sunshine. You were the music. You were the laughter. You were everything that was good, and it makes me so angry that no one wants to remember you. You were able to defy what everyone expected of you and make everyone love you. I looked up to that. I looked up to your radiance, and when you were taken from me it just hurt. Dad and I were ruined without you, and I tried too hard to be you. I hate to tell you, but Mom I suck at guitar, and I kind of burned your old one once I realized that I wasn't some secret virtuoso.  I can never live up to you, but I don't think I have to anymore. I just have to keep trying to be better, to be a good person, and I think that idea alone will make you happy. I think that just me trying to be happy will make you proud of me. God, I hope you're proud of me, and I don't know when or if I'll be back, so let me just tell you that I love you. I love you and if no one else in this world remembers you as a light, I will. I'll remember the music and laughs when I'm sad and it'll remind me to keep moving, to keep getting better. Well, I guess that's everything, and just in case I haven't said it enough, I love you. I love you forever and always."

494

I feel as if I have more to say to her, or at least I feel as if there's more that I should say because I know that I won't ever come back. I've laid it all out of the table. I put my heart out there and for some reason I feel at ease. I did my best starting over, I did my best growing up. If I end up coming up with something else later it'll be for the better. I don't want to upset myself, and some things are just better left unsaid.

With a cold core and a defrosted heart I walk past two empty plots, one for my Dad and one for me. The ground is uneven and I sit on my grave while staring at Charlie's. For the longest time I hated him. I blamed him for ruining me. I believed in the narrative that everyone forced onto me; Charlie was a monster. He was the demise of a "perfect" society that was corrupt to the core. Yet at the same time, I loved him. He was the one who protected me, he was the one who was by my side on a rainy day. Charlie was my brother and it hurt to balance the narratives of a murderer and a boy with a twisted soul.

"Hey Charlie. It's been awhile, I know you've missed me, haven't you? Your little pied Piper is all grown up, but my personality is the same. You know how I am. Always trying to figure out who I want to be and changing with the wind. I'm trying to stop that though. I don't think it makes me happier and I just want to be happy. You tried to do that too, didn't you? That's why you stopped taking your medicine and took up partying... That's why your life became one big game. I get it now. I've been living a lie too. You know what? We're the same person in a way. Changing ourselves for other people, trying to find the way to happiness in the most fucked up way. I remember telling you that I liked you as you were as a kid but it didn't make a difference in your eyes. I remember trying to help you when you were at your worst just like you tried to help me, but nothing I did worked. I guess that's because you never were a good listener. You were determined to be liked and lived a lonely existence because of it. That's why everything ended the way it did. You weren't a monster; you were simply a product of your own environment. I guess I am too. I guess that's why it's been so hard for me, but I'm getting better. I have someone in my life that reminds me that I'm fine as I am. I have a place that I call home. I don't have everything figured out, but I've escaped what you never could. I've escaped the idea that societal acceptance is the only path to happiness. You know I love you Charlie. You know, back when we were kids I saw you for who you really were, and now I'm finally able to see you as that person again. Now, I need you to know that I forgive you for everything. You were my best friend, my brother, my world, but I think it's time for me to let go. Though you and mom were such an important part of my life, I can't let you two be what defines me anymore. I have to figure out who I am without the baggage, without all the pain. I probably won't be back to this hell hole, but keep looking out for me, alright? I've escaped, and now I've broken every tie that connects me here. God, I hope you're in a better place too, but honestly, any place is better than here."

I laugh and wipe away a frigid tear rolling down my cheek. I'm done, and though my body is frozen and slowly losing feeling, I've never felt so relieved in my life.

Walking down the snowy roads, I know it's over. I know I did what I had to do and now it's time to go back to where I belong. It's time to go to the place that's name is as quaint as the sea, my home, Belfast.

# EPILOGUE (NOW):

In the middle of forgotten woods, there's a tiny cottage covered in snow and fairy lights. This is the place I call home. It used to be my escape from reality, where words were my only friends, but now things are different. The house doesn't echo the sad songs of singers who are long gone, it no longer smells permanently of tea and burnt toast. It's a happier place where I laugh more than I cry; it's a place where I can try to tackle everyday with a twisted sense of optimism.

I owe my Clark for that. I owe him for staying by my side and not giving up on me, though I often gave up on myself. If it wasn't for him, I'd be stuck playing a game. I'd be like Charlie, believing that the only purpose of life was being someone else. I know I may not be able to answer all the questions of life that I anguished over when I wrote, but it doesn't matter any more. None of it really matters now that I have a better outlook on things.

Now please don't get me wrong, there are some days where I feel completely lost. There are days when I can't get out of bed and my heart aches more than it should, but those days are far and in between the good ones. I think that fact should count for something, right? Maybe not, but I like to think it means I've grown.

498

As the holidays roll around, I miss my family more. I miss my Dad, and I wonder if he thinks of me as often as I think of him. I miss my Mom, and I wonder if she's teaching kids how to sing with their heart somewhere where the sky is blue and the clouds are pure. I miss Charlie, and I wonder if he ever found peace like me. I miss the memories and togetherness, but Clark has been trying to help. We spend every day together, and his family sees me as a part of theirs. We even plan to spend Christmas together and I'm excited. I don't know the last time I had to buy gifts for other people, or when anyone else thought of gifts for me.

"Hey sunshine," Clark walks in as my head's buried in my typewriter. I look up and smile at him. Ever since we got back he's been calling me that. I think it's because I told him about Charlie and I's song. When I asked him why he started calling me that he shrugged and didn't answer. Maybe it's because I stopped looking for the sun, I stopped waiting around to find my happiness and felt better in the process. I'm not sure, maybe it's just because he likes the sound of it, I know I do.

"Hi you, long time no see."

"Oh how I love your sense of humor," he says and I hear the underlying tone of sarcasm.

"You know you love me." I smirk.

"That I do. Are you writing again?"

I smile and nod. I've been thinking a lot lately and though my thoughts aren't like a stormy day, they're still muddled and I think writing will help me. I need to remember the good and the bad. I need to remember how far I've come because it's what makes me, well me. It defines me.

"Yeah, you know what? I think I've finally figured out how to start my story. Here, tell me what you think."

"Honestly, it's awful."

"What? Really? Oh god."

"No, no. I'm kidding. I swear."

"Promise me?"

"Yeah, it's perfect."

*There's something about being stuck on a bus for hours on end that makes you notice the little nuances in life.*